RAVEN STORM

Fire-Walker part three

Emma Miles

Chapter One

Kesta, Kingdom of Elden

Kesta tied her hair back as she strode across the great hall, heart racing. Several of the men at the long tables straightened up over their breakfast, but only Tantony got to his feet. Northold's steward met her gaze, grey eyes anxious, but she waved a discreet hand towards him and the Merkis sat back down.

The ravens were flying low beneath bruised and angry clouds as Kesta hurried down the shallow steps out of the keep. The Raven Tower cast a long shadow, the only light within coming from the uppermost room beneath the eaves. She heard a shriek, and pivoting on her heels she saw her daughter emerging from the pond, her dress muddy to the chest and water dripping from her arms and hair. For a moment Kesta's anxiety lost its tight grip on her lungs and she felt the flutter of amusement.

'Arridia!' Rosa stood with her hand over her mouth. The former lady-in-waiting to the queen's cheeks flushed, her brown eyes wide.

'It's all right.' Six-year-old Arridia smiled up at Kesta's closest friend. 'I'm not hurt and the mud will come out.' She began wading up out of the water while on the other side of the pond the geese screeched angrily.

Rosa pulled a handkerchief out of her pocket, looked the sodden girl up and down, then threw her arms up in a gesture of hopelessness. She sighed. 'Whatever is your mother going to say?'

'That no one is hurt and the mud will come out.'

Rosa spun about; her mouth open.

Arridia and Kesta grinned at each other.

Kesta held out her hand to help her daughter. 'But you do need to be more careful. What were you doing?'

Arridia pulled a face, wiping her black hair away from her brilliant blue eyes with her dirty fingers. 'Watching the water-boatmen.'

Kesta tried not to laugh and forced her facial muscles to relax. 'Well, perhaps you shouldn't watch them quite so closely. What have you learned?'

Arridia answered immediately with a scowl. 'That banks can crumble.'

'And what do you need to do?' Kesta glanced at Rosa, who was standing with her arms folded.

Arridia sucked at her bottom lip. 'Clean myself up?'

Kesta nodded. 'And?'

Arridia's eyes widened, and she blinked rapidly. 'Um... oh! I shall apologise to Rosa and the geese for scaring them.'

Rosa gave a shake of her head, but the older woman was smiling.

'Go on,' Kesta indicated the keep with her head.

'Is everything all right?' Rosa regarded the letters tucked under Kesta's arm.

Kesta placed a hand briefly on her friend's shoulder. 'We'll talk later.'

Rosa nodded, her eyebrows drawing in across her nose.

With a grin at Arridia, Kesta turned back toward the Raven Tower, crossing the lawn to the arched doorway. She took hold of the iron ring and pushed it open.

Only one candle lit the small hallway, and she felt her way up the familiar stairway, the stone rough beneath her fingers. She passed the two libraries and the storeroom, hearing voices as she neared the last door at the top.

Azrael was humming.

Kesta listened.

'And ssso the warrior cut off the head of the giant and the blood came pouring out—'

'Azra!'

Kesta had to bite her lip to stop herself chuckling at her husband's exasperated tone.

'What?' Azrael demanded, all innocence.

'Remember Joss is only three.'

'But I like this story,' Joss protested.

'I'm sure you do,' Jorrun replied reasonably. 'However, I like for you not to have nightmares.'

Kesta pushed the door open and stepped into the room. All three of its occupants turned to look at her guiltily.

'And what are you three up to?' Kesta cocked her head.

'Playing.' Joss held up a wooden statue of a cat to demonstrate. He perched beneath one of the windows on the dishevelled bed. His eyes were a lighter blue than his sister's, almost grey, but he had the same black hair, prone to curl if left to grow long.

'I see.' Kesta raised an eyebrow. She turned her gaze on Azrael. The fire-spirit altered his flickering shape to look more human, forming shoulders which he shrugged.

'Are those reports from Chem?' Jorrun pointed to the documents she carried.

Kesta met her husband's eyes as she sank into a chair. 'Yes. It isn't good.'

He pulled out a chair himself, studying her face with his pale-blue eyes.

She drew in a breath. 'Navere remains stable. A new head priest has taken over the temples and Rece says he seems to be much more open-minded and tolerant than his predecessor, although Calayna doesn't trust him.'

Jorrun winced. 'Sadly, trust is often repaid with a knife in the back these days.' He scratched at his short, black beard. There were a few grey hairs in it, the worry lines around her husband's face more pronounced than when she'd met him years ago.

'There have been more riots in Darva. Tembre has had two of his own Coven members executed for treason.' Kesta picked at the edge of one of the documents. 'In Parsiphay there was an uprising of women and slaves. It...' She swallowed, unable to meet his eyes. 'It was a massacre. They didn't stand a chance against armed and well-fed soldiers.' She shook a little as she breathed out.

Jorrun placed his hand over hers and stood to fetch a map from a bookcase.

'What's wrong, Mumma?' Joss asked anxiously.

Kesta forced a smile. 'It's all right, Joss, you play with your cat.'

With a little flash, Azrael moved from where he hovered by the table to the end of the bed and began to sing. Kesta gave him a grateful nod.

Jorrun spread the map of Chem on the table. They had altered it many times, the border between east and west moving as towns and cities changed allegiance. In the west each province was ruled by a democracy of sorts, overseen and protected by the Ravens. There was no slavery, women were equal, and they traded freely with Elden, the Fulmers, and the Borrows. To the right of the border, in the east, Covens of sorcerers still ruled most provinces; slavery was still their biggest economy and included every woman.

Jorrun's long forefinger touched the circle that indicated the city of Parsiphay. It lay a long way inside the eastern border, on the south coast. Kesta's heart clenched at the pain in his eyes.

'It's only been seven years.' She reached out to squeeze his arm. 'We've achieved more than we could ever have hoped.'

He moistened his bottom lip with his tongue and sighed. 'I know.'

His gaze moved to Joss and Kesta guessed Jorrun was thinking of his brother, the uncle after whom Joss was named but would never meet.

'There's something else.' Kesta leafed through the parchments for the one she needed. 'The Ravens think they've found your sister! Catya and Cassien are on their way to verify the reports.'

Jorrun stood so suddenly he almost knocked his chair over. He reached the fireplace in two long strides, grabbing the mantel and leaning to rest his head against it.

Azrael stopped singing. Joss sat upright, his wide eyes watering as he stared at his father. Kesta quickly moved around the table to hug Joss and kiss the top of his head, using the magic of a fire-walker to send him calm.

'I need to go back to Chem,' Jorrun said through gritted teeth.

Kesta winced. 'I know. But...'

Since Arridia had been born, they'd returned to Chem many times, but never together. One of them had always remained at Northold with the children. Despite how much safer Navere was now, they would never risk Joss and Arridia by taking them there. But Kesta hadn't given him all the news yet, and although she opened her mouth, it was a while before she could speak.

'There has been a rise in the so called 'Disciples of the Gods.' They've been carrying out small acts of violence all over the west in the name of their gods. Including in Navere. They are threatening to resurrect Hacren.'

Jorrun turned to look at her. 'They can't, we destroyed him.'

Kesta chewed at her bottom lip. 'But they could summon some other evil spirit instead.'

'More ssuch demons do exist,' Azrael whispered.

Both Kesta and Jorrun shushed him, glancing at Joss.

Jorrun came to sit back at the table. 'What do you suggest?'

She gave Joss a squeeze, sending out more calm before joining her husband. 'We need to both go out there, put this down quickly. We also...' she gave a slight shake of her head. 'We need to decide if we are going to liberate the rest of Chem.'

His eyes widened a little, and he glanced at Parsiphay on the map.

'We've given it time, and it isn't working,' she continued.

'The Ravens have smuggled hundreds of people across the border.'

'But thousands still suffer.'

'Osun's plan—'

An old wound opened in Kesta's chest, filling with the empty ache of loss. She didn't miss the Chemman as much as Jorrun did, but grief and guilt both stirred within her whenever she thought of the man who had quietly conquered half of his vile homeland.

'Osun's plan isn't working in the east,' she interrupted. 'Now we have more than half the country it might be time to try something else.'

'All-out war will cause thousands of deaths.' Jorrun shook his head.

She studied his face, sagging a little as she nodded. 'But I want to do something.'

He shuffled through the documents, picking up the one that reported the finding of his sister.

'Let's start with the things we can achieve. We would need to consult with the Ravens, anyway.'

Joss had returned to playing with his wooden statues, the carved image of Elden's goddess in his left hand, chasing after the wooden cat in his right.

'He's not going to summon anything, playing with your idols, is he?'

Jorrun smiled, and her heart eased. Her husband always looked so different when he smiled.

'I don't think so.'

'Am I coming with you to Shem?' Azrael asked.

Kesta and Jorrun looked at each other.

'No.' Jorrun turned to his fiery friend. 'We will need you to look after Arridia and Joss.'

'But Rosa is in charge,' Kesta added quickly.

Azrael made himself larger, pulling a terrifying face that had Joss in fits of laughter.

'They'll be ssafe with me.'

'I know they will,' Jorrun smiled fondly at the drake.

'When?' Kesta asked him.

Jorrun held up the report. 'As soon as you're ready.'

***

Kesta watched the door to the stairs, holding her wineglass in her lap. She could hear Jorrun's soft voice and Arridia's higher one in the tower above. She itched to be in the room with them, but Jorrun was always better at getting the children to sleep than she was.

'Kesta?'

Rosa brought her mind back to the room.

'They'll be fine.' Rosa came to sit beside her. Rosa's husband, Tantony, shifted awkwardly in his seat.

'I'm sure they will.' Kesta sighed. 'But I hate leaving them.'

'How are the kids taking it?' Rosa asked.

Kesta took another sip of her wine, trying to quell the churning of her stomach. Guilt was turning her inside out, at the same time as anxiety for the people she was responsible for in Chem had locked her shoulders and spine. She realised Rosa was awaiting an answer.

'Arridia took it in her stride, but Joss cried. Until Azrael distracted him.'

Rosa smiled. 'He's better than I am with the children.'

'A sheep would be better than me,' Tantony muttered. He shuffled a bit to sit on the edge of his seat and leaned toward Kesta, worry lines deep in the skin around his grey eyes. 'I didn't get to face that Hacren character seven years ago, thank the gods, but...' He rubbed at his greying beard. 'Well, you paid a high price to kill him. I don't like the thought of you facing another of those demons.'

'That's why we have to go.'

Tantony jumped as Jorrun appeared in the doorway. Even after all these years, Kesta was still impressed by how quietly the tall man moved. Jorrun strode across the room to sit beside her, placing a hand on Kesta's leg.

'We need to shut down these 'Disciples of the Gods' before they even get close to bringing a monster through into our world. And if they do...'

'And if they do, we know how to destroy one,' Kesta finished, taking his hand.

Tantony looked from Kesta back to Jorrun. 'Is one of you going to stay in Navere?'

'Kesta will,' Jorrun replied quickly.

They'd debated that point for nearly two hours, both of them wanting the other to remain where it was safer.

The old chieftain nodded. 'What do you need me to do?'

'Look after the hold as you always have,' Jorrun held his gaze. 'Protect our children and keep us advised of anything arising here.'

Tantony frowned. 'Is there anything happening in Taurmaline that I need to know of? Is King Bractius aware you're heading off?'

It had been a long time since Jorrun had needed to get permission from his king to do anything, but he was still technically under Bractius' rule and command.

'I've sent a message.' Jorrun glanced at Kesta, his pale-blue eyes seeming darker than usual in the candlelit room. 'As for court, no, nothing of note. Bractius is still wrangling taxes from his Jarls and Thanes. Ayline is busy with Lucien and the twins. Temerran is due to visit soon, I believe.'

Rosa sat up at that. 'Do you think the bard will come here?'

'He might.' Kesta smiled at the excitement in her friend's face. 'Keep a watch on the lake.'

'His sstories aren't as good as mine.' Azrael squeezed himself out of the flame of a lantern hung on the wall. The little fire-spirit shot across the room, taking on a more human shape as he came to hover close. 'I have sspoken to the other Drakes, they will keep an eye out for anyone ssummoning another demon.' He hissed and gave another shiver. 'We hate blood magic.'

'I'm not overly fond of it either,' Jorrun murmured.

Kesta looked down at her hands. Even she had touched on using blood magic to help defeat Hacren and liberate western Chem.

'Have you let the Icante know?' Rosa asked.

Kesta nodded and glanced at Jorrun. 'We send copies of all the reports from Chem to my mother.'

'Well.' Tantony got to his feet, putting down his glass and stretching his back. 'We'll let you get some sleep.'

Rosa blinked rapidly, but stood with her husband. 'We'll see you off tomorrow.'

Jorrun shook Tantony's hand, but Kesta remained in her seat, forcing a smile.

'You're still worried about leaving the children,' Jorrun said as they listened to their friends' footsteps drawing further away on the tower stairs.

'Of course.' She drew in a deep breath and sighed it out. 'But I'm worried about our friends and family in Chem as well. Have you heard from Kussim?' She looked up, Jorrun was gazing at the dark window.

He shook his head. 'Not for a couple of weeks.'

Jorrun's niece was an exceptionally strong magic user, she'd inherited his ability to dream-walk as well as being able to manipulate elemental magic. Kesta had to keep reminding herself that Kussim was about the same age she had been when she'd married Jorrun and twice saved their countries from slavery and destruction. Even so, she wished the young woman had someone experienced and steady with her in the border province of Caergard, like Captain Rece and Calayna, rather than a coven of mostly untried Ravens. Cassien based himself in Caergard and that gave her some comfort, although the Chemmish warrior spent a lot of time away on missions.

'Kes?' Jorrun broke into her thoughts and Kesta realised she was frowning.

'Thinking of Catya,' she winced.

The young woman had been Jorrun's ward once, and her maid for a short while. After spending time with Heara learning to be a scout and bodyguard, Catya had found the lifestyle of the Borrowmen more to her liking than the peaceful Fulmers and had spent more than two years sailing with Temerran the Bard. Then she'd set her inconstant heart on being a Raven and had trained hard in Chem under Rece and Calayna. All Ravens spent time in each of the four lands, learning every skill they could and trying to absorb the best of each culture. Catya, somehow, had absorbed the worst of each.

'She's still little more than a child—' Jorrun started, but Kesta shook her head.

'She always had an old head.' Kesta closed her eyes and gritted her teeth. 'Cass is the best person to temper that anger of hers.'

It was Jorrun's turn to blanch. 'I'm not sure poor Cass will agree. Still, this is an old problem and one we may never solve.'

'I wish I wass going to see our friends again.' Azrael's flames grew paler and his shape dissolved into a fat teardrop.

'Do you really want to cross the sea though, Azra?' Kesta asked him.

He made himself brighter and pulsed larger. 'I would go!'

'I know you would.' Jorrun smiled at him sadly. 'But there is no one else we trust to guard the children.'

The little fire-spirit's mouth elongated into an exaggerated smile that made Kesta laugh out loud.

Jorrun put down his glass and reached out his hand for Kesta. 'Come on, let's try to get some sleep.'

***

The sun was only a promise on the horizon when they finished stowing their supplies on Jorrun's small ship. They'd said their goodbyes to Arridia and Joss, insisting the children stay in bed and not come out to the lake. Azrael followed with Rosa and Tantony, Rosa's greying brown hair was loose about her shoulders and it made her appear younger, more fragile.

'Make sure you come back,' Rosa whispered into Kesta's ear as she hugged her goodbye.

'Of course.' Kesta nodded firmly. 'Good luck with the kids.'

'Oh, I'm sure they'll be good as gold,' Rosa replied optimistically.

Kesta made a noise in her throat, her eyes going to where Arridia peered at them from the tree she was hiding behind.

Jorrun jumped lightly from his ship onto the wooden wharf, striding to the lakeshore to clasp Tantony's wrist.

'Good luck, Thane.' Tantony gave a slight bow of his head.

'We'll see you soon, Merkis.' Jorrun promised, his blue eyes almost as clear as ice where the rising sun caught them.

Kesta drew in a breath, kissed Tantony's whiskery cheek, then with a glance at her daughter walked up the wooden wharf to the ship and jumped in. She waited for Jorrun to untie, before going to the mast to prepare to set the sail. Jorrun pushed them away from the wharf and took his accustomed place at the rudder.

Anxiety was a greedy worm eating at her stomach, but Kesta forced herself to turn her eyes away from Northold and her daughter's hiding place and looked instead northward to where the river Taur poured out from the lake. The wind took them, and Kesta called up her magic to add to it, speeding their journey through Elden toward the sea. Although they hadn't been to Chem together since Arridia's birth, they'd sailed together often, visiting her mother in the Fulmers or just taking some time for the two of them to be alone.

She turned to grin over her shoulder at Jorrun. 'You realise this ship is probably responsible for both our children?'

He smiled back at her, although it didn't spark in his eyes, and she knew he was still really worried. 'I'm willing to risk a third.'

She laughed, tying off the sail and edging her way around the cabin to stand at the prow. The wind whipped her long black hair across her eyes and she held it back with one hand to watch as the men at the bridge wound the winches to lift it and let them pass.

Arridia had been a blessing. Most fire-walkers struggled to conceive, but their daughter had come to them early in their marriage. Joss had been nothing less than a miracle. No one in the Fulmers could recall a *walker* ever bearing more than one child, even those who took husbands who weren't of Fulmer descent. As delighted as they were, their happiness was tinged with concern. Years ago, King Bractius had arranged their marriage to gain more magic users to serve Elden and the throne. Jorrun had initially pushed Kesta away, not wanting Bractius to use her or any child of theirs as he had been. Jorrun's relationship with the king had changed, but the trust between them was uneasy.

Kesta and Jorrun took turns using their magic to fill the sails and move them swiftly downriver. They paused at Taurmouth to pass on some letters, then headed out to sea. The amount of ships they passed had increased over the years, now there was no war between the four lands beneath the sky, trade prospered and more fishermen ventured out in smaller, lone vessels.

The Borrow Islands were still sparsely populated, the decimation of the Islands by the Chem necromancers would take a long time to recover from. As they passed between the ragged, dark cliffs, Kesta was surprised and relieved to see a new settlement. One woman paused, slowly raising a hand in greeting. Kesta raised her own hand, calling fire to dance across her fingertips to let the woman know who, and what, she was.

'Do you need anything?' Kesta yelled, not sure if her voice would carry to shore.

The woman shook her head, but placed her hand over her heart in a simple blessing.

Kesta's own heart clenched and for a moment emotion overwhelmed her. Peace between the Fulmers and Borrows was another miracle.

'Did you want to stop off at Nisten Island?'

Kesta jumped, clutching at her shirt as she turned to growl at Jorrun. Even though he no longer had his mother's amulet that had protected him from her *knowing*, he could still sneak up on her, and delighted in doing so. She narrowed her eyes at him and he watched her hands, waiting for her to give him a shove or a dead arm.

'No, it will take us out of our way and my mother mentioned recently Matriarch Grya is doing well.'

Jorrun turned his gaze to the closest shore. 'Do you feel any remnants of the blood curse?'

Kesta shuddered. 'Thankfully, no.'

He touched her cheek, then wrapped his arms around her in a tight hug. 'It will be all right, this time.'

'It better be.' Kesta scowled. 'I'm sick of having to rescue you.'

He pulled away, looking down at her with the most affronted expression he could muster, but it didn't last long against Kesta's mischievous grin.

He squeezed her arm. 'Come on, last leg.'

Kesta got some fitful sleep while Jorrun sailed them through the night. In the early hours Kesta took over, and she watched the sun rise over the sea, turning the sky red. She woke Jorrun when the dark shadow of Chem appeared on the horizon and they silently steered for the harbour city of Navere, Jorrun's birthplace and the people Jorrun's brother, Osun, had died to protect.

Kesta's breath caught in her throat.

A plume of black smoke billowed up from the heart of the walled city.

Navere was on fire.

Chapter Two

Dia, Fulmer Isle

Dia tried to ignore the man beside her as he sighed loudly. He was leaning back in his chair, his long boots crossed over on the edge of her desk. He picked up a piece of parchment, and it was hard not to follow his tanned fingers as they shaped it into a bird. He threw it at her, but it flew badly, looping to hit him in the thigh.

Dia gritted her teeth, trying to read the passage in the report before her for the second time.

'Haven't you finished yet?'

Dia put the report down and sat back in her chair to glare at him. 'Why don't you go out in the hall and find some pretty young woman to charm?'

'I'd rather charm you.'

He grinned, and Dia struggled to keep the smile from her own face. Humour danced in the bard's green eyes, and he gave a little flick of his head to jostle the red curls that obscured his vision. She imagined there were very few women this Borrowman couldn't charm. Had she been ten years younger and unmarried… well, maybe just unmarried.

'Don't let Arrus catch you saying that, he'll most likely challenge you to a fight,' she said.

Temerran laughed. 'Yeah, he'd beat me to a pulp, but he'd pour me a drink after.'

Dia did laugh at that. 'Yes, he probably would.' She sighed, pushing aside the reports. 'Come on then, this is meant to be your farewell feast.'

As they made their way down to the great hall, the sounds of celebration rose to meet them. Despite the Borrowman Bard being in residence, the Fulmer's own musicians were playing a rowdy tune and Arrus's distinctive laugh rolled above it like good-natured thunder. Dia pushed open the large door, and she blinked rapidly as the smoke from the central fire-pit drifted toward her. The far doors stood wide open, the pressing darkness kept at bay by fire and candlelight.

Temerran headed straight to the musicians, picking up his flute to join in at once with the tune, but not before he'd spared a smile and a wink for a group of Fulmer women. Dia placed a hand on her husband's shoulder and he reached up to squeeze it, turning from the men he was laughing with to look up at her.

'Is all well?'

Dia hesitated, sucking at her lower lip. 'Not well, but manageable.'

The lively tune ended, but Temerran leapt up onto a table, holding his hand out for someone's fiddle. With a grin that could set a room alight, the bard began a fast-paced reel, which had people in the hall shrieking in delight. Dia's eyes fell on a quiet, still couple who appeared at odds with the rest of the room; their calm was soothing, private. It had seemed for many years that Arrus's brother, Worvig, was determined to remain a bachelor. Worvig was a formidable warrior, but composed. A man of few words; almost the opposite of his brother. Just over a year ago he had hand-fasted to the freed Chemman slave, Milaiya, and Dia couldn't have been more delighted.

She'd become rather fond of the shy, but strong, woman her daughter had rescued from Chem; and gentle, protective Worvig was perfect for her.

Arrus stood up to regard Dia, rubbing his fingers down his beard to remove the foam of his beer. 'Do I need to be worried?'

She shook her head and forced a smile. 'The usual troubles in Chem. You can read the reports later when you tell me what Borrowman plots you're embroiled in.'

He showed his teeth in a grin and reached out to place his hand on her hips. 'It will be quiet when the Borrowmen go.'

'It will, although there's the harvest to prepare for.'

He leaned forward to kiss her forehead. 'Harvest can wait, how about a dance?'

Dia laughed. 'I'm not as young as I used to be.'

He gazed at her with his hazel-green eyes. 'Icante, you will always be young.'

'Oh, I don't know about that,' she protested, but she allowed Arrus to drag her out to a space in the hall.

The feast went on until the early hours, long after Temerran slipped away with one of the Fulmer women. Despite the peace between their lands, Dia couldn't help but regard the unsupervised Borrow warriors with an uncomfortable, unsettled feeling in her stomach. Whenever she made up her mind to leave the hall, uncertainty seemed to weigh down her limbs, and she'd watch a little longer. They weren't dissimilar to Fulmer warriors, including their respect for their own women, but historically what they'd done in their raids on the Fulmers still filled Dia with red rage.

She caught the eye of her bodyguard and Silene, Heara, and the woman stood and sauntered over to her at once. Heara was almost fifty now, but she didn't look it. Her body was still supple, muscular, and she moved with the ease of a cat. There was some steel in her black hair, more lines about her eyes, but Dia trusted her more than any warrior in the hold.

'Icante?' She raised an elegant eyebrow.

'I'm sorry to ask, but will you keep an eye on things?'

Heara glanced over her shoulder at Vilnue. The Elden Merkis and ambassador had been her lover for about eight years. There was none of the red left now in the man's hair and beard that had first attracted Heara to him, but she showed no inclination to either give him up, or marry him. Vilnue looked up and gave them a nod. He had a tankard in front of him, but the ale inside hadn't been touched in some time. Heara had chosen a clever man.

'We'll stay here,' Hera agreed.

'Thank you.' Dia squeezed her hand and then took Arrus's arm. 'It's not like you to not be the last man at the feast,' she said quietly to her husband.

'Maybe *I'm* getting old.' He waggled his bushy eyebrows. 'Seriously? It's all in hand. Temerran's men might be rough and uncouth, but he won't sail with anyone he doesn't trust. You know that, though.'

She pressed her lips together in a thin line and nodded.

'So why the caution?' He pushed open the door to their room.

'I... I'm not sure,' Dia replied. 'I just feel uneasy.'

Arrus halted to regard her. 'Then you're right to be cautious. Your instinct is never wrong.'

They stepped into their room and were greeted by a flare of orange light. Arrus blinked and raised a hand to shield his eyes. 'Hi Doraquael.'

'Something wrong?' Dia asked the fire-spirit.

Doraquael shot across the room, but settled quickly on the wick of a fat candle.

'I have had word from Azrael via the other drakes; Kessta and Jorrun have gone to Shem.'

'Both of them?' Arrus's head whipped about to glance from the drake to Dia.

'I'm not entirely surprised.' Dia sat on the edge of the bed. 'But I wonder if it's a bit foolish.'

'Hmm, well, I guess it depends.' Arrus scratched at his beard and pulled his shirt up over his head. 'They are stronger together.'

'They didn't take the children?' Dia demanded.

'No, Rosa hass them at Northold.' Doraquael brightened.

'Doraquael.' Dia wrapped her arms about herself. 'Have the spirits in the fire realm spoken of any danger?'

'Danger?' Doroqueal's shape altered. 'You mean troubles in Shem?'

'No.' Dia frowned. 'Something else. Like when Quinari was spying on us in our dreams, or when the priests were meddling with summoning gods.'

Doraquael made a buzzing sound. 'Nothing like that. I will keep my ears open though. I'll speak to Siveraell, of the ancient Drakes he is the only one who cares for humans and will talk to earth-bound spirits like Doraquael and Azra.'

Dia nodded. 'I'd appreciate it.'

Arrus yawned loudly, getting into bed. 'Come on, Dia, we'll worry about it in the morning. If there is any trouble, I'm sure it will find its own way to us without us looking.'

Dia snorted. 'I fear you're right.'

She got into bed; the sheets were cold, so she moved closer to Arrus. Doraquael remained for a while, before eventually vanishing up the chimney and plunging the room into darkness. It was a long while before Dia fell asleep.

***

Despite her late night, Heara was already running her trainees through their paces when Dia left the hold to make her way down to the beach. The Borrowmen had loaded their trade goods the day before, and most of their boats had left the beach and returned to the ship. The Undine was beautiful in a way that made you catch your breath; it was as though the ship were not just made for the sea, but made *of* the sea and the wind.

She spotted Temerran sitting alone in the dunes, his gaze lost somewhere out to sea. He'd tied his hair back in a small tail, but the wind still played with his red curls. Dia was reluctant to disturb him, but he sensed someone watching and looked up. A smile immediately replaced his pensive frown.

'Icante.' He stood, but she waved at him to stay where he was. Her knees protested with a sharp ache as she crouched to sit beside him.

'Will you follow your usual route?' she asked.

Temerran glanced at her and nodded. 'I'll spend two weeks in Taurmaline and then head up to Chem. I'll need to spend a couple of months in the Borrows after that.'

'My daughter and Jorrun have both headed for Chem.'

He turned to regard her. 'Trouble?'

'Isn't there always?'

A smile ghosted his lips as his eyes traversed the horizon. 'I'll let you know everything I see.'

Dia laughed, and Temerran's smile broadened. 'You're not my spy.'

'Aren't I?' He turned to look at her, eyebrows raised.

She gave a slight shake of her head and laughed again. 'Okay, perhaps you are.'

His face grew serious. 'Do you think you'll ever send another *walker* to Taurmaline?'

Dia's throat tightened. It was many years since Larissa's murder, but it still hurt. King Bractius might not have been to blame, but queen Ayline had most definitely played a part.

'No, I don't think I'll ever send another *walker* to Elden. Dorthai and Finian do well enough as ambassadors. Will you call in at Northold?'

'My visit there is what makes the Elden court tolerable. Mind you.' He smiled. 'I am looking forward to seeing Prince Lucien.' He turned and took her hand. 'Come with me. It's been months since you visited Taurmaline.'

Dia shook her head. 'It's harvest, I'm needed here.'

He let go of her hand and kissed her cheek. 'It was worth a try. But seriously, I think you should go sometime soon, your influence on Bractius is important, and the reminder to Ayline that there are consequences if she tries anything stupid is even more important.'

It was Dia's turn to stare out at the horizon. 'Perhaps you're right, but I don't exactly feel comfortable there.'

Temerran winced. 'That's hardly surprising.'

Loud male voices broke into their peace as Arrus and Vilnue made their way down the narrow path to the beach with the last of the Borrow warriors, Worvig tagging along at the rear.

'I guess we're ready to sail,' Temerran said, although it was a moment before he stood. 'As a bard my only home is my ship, but I'm always saddest leaving here.'

'Will you ever settle?'

He looked down at the sand, his eyebrows drawing in tight across his green eyes. 'The Bard of The Borrows cannot settle, he belongs to the sea, and to all the islands.'

Without a backward glance he strode down the beach to meet his men, falling in with them easily, his volume and tone matching theirs. Temerran shook hands with Arrus and Vilnue, exchanging a few words with Worvig who helped push the rowboat out onto the water before the Borrowmen jumped in.

Dia realised she hadn't moved and taking in a breath hurried to intercept her husband, linking her arm through his.

'How was he?' Arrus asked.

'A little melancholy, he always is when he leaves here. How about his men?'

Arrus snorted. 'From their stories of the deep sea and the strange lands they visited in the west, I'd say they miss the freedom. I'm not sure a bored Borrowman is a good thing.'

'Hmmm.'

'Hmmm what?' Arrus poked her in the ribs. 'You're plotting.'

'Always.' She grinned. 'Come on, we have a harvest to organise and I have letters to write.'

Chapter Three

Cassien, Eastern Chem

She didn't make a sound as she moved up the slope to join him, barely stirring the undergrowth. Catya's blue eyes narrowed as she surveyed the city below them before turning to regard him.

'What do you have?'

Cassien crawled back a little way, ensuring nothing of his silhouette could be seen against the sky, before sitting up. 'There are twelve guards on the gate, they question and search everyone who goes in. From older reports that's a new thing, Uldren used to be pretty open to trade.'

'They've likely been rattled by what happened in Parsiphay.' Her eyes were still fixed on the city. 'What else?'

'They pay more attention to any groups with women in them. It would be easier for me to get in alone.'

She hesitated. 'Maybe. But that's not a plan I like.'

She turned and met his eyes, and it sent a little jolt through his body. He clenched his fists briefly against the heat that rose to his cheeks. They'd trained together for four years in the Fulmers under Heara's expert tutelage and Dia's watchful eye. Although fierce Catya was almost Cassien's opposite in nature, or perhaps because of it, they'd become lovers. Cassien had been completely in love, and he'd assumed she felt the same way until the day she packed and left. No warning, no word, she'd taken her weapons and a few clothes and joined the Borrowmen on the Undine. Cassien had returned to Chem, to the Ravens, to the familiar comfort of Navere. Two years later Catya turned up there, having tired of life on the sea and looking for something more challenging, something bloodier, to throw herself into. Hoping to turn her from her destructive path, Jorrun and Kesta had allowed her to join the Ravens, and after a year's training, they'd sent her with him to support Kussim in Caergard. To all outward appearances, Catya was calm, disciplined; but Cassien knew her better.

'The only way we'll learn for sure is to get into the palace.'

Cassien shook his head. 'There are subtler, easier ways to gather information.'

'But they take time.' She moved back from the brow of the hill to sit beside him. Her light-brown hair was plaited in multiple braids in Borrow style.

'All we need is confirmation Dinari is alive and in Uldren. Osun would have—'

'You're not Osun. Cass, let's just get into the city, speak to our contact, and see where we can go from there.'

He ground his teeth, but didn't disagree. Once Catya set her mind on something, it was very hard to turn her aside. Catya un-plaited her hair, combing through it with her fingers and tying it back in a simple tail. Cassien kept a look out while she changed from her scouting clothes into a long, plain dress and tied a veil about the lower half of her face. Cassien helped her stow everything in their saddlebags, and they wound their way through the trees to the black-paved road.

As a native Chemman, Cassien found it easy to blend in and he'd run several missions for the Ravens in and out of Eastern Chem.

Most of those missions had been to scout and gain intelligence, or meet up with operatives of the Rowen Order. He'd been a part of several rescues, but this was the first in which he'd been partnered with Catya. There was no doubting she was good at what she did, excellent in fact, but the tightening of his stomach muscles was a result of his knowing she wouldn't hesitate to take huge risks, whereas he preferred caution.

When they reached the road, Cassien got up into his saddle, but Catya remained on foot; in Eastern Chem, women didn't ride. Cassien pushed back the hood of his long-sleeved, beige tunic. Although there was a bite to the early autumn wind, he didn't want to appear as though he was hiding who he was. He couldn't help checking the four daggers tucked into the wide belt at his waist, or the sword buckled at his side.

He kept his head up as they came into view of the city gates, its high walls a patchwork of granite and hard, black, volcanic rock. He didn't acknowledge any of the traders who passed him, but called Catya forward to walk at his stirrup when a group of mercenaries thundered by on their horses. He joined the short queue, dismounting to hold the harnesses of both horses. Catya stood silently at his side, head bowed.

'Who're you?' One guard stepped around the group in front of them to confront Cassien, while his colleagues finished with the others.

'Cassien,' he replied at once. 'Of Caergard province.'

The guard's nostrils flared and his eyes narrowed; Caergard had fallen to the Ravens less than a year ago and was the most turbulent area within the 'Free Provinces of Chem.' Although the city itself was secure, with help from warriors of Elden, the Fulmers, and even the Borrows, the smaller villages in the region were yet to comply with the abolition of slavery.

Cassien almost snarled. 'I didn't like the way things were going down.'

'This woman from there?' The guard indicated Catya with his head.

'She is. I had to take the back roads and swim the river at night to stop those cursed heathens forcing me to leave her behind. I paid a lot of money for this one.'

'Got her sales papers?'

Cassien scowled, but turned at once to dig them out of his saddlebags. He took a moment to breathe in deeply and compose himself. Osun had been a master at this kind of thing, but Cassien always struggled not to allow his guilt to show. He was sure his cheeks must be bright red.

He handed over the papers depicting Catya's supposed bloodlines and her sale. It was easy enough to have such documents created and no actual way for the guards to know if they were genuine. One of the other guards wandered over to look Cassien up and down.

'So, what are you here for?' The first guard demanded.

'If I want to live, I'll need to find work.'

The guard grunted, handing him back the papers. 'I'll have to check your woman for weapons.'

Cassien shrugged. 'Of course.'

In the past, what this man was about to do would have been considered a crime against property, but since the conquest of the west and the rise of women into power, they had to accept such measures. Cassien forced himself to watch with an air of disinterest as the guard ran his hands over Catya, placing them everywhere. Cassien's fingers twitched, wanting to form themselves into fists. Catya didn't so much as blink, but Cassien knew as soon as she got the chance, this guard would be dead.

'All clear.' The guard nodded to his colleague, then waved Cassien through the gate.

Cassien took his horses' halters and strode through the gates. From his research, he knew the market district stood in the southern part of the city, the palace and wealthier citizens in the north. To the west were Uldren's dirtier industries, the tanners, dyers and slaughter houses; in the centre the towering temple. Their contact was to meet them in an inn near the city's eastern exit.

The streets of Uldren were no shock to Cassien; as a slave there was little he hadn't witnessed, or experienced first-hand. Even so, the smell of the slave pens in the market hit him like a physical blow. The metallic tang of blood made the hairs on his arms and the back of his neck rise. The swish and crack of a whip caused him to flinch, and he tightened his grip on the halters, his fingers needing the reassuring feel of his sword hilt. One gelding snorted, rolling its eyes and trying to pull its head free. He wanted to reassure it, but it wasn't something an Eastern Chemman would do.

His lungs seemed to open up, and he breathed more easily as they left the market behind. He'd memorised a map of the streets but anxiety didn't leave him until he saw the hanging sign of the Cuckoo Inn; a crudely drawn bird perched on a rowan branch. It was a small three-story building with a narrow alley leading to a yard and stable.

34

The horses' hooves made a hollow-sounding echo on the cobbles, which brought a servant hurrying out. He was in his thirties, his brown hair thinning, and wore a silver ring about his neck that indicated he was a favoured employee; possibly one left to run the inn for its owner.

'Master, can I help you?'

'I'm Cassien, I believe I'm expected?'

The man gave a slight bow. 'You are, master.' His eyes made a swift survey of Cassien's face. 'Would you like to follow me?'

Cassien waved a hand toward the inn, and the man proceeded him, ringing a bell on the wall to summon a slave to tend to the horses. Catya silently brought up the rear, head bowed. The inside of the inn was dark, but clean; sage grass burned in a small bowl on the mantle above an ornate fireplace. The walls were whitewashed, the carpets and furnishings a deep burgundy.

'Master, this is the guest you had booked in,' the servant spoke to a man sitting behind a desk. He was so short Cassien could only see the top of his grey-haired head. 'This is master Cassien.'

The innkeeper stood, and Cassien saw a man in his sixties with a pleasant smile. As he came around the desk to give Cassien a bow, his head barely came up to Cassien's chest in height. 'Master Cassien, I'm Gunthe, welcome to the Cuckoo inn.' He clapped his hands together loudly and a slave who was standing in a corner scurried over. Gunthe reached under his desk and took out a key, which he placed in the slave's hand. 'Take them up to the best room, Tildy.'

The woman gave a low bow, waiting until Cassien stepped forward to follow her before straightening up and heading towards a door. She had light-brown hair which contained a few strands of grey;

Cassien guessed her to be in her early forties. She held the door open for them and she led them up a flight of stairs to a hallway with creaking floorboards. She unlocked one of the rooms, standing aside to bow, the key held out on her palm.

There was also a small piece of parchment in her hand.

Cassien took both quickly. 'The room is sufficient.'

Catya stepped silently past them, and the slave ducked back out into the corridor. The moment the door shut, Cassien opened up the piece of paper while Catya made a quick check of the room and peered at the street below the window.

'It says to stay in the room and wait.'

Cassien jumped when someone knocked at the door. Catya snatched a knife from his belt and darted forward to open it, keeping the knife behind her back.

The servant with the silver collar stood there with a young male slave, both of them carrying their bags from the horses.

'Your belongings, master.'

'Just place them there.' Cassien pointed to the floor and Catya stepped aside. Neither of the inn's staff spoke as they put everything carefully down and backed out, gently closing the door behind them.

Cassien realised his lungs were aching, and he drew in a breath. 'What do you think?'

Catya shrugged, handing him his knife and taking her own weapons from their luggage. 'We wait.'

Cassien nodded. Gunthe was one of their best operatives, he'd worked quietly for the Rowen order for many years in Margith, an unobtrusive and patient man who said little but heard everything. The Ravens had set him up successfully first in Darkhall, then in Uldren, with a genuine business which allowed him to gather information. The woman who'd brought them up to the room was Gunthe's daughter; the trusted servant was a stranger.

Catya changed back into her trousers and shirt in case they had to fight, then returned to watching out the window. The light that spilled in caught her eyes, turning them to a lighter blue, and gave her pale skin a rosy glow. He turned away quickly before she saw him looking, the knot tightening in his stomach, and in his heart.

It was almost an hour before someone knocked. Once again Catya moved to one side of the door to open it, drawing her sword.

Cassien exhaled loudly when he saw Gunthe standing there.

'Come on in,' he ushered with a wave of his hand.

Gunthe didn't hesitate, stepping forward to shake Cassien's hand the moment the door closed.

'Master Cassien, it's good to see you.'

'And you, brother,' Cassien replied. 'Are you well, are you safe?'

Gunthe nodded rapidly. 'As safe as anyone can be in these times.'

'This is Catya. Please, have a seat.'

'I'm sorry about all the sneaking about; only my daughter knows who you are and what I am. I care for my staff, but can't afford to trust them. My message got safely to Darkhold then?'

'And from there to Caergard.' Catya sat on the bed, leaning forward. 'So, tell us all you know.'

Gunthe gave another rapid nod. 'So, one of the Rowen order works in a geranna house, an exclusive one in the palace district. A merchant frequents it, an ambitious man name of Pytin. He's a skin trader.'

Cassien's nostrils flared, and he gritted his teeth.

'Well,' Gunthe continued as Catya watched him avidly. 'He was bragging of how he'd made a tidy fortune selling a woman of excellent blood. He'd bought her from the palace in Farport for a lot of gold, intending to use her himself to try to produce an heir with power. She's old for childbearing, in her early forties; but he thought it worth the risk. Anyway, after thinking about it, he thought he'd see if he could make a tidy profit, knowing the Coven here in Uldren is desperate for stronger blood. He asked them to make an offer, and allegedly they gave him twice what he'd paid.'

'What makes you think it's Dinari?' Catya asked.

Gunthe shrugged. 'It's the name he used, and he described her as a tattooed woman of strong Fulmer descent.'

Cassien closed his eyes and groaned. 'She's tattooed.'

Gunthe screwed up his face in sympathy. 'I'm afraid so. If this woman is Jorrun's sister, it makes sense she'd have enormous magical ability, and they'd have blocked them with inhibiting runes.'

'Have you found out any more since?' Catya frowned.

Gunthe held up his hands. 'I'm sorry, no. I have no Rowen operatives within the palace, and they're so paranoid these days it's hard to get anyone in. I thought of trying to bribe a slave, but I'd be risking my safety, and more importantly, that of my daughter.'

'No, you can't do that,' Cassien said quickly. Catya had opened her mouth to speak, and her scowl suggested she wasn't about to be as sympathetic as him. 'We can take it from here.'

Catya sat back, drawing one of her legs up onto the bed. 'I'll get into the palace—'

'No, you won't,' Cassien snapped. 'There is a less dangerous path to try first. Gunthe, where can I find this merchant?'

'I can give you his address and what I know of his haunts and movements.'

'Excellent.' Cassien nodded, running a hand through his short hair. 'We'll try to get a look at his sales records; he should have retained copies of Dinari's history and bloodlines.'

Gunthe folded his hands together. 'An admirable plan.'

'Right.' Cassien drew in a deep breath. 'Let's sort out the details.'

***

Like most skin traders, Pytin kept slaves in pens and a warehouse in the market district, but he did all his most important trading from the comfort of his own home. Cassien spent some time posing as a buyer, even spending time pretending to haggle with Pytin's overseer in his cramped office. There were record books in there, but he doubted they would be the ones he needed. He made a note of the building's security even so; perhaps it would be needed one day when the Ravens came to free the slaves. That thought was the only thing that kept him from slicing the overseer's throat then and there as he kicked at one already badly bruised woman who couldn't crawl quickly enough from his path.

He did learn the important news that Pytin was away again on a new trading venture further east. Cassien cursed silently. They might have to wait months, weeks, to question the merchant. His overseer didn't seem to know anything about Pytin's dealings with the palace, and Cassien didn't dare raise the man's suspicions by pushing him too hard for information.

There was one option left to try. They'd have to break into the merchant's house.

Cassien finished sharpening his daggers and slid all four of them into his wide belt, then buckled on his sword. He stood regarding Catya, who was leaning against the wall, arms folded and foot tapping.

She rolled her eyes. 'Stop looking so worried, Cass, it will be fine.'

He didn't reply, going to the door and waiting for her to step into the hall so he could lock up behind them. He pocketed the key, and they left the hotel through the reception room, ignoring Gunthe who was busy with a new guest. The stranger had two hired guards with him, who watched Cassien and Catya leave through narrowed eyes. It was dark outside, only two lamps hung from posts to illuminate the short street. Cassien set a steady, unhurried pace, keeping his head up and not looking around at Catya, much as he itched to do so.

The streets were fairly quiet, but there was a tension in the air that made Cassien's skin prickle. Unlike Parsiphay, there had been no uprising here in Uldren, which was more than partly due to the fact it was ruled by one of the strongest of the remaining Covens. Between rumours of war and disquiet, and the religious turmoil the killing of the demon posing as Hacren had caused, people were fearful. Most avoided eye contact with Cassien, but there were some who checked him out as either a threat, or a possible target. His open display of weaponry seemed to deter the latter.

They reached the northern palace district un-accosted. Cassien had already scouted out the area, and he headed for an alley between two properties. Cassien cursed under his breath; there were two men coming towards them who would most certainly wonder at him disappearing into a dark alley with his slave. He continued with only the slightest of catches in his pace, having no choice but to take a long detour around an expansive block of walled-off gardens. When they returned to the alley, this time there was no one in sight.

They worked in complete silence, Cassien jumping up to catch the top of the wall and lying across it to survey the garden below. He hadn't been able to find a way of checking each residence's security without risking being seen, so they had to scout as they went. It looked clear, so he reached back down the wall to help Catya up. She dropped into the garden, pulling off her dress and stashing it beneath a bush. Cassien handed her two of his daggers, which she pushed into her own belt. They set off across the garden, staying low and keeping close to the wall.

In the next garden, Cassien spotted a guard patrolling around the house. He gestured for Catya to follow quickly, and they both dropped to the lawn the moment she was over the wall. Cassien slowed his breathing, his leg muscles braced. As the guard reached the corner of the grand building, they sprinted for the next wall. Cassien crouched, allowing Catya to use his back to spring straight up and catch the jagged stones; there wasn't so much as a catch in her breath as her trousers tore. Her fingers wrapped around Cassien's wrist and she helped him haul himself up. They scanned Pytin's garden before slipping down into a scratchy bay bush.

They were in.

Rather than ornate flowerbeds, this garden contained a small orchard and several vegetable beds. They used the small crooked apple trees to weave their way closer to the house, their dark-green clothing melting into the shadows. They waited for half an hour, studying the windows from a distance, watching as light flickered behind the glass and a silhouette occasionally passed. Catya glanced at Cassien, and they nodded, running across the open area to the granite building. Catya went straight for the door and tried the handle, not surprisingly it was locked. She held a hand up for him to wait, then checked the windows, pressing her face up against the glass to peer within. She returned to Cassien, shaking her head.

'If we break a window, they'll hear it,' Cassien whispered.

Catya held his gaze. 'We might have to feign a robbery.'

'You mean kill people.'

She nodded.

Cassien's stomach flipped, leaving him nauseous. He swallowed, there might not be any choice. 'Let me try the lock first.'

He fumbled in his pocket for his picks. All the Ravens had taken lessons in picking both locks and pockets from a nefarious thief called Rothfel, recruited by Captain Rece. Cassien was no good at pockets, but had some success with locks. He gritted his teeth, blushing slightly at the shaking of his fingers; if Catya noticed, she refrained from commenting. He wet his bottom lip, feeling for the tumblers while Catya kept a lookout. He drew in a sharp breath as his pick caught and he lifted the handle, giving the door a tentative shove. It opened.

He pocketed his picks and drew a dagger, Catya moving ahead of him. From their observations there seemed to be at least one person still up and about. Catya turned right, ignoring the first two doors they came to and pausing at the third; Cassien guessed she'd discovered Pytin's study when she'd spied through the windows. Cassien tensed as she reached for the handle, half expecting it to also be locked. It wasn't. Catya opened the door a crack, then wider when she was sure it was safe. They slipped in, closing the door behind them.

They waited, taking a moment to check the room over with their eyes, then moved at the same time, going for a tall bookcase filled with ledgers behind the desk. Cassien stepped aside to let Catya proceed him, then squinted at the barely perceptible lettering on the thick spines.

A floorboard creaked above them, and with a glance at Cassien, Catya crept back to the door to listen. Cassien drew out one of the volumes, holding it closer to the window to gain a little light. It was a sales ledger, but not the right one. Cassien tried three more before he found the one he was looking for. He looked around at Catya; she hadn't moved. He quickly searched through the entries, sucking air in loudly through his teeth when he found it. Dinari, born in Navere, sired by Dryn Dunham, sold at age eight to Karinna of Mayliz.

His finger moved to the bottom of the page.

Sold to Pentok of Serin Coven, Uldren.

It was her; she was here. Osun's sister.

Cassien put the ledger back and joined Catya. She looked up, and he nodded, a smile spreading across his face.

Catya raised her eyebrows and carefully opened the door.

The corridor was empty. They hurried for the exit. It was light that warned them before sound. Someone was coming.

Rather than run for the way out, Catya spun about, pushing past Cassien to draw a dagger. A middle-aged man, wearing a servant's collar, stepped into the hallway. Catya threw her dagger, catching the man in the chest. She sprang at him as he toppled backward, dropping his lantern. Cassien hissed at her in alarm, but she'd slit his throat before he had time to catch hold of her arm.

'We could have just knocked him out!'

She yanked her arm free. 'He saw our faces.'

She retrieved her dagger, freezing momentarily as a door opened somewhere else in the house. With a glare at Cassien, she made another run for the exit. This time they made it uninterrupted.

As they checked the garden and sprinted for the wall, they heard a woman's scream from inside the house. Cassien closed his eyes briefly, clenching his jaw.

Catya sprang up to catch the top of the wall, pulling herself up and over. Cassien followed, quickly surveying the two gardens ahead of them. The scream had alerted Pytin's neighbours, the guard calling in to someone in his building before demanding to know what was occurring with a yell.

'Murder!' Was the reply he got, a man's voice, not the screaming woman.

Cassien and Catya were already in the last garden, Catya scrambling into her dress while Cassien climbed up to check the alley. He held out his hand and helped her up, both of them dropping to the muddy path at the same time.

There were voices in the street. Cassien's stomach dropped; if they left the alley, they'd be seen.

Catya sidled up to the end of the alley, staying out of the weak lamplight, a deep frown on her face. Her shoulders dropped, and she turned to beckon Cassien.

'You have a plan?' He whispered close to her ear.

'Wait just a moment.' Her breath tickled his cheek. 'If they look down here, we'll make out you pulled me in here as you couldn't wait until we got back to the inn.'

She grabbed hold of his hips, pulling him close. He pressed his cheek against her hair, heat rising up his neck to his face. Several times since Catya had come to Chem, Cassien had given in and found himself in her bed. He always hated himself afterwards for being so weak, promising himself he wouldn't let her hurt him again, knowing it was a promise he'd struggle to keep.

She shifted to better see out of the alley over his shoulder.

'I think it might be clear a moment.'

Cassien stepped back and Catya risked moving into the light to peer down the street.

'Okay.' She looked up into his eyes, slipping his daggers back into his belt. 'We walk toward them.'

He nodded; it was dangerous but made perfect sense. If someone stepped out into the street and saw them, they'd wonder why they hadn't seen them pass Pytin's house; whereas it was feasible they'd come from further down the street.

With a rapid check in both directions, Cassien stepped out and fell into the same casual walk he'd used before, knowing Catya would be right behind him. His heart gave a flip as two armed men burst out of Pytin's gate.

'Hey, you there! Have you passed anyone?'

Cassien glared at them, doing his best to look affronted at being addressed in such a manner.

'Not for some time.' He looked the men up and down. 'Why?'

'Master Pytin's manservant has just been murdered.'

'Gods!' Cassien's hand went to his sword hilt. 'When?'

'Just a few moments ago. Better watch yourself, master.'

'I will, my thanks.' He turned to snarl at Catya. 'Hurry up.'

He set off with a faster stride, taking the same circuit they had earlier, before turning off to head back to the inn. They didn't speak until they were safely in their room.

Cassien swore. 'They know my face, that servant died for nothing.'

Catya gave an exasperated snort. 'The servant also saw me, a woman, armed and in trousers. It would have given away the fact Ravens are operating here.'

Cassien's muscles sagged a little. 'Well, hopefully they didn't think me anything to do with it. We should leave soon though, before they think to question me again and give my description to the gate guards.'

'We can't go until sunup, so we might as well get some sleep.' She pulled the Chemman dress up over her head and removed her boots and clothes. Cassien gritted his teeth and dragged one of the chairs around, sitting in it with his back to her and putting his feet up on the other chair.

'There's plenty of room for both of us,' she said.

He heard the creak of the bed as she got in it. 'I'm fine here, thanks.'

'Please yourself.'

Cassien didn't reply. Eventually her soft breathing told him she was asleep, but it was a while before he could sleep himself.

Chapter Four

Kesta, The Free City of Navere

Kesta picked up a rope, standing with one foot on the side of the ship as Jorrun steered them in. As soon as they tied up a guard came hurrying down the wharf to meet them, Kesta recognised him but couldn't recall his name. She grabbed up a bag and the harbour master waved them through.

'It's the women's market,' the guard told them breathlessly as he led them along the wharf. He was dressed in the green uniform of Navere, but didn't wear the Raven crest. 'Someone threw two flaming bottles of alcohol. He claims to be a Disciple of the Gods.'

'Was anyone hurt?' Jorrun demanded.

The young guard shook his head. 'No, Master Raven, thankfully not. The fire spread quickly though and they are still putting it out.'

'Was the culprit caught?' Kesta asked.

'He was.' The guard's jaw muscles moved as he gritted his teeth. 'He's been taken to Captain Rece.'

Kesta couldn't help a smile. Captain Rece had been one of the first Ravens, yet people still called him Captain, including her.

'Has anything else like this happened recently?' Jorrun's long stride easily kept up with the guard.

He shook his head. 'There was a man loitering outside the women's temple who we suspected was up to no good, but the amount of guards there put him off doing anything. When one of them moved to challenge him, he scarpered.'

They reached the guardhouse that overlooked the harbour.

'Would you like an escort to the palace, masters?'

'No.' Both Kesta and Jorrun answered at once.

'Thank you, but we can take care of ourselves,' Kesta gave him a thin-lipped smile.

The young man gave a bow and went in to report to his superior.

Kesta looked up at Jorrun. 'Market?'

He nodded, his gaze on the smoke that still rose. It was thinner now, less black. The sky itself was brightening, red still clinging to the clouds. The market would have only just been setting up when it was attacked and Kesta wondered at the 'Disciple's' choice of timing.

The city seemed busier than the last time Kesta had been here, almost eight months ago. She hoped it was a sign of Navere prospering, rather than just morbid curiosity of the market fires.

'At least they're not scared to come out on the streets,' she murmured.

Jorrun glanced at her, his blue eyes narrowing as the rising sun caught them. 'It seems to be mostly women the Disciples are targeting.'

Kesta's feet faltered at that, but she clenched her teeth and sped up to catch up with Jorrun.

'Yes, well, just let them try to pick on me.'

Jorrun met her eyes and grinned, albeit briefly.

They heard the shouts of the men fighting the fire as they drew close to the market and were heartened to see women among those forming the bucket chain. Two guards made to stop them, before realising who they were.

'Clear everyone out of the way,' Jorrun said.

There were some protests from those throwing water at the burning stalls. The fire had caught at least half a dozen of them and a building close by. Jorrun called up his power and sent a blast of cold air at the flames. Kesta watched wide-eyed, biting her lower lip. She might be able to rip rock up from the earth below, but Jorrun had always been better at cooling air than she was; he could even raise an impressive fog.

The fires sputtered and died, frost forming on the charred wood. Murmurs of relief rippled through the waiting crowd.

'Kesta, Jorrun!' One of the women dashed over, holding her bucket against her chest. Her brown hair was bound back beneath a green scarf, and a raven crest was sewn above her heart.

'Jollen!' Kesta hurried to meet her, kissing the taller woman's cheek. 'It's good to see you.'

'I'm certainly glad to see you, my magic doesn't stretch to putting out fires.'

Jollen took Jorrun's offered hand and squeezed it as he also kissed her cheek. Jollen had been one of the first women they'd freed in Chem, and one of the first to learn to use her magic. She wasn't strong, but she was a patient and clever woman, and she trained most of their recruits through the first stages of developing their power.

'I'm surprised you're both here though.'

Kesta winced. 'It seemed like it was necessary.'

Jollen replied so quietly it was hard to catch her voice, 'I think it is.'

'Ravens,' a guard interrupted. 'Should we close off the market for now?'

Jorrun shook his head, surveying the destruction. 'Keep it open as much as possible. I'll send word to Northold and have timber brought from there as soon as I can. In the meantime, please take details of everyone affected and have them report to the palace this afternoon with an inventory of what they've lost. We'll help get them trading again.'

'I'll have it done, Master.' The guard gave a bow.

The use of the word 'master' still set Kesta's teeth on edge, but making changes in Chem had to be a steady progression; the fact many women were now called 'master' was a huge stride forward.

Jollen handed her bucket to a man who'd presumably lent it to her and indicated toward the palace. 'The guards caught the person who did this, they have taken him to Rece.'

'So we heard.' Kesta narrowed her eyes, her fingers playing with the end of her dagger.

'Are you heading back there now?' Jorrun asked the Chem woman.

She shook her head. 'I'll stay and help fix things here. I'll catch up with you for dinner later though.'

'We'll look forward to it.' Jorrun nodded politely.

'I'm looking forward to getting some answers.' Kesta's hand dropped away from her dagger as she kept pace beside Jorrun. He automatically took a route that would avoid any larger crowds, even though Kesta was more used to them now and didn't get quite so claustrophobic. 'Like who's behind this. My money is still on the priests.'

Jorrun didn't answer, and she looked up to study his face. Worry lines creased around his eyes.

She swallowed. 'Are you thinking of Hacren?'

He turned his head, his eyes meeting hers, and reached out to take her hand. 'I can't not think of that demon since word of the threats the Ravens have received. I have an idea though, but...'

'But what?'

He squeezed her fingers. 'I don't think you'll like it.'

She sighed. 'Just because I don't like it, doesn't necessarily mean it will be a bad plan.'

He smiled, and her heart gave a skip, feeling lighter at once. Her cheeks tightened and warmed as his eyes travelling over her face.

'You're amazing Kesta.'

She snorted. 'We'll see how amazing you think I am when you tell me your plan and I shriek at you like a herring gull.' She pulled her hand free, but only to lace her fingers between his.

He almost laughed, but she could see he was still anxious. 'Not in the street, we'll discuss it in private with Calayna and Rece.'

Kesta nodded.

***

Navere palace loomed above the city, its high walls surrounding an expansive garden that for many weeks had provided Kesta with a calm sanctuary, a place of almost-freedom. The trees were just starting to turn, here and there a fallen leaf lay on the grass. The sound of children playing caused both Jorrun and Kesta to halt a moment. Sonnet and Ursaith were chasing each other around one of the flower beds. Sonnet's mother, Beth, kept an eye on the Navere children, looking up to smile and wave at Kesta and Jorrun.

Kesta drew in a deep breath. This was what they were fighting for.

Beth's smile faded a little, and she called out, 'Rece and Calayna are down in the old dungeons!'

The children spotted them then and came tearing over.

'Aunty Kesta, Uncle Jorrun,' Ursaith called out.

Kesta staggered back at the impact as the nine-year-old collided with her, gazing up at her with her bright, brown eyes. Sonnet was a little shyer, hanging back as Beth hurried over to apologise.

'Where's Sirelle?' Kesta asked the dark-haired girl who still clung to her waist.

'Mumma is taking the lessons today. Fire-balls!' Ursaith's eyes widened.

'Girls, leave them be,' Beth scolded. Like Sirelle and Jollen, this pretty blonde woman was one of the first Kesta had trained to use magic; Beth was one of the strongest in magic they'd found so far and also had an aptitude for midwifery. 'Are you heading down there? I don't envy you.'

Kesta's stomach tightened at the thought of the dungeons, they'd avoided using them since taking over Navere. If Rece had chosen to use them though, it was with good reason.

Kesta freed herself from the young girl. 'We are, thanks Beth, we'll see you later.'

Beth nodded, her smile slipping a little as she pulled Sonnet closer to her side.

The guards at the doors to the palace straightened on seeing them, and Jorrun gave a nod in greeting. A steward was waiting to see them, Zardin, an older man with thinning grey hair and hazel eyes.

He'd been a member of the Rowan order for years and had a lot to do with the subtle changing of opinion and behaviour of the men working within the palace.

'Ravens.' He gave a small bow. 'Calayna asked for you to be taken straight to them.'

Kesta dropped her bag to the side out of the way.

'How are you, Zardin?' she asked as they followed him through the hallway.

'I'm well, master, thank you for asking.' He looked around at her and smiled. 'I take it you want a report?'

She grinned, and he responded in kind, formality falling away.

'Mostly things have been settled since Master Jorrun was last here,' Zardin glanced at Jorrun. 'We've had no incidents in the palace itself. As for Navere, we've had the usual grumblings from the guild leaders. The so-called Disciples of the Gods have only shown their faces here in the last month.'

Two guards stood at the door leading down to the dungeons, something Kesta had never seen before. They moved aside at once for Zardin, and the Chemman steward opened the door.

'Did you ever...' Kesta hesitated, realising this wasn't the best time to ask Jorrun a difficult question.

'It's okay, go on,' Jorrun prompted.

She swallowed. 'Did you ever come down here as a child?'

Jorrun studied her face, glancing at Zardin. For a moment she thought he wouldn't answer. He opened his mouth, but it was a moment before he spoke. 'Yes. I was brought down here twice for lessons.'

'Lessons?' she asked in horror.

'Lessons in obedience and death.' His face had gone pale.

Kesta placed a hand on his arm. Zardin chose to diplomatically pretend he hadn't heard.

They had to take the steps single file, the lonely candle at the top of the stairs flickering so their shadows danced before them. Their footsteps echoed, particularly those of Zardin who wasn't used to treading softly.

The steward knocked at an old wooden door, its planks going green at the bottom from the damp. Kesta imagined Dryn Dunham had taken better care of the dungeon's maintenance than they had. She shuddered.

A bolt was drawn back and a young man peeped out at them, opening the door wider when he saw who it was. Kesta recognised him at once, he'd been a child when she'd first come to Chem, one of many who'd come to manhood in a very different Chem than he'd expected. She couldn't help but wonder if there was resentment behind that handsome face.

'Masters, please come through.' He gave a slight bow and gestured with his hand.

Torches burned on the wall; their flames steady without the hint of a breeze.

Kesta heard Rece's voice and saw Zardin blanch at the angry volume of it.

'Did you want to wait here for us?' she asked the steward. 'Or perhaps see to our belongings being taken to our rooms?'

'I will arrange that at once,' Zardin replied eagerly.

Jorrun shrugged his own bag off his shoulder and handed it to him. 'There are two small trunks also on my ship, in the cabin. Please see that nothing else in there is touched.'

Zardin gave a low bow and glanced at Kesta, a slight smile curving his lips. He knew as much as she did how much Jorrun loved his books.

Jorrun's chest rose as he drew in a deep breath and started toward the sound of the voices. As far as Kesta was aware, this was the first time in the seven years they'd held Navere, that Jorrun had ventured down here. She'd only been once, just to explore and ensure she knew everything she could about the palace. Osun had locked the place up; she'd never asked what he'd found down here.

Calayna's voice came softly to them and Jorrun's pace slowed. 'If you talk to us, we can help you. If you don't, we'll have to treat you as an enemy of Free Chem.'

Kesta tensed, holding her breath as they reached the open cell. A guard stood waiting outside, shifting his feet and appearing almost guilty. Jorrun froze, his eyes widening. Kesta moved to peer around her husband.

Calayna and Rece were standing with their backs to the door, a single torch was mounted in a bracket on the wall. Slumped on the stone floor was a small ragged figure.

Kesta gasped. 'It's just a boy!'

Calayna and Rece both spun about to look at her. The tattooed woman's mismatched brown eyes were hard, but softened, as did her posture.

'Kesta, Jorrun.' Rece stepped forward to shake Jorrun's hand and kiss Kesta's cheek. Calayna's greeting was more reserved. She and

Kesta had never completely warmed to each other, although there was plenty of respect there.

All of them watched as Jorrun took a few steps into the cell, his eyes fixed on the boy. He couldn't have been much more than nine, his clothes were ragged and thin, his dark-brown hair hung in curly strands down his dirty face. With a jolt, Kesta was suddenly reminded of Catya.

'What's your name?' Jorrun asked softly.

Rece opened his mouth, but Calayna touched his arm to hush him.

The boy didn't stir.

Jorrun turned his blue eyes on Kesta. She nodded and called up her *knowing*.

Jorrun's emotions were sharp. It hurt him being here, seeing this bedraggled boy in the cell. From Rece there was frustration and anxiety. Calayna was fighting hard to quell her pity, aware of the thousands of lives that depended on her.

From the boy… she felt fear, defiance… defeat. He desperately wanted to cry and was stretching for every ounce of hatred he could find to strengthen his resolve. Carefully, subtly, Kesta sent calm, trying to ease his fear, letting him know he could trust them.

He recoiled, spitting at her and showing his teeth. His wide eyes were a startling pale amber with bright flecks of green.

Kesta turned to look at the others, her mouth hanging open. 'He has power! He has the potential for magic.'

'This isn't working,' Jorrun said. Through her *knowing*, Kesta experienced his nausea. 'I have another idea. We should talk upstairs.'

'The boy?' Rece asked, his eyebrows drawn inward in concern. The ex-captain of the Navere palace guard was a tall man, though a good three inches shorter than Jorrun. His hair had gathered more grey in the years Kesta had known him and was almost silver above his ears.

Jorrun closed his eyes and sighed. 'Leave him here for now, with a guard present at all times. He is not to be left in the dark. Have him given food, hot water and a decent meal.'

Rece narrowed his eyes, but nodded.

Calayna's muscles seemed to relax a little. She turned to look at the boy. 'We will be back tomorrow. Think about what we've said.'

The boy snarled, but Kesta still had her *knowing* open and she felt his spark of hope, warring with the stinging resentment.

The guard closed and bolted the cell door, and they waited until they were up the stairs and out of hearing before they spoke.

'Are you both all right?' Kesta asked.

Rece sagged, pulling at his earlobe and rubbing the side of his face. 'It's been tense the last few days, I have to admit.'

'It hasn't been easy,' Calayna admitted reluctantly. 'But then none of it has been, and we didn't expect it to be.'

'What's your plan?' Rece regarded Jorrun.

Jorrun moistened his lower lip with his tongue and rubbed at his short beard. 'I'll dream-walk, see what I pick up from his subconscious.'

Rece grunted, and Kesta wasn't sure if it was surprise or approval.

'I hope it works,' Calayna said. 'I'm really not keen on torture, but we have to think of everyone's safety.'

'I can keep working on him with my *knowing*,' Kesta spoke up as they ascended the stairs to the main part of the palace. 'Try to win his trust.'

'We should try everything before we resort to violence,' Jorrun said quietly. 'A boy with power in Chem...'

Kesta's heart constricted. A boy with power in Chem would have been brutalised, brainwashed, just as they'd tried with Jorrun.

She froze. 'Wait, a moment. Does that mean a Coven sent him here? Eastern Chem?'

'It's a possibility to consider.' Jorrun headed automatically to the room that would forever be known as Osun's study. A young servant was waiting outside the room, and Rece quickly instructed him to fetch them some refreshments. The servant hurried away; he wore no collar, only a smart uniform.

Kesta tensed as she entered the room. There were still traces of Osun here, almost like a shrine. Jorrun ran a finger down Osun's blue quill pen, now covered in dust, and Kesta had to fight against the tight knot in her throat.

'Would you bring us up to date?'

'Of course.' Rece moved around the desk, Calayna sitting in one of the high-backed chairs to regard her and Jorrun. Rece drew out a map and unrolled it, Jorrun reaching out to hold a corner in place with his long fingers. Rece looked up to meet Kesta's eyes. 'So; as when you were last here, Chem is divided east from west by Warenna's River. Rey is doing well in Darkhall with her daughter, and our Sevi.' Rece turned to smile at Calayna. Sevi wasn't his biologically, and had been born, sold, then rescued before the two of them had married, but as far as Rece was concerned, the young woman of

Fulmer descent was his daughter. 'It still remains our best way of smuggling rescued slaves from the east.'

Kesta's eyes scanned the heavily forested area on the map, nestled in the mountains near the source of Warenna's River.

'Caergard holds fast, but as you know receives the brunt of the attacks from the east. The posting is as when you left it; so, your niece Kussim, with Pirelle, Merkis Dalton, Cassien and Catya and their Coven. The reports from Jagna and Estre have been good of late, the old capital of Arkoom is settling, although I fear getting my hope up on that. The rebuilding of Arkoom's palace is going well and has helped a lot of labourers get back on their feet.'

Jorrun looked up. 'And Tembre's Coven in Darva?'

Rece rubbed at his mouth. 'He has sent reports that all is under control in Darva…'

'But?' Jorrun raised his eyebrows.

Rece straightened up. 'But our Raven and Rowen intelligence suggest they're experiencing the same resistance as Caergard and Tembre's way of dealing with it can be a little… extreme.'

Kesta folded her arms across her chest. Tembre remained a tentative ally at best. He'd requested control of a coastal province to allow for trade with the Borrows and Elden, and they'd been happy, if wary, to help him take Darva.

'The last thing we need is for Darva to fall,' Jorrun murmured.

'And inside our borders?' Kesta asked.

Rece glanced at his wife. 'A few teething problems, a few minor clashes, the same as we get all over the Free Provinces.'

Jorrun reached out to pat the Chemman hard on the shoulder. 'You're doing an amazing job, both of you.'

Rece coloured slightly.

They were interrupted by a knock at the door and the young servant opened it.

'Come in,' Rece invited.

Two smiling women brought in trays of steaming violet and chamomile tea, and an array of breads, cheese and pastries. They waited until the servants had left before continuing.

'You know of the rebellion in Parsiphay and the report Dinari is believed to be in Uldren.' Calayna regarded them both.

Both Kesta and Jorrun turned back to the map, Kesta sipping carefully at her hot tea.

'I've been thinking about Parsiphay,' Jorrun said slowly. He worried at his bottom lip with his teeth. 'It wouldn't be impossible to take the city.'

Rece shook his head. 'I'm not sure our usual tactic of taking the palace and assuming rule would work there. Their 'Coven' is run by some kind of pirate lord and the citizens likely to turn on any guards who support Ravens. There's also the fact it would be difficult to hold the province and its borders. Warenna's River is pretty much the only reason we've kept our present border.'

Jorrun sagged a little, but the determined line above his nose remained. 'I was contemplating taking the city by sea, offering it to the Borrows with our support.'

Rece stared at him, mouth open. 'You want to give a Chemman city to the Borrows?'

'I'm not sure that's wise,' Calayna shook her head.

'Neither am I.' The corner of his mouth twitched up in a grim smile. 'But there were women and slaves in that city desperate enough to make an attempt alone. I... I feel I owe it to them to try something.'

Kesta straightened her spine. 'I think it's worth considering, certainly worth discussing with Temerran next time he's here. If... if we went for that though, we'd need to look at striking at some of the remaining inland cities at the same time to advance our border and weaken them. We hold over half the provinces. If we take Uldren and Parsiphay, it leaves them with only four. Three really, with Snowhold being isolated over our northern borders.'

'Are you suggesting Uldren because of Dinari?' Calayna narrowed her eyes.

Kesta shook her head. 'No, we'd be better off retrieving her in a more subtle and careful way. I only suggest Uldren because it's closest to our borders.'

'Has there been any more news on my sister?' Jorrun asked.

Rece shook his head. 'I only know Kussim has sent in Raven scouts to verify the rumour.'

Jorrun continued to stare at the map, his eyes fixed on the small red dot that marked Uldren.

Rece cleared his throat. 'So; what do we do about the boy?'

Jorrun stirred. 'I dream-walk.'

Rece raised his eyebrows.

'And Kesta should keep trying her *knowing* to win him over. If neither of our subtle magics work... well, we'll have no choice but to use stronger measures. In the meantime...' He turned to regard Kesta. 'We need to talk to the priests.'

Chapter Five

Temerran; Kingdom of Elden

'Temerran!' King Bractius stood, holding his arms out wide as Temerran approached the throne. His brown eyes seemed to hold genuine warmth, as did the tone of his voice; but you could never be sure with the King of Elden.

'Your majesty.' Temerran halted to give a dramatic bow, a charming grin lighting his face. 'I am honoured to be here.' He turned his gaze on the young queen who remained seated at the king's side on a smaller throne padded with purple satin. She'd gained a little weight in the last three years and it looked good on her, softening her face and giving shape to her figure. They had relegated the harsh black chair that had once stood beside the king for the use of his sorcerer, to the corner of the room. Jorrun did still sometimes sit in on audiences with the King, but it was much rarer these days.

'How are the twins, your majesty?' Temerran had no real interest in the princesses, other than to be polite. Babies and children weren't something that appealed to him. The prince, however, was a different matter. Young Lucien had started to develop a very interesting personality.

Ayline's face lit up with a smile. 'They keep me busy. Eleanor is a quiet baby, but Scarlet is already walking and interested in everything.'

That was one thing Temerran had to give the queen credit for; she hadn't handed her children off to a nurse, as most women in her position would, but was raising them herself for the most part.

'And Lucien?'

'With the arms master.' Bractius frowned. 'Although he doesn't seem to have taken to the sword as much as I'd like.'

'He's only seven,' Ayline muttered.

'At seven I could kill a man,' Bractius scowled. He sprang forward suddenly, jumping off the raised dais. 'Come, Temerran, have a drink with me. Tell me news of the world; I have something intriguing for you in return. The timing of your visit couldn't be better.'

Temerran smiled and followed the king to the long table at the side of the room. Bractius grabbed up a pitcher of foamy dark beer and poured them both a tankard. Seven years ago, this man had accused Temerran of murder and had him imprisoned within the castle with his men from the Undine; now he acted as though they were the best of friends and that chapter of their lives had never happened.

Temerran told Bractius all he believed it was wise to divulge of his recent visits to Chem, the Fulmers and his own Borrow Islands.

'You're aware Jorrun and Kesta have both gone off to Chem?' Bractius drained his tankard and re-filled it.

Temerran glanced up at Ayline. The queen hadn't moved from her seat but was watching them avidly.

'Typical when I could do with them here,' the king continued. 'Although you might stay and give me a good pair of eyes and ears?'

'What's happening?' Temerran's curiosity woke as he picked up on the king's excitement and wariness.

'We have visitors coming. Just over a week ago a large ship found its way to our southern coast carrying a delegation from a far-off land. I've sent warriors to meet them and escort them here.'

Dread slowly crept through Temerran, stiffening his muscles. 'What land?'

'They call it Geladan.'

Temerran froze. 'I have heard of it.'

'You have?' Bractius lowered his tankard. Ayline stood, catching the concern in Temerran's voice.

Temerran nodded once. 'I've not been there, but I have visited another land which traded with Geladan.'

'Well, tell me, man!' Bractius was smiling, but his eyes had hardened.

'I don't know much.' Temerran turned to perch on the edge of the table. 'They have magic in Geladan and are ruled by a woman. They say she is some kind of god and has lived for…' He ground his teeth. 'Well, according to the legends, she is hundreds of years old.'

'Really?' Ayline had moved closer to them across the hall.

Temerran shrugged. 'It's just legend and rumour. The people I visited were wary of trading with Geladan, partially because of the distance over hostile seas, partially because those people were without magic and intimidated by it. They seemed to think Geladan strange, but not barbaric, more… I would say they considered Geladan to be an advanced and perhaps overly religious people.'

Bractius snorted. 'Well, if they're ruled by what they consider to be a god, I guess they have to be. You don't think it's another of those demons, like Hacren, do you? One of the reasons Jorrun went running off was rumours some priests were threatening his Ravens with raising another so-called god.'

Temerran raised his eyebrows. 'We can't completely rule it out. We might have to be careful of what we say.'

'Well, yes, of course.' Bractius stared down into his tankard.

'When are they expected?'

It was Ayline who answered. 'Three days.'

'And you'd like a bard to entertain them?'

'That's very kind of you.' Bractius grinned.

Temerran couldn't help a chuckle. 'All right. And my men?'

Since Quinari's attack on the king and the murder of Larissa, they'd allowed only a limited amount of Borrowmen into Taurmaline castle with each of Temerran's visits. Although completely exonerated, Bractius was still overly cautious of the slightly wild Borrow warriors. Temerran hoped Elden's king would show the same reservation with his new guests.

Bractius rubbed at his sandy-coloured beard. 'Find me a couple of dozen you trust and brief them, if you're willing. Closed mouths, open ears. It will be good to show our lands are peaceful, but united if there's trouble.'

'I can find you the men.'

'Good.' Bractius thumped him hard on the back. 'Come man, get settled in your room, eat with us tonight.'

Temerran thanked him, putting down his tankard and allowing a page to lead him away.

***

As soon as he'd made arrangements with his first mate and seen his men settled, Temerran found his way to the training yard. He winced when he saw the young prince was still there, wooden sword in hand. The burly warrior who was teaching him wore a scowl of annoyance on his face. No doubt the king would blame him if his son failed to become the skilled fighter he demanded.

Lucien was the picture of concentration, his fair eyebrows drawn in over his large, brown eyes. His hair fell in tight curls about five inches long, brown but with a hint of red. He had the positioning of his feet correct, but his shoulders were hunched over as though he were expecting a blow. To an extent, Temerran supposed he was.

Lucien looked up as Temerran approached across the yard and the boy immediately straightened up, a smile spreading across his face. 'Tem!'

The warrior gave Lucien a clout about the head. 'What have I told you about concentrating?'

Temerran clenched his fists and had to stop himself growling. He had an overwhelming desire to punch the warrior and teach him a lesson in saving his aggression for someone his own size.

Lucien's face reddened, his small nostrils flaring. He sniffed, but refused to cry.

Temerran raised his hands. 'That was entirely my fault, I should have held back and waited. Young children are easily distracted.'

'Lucien is a prince, not a boy,' the warrior snapped.

Temerran had to bite his tongue. 'I wondered if I might speak with his highness?'

'He has another half an hour of training yet.' The warrior's dark eyebrows almost seemed to bristle. Temerran held his gaze, a pleasant smile on his face. The warrior's posture relaxed a little. 'I suppose it won't hurt. Gods know he isn't getting anywhere.'

Temerran's spine locked. His smile froze, but he said nothing. His temperature rose as he saw the trembling of Lucien's jaw out the corner of his eye.

'Make sure you put your sword away,' the warrior snapped at Lucien.

Neither Temerran nor the boy relaxed until the warrior had left the courtyard.

'The man's a vile bully,' Temerran growled.

Lucien's eyes widened, and he stared up at Temerran. The bard smiled, holding his arms open, and Lucien darted forward to give him a hug.

'You could ask for someone else to train you,' Temerran suggested.

Lucien bit his lip and shook his head. 'If I asked for someone else, I would have failed.'

Temerran regarded the boy. As Bard of the Borrows, Temerran would eventually have to choose an apprentice, someone who could be neutral in dealing with each settlement on the Islands, someone with the ability to work the magic of a bard. Lucien loved music and absorbed every story into his soul with the eagerness of a starving pup. He was also incredibly sensitive to those around him, aware of emotion and subtext far more than a child his age should be. The Matriarchs of the Borrows would say Lucien was an old soul in a new body. If he'd been of the Borrows, had he not been a prince, Temerran would have chosen him without hesitation. It broke

Temerran's heart to see how much Lucien's sensitivity and intelligence was already causing the boy pain.

'I understand,' Temerran replied sadly. 'What is it that makes you struggle, do you think?' He walked over to a low wall and sat; Lucien followed, putting down his wooden sword to pull himself up.

'I think…' Lucien shifted a little. 'I'm not sure it's in me to be a warrior.'

'Hmm.' Temerran gazed across the courtyard. 'I imagine you've been taught that being a warrior is all about being aggressive, strong, loud, and absolute.'

Lucien nodded.

'Let me tell you about some of the best warriors I know. Have you met Cassien?'

'I think so.' Lucien frowned. 'I've heard of him.'

'Cassien is the finest swordsman I've seen, faster than a hawk striking, precise, almost genius; but he hates killing. He was a slave, forced to fight to live, but he didn't want to fight, and it hurt his soul. He was rescued by Osun, and now he fights for the people who are like he used to be, and for the people who can't fight. He doesn't like to be called a warrior, but he is one of the best.'

'Is he a Raven?' Lucien blinked up at him.

Temerran's smile broadened. 'He is. I'll tell you of another warrior. I think you know her very well. She doesn't fight with a sword, she fights with her mind, with her cleverness, and with her magic. She isn't physically strong, but she thinks, and she plans, and she learns. She defends her people with the skills she has. Do you know who I'm talking about?'

'Raven Kesta?'

Temerran laughed. 'Very similar, but I was talking of her mother, the Icante.'

'Grandma Dia?' Lucien exclaimed in surprise.

Temerran winced, wondering if Ayline knew her son called the leader of the fire-walkers, 'grandma.' It was hardly surprising though; Lucien spent a lot of time with Arridia and Joss.

'Yes, Dia. Being a warrior is more than being a swordsman or a brute, it's about using the strengths you have to protect others. Does that make sense?'

Lucien leaned back a little to gaze up at the sky. 'Yes, it does make sense.'

'Good.' Temerran hopped down off the wall. 'In the meantime, though, let's see if we can improve your technique and save you a few clouts about the head.'

***

Temerran sat cross-legged, his back against the tree. Around him leaves slowly fell, and shafts of sunlight caught the dancing insects. He took in a deep breath, enjoying the warmth of the sun against his skin.

The skittering of a stone caused him to open his eyes, and he turned to see his two men returning. Both Nolv and Sion had smeared ash around their eyes in Borrow raider fashion, giving them the appearance of wearing masks.

'They're coming,' Sion said, moving to stand behind Temerran's tree.

They waited, hearing the clip of hooves before the group came within sight on the road below. Elden warriors took the lead, but

Temerran sat up straighter when the Geladanians came into view. At their head were a man and a woman; she was tall with straight black hair, riding side-saddle with a long staff across her lap. She wore a headdress of red and gold that reminded him of the rays of the sun. The man was thin, with blonde hair and sharp blue eyes, his clothing was dark green with intricate and expensive-looking silver embroidery.

Behind them rode a muscular warrior, his arms bare, with dark hair and short stubble. He had a long-handled axe strapped to his back and both sword and dagger at his belt. Behind him was an older man with long grey hair tied back in a tail and a neat beard cut close to his face; at his side was a younger woman with soft grey eyes and curling black hair. All of them were richly clothed and wore jewelled accessories.

Five warriors came next, in plain clothing and outfitted with swords and bows. Just before the Elden warriors brought up the rear, a wagon trundled, carrying luggage and a huddle of servants. One caught Temerran's eye and he didn't realise he was holding his breath until his lungs ached. She was wearing a dark-red cloak, the hood down, showing soft brown hair with golden highlights. She had a small nose and rounded cheeks, flushed almost as red as her lips. She looked up, and Temerran's eyes widened as her blue-green ones met his. She didn't say a word to anyone else, but she held his gaze for as long as the wagon remained in sight.

'Captain?' Sion prompted.

It was a moment before Temerran shook himself and got to his feet, brushing the forest debris from his trousers. 'Come on, let's get back to the castle before them.'

'Did you learn anything?' Nolv asked.

Temerran frowned. 'Just a little. Come on.'

They hurried up the hill to their horses, riding out of sight of the road toward Taurmaline. Many of the city's residents were loitering in the streets ready to catch a glimpse of the strange guests from a far-off land and in places it was hard to get the horses through. Merkis Teliff was waiting at the stables; the Eldeman was an able captain and advisor to the king and often spent time away on trade runs to the other lands in their new alliance. He took hold of Temerran's rein to help him dismount.

'Anything useful?'

Temerran sucked air in through his teeth. 'At least two magic wielders. Plenty of muscle, too. If I were you, I'd send to the Fulmers at once and see if they'll send a *walker* to keep an eye, if not them, one of the Ravens who are training there.'

Teliff narrowed his eyes and nodded, handing the horse over to a stable boy. All four of them headed into the great hall, Temerran and his two scouts taking up position at a guest table while Teliff hurried to speak quietly with his king. Bractius nodded, and Teliff moved to speak to a steward. Something else caught Temerran's attention, prickling at the back of his neck. He spotted Merkis Adrin seated almost opposite on the other side of the room. The handsome, but arrogant warrior was still in favour with the king, although not as much as he'd been after the saving of Mantu island. He sensed he was being watched, but Temerran looked away before Adrin caught him studying him.

A guard at the main door banged his pike down on the floor thrice; a warning that their guests were imminent. Many in the hall hushed, but others continued talking, their voices rising a little higher in pitch. Several warriors lined the wall, all smartly dressed in the same light armour. Several others sat more discreetly among the guests, armed only with long knives.

The Elden escort appeared first in the doorway of the great hall and a hush fell, Teliff gesturing for everyone to stand. Only Bractius and Ayline remained seated in their ornate chairs. Temerran was relieved Lucien had been kept away from the hall; the queen's ladies-in-waiting were also absent. The chieftain who'd led the escort strode to the base of the dais below the high table and gave a bow, turning to gesture as their strange guests entered. All but two of them had olive skin like the people of the Fulmers, only the woman in the red cloak and the blond man who stood at their head were pale skinned.

'Your majesty, Bractius, King of Elden, I introduce to you visitors from the far-off land of Geladan.'

Temerran didn't miss the tightening of Ayline's jaw at her being omitted.

The chieftain continued, waving a hand toward the tall, dark woman and the grey-haired man. 'Yalla, High Priestess of Geladan, and Lorev, a sorcerer of Geladan.'

Both bowed toward the king, Lorev much lower than the priestess who held her ornate staff. It seemed to be made of gold and was embossed to resemble the scales of a snake, the head of the staff that of a dragon, mouth open to strike.

'May I introduce, Ren, ambassador of Geladan, Efrin, a Guardian of Geladan, and Kichi, a bard of Geladan.'

Temerran sat up straighter, studying the short, smiling woman with black hair and soft grey eyes. The thin blond man stepped forward, and Temerran guessed he must be the one named as Ren.

The ambassador gave a low bow, bending gracefully at the hips, rather than the waist. 'Your majesties, it is our great honour to be invited here, to be received by you.'

'And you are most welcome.' Bractius wore his most charming smile, the one that had fooled many into thinking he was a kind and light-hearted man. 'What brings you many miles across the sea to our shore?'

Ren's smile broadened a little at Bractius coming straight to the point. The 'Guardian,' Efrin, shifted his feet. 'We heard rumour of your land through a people we trade with and wished to explore and meet you.'

A jolt ran through Temerran's nerves. So, this *was* down to him and the Undine. There was something else, something beneath this smiling man's words…

'We look forward to getting to know you.' Bractius regarded them all, taking their measure. 'Would you join us? Or do you wish to refresh yourself first?'

'We would be honoured to join your meal.' Ren gave another bow.

Bractius gestured to Teliff, who quickly deployed pages to guide their guests to their seats. Like Temerran, Bractius had already spied out who to expect and had briefed his staff. Ren was led to the seat beside Ayline, and Teliff sat to the other side of him. Yalla was offered the seat on the king's left and Temerran was called up to sit between her and the Geladan bard, Kichi. Adrin strode across the hall

73

to take the seat beside Kichi, and the remaining two visitors from Geladan sat at the opposite ends of the long table, Efrin beside Adrin.

Temerran looked back down the hall. The woman in the red cloak had remained with the five Geladanian warriors who hadn't been introduced. They were all found seats among the lower tables; presumably the other Geladanian servants had remained in their rooms. Temerran noticed the Fulmer ambassadors, Dorthai and Finian, were placed with his own Borrowmen; he imagined the Fulmer ambassador would have been seated at the top table and used differently by the king if they'd had magical power.

Adrin didn't waste any time, introducing himself to Kichi and being sure to mention as soon as possible his greatest achievements as a warrior. Efrin appeared thoroughly unimpressed, reaching for a leg of chicken and eating slowly, his brown eyes tracking the movement of the people in the room. Ayline and Ren had already engaged in a lively and cheerful conversation, comparing the food and drinks of their countries. Temerran had to admit the queen was as good as her husband at this game, perhaps better. Bractius had begun with safe ground, enquiring of Yalla how she'd found her journey here and her initial impressions of his kingdom. A young woman brought a carafe of wine to the high table to fill their glasses, Temerran noted only Efrin declined. The serving woman smiled down at Temerran, her cheeks flushing slightly. She'd shared his bed the last two nights and probably would again.

Temerran looked up and automatically his gaze searched out the red cloak. The nameless woman was eating daintily, head down. She glanced up, meeting his eyes, and he quickly looked away. Time to get to work.

He introduced himself to Efrin first, explaining a little of his land and who he was to the Borrows and to Elden. When it came to his ship, he didn't hold back his talent as a bard, and he gained a little information about the Geladanian ship and their fleet back home in return. Efrin wasn't particularly talkative, but unsurprisingly Kichi was. Frustratingly Adrin was more so, spilling his guts to the attractive woman. Temerran found it hard not to let his frustration show, the narcissistic warrior was the worst person Bractius could have seated here, although … he doubted the king would have been thoughtless in his choice. The fact Adrin's young wife, Lady Sonay, was not present suggested Bractius expected Adrin to charm the women of the Geladanian delegation.

Temerran realised Bractius and the High Priestess of Geladan were discussing religion; dangerous and delicate ground. Bractius told of the God and Goddess of the Elden people, and Yalla nodded politely, a soft smile on her face. Temerran pretended to be paying Adrin all his attention, sometimes even exchanging a conspiratorial roll of the eyes with Kichi, while in reality he was listening to Yalla.

'We are lucky, blessed, in Geladan. Our Goddess came to dwell amongst us, to be close and protect us. She took the body of a priestess who gave up her vessel willingly and has guided us for many years.'

'It's not intimidating facing your god every day?' Bractius asked.

Yalla tilted her head a little, her eyes un-focusing as she considered it. 'Jderha is unforgiving of betrayal and swift to destroy those who would threaten the peace of Geladan, but she is otherwise generous, benevolent and wise beyond words.'

'And powerful no doubt.'

Temerran winced. That had been less than subtle.

'Oh, of course,' Yalla replied. 'She commands the spirits.'

'You mean like fire-spirits?' Ayline broke in.

The hairs on Temerran's arms prickled and foreboding blew like a cold wind across his spine. Efrin had looked up, Kichi turned a little in her seat, and Ren ceased speaking.

'You know of fire-spirits?' Yalla asked brightly.

'We have heard of them in tales,' Temerran said quickly. 'But sea-spirits I do know, for I sing to them myself.'

Ayline frowned a little, but she didn't correct him.

'You can control sea-spirits?' Kichi asked, her eyebrows raised.

Temerran chuckled. 'I wouldn't call it control. Calm, influence perhaps, but sea-spirits are wild and slippery, as I'm sure you're aware.'

'All spirits serve Jderha.' Yalla frowned, her voice deep and low. 'Those who do not—'

'Come to love her anyway,' Ren interrupted, showing his teeth in a fixed smile. 'You say you know tales of spirits?'

Bractius took his cue. 'Temerran, would you sing for us?' The king beamed at him. 'If you would be kind enough to indulge me, I'd be grateful if you could sing some Elden songs for our guests.'

Temerran stood and gave a small bow. 'I would be honoured to, your majesty.'

Moving around the high table, he gestured toward the musicians and called out the name of the song he wished them to play. His own instruments were there waiting for him, and he picked up his fiddle. Something lively to begin, a classic tale of foolish love. He followed with a traditional folk song for the harvest, dared a song of praise to the goddess and then moved onto a ballad which had several people in the room in tears. He used his voice but was careful not to draw on his subtle magic, the power of his soul. He'd noticed in the conversation at the high table that Ren, the ambassador, used the same magic, and he had no doubt Kichi would possess it too, or something similar.

He took a break, making his apologies and leaving the Elden musicians to play alone. He noted Kichi made no offer to sing for them; unusual for a bard not to want to show off their skills. Teliff sought him out immediately, handing him a chalice of wine. He spoke quickly and quietly.

'Bractius asked me to tell you he has sent a message to Northold to warn Azrael and see if the creature knows anything of these people. He'll also write to Dia and see if she's willing to come and meet them.'

Temerran nodded. 'I didn't hear much from the sorcerer.'

'We'll meet early tomorrow and discuss everything; I'll send a page to you.'

'Good evening.'

Temerran startled, Teliff took a step back. The woman in the red cloak stood looking up at him. Her green eyes were darker than his, almost turquoise. Teliff cleared his throat and made his way back toward the high table.

'Good evening.' Temerran's mouth curled up in a smile, and she didn't look away as he studied her face. 'So, do you have a name?'

'Linea.'

'You weren't introduced to the king, Linea.'

'I'm merely a servant.'

Temerran narrowed his eyes. Somehow, he doubted that. She was too confident, too poised, too at ease; someone who was used to moving where she liked.

'And whom do you serve?'

She smiled at that; her rounded cheeks dimpling and Temerran's heart beat just a little faster. 'I serve Jderha.'

A touch of dread mixed with the fluttering in his chest. 'And are you enjoying your visit to Taurmaline?'

'I especially enjoyed your singing.' She lowered her head as though shy, although she maintained eye contact. 'And your ambassadors from the Fulmer islands are interesting, the islands sound wonderful. Fire-walkers.'

'They are the best of people.' He wondered if she'd caught the flicker of fear in his eyes.

She looked away and wet her lips. He couldn't help but wonder why she'd let him know she'd caught him out on his lie of omission. Was she warning him they knew there were fire-spirits here? He took a risk.

'Do your people have a dislike of fire-spirits?'

She turned back to him, shaking her head. 'Not at all. But Jderha has a dislike of those who disobey. In Geladan all spirits serve the god. Many, many years ago priestesses of the flame and their families rebelled, freeing their fire-spirits and escaping over the sea. It was said those priestesses who served the flame had mis-matched eyes.'

'But…' Temerran shook his head. 'You are talking of hundreds of years ago, surely.'

She quickly looked around her. 'Many generations, yes.'

'A long time to hold a grudge.'

'Gods have long memories.'

Temerran felt sick. Surely these people hadn't come all this way to look for escaped fire-spirits from some bygone age? If they had… it was down to him and his vain exploration of the seas.

'Why are you telling me this?'

She shrugged. 'Why not? There is no reason to hide our history.'

Because it meant nothing, or because they thought there was nothing anyone could do to stop them?

He held her gaze. 'Why did your people come here?'

She took a step back. 'You are very direct, Temerran of the Borrows. We came here to explore and to learn.'

Was it a lie? Despite all his bard's training, he couldn't tell. He mustered his most charming smile and bowed. 'I certainly look forward to learning more about you, Linea. But at the moment I'm neglecting my obligation to our host, the king. Please excuse me.'

He held her gaze as he took two steps back, then turned around to make his way slowly toward the musicians. As he passed his men, he bent to whisper to Nolv.

'Tell Teliff to send another message to Northold; Tantony needs to get the kids and Azrael out of there and to the Fulmers, I think they may be in danger. And Dia and the *walkers* must not come to Elden.'

Chapter Six

Catya, Eastern Chem

As soon as they were clear of the road, Catya ripped off her veil and pulled the long dress up over her head. She dug in her saddlebags and took out a shirt, buttoning it as she caught up to Cassien. He handed her sword to her and pushed his hood back. His hair was cut a lot shorter than it had been when they'd first met; she missed his soft curls, there had been something endearingly innocent about them. When she was ready, she swung up into his saddle and they set off through the pine trees at a steady canter, putting distance between themselves and the city. Catya closed her eyes, letting the wind blow back her hair. She loved riding; it didn't give her quite the same feeling of freedom as being on the sea, but it was close.

Avoiding the roads, villages, and towns also meant for the most part they avoided the patrols of the province's guard, but it put them in danger of crossing the path of the increasing number of bandits and thieves. Catya wasn't as good a scout as her mentor, Heara – she doubted anyone was – but she prided herself she was close. The only time bandits found them was when she wanted them to.

The easiest way back into western Chem and the Free Provinces was through a dense and mountainous forest and the source of Warenna's River. Here, Uldren's north-west border met the eastern edge of smaller Darkhall province. Cassien had considered going that way and sending a message from Darkhall to Caergard by bird but had decided on the quicker but more challenging route, directly west to Caergard and through the river.

The Warenna had three fording points and once had two bridges between Caergard and Uldren, both of which had been destroyed to prevent invasion or the escape of slaves. The fording points were guarded on both sides, the only way to cross was to swim or sail the wide river or pass a post unseen.

Not wanting to leave their horses, they opted for the former, spying on one of Uldren's guard posts while they waited for nightfall. Catya plaited back her hair again and smeared ashes across her cheeks and around her eyes in Borrow raider fashion, masking her pale skin and making the round shape of her face less obvious.

Cassien had changed into a green tunic, its hood up, although it didn't hide his disapproving looks. He hated that she loved the culture of the Borrows best of all the lands she'd apprenticed in. Not surprisingly, he favoured the Fulmers.

'Thirty-seven,' he whispered. 'But there's no way of knowing how many are inside the buildings.'

Catya gave a distracted nod, her eyes following the men below. 'I concur. They obviously don't expect us to attack anytime soon, it would only take a small force to wipe out that post, a couple of magic wielders could do it.'

'It's not the way the Ravens work.'

'Precisely.' She jabbed him in the arm with one finger. 'It's time we changed how we work. Osun's plan may have gained us a foothold and taken the west, but the same thing won't work anymore.' She had to refrain from rolling her eyes when she saw his jaw tighten; Cassien couldn't bear for anyone to criticise his hero, Osun.

He crawled back a little way. 'Come on, we should get into position to cross.'

Catya lingered a moment longer, watching as the Chemman guards sauntered about the village they'd commandeered. Her nostrils flared a little, her heart beating strongly. She would have loved to go down there and take out as many as possible, just to test herself. She wondered how many she could get on her own before being discovered.

'Cat!' Cassien hissed.

With a huff, she edged back and followed him to where they'd left the horses.

It was pitch-black when they reached the point they'd chosen to make their crossing. A long, narrow copse ran along the path of a stream that fed into the wider river. They'd already stowed their gear carefully to avoid losing it in the wild water.

The horses weren't going to like it.

They edged them into the stream where the bank was shallow, and Catya winced at the splashing they made. Her horse snorted as the water deepened and tugged at the reins.

'It's okay.' She leaned forward, rubbing its neck.

She urged it towards the water, and it blew out air loudly as they hit the current of the faster river, its eyes rolling as its hooves found only water instead of ground.

'Go on, it's not far,' Catya reassured it, shifting her position in the saddle to help it swim more easily. There was a loud splash as Cassien's horse followed. They were out in the open now and she peered at the bank ahead, before twisting to watch behind them. Cassien's eyes were bright, almost the same colour as the moon that caught in them. She gritted her teeth and turned back to the far shore, pushing aside any weak sentimentality. Caring about people was how you got hurt, it made you vulnerable, just as Osun's death had weakened Cass; and Jorrun.

Her horse's hooves touched ground and it surged forward, its muscles bunching beneath her. She didn't wait for Cassien but headed straight for cover.

Something moved. The glint of metal.

She threw herself from the saddle as an arrow came whining out of the trees, rolling as she hit the ground and coming up onto her feet in a crouch with one of her daggers drawn. Her horse gave a scream and thundered away into the darkness. Cassien's horse followed; without a rider.

Catya calmed her breathing, widening and un-focusing her eyes to let as much light as possible in. She dropped to the grass, crawling almost soundlessly, using her knees, toes, and forearms to propel herself forward quickly.

There.

She sprang up, throwing her dagger and grinning as it went straight into a man's eye. She drew another dagger and raced for the trees, twisting aside to avoid the swing of a sword and slicing her blade through a second man's throat.

Cassien was in the trees beside her, sword drawn. With a cry three men rushed them and Catya stepped back, letting Cassien engage. She couldn't help but be mesmerised at the way he moved. He was a master at sword as Temerran was a master with words, able to shape sounds into magic. Heara was the same; with her outstanding speed and grace, she was a joy to watch. The difference was both Heara and Temerran took great pleasure in their skill, Cassien somehow seemed to resent it.

He took out one man with a swift thrust and the Chemman stared down at the wound, wide-eyed and open-mouthed, as though he didn't understand how it had gotten there. Cassien engaged the second's sword, barely a flicker on his face as he ducked, swapped the sword to his left hand, and sliced across the third man's chest as he tried to cut in on his other side. Catya darted in to finish him with her dagger. Cassien changed his sword back to his right hand in time to block an overhead, two handed blow from the remaining man. He stepped forward, drawing a dagger, and thrusting it into the man's stomach.

With a curl of his lips and an anguished groan, Cassien slit the man's throat to end his pain and save him from a slow death.

Catya didn't waste any time, but quickly examined the men and what she could of their tracks.

'Was that all of them?' Cassien asked. He wasn't even slightly out of breath.

'It's too dark to be sure.' She grasped a silver broach on the chest of one of the men, unpinning it to hold it closer to her face. 'A wolf insignia. They all seem to wear one.'

Cassien crouched beside her and she handed it to him. He ran a finger over the engraving. 'It's not an emblem I'm familiar with. A new Coven perhaps?'

'But they didn't have any magic users with them.'

'Not all of them have these days.' Cassien looked up, his gaze somewhere beyond the trees, his forehead wrinkled in concern as he rubbed at the brooch with his thumb. 'Parsiphay doesn't rely on magic, but their emblem is a Kraken.'

She studied his face. 'What are you thinking?'

'I'm thinking we have Ravens.' He stood up and handed her back the brooch. 'Maybe they now have Wolves.'

Catya raised her eyebrows. It made sense. These men dressed and acted like scouts, not bandits.

'Let's take what's useful and find our horses.' Cassien looked around them quickly. 'We need to get this news to Caergard and Navere as soon as possible. If they are scouts, it means a prelude to something.'

Catya didn't need telling twice. She picked only small valuable items, including the wolf emblems, not wanting to weigh herself down. It took them only a moment, then with unspoken agreement, they made a last sweep of the copse in case they'd missed anything before circling back. The moon was already dipping toward the horizon, and it wouldn't be long before they lost its light.

They set off at a jog in the direction the horses had gone, frequently scanning the meadow around them for danger. Catya's limbs loosened in relief when she spotted the silhouette of one of the animals. She slowed to a walk, approaching calmly. The horse lifted its head, scenting them. It stamped a hoof, but otherwise didn't move. Catya's mare wasn't far beyond it and came trotting over when Cassien took a carrot out of his saddlebag.

'We should get some more distance between us and the river,' Catya suggested.

'Agreed.'

Cassien quickly checked his horse over for injuries, and with a twinge of guilt, Catya copied him. They mounted up and headed into the darkness of the west.

***

Catya looked up at the walls of Caergard with a mixture of trepidation and relief. She tried to tell herself it was just a posting, a job to do, but her heart told her it wasn't her home. For a while the Undine had been, but she shied away from thinking of it as a stab of pain ripped through her heart. When she thought of home, she thought of Northold, of Rosa's gentle hugs and her warm lavender smell. She hadn't been able to face going back since falling out with Kesta and Jorrun over Cassien. They'd been furious with her treatment of him and her running off on the Undine. Heara had understood to an extent, but even the wild Fulmer woman had looked at her with disappointment in her eyes. The only person who hadn't expressed their opinion on her behaviour had been Cassien himself.

The guards at the gate straightened up to salute them as they passed, their Raven crests giving them swift admission. Her horse picked up its pace, knowing it was near its stable and a generous helping of good feed. A runner went ahead of them to report their return to the palace as they handed their animals over to a groom.

Cassien strode eagerly to the doors, his gaze focused on the ornate wood and flickering up to the windows as though he thought someone were watching for him. Catya's stomach cramped a little and she glanced around them. The palace grounds were quiet, unlike the cheerful gardens in Navere.

They were ushered straight through to the audience room, one of the four guards outside opening the door for them. There were three people present and they ceased their conversation at once.

'Cassien.'

The youngest of the two women hurried gracefully over, holding out a hand which Cassien took to kiss. Catya narrowed her eyes, as Kussim's dark skin flushed ever so slightly.

Cassien's grey eyes were wide as he looked down at the petite woman.

'We've found her,' he said breathlessly. 'We've found your mother.'

Kussim took a staggered step back, and Cassien darted forward to put a hand to her waist to steady her. Catya realised she was scowling and quickly softened her expression.

Kussim was a little older than her, with straight black hair, the darker skin of the Fulmers, and stunning silver-blue eyes. She was a quiet young woman with a soft, deep voice. When Catya had first met her, she'd wrongly assumed Kussim had only been given charge of Caergard because she was Jorrun's niece and very strong in power, but she'd soon learned this unimposing, somewhat shy girl, was shrewd, even genius.

'Uldren?' Kussim's voice was hoarse.

Cassien nodded. 'In the palace.'

Kussim swallowed, touching Cassien's hand briefly before stepping away from his support. She was wearing a green, sleeveless dress over which she wore a thin netting of chainmail.

The other woman cleared her throat. Pirelle was from the Fulmers and had been the Icante's own apprentice despite her *walker's* powers being weak. She'd mainly come to Caergard to give Kussim assistance in administration, as well as being the Fulmer's representative on the border.

'And is Uldren as solid in its defence as previously reported?'

'It is,' Catya replied. 'Even the Rowan Order is struggling to get a foothold in the city. There's also this.' She pulled one of the wolf brooches from the pouch on her belt.

The Eldeman, who'd so far remained silent, came forward to stand beside Pirelle to study it.

'What does it signify?'

Dalton had been used as something of a scapegoat after Quinari's almost successful attack on King Bractius and Elden. Out of favour in court, he'd jumped at the opportunity to become Elden's permanent ambassador to the Free Provinces of Chem.

'They might be scouts.' Catya looked from Dalton to Kussim. 'They were within our borders and attempted to prevent our return.'

Kussim looked up sharply at Cassien. 'It might be a prelude to an attack.'

'Or it could be just to prevent our scouts getting back here with information,' Cassien replied. 'Whatever the case, it would be wise to increase the patrols of people we can trust.'

Kussim sighed. 'It's people we can trust that's the problem.'

'More of these Disciples?' Catya folded her arms across her chest.

'A woman walking alone from her job to her home was murdered last night,' Pirelle told her. 'There was a note left on the body. It said, "a woman without a man belongs to any man."'

Catya swore and Dalton raised his eyebrows.

'What's been done?' Cassien asked.

'That's what we've been debating.' Kussim gestured towards Dalton and Pirelle. 'We've agreed to post a reward for the capture of those responsible, even though we risk false accusations. Dalton suggested we hang some of those we've imprisoned for crimes against women. My fear is that it might escalate things and place the women of this province in greater danger.'

'These people are used to being ruled by a strong hand,' Catya stated. 'They used to fear the consequences of breaking the law. From what I've heard, punishment used to be much worse than hanging.'

Kussim bit at her lower lip and nodded. 'But the point is we don't want to be old Chem. We're supposed to be better.'

'I agree,' Cassien said.

Catya rolled her eyes. He would. She unfolded her arms and placed a hand on her sword hilt. 'I disagree. Well, kind of. Yes, we want to be better than old Chem, but we won't get that way if we lose the border towns. We won't stand up against invasion unless we have the people to fight for us, the men to fight for us. Navere, Mayliz, and Margith might be a strong anchor of relative stability through the centre of Chem, but everywhere else is still too unsettled. Most of the men here would turn on you and join Eastern Chem given half a chance.'

'But would threatening them win loyalty or make them any more likely to fight willingly for us?' Kussim tilted her head. 'I'm starting to think the best solution is to take Eastern Chem.'

Catya straightened up. She hadn't expected Kussim to be an advocate for an all-out war. Neither had Cassien from the look on his face.

'My uncle and Kesta are in Navere,' Kussim continued quietly. 'I expect Jorrun will want to come here himself to plan my mother's rescue. I wonder if he'll try to take Uldren.'

'I still think it will be a step too far, too soon.' Dalton shook his head. 'If we can't hold Uldren, we'll likely lose Caergard and Darva also.'

Kussim looked down at the floor and Catya almost felt sorry for her. They needed an army; they needed more strong magic users, but all of those would take time, time Dinari didn't have.

'I'm going to consider things a bit more.' Kussim glanced up at them all, her eyes lingering longest on Cassien. 'And we'll have a Coven meeting tomorrow. In the meantime, I'll send word to Navere of Dinari and these 'wolves' and see if there's any way the other cities can spare us more men.'

'Would you like me to request warriors from Elden?' Dalton asked.

Kussim hesitated, then sighed. 'I think we'll have to.'

Catya excused herself, heading not to her chamber but to a much larger room on the ground floor that had been used for holding feasts. It was rarely used these days but provided a space in which she could leave her best friend. The staff of the palace had strict instructions to be careful going in and out, and to ensure the windows stayed shut and the door was firmly closed behind anyone who entered. If he could, Ruak would follow Catya and he would most certainly give her away. He was excellent for scouting, however, would stand out as something much too odd for a woman in an eastern city.

A guard stood outside the door and he started at Catya's appearance; she realised she still wore the charcoal Borrow mask on her face. But the young man obviously recognised who she was as he moved aside to let her into the room without a word.

As soon as she stepped inside, there was a harsh cry and a dark shape swooped down toward her. She raised her arm, but the raven ignored it, landing instead on her shoulder and picking at the loose strands of her long, brown hair.

She laughed as he tickled her ear and reached up to stroke his chest feathers.

'I missed you too, Ruak. Have you been giving Cella trouble?'

Ruak stretched out his neck and gave another raucous caw.

Chapter Seven

Jorrun; Free city of Navere

Jorrun gazed through the open window across the tidy lawns; a few lanterns lit the path between the palace and the gates, casting long shadows. Stars glimmered intermittently between the thin, fleeting clouds. A fire crackled in the small fireplace behind him, but a cold breeze tickled his skin and he shivered.

He heard Kesta's soft tread but didn't turn. She placed a hand against his back and leaned against his arm.

'What are you thinking?' she asked softly.

He swallowed; his stomach was churning. 'I'm thinking we don't have the resources to take and hold Eastern Chem, but if we do nothing people will suffer and they get time to build its strength while undermining us in the west.'

Kesta moved around so she could look up at him. Her mismatched eyes were wide in the darkness. 'We can't take and hold the east, but we can stop them getting strong, and we can stop them undermining us.'

Relief flowed through him, warming his veins. He should have known she'd be on the same page as him. 'Yes. We get to the root of these Disciples of the Gods and rip them out.' He drew in a deep breath. 'And we can weaken Eastern Chem by freeing slaves with power and taking out their strongest Coven members, keep the Covens in disarray, prevent them from uniting.'

'It's a good idea.' She held his gaze. 'But I can see you don't like your own plan.'

'It feels…' He clenched his jaw. 'Underhand, cowardly, although at the same time whoever we sent would be at serious risk of never returning.'

She stiffened, leaning back a little. 'You still intend to go yourself to Uldren.'

He nodded. 'I do.' He held up his hand as she opened her mouth to protest. 'I want you to stay in Navere where you can get back to Northold if you need to. I'd also like you to take charge of dealing with the Disciples, your *knowing* will be invaluable in doing so.'

He saw her deflate a little, her fingers unclenching, but she folded her arms across her chest and turned to scan the wall around the garden. 'I should go with you; we have more chance of getting your sister out of Uldren together.'

'We don't even know for sure she's there yet. It isn't just about us though.'

She sighed loudly. 'I know.'

He opened his mouth to find the words to reassure her, but she gave him a light slap on the arm. 'I just better not have to rescue you.'

A smile twitched on his lips. 'Perhaps I can rescue you this time.'

She stood on her toes to kiss him, then turned her attention back to the room. 'Are you ready to dream-walk? I came to let you know the guard thinks the boy is asleep.'

Jorrun followed her gaze; he'd lain out the objects representing the five elements in a star and placed the candles in their positions.

Kesta squeezed his arm, going over to the bed to sit cross-legged on it. Jorrun called flame to his fingertips and lit the candles, moving in a sun wise fashion, then threw a handful of herbs onto the fire. He looked up at Kesta, giving her a smile of reassurance before stepping into the 'star' and lying down.

It was a long while since he'd feared dream-walking after being captured and tortured by Karinna Dunham, but it was still reassuring to have his wife watching over him.

He closed his eyes, calling his power and triggering the part of his brain that allowed him to enter a dream trance and break free from his body. Almost at once snatches of emotion reached him like drifting strands of spider's web. Some personalities he recognised, but most were strangers to him. One of the guards had snatched a few hairs from the boy's head, and as they burned among the sage in the bowl beside Jorrun, he followed the smoke down to the dungeon and found the wisps of the boy's dream.

Colours came first, muted but edging towards reds and crimsons like the leaves of a maple. The emotions grew stronger as Jorrun sank with practised subtlety into the dream. The images came into focus and Jorrun saw the boy was in a richly furnished room; it was dark, and shadows seemed to move. The boy was staring at the door in dread, the sound of heavy footsteps drawing closer, but taking a long time to arrive. The boy was so afraid his physical body was close to loosing its bladder. Jorrun struggled for the first time in many years to hold back his own emotion.

He's going past, Jorrun pressed gently into the dream.

Sure enough, the footsteps faded away.

Confusion flowed through the boy, and he couldn't quite relax. Jorrun was struck by inspiration and he created the image of a small black cat. It was risky, but worth a try.

Hello.

The boy jumped, spinning about, his eyes widening when he spotted the cat. His soul's representation of his eyes were a dark, glowing amber.

Don't be afraid, I'm here to help you.

'Who are you?' The boy backed away.

I'm the cat. What's your name?

The boy took a hesitant step forward. 'I'm Alikan.'

Who wants to hurt you, Alikan?

The boy's voice came out in a whisper. 'Voxen.'

Immediately the sound of the footsteps returned, louder, faster. The boy hunched in on himself, his hands going up to his ears. Jorrun recognised that posture, it was that of someone defenceless expecting a brutal beating.

Quickly, Alikan, tell me your favourite place to be and I'll take us there.

Jorrun saw it as soon as it came to the boy's mind; a fast stream running through some bushes, a child's den made beneath a holly bush. He shifted the dream subtly, sitting in his cat form up on one of the narrow branches.

'Oh, but, cat!' Alikan's lip trembled and the skin around his eyes reddened. 'If I'm not there to take my punishment it will be worse for me!'

Jorrun's heart ached and he had to gather himself for a moment.

No one will hurt you again. I have friends who can deal with Voxen, just tell me who he is and where to find him.

The boy screwed his face up. 'Well, he's my master; my father. We used to live in the palace of Caergard, but when the Ravens took it, we escaped into the countryside. My master wants to teach them a lesson and the gods came and asked him to serve them, he said he would if he could have his palace back. I have two brothers and they both have power, but I didn't get any. So, when the gods said Master had to prove himself and his loyalty by sending one of us to...'

The dream started to break up as Alikan remembered he wasn't in his hiding place in the province of Caergard, but in a dungeon all alone in far-off Navere.

No, not alone, Jorrun pressed towards him quickly. *I'm here, and the Ravens are your friends.*

Jorrun found himself back in the blackness of the spirit realm, threads of dreamers reached out to him, but none were the boy. He followed the pull of his body and returned to it, slowly opening his eyes and blinking at the candlelight.

The emotions he'd held at bay hit him like flung stones and he sat up quickly, holding his head in his hands.

'Jorrun?' Kesta scrambled off the bed, her arms reaching around him to hold him tightly, enfolding his soul, making him safe. 'What happened?'

He lowered his hands, finding Kesta's and lacing his fingers between hers. He told her everything he'd learned from the boy's dream and Kesta grew still. He knew without seeing her face she wanted to give Master Voxen what he deserved.

Jorrun drew in a breath. 'We need to get the boy a cat, preferably a black one; and he likes to be outside. I'll send word to Caergard of Voxen and see if Catya is free to search for him.'

He felt Kesta nod. 'Should we see Alikan now? I hate to think of him down in the dungeon.'

Jorrun rubbed at his beard. 'No, let him be. He didn't quite believe Cat about Raven's being friends. It's a shame Ruak isn't here.'

Kesta laughed quietly, then stood and reached out to help him up. 'Come on, you've made amazing progress tonight, let's get some sleep.'

He snuffed out the candles while she got into bed, and undressing quickly, he snuggled in beside her.

***

Jorrun had to resist the temptation to head straight down to the dungeons to check on Alikan, and he realised it wasn't just concern for the Chemman boy; he was missing Arridia and Joss. Azrael too, for that matter. He slipped out of bed and went to the desk, composing a letter to his children for Rosa to read to them.

The bed creaked as Kesta stirred.

'Jorrun?'

'It's okay, I was just writing to the kids.'

Kesta stretched and slowly got up, padding softly over to kiss his cheek. 'Ask them what they've learned since we've been gone.'

He smiled, dipping the quill. He loved the Fulmer way of raising children, giving them responsibility while demonstrating consequence.

Kesta called up her magic and heated a bucket of water to wash with. He got a strong waft of mint as she broke up a leaf to clean her teeth with. He was about to sign the letter, 'Jorrun,' but stopped himself and wrote instead, 'Dad.' It still shocked and amazed him that he was a father, something he thought life would never allow him.

Kesta broke into his daydreaming. 'We need to get to the audience room.'

He put away his writing materials, shaking thin sand over his letter and neatly tipping it from the parchment into a small dish. He tidied his hair and beard and took the proffered mint leaf as he followed her out into the corridor.

Despite Kesta's concern, they were the first to arrive. The softly cushioned but plain and practical chairs were set in a circle ready for the Coven's meeting. Jorrun's gaze was caught as always by the green banner with their raven emblem sewn into it that hung on the far wall, made around seven years ago by the Raven Sisters for himself and Osun.

Calayna and Rece were the next to arrive, and Jorrun quickly filled them in with all he'd learned and warned them in advance of his proposal for the future of Chem. A larger group entered; Beth, Jollen, and Sirelle, with a red-haired boy in his late teens. Tyrin had been the son of a member of Margith Coven but had joined them willingly with three other younger boys.

Next came Harta who'd been saved three years ago from Darkhall, and her sister, Chari, both of whom had developed their magical ability under the tutelage of Jollen. The last to enter the audience hall was a man in plain, but neat clothing. He was Chemman with short brown hair and brown eyes, possibly in his thirties, although there was a touch of grey in his beard and the skin around his eyes crinkled considerably as he smiled.

'Rothfel,' Rece greeted the thief. There had been plenty of resistance to the man joining the Ravens, although Rece had spoken for him and explained Rothfel had always worked against the old Covens, particularly the Dunhams, in his own dubious way. Rothfel strode straight over to Jorrun, hand out to shake his. Jorrun sighed as the man picked Kesta up in a brief but enthusiastic hug.

'Jorrun, Kes, how in the Gods' names are you?'

'We're good,' Jorrun replied, and he made his way to his accustomed seat to settle everyone down. He quickly recounted his dream-walk and, with a flutter of apprehension, outlined what he thought would be their best course to secure the future of the Free Provinces.

'As has always been the case, we are in a race to see who rebuilds power first.' Rece gave a slight shake of his head. 'It makes sense to prevent them building theirs, but as you say, they seem to have the same plan.'

Calayna stood and took a few steps toward their banner. 'My fear is that we'll have to use Ravens to carry out the work, the very ones we can least afford to lose.'

Jorrun cleared his throat. 'Yes, that would be so.'

'There are other methods.' Rothfel leaned forward, his head cocked to one side. 'Small but strategically planned acts of sabotage could prevent them increasing their power. Interrupting their communications to keep their cities isolated. False rumours to start conflict between the eastern cities even.'

'We'd be wise to use every means available to us,' Jollen spoke up.

Jorrun rubbed at his forehead with his fingertips; his lungs ached. 'It all feels so underhand, though, almost evil.'

'Evil is what will come if we do nothing,' Calayna said.

Jorrun turned to regard the tattooed woman. Like all of those who'd lived in Chem, she'd experienced evil first-hand. His thoughts shifted to the young boy down in the dungeons. There were possibly hundreds of boys just like him in Eastern–even Western–Chem, waiting to see if their powers would come through, or if they'd be slaughtered by their own fathers as a useless waste of their resources.

He drew in a breath and nodded. 'Let's do it. Rothfel, start working on some strategies for us to consider. Have we heard anything from Caergard yet?' He pivoted to look from Calayna to Rece.

The Captain shook his head. 'Nothing yet.'

'We'll wait for word before we head off to do anything, we don't want to go into Caergard Province missing any vital information. Do we have other matters on our agenda?'

'We do,' Rece said almost apologetically. 'We arranged for you to meet the new High Priest of Navere's temple. He… well, he was eager to meet with you and invited you to come and visit the temple as soon as it's convenient.'

Jorrun turned to look at Kesta, her eyebrows were drawn in a heavy frown. She looked up at him and gave a resigned shrug.

'We'll go as soon as we're finished here,' Jorrun said.

It took them almost two hours to go through everything that needed to be addressed, including resolving disputes between guild members, granting petitions for aid in setting up new businesses, marriage agreements, and the division of guard patrols within the wider province. Zardin entered the room at one point, waiting patiently and discreetly until Rece beckoned him over.

The steward gave a slight bow. 'Just to let you know we have procured a black kitten. How would you like to proceed?'

'Let it seem as if it found its own way to the boy,' Jorrun instructed. 'Give Alikan a generous lunch with chicken or fish. Leave the cell's food hatch open as though accidentally and push the kitten through soon after. Tell the guard to stay back and listen discreetly.'

'As you say.' Zardin bowed again and backed out of the room.

Jorrun turned to Kesta. 'We'd better go and see this priest.'

She followed him out of the palace, and they walked together in companionable silence through the busy city. Most people ignored them. Some, mostly women, nodded in greeting. There were few scowls and Jorrun began to relax. The main trading areas seemed to be prospering and the small women's temple that had been built had a slow but steady stream of visitors.

They came to the temple gate and took the wooden path suspended along the cliff face. The surf shushed rhythmically below them, throwing up spray that left tiny white stains on their clothing. Jorrun took in a deep breath. The briny smell of seaweed was sharp, igniting memories of his childhood, of Osun, and of his mother.

Outside the temple cave, an endless age of candles deposited their ivory legacy in waxy stalactites down the black rock, several flames flickering bravely against the wind. He turned to see Kesta pause to look up at it, her lips slightly parted.

'Kes?'

She started. 'It… it's strangely beautiful.'

He reached out for her hand and she stepped quickly toward him to take it. He held her gaze, his heart seeming to swell inside his chest.

'In the Fulmers you believe in yourselves. It's always amazed me, that kind of inner faith. Here, in Chem, they depend on the Gods for validation. Do you understand?'

She placed her free hand against his rib cage as though to feel for his heart. 'Of course, I understand, I'm a *walker*. Are you asking me to be diplomatic?'

He tried to suppress his smile. Kesta had more empathy than any other human he knew, but her nature was fierier than Azrael; and she more often than not was sure to let people know how she felt.

He stepped closer to her, placing his free hand against the small of her back. 'I'm asking you, to be you.'

The smile that lit her eyes made his heart beat faster. 'I think I can manage that.'

He kissed her forehead, then closed his eyes and breathed in the saline air to compose himself. 'Let's see what this new priest has to say for himself.'

The entrance into the caves was small, but once inside it opened up into a series of huge caverns. Soft voices echoed, rising and falling like the sea below or wind in the trees. It was hard to determine the direction. Large iron candelabras stood on the uneven floor, barely flickering in the temple's stillness. A priest spotted them at once, his face reddening at the sight of a woman daring to enter the temple. He was dressed in the light green robes of the god of healing, Seveda. The man hurried forward but was cut off by another who wore plain brown robes.

'It's okay.' The priest held a hand up to halt his colleague. He had short grey hair and soft brown eyes, a smile crinkling the skin around them. Beside him scuttled a taller man in the purple robes of Warenna. 'They are invited.'

Jorrun and Kesta stopped to wait as the priests approached. 'You're the High Priest?'

'I am.' He gave a polite bow of his head. 'My name is Bantu, and this is Kerzin who is my administrator.'

'Jorrun, and this is my wife, Kesta.'

Jorrun sensed Kesta call up her *knowing*.

'Welcome, both of you.' The smile remained on Bantu's face. 'Have you visited Navere temple before?'

'I have,' Jorrun replied. The priests knew Kesta hadn't set foot in the caverns before; he was obviously just attempting to open up a polite dialogue.

'May I show you around?' He indicated the wide space with one hand.

Jorrun wished he knew what Kesta was sensing from these men. He glanced up at her; she wasn't smiling, but she didn't appear concerned either. 'We would be honoured.'

'Do you follow a particular god, Raven Jorrun?' Bantu asked as he headed toward a corridor leading off the main cavern.

'I do not,' he replied at once, a little more sternly than he intended.

Kerzin started to speak, but Kesta cut him off. 'I believe you served Hacren before they appointed you High Priest?'

Bantu twisted to regard her over his shoulder. 'I did, I still do. But I serve the God Hacren, not the creature summoned by the priests of Arkoom.'

They entered a small cavern, maybe twelve feet across. A huge statue towered above them in a man-made alcove. It was a typical depiction of the god of healing, a clean-shaven male with a high forehead and long, curling hair. He held a pestle and mortar in one hand and a burning brand in the other.

'Then you're not a part of this alleged movement to call up another demon?' Kesta asked.

Kerzin gasped, freezing in the midst of reaching for a candle to light.

Bantu looked from Jorrun to Kesta. 'You are very direct.'

'I don't have the patience for deception,' she replied.

Jorrun narrowed his eyes. Was she suggesting there was deception here?

Bantu's smile faded and he regarded her seriously. She didn't look away as he studied her mismatched eyes. 'I am neither foolish nor conceited enough to dare to bring gods to our mortal realm. My thinking is, if they wished to be here, they would be.'

Kesta drew in a breath, but she said nothing.

'You would warn us if any of your priests tried to summon a demon?' Jorrun asked.

'No.' Bantu's smile returned. 'I wouldn't warn you. I would deal with them myself and then tell you I'd done so.'

Kesta glanced at Jorrun and nodded.

'And the Disciples of the Gods?' Jorrun prompted.

Kesta spun toward Kerzin, biting her lower lip. The priest of Warenna's knuckles had turned white as he gripped the candle he placed.

Bantu sighed, frowning as he gazed down at the uneven floor. 'That is a more complex matter. Although they say they serve the gods, I fear they serve their own purposes. That being said, there are many who believe what you have done goes against the order of the gods.'

'And what do you believe?' Jorrun asked him.

Bantu looked up at the much taller man. 'That we should not presume to know the will of the gods. All we have to guide us are the ancient texts—'

'Which say a woman must serve men,' Kerzin interrupted vehemently.

'They do.' Bantu gave an apologetic shrug to Kesta. 'But that is not to say things cannot grow, or change. A woman can serve a man without being a slave, and there is nothing in the texts to say it cannot be a reciprocal thing.'

Kerzin's face reddened.

'That's not how the texts are interpreted though.' Jorrun studied him warily.

'It is not.' Bantu winced. 'But then the texts have always been interpreted by men, have they not?'

Jorrun nodded, unsure of where this man was going. It was frustratingly hard to judge if he were being open-minded and liberal, or just slippery.

'Come, I'll show you the other caverns, some of them are quite magnificent.'

They spoke little as they were escorted around the rest of the temple, Kesta stoically ignoring the outraged muttering of the other priests and visiting men. The caverns were wondrous, the temple of Warenna particularly so. Pearly stalactites hung down from the ceiling in narrow strands, some of them merging with the wider stalagmites to create a maze of pillars. The statue of Warenna appeared to be juggling worlds in his hands, a star emblem tied to his forehead.

'A magical place, is it not?' Bantu asked Kesta.

'It appears to be so,' she replied. 'And do you have power, Bantu?'

Jorrun's eyes widened. What had his wife sensed or guessed?

'Those with power do not go into the priesthood.' Bantu's eyebrows drew closer together.

Kesta folded her arms over her chest.

'I must get back to my duties,' Bantu apologised. 'Would you like to take a private moment in one of the shrines?'

'No, thank you,' Jorrun replied at once. Despite the size of the caverns, Jorrun had the uncomfortable sensation that the rugged walls were closing in. He cleared his throat, forcing himself to breathe slowly. 'We also have much to see to.'

Bantu walked with them to the exit, the sky outside seeming blindingly bright. Kerzin followed behind at a distance, not saying a word or even looking at them.

'Thank you for visiting us. Please come and speak to me any time.' Bantu gave them a polite bow.

'I'm sure we'll talk again soon,' Jorrun replied.

Kesta proceeded him along the cliff walk. He wasn't surprised at the pace she set. She didn't say a word until they were back on the solid street where she put both her hands over her face and shuddered.

'What an awful place, did you feel all that animosity?'

Jorrun placed an arm around her, matching his long stride to her swift, small steps. 'It was uncomfortable, that's for certain. What of Bantu?'

Kesta gave a short bark of a laugh. 'Our High Priest has been very clever. I could sense nothing through my *knowing*. He may be wearing an amulet against my magic.'

Jorrun halted and she'd taken two steps before spinning about to regard him.

'Is that an unusual thing?'

'For a priest to wear an amulet against *walkers*?' Jorrun shrugged. 'To be honest, I have no idea, but it wasn't something I'd considered.'

He realised where they were, and glancing around the street, he caught up with her and they continued toward the palace.

'Kerzin was very interesting though.' She looked up at him, eyebrows raised. 'He was scared and excited at the same time. His anger… well, his supposed anger was somewhat shallow and sometimes in the wrong places.'

'What do you mean?'

'I mean he was acting.' The corner of her mouth twitched up. 'He was being deceitful. He was also afraid. Of us, or Bantu, I couldn't say.'

'And your impressions of Bantu?'

She grunted. 'His words and behaviour made me want to trust him, but I don't.'

'Then we don't,' Jorrun said firmly. 'But we keep up a frequent dialogue with him to work him out. It won't hurt for people to see closer ties between the temple and the palace, even if the temple remains against what we are doing in Chem.'

'Something's up.' Kesta gave his arm a squeeze. She still had her *knowing* open. 'There's excitement and apprehension in the palace.' She grinned. 'I think it's something good.'

She almost ran when they stepped within the large, ornate building, heading straight for Osun's old study. They found Calayna and Rece inside with Rothfel; the latter holding a tiny roll of parchment in his hand.

'Jorrun!' Calayna clasped her hands together beneath her chin. 'Word from Caergard. They confirm your sister is in Uldren.'

Jorrun grabbed for the doorframe as his vision blurred for a brief moment. 'Where?'

'The palace,' Rece told him seriously. 'Will you go?'

Jorrun clenched his left fist. 'Of course.'

Chapter Eight

Rosa, Kingdom of Elden

Rosa and Tantony watched the fire-spirit's reaction as the Merkis read out the odd and startling messages. The first had come from King Bractius himself. The second was allegedly from Temerran, although Rosa was certain the tiny writing was that of Merkis Teliff.

It was a moment before Azrael replied, and Rosa was sure the little spirit appeared guilty about something.

'We musst heed the warning.' Azrael darted about in a loop.

'Do you know anything of these people who claim to rule spirits?' Tantony demanded.

'Noooo!' Azrael made himself slightly larger. 'Azra wass born in the fire-realm deep below Shem, he has never been to faraway lands.'

Rosa frowned. 'What of the other Drakes?'

'Let Azra assk.'

Before either of them had time to protest, Azrael had vanished into the fireplace.

Rosa stared after him open-mouthed for a moment, before turning to regard her husband. 'What do you think?'

Tantony pressed his lips together into a thin line. 'We have to take it seriously. We should write to Jorrun and Kesta.'

Rosa drew in a deep breath, her eyebrows drawn in tightly. 'If there is even the slightest chance the children are in danger, we have to get them away.'

'To Chem?' Tantony said in alarm.

'No.' Rosa took a step forward, placing two fingers against the cold marble of the tabletop. 'Somewhere closer and safer, somewhere it wouldn't look suspicious for them to go.' She looked up at him. 'I should take them to visit their grandmother.'

Tantony brightened and straightened up. 'That's a good idea, we'll get going as soon as it's light.'

'Oh.' Rosa's heart fluttered a little. Tantony had never given her any reason to fear contradicting him, but it went both against her nature and the ways of the Elden court. She drew in a deep breath. 'But are you not needed here to run Northold? What if Temerran needs help?'

Tantony gave a frustrated sigh. 'The children are my responsibility. I'd never forgive myself if anything happened to them.'

'They're also mine and Azrael's responsibility. Azra should come with us.' She glanced toward the fireplace. 'If he comes back.'

The muscles of Tantony's jaw moved as he considered it. 'Very well, Azrael should be powerful enough to protect you. I'll go wake Kurghan and see how he feels about another secret mission.'

Rosa smiled at that. 'I'll get a couple of men to stand guard at the base of the Ivy Tower and get back there myself. I'm a bit anxious with the children being alone there.'

'Didn't you leave Marra there?'

Rosa winced. Her maid, Marra, was a sweet girl, but a bit empty-headed.

Tantony laughed. 'You make a good point without speaking. I'll be with you as soon as I can, I want to guard those kids myself tonight.'

They quickly checked on the Ravens in the loft, before hurrying down to the ward. While Tantony headed for the gate, Rosa scurried into the hold, instructing the warriors on duty in the great hall to take turns posting themselves at the base of the Ivy Tower. She lifted the hem of her long skirt as she climbed the steep spiral staircase, groaning when she saw Marra fast asleep in one of the soft chairs in the receiving room. Heart in her mouth, she continued up two more flights to the children's room. She hesitated, her hand shaking a little as she reached out to push the door open.

She breathed out when she saw the room was empty but for the two small mounds in the beds. Joss's still had a small frame around it, and she crept across the carpet of what once had been her room, to peep inside. The dark-haired boy was sleeping soundly, and Rosa resisted the temptation to touch his soft cheek.

She heard the rustle of fabric behind her as Arridia stirred. 'Rosa?'

'It's okay.' Rosa smiled, straightening.

A light thud upstairs stopped Rosa's heart. No one should be up there.

'Is Mumma home?' Arridia asked wide-eyed, her hair was a black nest of tangles as she sat up.

Rosa put a finger to her lips and Arridia stilled.

Heart racing, Rosa hurried to the door and closed it, pushing the bolt across. Her chest muscles tightened when she thought of Marra alone downstairs. Despite wearing her house dress, Rosa wasn't without the influence of her Fulmer best friend. She hitched up her skirt and took a dagger from her boot.

'Are we in danger?' Arridia whispered.

Rosa put a finger to her lips again and nodded. She pointed toward Joss, and Arridia didn't need telling twice. The young girl slipped out of bed, picking up a silver candlestick before padding almost silently to her still sleeping brother. Admiration surged though Rosa, there wasn't even a glimmer of a tear from the girl; she was her mother's daughter.

A floorboard creaked above them and Rosa thought her heart would race right out of her body. She surveyed the room. She wouldn't be able to move anything heavy in front of the door without giving their presence away. Perhaps she was being foolish, she hoped she was, after all, how could someone get into the Ivy Tower without being spotted by the warriors in the great hall?

She sagged a little. It must be just Marra, or perhaps one of the warriors was making a check of the tower before taking up his post downstairs.

The door handle moved. Rosa gasped, clamping a hand over her own mouth.

It's just Tantony, she told herself.

The handle moved slowly downward and the door was pushed but held in place by the small bolt. Rosa drew in a breath to ask who was there, but Arridia hissed, 'No, Rosa, it's a bad man!'

Rosa glanced at the girl, then turned her wide eyes back to the door. She spotted the handle of a bed warmer poking out from under Arridia's bed and darted forward to snatch it up just as the door burst open. Rosa swung the warmer with all her strength, and it connected with the side of the man's head. He staggered, falling against the wall.

'Get out,' Rosa yelled at Arridia, who was trying to rouse her brother and drag him out of his cot.

The man shook his head. Blood trickled down the part of his face that wasn't hidden by a scarf. He had the darker skin and black hair of someone from the Fulmers. He was dressed in tight-fitting blue, the colour of a sky near full dark. He raised his head to glare at Rosa, his brown eyes fierce. In his left hand, a long knife glinted as it caught the candlelight from the hallway.

Rosa swelled her lungs with air. 'Tantony!'

As the man straightened, she grabbed the blankets off Arridia's bed and flung them at him. As the man reflexively raised an arm Rosa swung the bed warmer again and the man bellowed as his bone gave a nasty crack, but the bed warmer spun away as the handle snapped off.

Arridia collided with the back of Rosa's legs, dragging a bewildered Joss behind her. The man was still between them and the door. He reached up his good hand, gripping his long knife, to pull down his scarf. His teeth showed between his lips in a snarl. Rosa pushed Arridia out of the way, altering her posture to turn side on to the man and trying to steady her breathing as Kesta had taught her.

She had to buy them time.

'What do you want? What kind of coward attacks children in their beds?'

For a moment she didn't think he'd answer, but he stepped forward and Rosa backed up. Arridia gave a small whimper.

'Jderha demands it,' the man said, his voice softer than Rosa expected.

Rosa swallowed back her nausea. 'Never heard of him.'

'Her,' the man corrected with a snarl. 'Ignorant heathen.'

He lashed out, Rosa screamed, flinching back and almost falling over Arridia who clung to her skirt. Bright light blinded her, and she turned to protect her eyes. A nasty, charring smell stung her nostrils and she realised the high-pitched scream was no longer her own. Snatching up the children, she bundled them behind the bed, daring to glance up to see the man stumbling toward the door and the stairs, his whole body alight. As he crumpled to the stone steps, a small ball of fury lifted away from him and hurtled around the room like a demented bluebottle.

'Kill you, kill you, kill you!' Azrael shrieked as he continued to dash about in mad loops.

Scuffling came from downstairs and the sound of Tantony swearing. She almost laughed at the same time as a tear slipped down her cheek.

'Wait here,' she told the children. Rosa got unsteadily to her feet, and pushed the door closed to stop the foul smoke that was coming in and opened all the windows to banish the vile odour. Azra's mad dashes were slowing and he gradually quieted. The children sat on the floor beside the bed, their arms around each other.

'It's all right.' Rosa had to clear her throat to try to loosen the tight knot there. Her heart was still rapidly thudding in her chest. 'Tantony will put out the fire.' She looked up at Azrael, who had halted to hover above the fireplace. 'Who was he?'

'Assassin.' Azrael buzzed and hummed. 'Azrael knows a lot now, friend Siveraell has told him. I'll tell you and the children when Tantony isss here.'

'The children?' Rosa glanced down. Both Arridia and Joss were watching her, their blue eyes bright and wide.

'Yesss.' Azrael bobbed and made himself a little larger. 'It concerns them most of all.'

114

The door came flying open and Tantony stood there panting, soot on his face and in his beard. Rosa shuddered when she thought about where that soot was from.

'Rosa! Are any of you hurt?'

She shook her head and in three swift strides he had his strong arms around her. Rosa allowed herself to sag, but not to cry.

'Are there any others?' she asked.

'I have every man, woman, and child searching the hold.' His face was flushed, his eyes were alight with fury. 'We think he must have climbed the ivy to an open window in Kesta's room, which means he got over both our walls or through both our gates. I should flog every warrior on duty!'

Rosa drew in a shaky breath. 'Azrael has news. When he's finished telling us, I think we need to leave for the Fulmers.' She nodded her head toward the children.

Tantony scratched at his beard, but he grunted his agreement. He stepped away from Rosa to regard Azrael. 'What's this news?'

Azrael made himself small, dropping down a couple of feet. Arridia climbed onto the bed, helping her brother up.

'Long ago,' Azrael began. 'Fire-spirits lived in a land called Geladan, ruled by a goddess called Jderha. They were her servants, her slaves, as were all spirits.'

'Jderha!' Rosa grabbed Tantony's arm. 'The assassin said he was from her.'

'Hang on.' Tantony frowned at the fire-spirit. 'I'm sure I heard that fire-spirits had supposedly never met a real god?'

'Oh.' Azrael made himself even smaller. 'Um... they lied a bit.'

Tantony almost choked. 'Lied a bit!'

'Well, technically they haven't met a god, and certainly not a ssupposed god of Chem…'

'But they have met a goddess,' Tantony growled.

'Yeessss,' Azrael wailed. 'Ssiveraell says he is sorry, but he wasn't allowed to tell. Drakes were slaves, bound and commanded by Jderha. There are many magics in Geladan and the Drakes had their own priestesses. They loved their fire-spirit friends. There wass a rebellion and the fire-spirits were freed. They fled the land of Geladan through the fiery earth and came to Shem and Elden. The fire-priestesses and their families escaped by sship, some were hunted down and killed, some made it all the way to the Fulmers. An earth-bound spirit led those who reached the Fulmers, after making a forbidden exchange of souls.

'The rebellion was sparked by a prophecy, a prophecy that a fire-priestess's child would be the one to slay Jderha. The prophet said that the child would be born of a fire-priestess and a man with the blood of many lands.'

'Gods!' Rosa sat down heavily on the bed, almost missing the edge. She glanced at the quiet children. 'You're talking about Jorrun, aren't you? Jorrun and Kesta.'

'I think ssso.' Azrael pulled a crazy face. 'Jderha certainly thinks so. There's more. The prophet also said the child would be protected by an earth-bound spirit. Jderha had all earth-bound spirits killed.'

Tantony paced across to the window. 'Do Jorrun and Kesta know of this?'

'No.' Azrael drifted a little closer to the Merkis. 'Azrael only jusst learned. Siveraell is an old spirit, but even he was born here, beneath Elden. The ancient ones do not speak of it. They are bound

116

to aid fire-walkers through debt and promise, but have little love or time for humans these dayss, particularly those who indulge in the vile blood magic of necromancy.'

'What do we do?' Rosa asked.

'We should go to grandma's,' Arridia said. 'She's stronger than anyone.'

'That's the plan.' Rosa reached out to stroke Arridia's dark hair. 'Get yourself washed and dressed and pack some sensible things to take with you to the Fulmers. I'll send Marra up to help you and Joss. We'll leave as soon as Kurghan can have a boat ready.'

Tantony opened his mouth and drew in a deep breath. 'Yes, go at once. I'll pick two good warriors. I bumped into young Nip on my way back from Kurghan's, he'll go with you too.'

'What will you do?' She searched her husband's kind but determined eyes.

'I'll set off for Taurmaline as soon as you're safely on your way, try to speak to Temerran and then Bractius. I don't trust a message bird, not to there, not to the Fulmers and certainly not to Chem; not when there're assassins and magic about.' He looked at Azrael.

'I go with the children.' Azrael flared brighter.

***

The boat rocked as Nip jumped in. He wrapped a blanket around Rosa and the children and gave them a reassuring smile. The stable master's son was only a teenager, but years of hard work in the stables and training as a warrior under Tantony had filled him out. His hair was such a colourless brown it almost appeared grey, the same colour as his friendly eyes. The children adored him, particularly Arridia who loved horses, and his presence had settled them at once. Rosa glanced down at the lantern by her feet, Azrael a tiny figure sitting on the wick.

'Quick as we can, fellows,' Kurghan said, taking a seat beside Nip and picking up an oar. The two warriors had split themselves between the prow and the stern to keep a lookout and would take a turn at rowing later. Rosa's stomach gave a lurch as they moved out onto the lake, and she squeezed the children a little tighter. Looking up she saw Tantony watching them from the narrow wharf, he remained there until the darkness made him invisible to her. Joss crawled down into the bottom of the boat and curled up to sleep, his face close to Azrael's lantern. Arridia was wakeful, but silent, taking everything in.

Rosa dozed, the swift flow of the water and the rhythmic splash of the oars somehow soothing. The ache in her back woke her not long before the men changed seats, the sky brightening as the sun drew near to the horizon. Joss was awake. His hands gripped the boat, his chin resting on the edge as he watched the shore passing them by. Arridia stirred in Rosa's lap, sitting up and rubbing at her eyes.

'Where are we?'

'I think we are still about half a day from Taurmouth,' Rosa replied.

Arridia shuffled closer to her brother. 'Do you see any bad men, Jossy?'

'No, Riddi.' He glanced over his shoulder.

'Nip, can I watch with you?'

Nip looked around from his seat at the prow. He stood and held out a hand, helping Arridia keep her balance and settling her in front of him. 'Tell me when you see anyone,' Nip said.

'I'll feel the badness first,' Arridia muttered.

Rosa straightened in her seat. 'You feel the badness, Arridia?'

The little girl nodded but didn't speak, her face serious as she watched the river ahead. A cold hand crept down Rosa's spine. They didn't have magic in Elden, and Gods knew she had none herself, but with her closest friend and her Thane both being magic users, she'd picked up a few things. Fire-walkers didn't develop their powers on the whole until they reached puberty. The magic users of Chem gained theirs earlier, from about eight, two years older than Arridia was now.

'Hope you brought your bed warmer, my lady,' one warrior said.

The other chuckled, and Rosa's cheeks flushed. She'd no doubt they'd be telling the tale for years of how she'd saved the Thane's children with a bed warmer. She straightened her spine and raised her chin a little, allowing herself to smile about it for the first time.

***

Taurmouth harbour was busy, fishing boats returning with their entourage of screaming gulls, traders haggling over the best catches. Kurghan found somewhere to tie up their small boat, and one of the harbourmaster's assistants hurried over to them as they were climbing the ladder up to the solid stone of the wharf.

'We're from Northold,' Kurghan called up as he passed Azrael's lantern to Nip. 'We need passage to the Fulmers on authority from the king.'

Rosa bit her lip, holding her breath. As the king's advisor and sorcerer, Jorrun carried the king's seal and Tantony had 'borrowed' it from the Raven Tower to ensure they got assistance without question. Kurghan may have had greyer hair and more wrinkles than when Rosa had first met him, but none of his age showed as he sprang up the ladder and dug in the inside pocket of his coat for Tantony's letter.

The master's assistant looked at the words on the parchment with narrowed eyes, bringing the seal closer to his thin face. Arridia was holding onto Nip's hand, gazing up at the street on a level higher above them. Rosa shivered, wondering if the girl could sense any 'bad men' up there.

'Well, your letter seems in order, but it doesn't mean I can get you passage just like that.' The man glared at Kurghan over the parchment. 'There's nothing sailing to the Fulmers this afternoon.'

'And in the morning?' Kurghan prompted. There was almost a growl in his voice.

'Where will you be staying? I'll send word as soon as I procure anything.'

Kurghan's face reddened. 'We'll stay in the Green Inn, but if I don't hear from you first thing, you'll be hearing from the king.'

The officious man swallowed. 'I will do what I can.'

Kurghan leaned toward him. 'See that you do.'

'Come on, then.' Nip turned and picked up Joss, hoisting him up onto his shoulder and picking up his own heavy pack in his other hand. Kurghan and the warriors divided the rest of their luggage between them, leaving Rosa to carry Arridia's small bag, and the young girl to take charge of Azrael's lamp.

Rosa kept close to Nip, ensuring Arridia walked between the two of them. Her knife was tucked safely in her belt sheath, and she had another in her boot. Not surprisingly, Nip and the warriors were better armed than she, even Kurghan wore a sword. As far as she knew, the carpenter had never been a warrior as such, but strangely it seemed to be him, rather than any chieftain of the hold, who they turned to for anything of dire importance.

The Green Inn was far enough from the harbour to be a little less rough and a touch cleaner, even so Rosa's heart sank when she gazed up at the crooked building and its mud-splashed walls.

'I, um…' Kurghan shifted his feet, scratching at his beard as he regarded Rosa. 'I know you have the lantern, and as good as you are at taking care of yourself, I'd like to put a man in the room with you and another outside your door, if…if you don't object, my lady.'

'It sounds like a perfectly sensible idea to me,' Rosa replied at once.

'Can Nip stay with us?' Arridia tugged at her hand.

'If he wants to.' Rosa turned to the older boy.

'Of course, I will.' Nip smiled.

They waited in the reception area while Kurghan haggled for two rooms and arranged for some food, showing again the king's seal. When Rosa saw what was considered to be the inn's best room, she groaned. There were three pallets on the floor and one table with three crooked chairs set below the small window. At least it seemed clean and there was a strong smell of recently burned sage. A maid and a boy carried in some trays of steaming food for them, depositing them on the table.

As soon as the door was closed behind them, Azrael came flying out of the lantern.

'Azra!' Joss immediately brightened; all tiredness forgotten. Azrael flew up to the boy, pulling faces to make him laugh.

Nip crossed to the window, checking the street below, and ensuring it was locked and secure.

'Okay, let's eat some supper and then get some sleep.' Rosa ushered the children over to the table, lifting Joss up into a chair. Azrael was buzzing unhappily to himself. 'What is it?'

'I want to sspeak with the other spirits and see if there is any news, but Azrael is afraid to leave the children.'

Nip straightened up. 'We should be able to hold off any assassins between us.'

Azrael made a miserable sound. 'They brought people with powerful magic from Geladan. Stronger than Azra.'

Rosa's heart seemed to stop. 'Stronger than Jorrun?'

Azrael's voice came out in a sibilant whisper. 'Sstronger than Dia.'

Rosa reached out to steady herself against the wall. She glanced up to check the children hadn't heard. They were both busy eating, Arridia helping Joss to reach what he wanted.

'Then you stay here, Azra,' Rosa said through gritted teeth. 'News can wait until we're safely in the Fulmers.'

The decision made for him, Azrael seemed to calm a little, burning more steadily.

'Nip, eat something.' Rosa waved toward the table. She drew in a deep breath and fixed a smile to her face, before joining them herself. Nip insisted she take the remaining chair.

'Let's have a story,' Nip suggested as they later tucked the children into the bed furthest from the door.

'I'll do it!' Azrael turned about in a loop.

Nip nodded at Rosa, taking a chair and putting its back against the door. He drew his sword before he sat and placed it across his lap, his gaze fixed on the window. Rosa took a blanket from one of the other beds and went to sit beside the children as Azrael started the first of several tales.

She awoke with a start. Someone had knocked and Nip scrambled to his feet.

'Who is it?' the young lad demanded.

Grey light shone through the window, showing the dust motes that stirred in the room as Rosa threw aside her blanket and stood. The children were sleeping, Azrael darted to Nip's shoulder.

'It's Kurghan. We have a ship.'

Rosa's hand went to her chest and she turned to wake Arridia and Joss as Nip let the carpenter in.

'It's not ideal,' Kurghan told them with a wince. 'It's just a large sea-fishing vessel, and the scoundrel of a captain wants plenty of coin to take us to Fulmer Hold. It will have to do though, we can't afford to wait for one of the king's warships, and to do so will tip the Geladanians off that Bractius knows why they're here.'

'Are the bad men here?' Joss asked sleepily.

'No, Jossy,' Arridia whispered. 'We're going to see grandma.'

'Quickly, get your shoes on,' Rosa prompted. They'd remained almost fully clothed in case of a swift flight, or a fight.

Rosa was proud of how soon the children stood at the door, looking up at Kurghan. Azrael squeezed himself into the lantern, rapidly shrinking to the size of a flame.

'Right then.' Kurghan looked them all over. 'The warriors have gone ahead to check the ship over and make sure of this fisherman's crew. We head straight there, no lollygagging.' He pointed a finger at Rosa and Arridia giggled. The old carpenter gave Rosa an apologetic wince, before spinning on his heels and heading for the stairs.

Kurghan set a spirited pace and Nip once again hoisted Joss up onto his shoulder. Poor Arridia almost had to run, but she didn't complain, her wide blue eyes taking in everything as she surveyed the streets.

Rosa felt uncomfortable asking, but they needed to know. 'Do you sense anything, Arridia?'

The little girl pursed her lips together. 'Just normal people, Rosa.'

Anxiety tumbled and gnawed inside Rosa's chest.

'There.' Kurghan pointed to the wharves below them, reaching a gap in the harbour wall and glancing at Nip before climbing down the ladder. Rosa looked quickly around them before sending Arridia down after him, then Joss. Nip took the lantern and insisted she go next, and as Rosa climbed down one of their warriors hurried to meet them.

'It all seems legitimate, Kurghan.'

The carpenter gave the man's arm a hard pat. 'Help me get the luggage on.'

They hurried along the wharf. The small ship stank of decomposing fish, but was surprisingly clean, and although crowded with fishing gear, it was carefully stowed.

'Don't touch anything,' she warned the children. 'There are sharp things on fishing boats.'

The captain was waiting for them. He was a tall man, clean shaven, and almost completely bald. He looked them all up and down.

'Welcome.'

He held out a hand, and with a scowl Kurghan placed a bag of coins on it. The captain hefted its weight, then pushed it into a pocket.

'I like timely passengers.' He grinned. 'Come aboard. I've made room in the cabin for the lady and the little ones.'

He held out a hand and Arridia took it without hesitation, allowing him to help her onto the ship. Rosa felt guilty at how reassured the child's trust made her. She grabbed up a handful of her skirt and lifted the hem out the way of her boots; the captain didn't miss the handle of her knife that showed briefly. His mouth quirked up in a smile. Rosa blushed.

'Welcome aboard, my lady. Have you been to the Fulmers before?'

'No, I haven't,' she replied, taking his offered rough and calloused hand. 'But I always meant to.'

Not quite like this though, she thought.

Chapter Nine

Temerran; Kingdom of Elden

Temerran halted in his quiet pacing, hearing the steps in the corridor before the light tap at his door. A young page waited there, candle in hand. It was two hours before dawn, but the bard hadn't yet slept.

'His majesty would see you,' the boy said.

'I should think so,' Temerran muttered. He blew out the candle that stood on the mantlepiece. With a glance at the woman sleeping in his bed, he followed the page to the king's private audience room. The king sat behind his desk, sipping at a steaming mug of what smelt like camomile tea. Teliff was also there, as was a disgruntled Ayline and the castle's captain of the guard. Adrin sat in the corner, his chair tipped back, and his long legs stretched out in front of him. Bractius clapped his hands together.

'What do we know?'

Temerran stepped into the centre of the room and recounted everything he'd heard and observed.

King Bractius placed his elbows on his desk and leaned his head in both hands.

'So, these people are here because of some prophesy that the children will kill their god.'

'Prophesy is for fools.' Temerran clenched his fists and strode across the confining space of the room. 'We can all see this is utter nonsense. Have any of you ever heard of Geladan before today?'

'Not I,' Teliff spoke up.

'I had.' Temerran admitted. 'As a distant place to be wary of. But they have heard of us because of me. Because I sailed across the sea to explore, to find new lands.'

Bractius sat back in his chair and waved a hand in the air. 'This isn't about fault, whatever the reason, they're here, and I take it they're powerful.'

'That they are.' Temerran sighed. 'And I would advise you to tread carefully. Their interest is not Elden.'

'Even so.' Bractius stood and turned to gaze up at the portrait of his father. 'Elden would not stand today were it not for Jorrun and the Fulmers.'

'But we cannot sacrifice our kingdom for heathens,' Ayline said, waving her hand before her face as though it were a fan, and the room too warm.

Bractius spun about. 'I can think of no delicate way to dismiss them. I fear we must dance this deceptive dance of polite discourse. Either that or we slaughter them all and burn their ship, ensure none return to Geladan.'

Teliff put his fist to his mouth and coughed loudly.

'While that might be prudent'—Temerran drew in a deep breath—'I don't think it will be easy. I think you're right, sire, that we must step through this diplomatic dance. I would say we should avoid all talk of the Fulmers, but I fear they've already learned all they needed on that score. Too many are aware of how the fire-spirits helped to save us, particularly at Mantu. Too many know the tale of the Icante saving us against Chem and against Inari.'

Ayline coloured slightly and looked down at her perfectly manicured nails.

'Aye.' Bractius picked up his tea and put it down again. 'There is no point lying now, but we can make it known the Fulmer Islands are our allies.'

'But that will put Elden in danger!' Ayline sat up straighter.

'The Queen is right.' Adrin tipped himself forward so the front legs of his chair hit the floor with a thud. 'It would be wise to put distance between us.'

It was Bractius's turn to redden. 'Wise if we are cowards. Wise if we wish to betray our friends.'

'But…' Teliff drew in a deep breath. 'What are we to do against strong magic? It would be sensible not to get drawn in.'

Temerran shook his head impatiently, slapping his hand down on the king's desk. 'We're already drawn in. If these people attack the Fulmers, we can't do nothing.'

Bractius held his hands up. 'Let's just slow down a moment, no one has attacked anyone yet. Perhaps they won't. From what you say, Temerran, the ancestors of those on the Fulmers fled Geladan many, many years ago. Surely even this god of theirs wouldn't hold a grudge that long?'

'Maybe not a grudge.' Temerran looked around at the portraits on the wall. 'But they spoke of prophesy.'

'Is such stuff even real?' Bractius scowled.

'If I'm honest, I don't believe so, but I might be wrong. In any case, it's easy enough to force prophesy to come true.'

They were all silent a while as they considered.

Bractius breathed out loudly. 'Well then. We'll continue to discover as much as we can, keep an eye on them. If they turn their ship toward the Fulmers, then my warships follow.'

'Very good, majesty,' Teliff said.

Temerran didn't miss the exchanged glance between Adrin and Ayline.

'We should try to keep them together if possible,' Teliff continued.

'We'll think of entertainments to invite them to, play the generous hosts.' Bractius nodded. 'The sky looks clear, we'll offer to take them out on the lake today on my warship, then a dinner in my private rooms. If anyone has any other ideas to occupy them, tell me.'

Temerran accepted his dismissal, snorting at the indignity of it. He wasn't a leader of his people, the Bard of the Borrows had no leader and led no one but his crew, but he certainly didn't serve Elden.

The Fulmers, though, the Fulmers he could serve.

He took a quick look in the great hall and the other communal areas of the castle but saw no sign as yet of the Geladan delegation stirring. With a nod to the guards at the gate, he left the castle and hurried down to the docks, the sight of his beloved *Undine* filling his soul like sunlight.

'Tem.' The lookout touched a finger to his forehead. The man's hair was braided back, and he'd painted his eyes with charcoal as though he were going on a raid.

'Anything?' Temerran asked as he made for the gangplank.

'No, Captain, but there's a small boat heading into the harbour 'cross the lake.'

Temerran strode up the plank and crossed the deck to the stern. Two of his men were leaning on the railing, watching the progress of the lone oarsman. Temerran narrowed his eyes. He recognised that bearded and determined man. He relaxed his body and drew air into his lungs.

'Tantony! Come to.'

The man's head came up and he shipped one oar, using the other to change his direction toward the *Undine*. When he came aside, Temerran threw down a knotted rope. He tried hard not to laugh when the Merkis cursed. Tantony tied the end of the rope securely to an iron ring on his boat, and with several more curses and a rather red face, he boarded the *Undine*.

'What brings you to Taurmouth?' Temerran asked, a twinkle in his eye.

'An attack on the children.'

Humour bled from Temerran faster than a slit throat. 'Please tell me they weren't hurt?'

'No, my wife saw him off.'

Temerran shared the man's grin.

'We got your warning; Rosa and the children are on their way to their grandmother. I came to tell the king. Listen, Temerran, the man had the darker skin of an islander. He is one of the foreigners?'

Temerran nodded. 'He is, and I can tell you the foolish reason they went after the children.' Temerran told him everything and wasn't surprised when the bearded Eldeman swore again. 'You've sent word to Kesta and Jorrun?'

Temerran nodded. 'Via the Fulmers. My friend, I could do with your assistance here at Taurmaline. I believe Bractius will stand with the Fulmers, but I don't trust his scheming wife. Another set of eyes and ears will be welcome.'

Tantony clasped his wrist firmly. 'I'll head to the castle now.'

Temerran watched him leave before gathering his men and giving them his instructions. As he headed back toward the castle, he spotted a bright red cloak swirling out behind its wearer as she hurried through the harbour gates. Temerran increased his pace, but somehow, he couldn't seem to shorten the distance between them.

'That woman,' he demanded of the harbour guards. 'When did she leave the city?'

'About an hour before dawn, sir, what business is it of yours?'

'It's the king's business.' Temerran held the man's gaze, calling a little of his power into his voice. 'Did you not think to ask what she was doing?'

'Of course.' The guard stiffened. 'She said she wanted some air and wished to see the sun rise over the lake.'

'And you didn't try to stop her leaving?'

'Why would we? The king has not ordered the visitors from Geladan confined.'

'All right.' Temerran relaxed his posture a little. 'If she leaves the city again, you'll tell me at once.'

'Yes, my Lord.'

Temerran almost ran to make up the distance he'd lost, finally catching sight of Linea's red cloak again as he reached the fish market. She glanced back only once over her shoulder but didn't seem to spot him. As far as he could see, she spoke to no one and returned straight to her room.

As he entered the great hall, he couldn't help his feet faltering. The five Geladanian warriors sat together at a long table, talking among themselves and hungrily eating the breakfast they'd been served. If it hadn't been one of the main party who had attacked the

Raven Tower, the assassin must have made his own way from their ship at Southport. There could be any number of them in Elden.

With a curse, Temerran hurried back to his room. The young blonde servant was still fast asleep in his bed. He brushed a strand of her hair from her face and she stirred.

'Jen.' He sat on the edge of the bed. 'Jen, I need a favour of you.'

She blinked up at him, her cheeks still flushed from sleep. 'Mmm?'

'Jen, I need you to speak with the other servants. Be discreet, and be very, very careful. I'd like you all to watch and listen to the Geladanian delegation. All of them. I don't mean follow them down dark corridors and listen at their doors, just pay attention as you serve them, alert Teliff or myself of anything that concerns you. Would you do that, Jen?'

She nodded, wide-eyed.

Temerran bent down to kiss her. 'Thanks, Jen. Nothing foolish, mind, they're dangerous people, they mustn't know we are watching them.'

***

Temerran wasn't surprised when he was invited to join Bractius and the Geladanian delegation on the king's warship for their lunch out on the lake. He leaned against the ship's railing, gazing out across the grey water, while keeping half an eye on those boarding. When the gangplank was pulled up, he straightened, his eyes surveying the group of guests again. He'd expected Linea and the warriors not to come, but she wasn't the only one missing.

Putting on a pleasant smile, he approached the group, singling out Kichi. 'Your sorcerer isn't joining us today?'

Kichi gave him a charming grin. 'Oh, no, Lorev doesn't sail well.' She laughed at Temerran's puzzled frown. 'It sounds strange that he would cross a sea but not a quiet lake, but the sea he was ordered to traverse by Jderha.'

'Would you tell me about Jderha?' Temerran turned his back to the railing, pulling himself up to perch on it.

The shorter Kichi pulled herself up to balance with ease beside him. A bard was a bard.

'Most of our communities have a bard, and from what you've said, they perform a similar role as you do in the Borrows.' Kichi's arm brushed his as she gesticulated. He doubted it was accidental. 'We keep records, elevate or destroy a reputation with our tales. The pinnacle of any bard's career is to become a Voice for Jderha. I attained that position three years ago.'

'But you have not sung for us.'

'My voice contains power.' She held his gaze. 'I have to be careful of its use.'

How much power, Temerran wondered, *more than me who was blessed by the spirits of the sea?*

'And your goddess, Jderha?' He prompted.

'It must seem strange to you, a living god.'

Evasive. 'On the Borrows we believe in the spirits who alter our destiny, in the harshness and benevolence of nature, of the strength of family, clan, and purpose. We have the gods of Chem to the north, the god and goddess of Elden to the south. We prefer to trust in ourselves and each other.'

'And the Fulmers?'

He sensed the subtle stirring of her magic in the question and resisted the need to smile. 'They are an insular people, respectful of life and nature. You have yet to tell me of your god.'

Her grey eyes narrowed slightly for the briefest of moments. 'To serve her directly is the greatest of privileges. Her wisdom is beyond anything human, or even of spirit. It… it is hard to describe. Think of the one you love the most and how it feels to win their approval, even their love. Multiply it and that is what a true god gives you.'

'I have only met a false god,' Temerran confessed, paying close attention to her reaction as he told her of Hacren. He had no doubt she'd already heard the tale, but he found himself leaving out the important parts Dia and Kesta had played in destroying the demon.

'So, you control sea-spirits?' Her gaze was intense.

He breathed in slowly. 'I have a relationship with the local sea-spirts. I no more control them than I do the sea.'

'Kichi!'

Temerran didn't miss the split-second scowl that marred Kichi's jovial face as Adrin approached, a broad grin on his face.

'My Lady.' Adrin's bow was too contrived.

Temerran winced as he hopped down from the railing. 'Please excuse me, bard, I have not met some of your fellow countrymen yet.'

He could almost feel the dagger between his shoulder blades for leaving her with the Elden Merkis. The handsome ambassador, Ren, was at the prow with King Bractius; the High Priestess stood a little apart and Temerran's stomach flipped when he realised her gaze was set toward the distant silhouette of the Raven Tower. The warmth of anger spread out from his chest and his toes clenched inside his boots, even as he kept a pleasant smile fixed to his face.

Temerran approached her with a chivalrous bow. 'Forgive me, I do not know by what title to address you.'

'Yalla is fine,' the woman replied without a smile.

Temerran didn't disguise his interest in the serpent staff she carried. There were two small emeralds set within the eyes, and he couldn't help but think of Linea. A shudder ran through him. The staff contained a huge amount of power, and it didn't feel good.

He cleared his throat. 'I hope it isn't rude of me to ask, do you have the honour of serving Jderha as her only High Priestess, or do others hold such a title? You must excuse my ignorance of your people.'

'You sailed to Hidarra, and to Mereck, did you not?' She tilted her head; she was almost as tall as he.

'I did. There was rumour of your land there, but little more than a name.' He didn't doubt she caught the careful lie. He'd heard enough; enough to cause him to stay away. 'I was called back to my home by the sea, a dire catastrophe had befallen my people.'

Yalla frowned and nodded. 'The Chemmish massacre and then the demon who claimed the name Hacren.'

Temerran gritted his teeth, more than a little concerned at how much she knew. 'Have you met such creatures in Geladan?'

'Not for many a year, they would not dare Jderha's wrath. In answer to your question, we have many temples in Geladan, each one has a High Priestess. I serve in the Goddess's own temple in Ramuth, the city in which she dwells. I am her most trusted servant.'

Temerran gave another low bow. 'Then I am most honoured.' He could tell his flattery was getting him nowhere. 'I imagine the rule of a god is absolute. Geladan must be a land of peace and prosperity.'

There was the slightest fluttering of the proud woman's eyelids. 'Jderha is wise and benevolent.'

Temerran turned to look out at the lake, taking a moment to compose himself. There were few people under the sky that he took a dislike to, but he really didn't like this woman. 'Do you have lakes such as this?'

'Of course.' She raised her chin a little, flicking back her black hair. 'Although much of Geladan is drier than Elden.'

'My land, the Borrows, appears barren to those who do not know it, but there are treasures in the rocks, in the earth, and in the sea.'

'And in its people?'

Temerran smiled. 'There is much that is rare and precious within people.'

'You know the people of the Fulmers?'

Every muscle in Temerran's body tensed. There was no point in lying anymore. The Geladanian delegation had done their research. 'I do. They were considered the enemies of the Borrows once, or at the very least a rich target for raiding. They saved the Borrows, they saved Elden. They are the best of people.'

Yalla blinked once, not meeting his eyes. 'They dwell with fire-spirits.'

Temerran resisted the urge to clench his fists. It was on the tip of his tongue to demand if they were here to harm the fire-walkers, but once it was spoken, the dance would be over and they'd have to act. He had a horrible feeling it wouldn't turn out well for Elden, or anyone in it.

'I dwell with sea-spirits,' he said. 'They are treacherous more often than benevolent. They have aided me from time to time, though.'

'All spirits serve Jderha.'

Spirits did he want to knock the superiority out of her. He doubted any elemental creature served in Geladan out of choice. 'I have never met a spirit of earth, and only rarely of air, have you such beings in Geladan?'

She glanced at her staff and once again it sent a shiver through Temerran. The emerald eyes almost seemed to watch him.

'We do. There seem to be none here in Elden, and no magic.'

Temerran suddenly saw safer ground and he flung himself at it, telling Yalla what he knew of Elden's history and its witch trials, while she pretended interest. He was relieved when King Bractius turned and gestured for Temerran to join him at the prow. They were nearing the lifting bridge that spanned the River Taur where it left the lake to run to the sea. Kichi had extricated herself from Adrin and was laughing with Ayline. The warrior, Efrin, was standing alone observing them all. His eyes met Temerran's briefly before moving on. He excused himself from Yalla and joined the king.

'Your majesty?'

'I was telling ambassador Ren here that you are the closest thing the Borrows has to an ambassador.'

'I guess that's so.' Temerran turned to the blond man who was smiling at him amiably. 'The Borrows have historically not been a people that bothered much with diplomacy.'

Ren raised a narrow eyebrow. 'You are of a warlike people?'

Temerran gave a chuckle and winced, although inside his humour was non-existent. He found it hard to believe these people had done their research on Elden and the Fulmers, but not on his own land. 'Until Chem conquered us, yes, that was so. We were raiders. Now we are traders.'

'But what do you have to trade?' Ren's smile remained, but Temerran couldn't help but feel the deep stab of an insult.

'Our strength and labour, when there is nought else.'

'Temerran's songs are worth a chest of gold.' Bractius gave him an encouraging thump on the back.

'Yes, you are a very fine musician.' Ren gave a slight nod of his head.

'You are kind,' Temerran replied, while telling himself not to be so paranoid. Any condescension from the polite ambassador was surely imagined.

Or was it? Temerran knew the man had power in his voice, but what would Ren gain by antagonising him?

'I have not yet heard Kichi sing,' Temerran said.

'Well, no.' Faint lines formed on Ren's forehead. 'The bards of Geladan have power in their voices, magic. We did not want to risk offence or startle anyone.'

'That was thoughtful.' Temerran smiled politely.

So that was it. They were still unsure of him; they were trying to determine if Temerran had power.

A servant approached, offering glasses of wine, and Temerran took one with quiet thanks. 'I would love to listen to the songs and tales of Geladan.'

'As would I,' Bractius said. 'People can learn much of each other from their music.'

'Then I am sure Kichi would be delighted to oblige us later.'

The ship continued its slow tour of the lake, and by the time they'd returned to Taur Castle, Temerran had had more than enough of diplomacy. His jaw ached from maintaining a pleasant smile. He slipped away to his room for a few moments of peace, but it was less than an hour before someone hammered loudly at his door. He was shocked when the king himself stepped in.

'Your majesty?' Temerran scrambled to his feet.

Bractius waved a hand at him. 'Tantony came to me. Gods, Temerran, they attacked the children! I couldn't say anything to you on the ship.'

Temerran pulled out a chair for Bractius. 'So it seems. None of their party were missing last night, they must have sent assassins out from their ship.'

'I've sent word to double the watch on the Geladanians in Southport, but it's probably too late. I've stashed Tantony in Jorrun's rooms here, he's too furious to be diplomatic… I shall have to send him back to Northold.' Bractius gritted his teeth and breathed out loudly. 'This is a mess, bard. If we were more powerful, or they less, I'd have done away with the lot of them.'

'We may have to find a way to do that yet,' Temerran said quietly. 'Have you seen anything in the last couple of days that would lead you to believe they're anything other than fanatical? And when they've destroyed the Fulmers and enslaved the fire-spirits, do you think they'll sail away without gaining a new land to worship their god?'

Bractius rubbed at his beard. 'That is the impression I got also. I'm having my own children sent away, then we must decide when, and how, to act. How much can your magic do?'

'Not enough.' Temerran shook his head.

'Dia?'

Temerran stood and went over to the window. 'She would come, of course she would, in fact I expect she will the moment she learns her family are at risk. I'm thinking Ravens.'

'Aye, Ravens might be the answer. But as always, Jorrun has his own mess in Chem.'

Temerran snorted a laugh. 'And you think he'll stay in Chem when he hears what's happened to his children?'

'No, I don't imagine he will.' Bractius raised his eyebrows. 'So, we try to keep the peace, buy some time.'

Temerran clenched his jaw. 'And we try to learn their weaknesses.'

***

Temerran made a point of visiting Lucien before going to dinner and learned that he was being sent to Taurmouth along with his sisters.

'It's not fair.' Lucien sighed. 'I don't get to see you much and now I'm being sent away. I don't want to go.'

'Life isn't fair,' Temerran said as he sat on the end of the boy's bed and watched him pack. 'And you'll find that having to do what you don't want happens frequently.'

'Could you not take me to Taurmouth? I'd love to sail on the *Undine*.' Lucien dropped a shirt into his small chest and hopped up onto the bed beside the bard.

'I promise, if fate does not forbid, that you shall sail with me on my ship one day.' He drew in a deep, quiet breath through his mouth. 'But it cannot be now. Your father needs me to help protect your kingdom.'

'I wish I could just be a sailor. I don't want to be a prince.'

Temerran shifted uncomfortably. 'It is what you were born to be. How you behave as a prince is down to you.'

'My father wants me to behave like him.'

'Most fathers do.'

'Was your father a bard?'

Temerran smiled. 'No. Bards on the Borrows are chosen. The bard finds someone with the potential for diplomacy, wisdom, discretion, and a talent for music. They also have to be able to summon the magic of the bard, an uncommon thing in the Borrows. I am from the small island of Baldec. My father was a fisherman, as most are. He was a rare man, though, he refused to raid. My mother wasn't pleased, especially when we were cold and hungry. She threw my father out and took in another man, one willing to provide what we needed to survive by any means. I didn't like him much, so I left, taking our small boat without even a hint of a plan. I was lucky. The old Bard, Falamin, found me at sea and took me onto his ship. He told me the sea-spirits had brought me to him.'

'Did you ever find your father again?' Lucien peered up at him.

'I never did.' Temerran was surprised at the slow, seeping sadness, like a shadow stealing the sun's warmth. He hadn't allowed himself to indulge in such self-pity for a long time. 'Come on, I'll help you finish your packing, then I'd best go down and be polite and smile a lot to people I don't like. See? Even grown up bards have to do things they don't like.'

Lucien grinned at him, though his quiet and sombre mood resumed as they packed. Temerran hugged him when he couldn't put off leaving any longer and hurried back to his room to make himself presentable. He wasn't quite the last to arrive in the king's private dining room. The Geladanian sorcerer, Lorev, and Efrin the Guardian had yet to show their faces. Temerran noted the ambassadors from the Fulmers had been omitted again, as had Adrin's wife. He'd have to seek Dorthai as soon as possible and see what the young warrior knew, and if there had been any word from Dia.

Efrin came hurrying into the room, giving a clumsy bow. 'Your majesties, I must apologise. Lorev has not yet returned and will not be joining us.'

'Returned?' Bractius demanded, his face reddening.

'He was inspired by your trip around the lake and set off to explore more of Elden with one of our warriors by land.'

Bractius's chest swelled and he opened his mouth; it was Ayline who stepped in smoothly, placing a hand on her husband's arm.

'I wish you had told us, we would have arranged a guide and an escort, then perhaps he would not have missed dinner.'

Ren regarded the king and Teliff and gave a dramatically low bow. 'I see we have offended. My deepest apologies. We are not entirely familiar with your ways. As guests, are we not free to come and go as we please?'

Temerran saw Bractius's jaw muscles move and he spoke quickly. 'I made many an error myself until I learned proper protocol.

It is considered offensive, an act of rebellion, even an act of war, to decline an invitation from the king. Leaving the king's court without leave is viewed in a similar way.'

'Then we have transgressed on two counts.' Kichi appeared genuinely mortified, although Temerran didn't believe it for a moment. 'How do we make amends?'

Temerran regarded to Bractius. The king's eyes were still narrowed, his colour high as he regarded the Geladanians. He relaxed his posture with some effort. 'I will choose to take no offense; however, I would like to hear a tale of your lands and a song or two as compensation.' He turned to Kichi.

The small woman gave a bow. 'I would be honoured.'

'Come then.' Bractius forced a smile to his face. 'Let us be seated.'

The king glanced at Temerran as they sat; he didn't need to speak to tell Temerran how much it galled him to both let the slight go and pretend they didn't know what these people were up to. They needed to know where Lorev had gone, Temerran prayed Arridia and Joss were far out of his reach.

The dinner was strained despite the efforts of both Kichi and Temerran to lighten the mood. Kichi's tale was interesting and they learned a little of the history of her land, and how firmly and relentlessly their goddess held sway over them. Temerran detected only the slightest traces of power in Kichi's words as she sang. Was she not as powerful as he'd feared, or pretending she wasn't so as he had done?

He had no doubt the others were as relieved as he when their dinner ended. Ayline issued them an invitation to take a tour of the city the following morning, and having been told of etiquette in Elden, they were not in a position to refuse. Temerran wondered if they would see Lorev in the morning. The prickling sensation down his spine told him the answer would be no, and they couldn't ignore his absence forever.

After excusing himself, Temerran made his way onto the walls to breathe in the outside air. It was chilly, but not biting, the silty smell of the lake brought to him on the soft wind. He turned his gaze from the water to the road below and froze. A woman in a red cloak hurried along the cobbles. Temerran swore, running for the door and taking the uneven stairs down two at a time. By the time he'd left the castle and ducked beneath the portcullis, there was no sign of her. She'd taken the forest gate before. It made sense she'd go the same way again. He set off at a jog and finally caught sight of Linea as she neared the high wall surrounding the city. He slowed, keeping to the shadows, and watched as she approached the gates. A skinny-looking dog came trotting out of a side street and took up an incessant barking toward the guards.

'Clear off!' one of the men yelled.

The dog took a few steps forward and continued its yapping.

'Get out of here.' The guard strode toward it, drawing a sword and waving it at the animal. It growled, its demeanour suddenly threatening. The other guard hurried up to join his colleague.

Temerran's eyebrows rose, and he observed with some admiration as Linea slipped through the gate. The guards didn't see her. As Temerran drew close to the gate, the dog backed away and ran off.

'You there!'

144

Temerran rolled his eyes but turned to smile at the guards. 'It's me.'

'Where are you going at this time of night?'

Temerran sighed, trying to keep the frustration from his face. 'I'm following the woman you just let through the gates.'

'What woman?'

'Spirits save us,' Temerran muttered. 'If you don't let me get after her, the king will have your hide.'

He put power into his voice and both guards shrank back.

'Yes, sir,' one of them said.

Temerran hurried through the gate and growled in frustration when he could see no sign of the Geladanian servant. He halted, relaxing his breathing and closing his eyes.

The lake was barely a whisper with only a gentle wind to stir it, but some of the boats moved and creaked away in the harbour. An occasional voice rose in the city behind him, and he heard the scuttling of rats among the fishing nets and the small boats pulled up on the muddy shore. A blackbird startled a short distance ahead to the north, and Temerran smiled to himself.

He followed the road for some way before spotting the red cloak again. She'd moved off the path and closer to the water as a wagon came toward them out of the darkness, a trader reaching the capital late. Temerran also slipped off the path, stepping carefully on the short grass leading down to the soft mud and black water.

They had gone almost a mile from the city walls when Linea stopped, making her way through a stand of five large trees to the water's edge where she knelt and sat back on her heels, head bowed. Temerran was out in the open but didn't dare get closer to the shelter of the trees. He crouched himself, keeping low to the ground. Linea untied her cloak and let it fall behind her, raising her face and opening her eyes as the moon rose over the lake. He drew in a sharp breath as she reached down and grabbed the bottom of her dress, rising up onto her knees to pull it over her head. He instinctively looked away, feeling suddenly warm. He shifted his position, pushing aside guilt at his intrusion and turning back. Linea was walking slowly into the water, the moonlight a soft glow around the edges of her silhouette. Temerran realised he was holding his breath and forced himself to breathe.

He shook his head at himself. There was a time and a place to be distracted by a beautiful woman, but this wasn't it.

For a moment he lost sight of her, but she appeared again between the trees, only her head now above the slow ripples of the lake. She remained where she was for several minutes, before swimming back to the shore.

Temerran considered his options. He'd learned nothing. Perhaps there was nothing to learn, but his instincts told him otherwise.

He sat up, crossing his legs, and looking out across the lake. He didn't have to wait long before the softest of footfalls landed beside him.

'Good evening, Temerran of the Borrows.' She sat slowly, tucking her feet up beneath her.

'Good evening, Linea. It's late for you to be far from the city alone.'

She smiled as she followed his gaze out over the water to the moon. 'I don't appear to be alone.'

'I'm sure the castle servants would have obliged you with some hot water for a bath.'

'I find fresh water and moonlight renews me. What of you? Will your lady not miss you?'

Temerran hesitated. He had no idea how conservative the Geladanian people were when it came to physical relationships. His behaviour was considered normal in both the Borrows and the Fulmers, but somewhat frowned upon in Elden. He thought he'd been discreet, perhaps he had, Linea might just be fishing to find out if he were available. He dismissed the thought at once; she was both intelligent and perceptive.

He turned to look at her, and his heart beat just a little faster as her eyes met his. 'In Geladan, do you choose just one person with whom to spend your life?'

The slightest of frowns creased the skin above her nose. 'Those of us who serve Jderha do not take a permanent life partner, our devotion must first and foremost always be to our goddess. Those who do not serve such a high calling are bound to one partner who must be approved by a priestess.'

'And are you bound?'

She smiled, her lips parting slightly. 'I am not.'

Temerran broke their eye contact, turning back toward the lake. 'Neither am I. The Bard of the Borrows is not meant to favour any one person.'

'That sounds lonely.'

Temerran swallowed. Loneliness was something he'd pretended not to feel all of his life, through pride, or self-denial. He had friends who meant the world to him, lovers who fulfilled his passions, but only his friendship with Dia had eased the ache in his soul.

'Let me walk you back to the castle.'

He got to his feet and held out a hand. She took it and he pulled her up. Her hand was soft, too soft for a servant. A warning scrabbled at the back of his brain, but as she stood, she seemingly lost her balance and staggered against him. His body responded before his brain and he reached out a hand to tilt her chin upward so his mouth could meet hers.

'I'm sorry.' He shook his head, taking three rapid steps back.

'I'm not.' She smiled, peering up at him from under her dark lashes. She laughed at his bewildered expression and linked her arm through his. 'Take me back, then.'

Temerran took a moment to gather himself, then headed slowly up the slope of the grass toward the road.

He cleared his throat. 'Lorev was not at dinner this evening, do you know where he went?'

'I only know that your tour of the lake inspired him to take a closer look at the beautiful land around it.'

Temerran frowned. There was warning in her words, the bard in him knew it, but the man in him couldn't quite shake himself free of the fog he was falling into.

He steeled himself and chose honesty. 'I am from the Borrows, but I care for the fate of Elden. Should the king fear your countrymen?'

Her pace slowed a little and he matched it, fearing he'd asked too much of her.

'That would depend on whether they opposed the will of Jderha.'

'And what is her *will* regarding Elden?'

'No more than trade, cooperation, and friendship for the moment.'

For the moment. The words sent a chill down his spine. It didn't take much imagination to guess what the Geladanian's goddess wanted in the long term; the same thing the lands he'd visited far across the sea were facing. Total, unquestioning devotion. Slavery of the soul. He wanted to ask what their intention was towards the Fulmers, but he recoiled from doing so. She might just be a servant, but even admittance from her would end their careful dance.

'You are very quiet for a bard,' she observed.

'Sometimes too many words can spoil a moment.'

She squeezed his arm a little more tightly, and he had to fight his desire to kiss her again.

When they reached the gates, the two guards stepped forward to bar their way. Temerran let out a loud sigh. 'I'm escorting the king's guest back to the castle.'

The two men glanced at each other in confusion. Temerran wanted to put his head in his hands and swear. Instead, he kept his smile on his face. He put power into his voice.

'You'll let us through to the castle.'

'Of course, Bard,' one of the guards stepped aside with a bow.

Temerran dipped his head in polite reply and guided Linea past them and through the gate. They spoke little as they wove their way through the city toward the castle, but Temerran was acutely aware of her warm hand on his arm. There were still a few people about, including the lampman who kept the street lanterns burning. Temerran realised his steps had slowed the closer they got to the castle gates.

'We are taking a tour of the city tomorrow, will you be joining us?' he asked.

'I wish I could, but it would not be appropriate.'

'Because you're a servant?'

She glanced at him and nodded.

'Will you be taking another walk to the lake tomorrow night?'

She shook her head. 'No. I may take up your suggestion of hot water.'

He laughed and placed his hand over hers. He quickly grew serious, nodding to the castle guards as they ushered them through. 'If you do not slip out of the castle tomorrow night, how will I find you?'

She halted, turning her face away a little. 'Perhaps I will find you.'

For the first time in many years, Temerran stumbled over his words. 'I would like that.'

'And your lady?'

Unwanted guilt stabbed at his heart again. Jen knew who and what he was, he'd been clear their dalliance was just for fun; even so, he couldn't help but think he was betraying her. His heart was screaming at him like never before, fear and excitement almost made his body freeze. It was as though some greater power had taken over control of Temerran's all too human mind.

He took a step back, pulling his arm free to make a heartfelt and courteous bow. 'Linea, my only lady is you.'

She froze, her eyes widening, her hand going to her chest. Linea turned away, clearing her throat. 'My room is this way.'

Not wanting her to know he'd followed her before, he let her lead the way. Temerran pushed open the door to her room, then stepped aside to allow her entry. 'Good night, Linea.'

It was a moment before she replied. 'Goodnight, Bard of the Borrows.'

She stepped into the room and he pulled the door closed behind her, gasping in air and forcing his muscles to relax. This was foolish, even for him.

And she was the enemy of the people he loved.

Chapter Ten

Kesta; Free city of Navere

Kesta watched as Jorrun packed the few things he was taking with him. She longed to tell him not to go; she wanted to insist she go with him, but to do either would be selfish, so she passed him the last of his folded shirts.

'Thank you.' He glanced up at her, stuffing the shirt into the top of his bag with less care than he'd taken with the two books he'd chosen to take. He stood, touching the small vial of his blood that she wore hidden below her tunic. A wave of guilt stung her, and her cheeks warmed a little. She still feared some terrible consequence for using even this seemingly harmless form of blood magic, but she couldn't let him go without knowing he could contact her quickly.

'It will take about nine or ten days to get to Caergard,' he told her. 'Then two to travel on to Uldren. It…it's likely to be a month before I make it back.'

'Well, that gives me plenty of time to sort things out here.' She forced a smile, but his face remained serious as he held her gaze.

'Take care of yourself.' He bent his head to give her a long, slow kiss and Kesta couldn't stop the few tears that escaped. She quickly wiped her face and picked up his bag.

'Come on, then.'

The others were waiting in the courtyard. They were a small party, only Tyrin, Rothfel, and two Raven Scouts were accompanying him to Caergard. Rothfel had hold of two supply horses.

Calayna and Rece came to see them away and Rece had a few swift, quiet words with Rothfel.

'I hope you recover your sister.' Calayna stepped up to hold the halter of Jorrun's horse as he swung up into the saddle. He gave her a nod, his gaze going straight back to Kesta. Without a word he turned his horse toward the road and set off at a trot towards the gate.

Kesta drew in a deep breath and headed back inside the palace.

'Kesta?' Rece called after her. He sounded worried.

'I'm fine,' she called back over her shoulder. 'I'm going to spend a bit of time with our prisoner.'

She made her way to the dungeons, trying to push her fears for Jorrun aside. She had work of her own to do. The guard let her past at once and she opened up her *knowing* as she approached Alikan's cell. She could hear a soft voice murmuring and the guard standing in the corner turned to her and smiled. He silently mouthed to her.

'He's talking to the cat. He often asks for its name.'

Kesta returned the smile and crept closer, the guard stepping out of her way.

Alikan laughed and a tingling hurt spread out from Kesta's heart. Calling up the same calm she would use for an injured animal, Kesta pulled back the bolt and opened the door.

The boy froze, his amber eyes wide. The small black kitten continued to play with the end of the shoelace which dangled from his hand.

Kesta closed the door behind her and slowly sat on the floor while the boy watched her every move without blinking.

'Hello, Alikan, my name is Kesta.'

He snatched up the wriggling kitten and shuffled back against the wall.

'How do you know my name?'

'The cat told me.'

He narrowed his eyes at her, glancing at the door. 'You're not supposed to speak to me.'

'Why? Because you think I'm your enemy?'

'Because you're a woman.' Alikan scowled.

'I'm from the Fulmers where women rule,' she replied gently. 'And we do not beat boys to make them fear their fathers.'

Alikan's eyes widened again and he let the struggling cat escape.

'Demons rule the Fulmers.'

Kesta opened her mouth to reply, but hesitated. This wasn't going to be easy. 'Some men call women with power demons because they are afraid of us.'

'Do you have power?'

Kesta called a small amount of flame to her fingertips. Alikan leapt to his feet and snatched up his kitten, turning to keep his own body between Kesta and the cat. Kesta withdrew her power and closed her eyes briefly. She could have wept for yet one more scarred soul in Chem. Here was another boy, who despite what had been done to him, was instinctively kind. She couldn't help but wonder when Alikan had last felt the comfort of a hug.

'I won't hurt you,' she said. 'I actually need your help, but I don't imagine for a moment you want to trust me.' She looked around the room. They had given him a straw pallet and several blankets and cushions. 'Do you read?'

Alikan screwed up his nose, but his posture became less defensive. The kitten had fallen asleep in his arms.

'What about drawing?'

Alikan made a disgusted sound. 'Drawing is for babies and the Coven's women.'

'I see.' Kesta pushed her momentary anger aside. 'So, what do you do with your time?'

'I train to fight, of course.'

'Of course.' A smile twitched Kesta's lips. 'Do you want to know what your cat's name is?'

Alikan drew himself up and scowled at her. 'I know its name. Anyway, he doesn't want to talk to you.'

Kesta let him feel her disappointment. 'I will leave you both alone then. May I visit you tomorrow?'

He shrugged, but she could sense his conflicting emotions. He was lonely and afraid, confused by the fact he was supposed to hate her, but didn't.

'Goodbye then, Alikan, and you, Trouble.' She looked at the cat.

Alikan glanced down at the little creature but said nothing as Kesta left the room.

Kesta touched the guard's arm as she passed him. 'Thank you.'

He gave a slight bow. 'Raven.'

She sought out Rece who was dealing with one of their food suppliers. As soon as they were alone, he asked her how she'd got on.

Kesta sighed. 'I'm going to have to take it slowly to win his trust, which means we have to wait for information. We could have someone else scare it from him, but I'd rather not.'

'I'd rather not either.' Rece winced. 'But we might have to.'

'Give me two or three more days,' Kesta asked him. 'Of the two boys we recruited with Tyrin, which would you say would be best to handle Alikan with sensitivity?'

'I'd say Ovey. What are you thinking?'

'Have Ovey train Alikan for an hour this afternoon, see what fighting skills the boy has. Let him use up some energy, keep his mind busy, and let out a bit of those emotions he's holding back.'

Rece gave a grunt of approval. 'That's not a bad plan.'

'Thanks.' Kesta grinned. 'And send out an invitation for the High Priest and his administrator, Kerzin to come and dine with us in a couple of days' time.'

'You want to invite priests for dinner?' He stared at her incredulously.

Her grin widened. 'I do.'

***

Kesta pressed her face into the pillow and drew in a deep breath. It still smelt of Jorrun. With a groan she forced herself to get up, using her magic to warm her water. She'd made little progress with Alikan over the past two days and setting a Raven scout to spy on Kerzin had as yet yielded nothing. She put a long, warm robe on over her tunic and trousers, fastening it at the front with a raven brooch and buckling her dagger belt around her waist. She strode straight to Osun's study to see if there were any new reports. Calayna was sitting at the desk, leaning her head on her hand as she read the parchment in front of her.

'Good morning.'

Calayna looked up, then sat back in her chair with a sigh. 'Morning. I'm just going over the accounts and they don't make good reading. I don't want to raise guild taxes, but we have a lot of guards and staff to feed through the winter and reports suggest the harvest will be poor this year.'

'In the Fulmers we tithe, rather than tax.'

'Tithe?' Calayna cocked her head.

'We ask for a portion of each harvest. Generally, people just donate what they can to the Hold's stores to be shared out as needed. I'm not sure that would work well in Chem though.'

Calayna winced. 'No. But we might offer some kind of tax relief or incentive for donations of winter stores. The last few years have been struggle enough, but this year we have little left to barter with Elden. We can't manage without their help.'

Kesta sat down heavily in a chair. 'And we're well aware Bractius gives nothing for free. Rothfel intends to borrow what he can from Uldren for us.' She grinned, but Calayna just snorted.

'I'm sure that thief will snatch what he's able, but we don't even know if—'

She halted, her eyes widening as she met Kesta's.

Kesta waved a hand at her, trying not to let a painful lump form in her throat. 'It's okay, we can't pretend Jorrun isn't taking a huge risk. Any Raven reports this morning?'

Calayna shook her head. 'It's gone quiet.'

Kesta raised her eyebrows. 'I don't like quiet.'

'Neither do I.'

Their eyes met and they both smiled tentatively.

'I'll try again with Alikan this morning. If Ovey or I don't get anywhere today, I fear we'll have to get a couple of the guards to attempt to scare some information out of him.'

Calayna rubbed at her mouth. 'A boy in Chem faces a lot of fear, particularly one born to a Coven. It might not be easy to shake him.'

Kesta looked down at her hands. 'No, I imagine not.' She stood up and made her way to the door. 'I'll let you know how I get on.'

She went to find Ovey first before going to the dungeon. The boy was eating in the common room next to the kitchen where the guards took their meals. Most of the Ravens ate in a dining hall on the upper floor, but those who trained to fight with the men under Captain Rece tended to eat with their comrades.

Several men scrambled to their feet on seeing Kesta, but she waved a hand at them. 'Go on and eat.' Ovey caught her gaze and remained standing.

'Did you need me, Master Raven?'

'Would you meet me in the Library when you've eaten?'

Ovey immediately pushed aside his chair and stepped away from the table. 'I'm ready at once, Master.'

Kesta opened her mouth to tell him to finish his food, but she realised it would embarrass, possibly even shame the boy in front of his comrades. 'This way, then.'

Ovey was somewhere around fourteen years old and hadn't quite taken on the build of a man, although his voice had broken. He had short blond hair with a hint of red and large brown eyes in a freckled face. Magically he was already strong and he knew Calayna and Rece held out hopes that he might one day lead one of the provinces, perhaps even help them take one in the east.

'How did things go with Alikan yesterday?'

The boy's eyebrows drew together in a frown. 'He still won't talk much, but he showed no reluctance this time when I arrived to train him. He's pretty good, actually. Intuitive, thoughtful. I still don't sense any magic in him, though.'

'It's there,' Kesta reassured him. 'He's young yet.'

Ovey nodded.

'How old were you when your power came through?'

'I was early, I gained mine the year they took me from my mother.'

'So, you were eight?' Kesta glanced around at the boy.

'I was.'

'Yet you didn't fight the Ravens who came to take Darkhall.'

'Our mothers spoke of the Ravens as being liberators, heroes, they prayed every night that you would come to save them. Some of us boys did too.'

Kesta's eyes prickled and she blinked rapidly. 'I see. Are you due to serve a term in the Fulmers?'

'Yes, I am to go there in the spring. I've heard Heara is a fearsome teacher!'

Kesta laughed. 'She's the best scout there is. When you're there though, be sure to get to know my uncle Worvig. He's a quiet man, but you'll learn things from him that will save your life.'

He turned to study her face; his brown eyes wide. 'I'll be certain to find him, Master.'

Kesta smiled at him. 'Go finish your food.'

He gave a shy smile back, then with a bob of his head, hurried back to the food hall.

Hope and guilt warred within Kesta. So, the women in the east were teaching their sons to respect and support the Ravens, laying a subtle but essential foundation. But when the Ravens didn't come, when the people got desperate… then there were massacres like the one in Parsiphay.

Kesta shuddered and stretching her spine strode to the dungeons.

The usual young guard was there, and he straightened up with a smile on seeing her.

'How has he been?' Kesta asked.

The guard frowned a little. 'Quiet this morning, actually.'

Concern made Kesta's limbs heavy and she hurried to unbolt the door to Alikan's cell. He was sitting on the floor with his back to the wall, the kitten asleep in his lap. Kesta felt his unease through her *knowing* and the redness around his eyes told her he'd been crying. She softly closed the door and sat on the floor, keeping some distance between them so as not to make him uncomfortable.

'What's wrong, Alikan?'

His nostrils flared a little, but he didn't reply.

She indicated the kitten with her head. 'Trouble says you're very sad.'

Alikan glanced down at the cat and shifted a little.

'You know, cats don't speak in words, not like people do.' Kesta made herself more comfortable, sending out subtle calm. Trouble started purring and Alikan's amber eyes widened. 'They comprehend a lot of our words, but they understand more our feelings, our tone of

160

voice, the way we move. They invent meows to tell us what they want and get us to cater to their demands. Trouble will learn his own special language just for you and him. I... I can't hear his words, but I see the images that form in his mind and can send him the same to communicate. Trouble thinks of his mum often, he feels and sees her as a softness, safety. Do you miss your mother, Alikan? Was she at Caergard?'

He scowled and looked away.

Kesta cursed herself for not thinking of this before. 'If you tell me her name, I can write to Caergard and see if she's there.'

Alikan sprang to his feet, dislodging the disgruntled Trouble. 'She's dead.'

Alikan's pain ripped through her and she grabbed at her stomach, quickly reducing her *knowing* and forcing herself to serenity before calling it back.

'I'm very sorry—'

'What do you want?' The boy rounded on her; fists clenched. 'I'm being kept in a dungeon, but you give me all these nice things and have me train. I know you want me to tell you stuff, what happens if I don't?'

Kesta drew in a breath and chewed at her lower lip. 'I'll be completely honest with you. I have to protect the people I care about. There are people who want to harm those under my protection, and I have to try to stop them. You know who those people are, and where they are, but I imagine they are people you care about and don't want to betray.' She sighed. 'Alikan, we don't want to hurt you but we can't let you go, not if you're going to go back and help them. Not if you're going to do bad things to the people I'm protecting.'

'You are the bad people,' he said, although she sensed his doubt and confusion.

Kesta stood up quickly and he backed away. She opened the door. 'Come with me.'

He stared at the door; his body frozen. Trouble chased about on the bed making little prooping noises.

'I promise you won't be harmed.' Kesta stepped out into the hall. 'I want to show you the palace, let you see the people we are.'

'Aren't you afraid I'll try to run away?'

'I'll be sad if you try to escape, I hope that you'll come to like us.'

She took a few more steps out into the hallway and Alikan tentatively followed. He jumped when he saw the guard. The young man smiled at him and moved out of the way.

Alikan gasped. 'What about Trouble?'

'He'll be fine here. We won't leave him for long.'

'I'll keep an eye on him,' the young guard offered.

After a moment, Alikan nodded.

Both the guards at the top of the stairs looked startled when Alikan followed Kesta out, but neither said a word. The boy stood blinking in the brighter light of the hallway.

'Let's go to the library first,' Kesta suggested. She didn't wait for a reply but set off at once, listening and using her *knowing* to make sure the boy stayed close.

When they'd first taken Navere, the library had become her and Jorrun's sanctuary. Now it was open to any of the Ravens and was used as a meeting place for the guild leaders. Kesta pushed the heavy doors open and peered in. It was empty. Light streamed in through the round window high up in the wall, the glass that had replaced the one Kesta had smashed years ago clear, rather than stained in bright colours. She glanced up at the high balcony that had once served as her and Jorrun's bedroom and smiled.

'Do you read?' she asked Alikan.

He took a tentative step into the room and looked around; his mouth slightly open.

'Would you like to pick a couple of books to take back to your room?' She winced at her last word, but he didn't correct her. Alikan took a tentative step, then another, glancing over his shoulder at her. Kesta moved over to one of the shelves to look at the books herself, using her *knowing* to track his progress. She was hit by a sudden surge of emotion as he glanced at the open library door, but he controlled himself and forced his feet towards the shelves instead of making a desperate run for freedom. Kesta's muscles relaxed a little and she sent him courage, she longed with every fibre of her being to send the boy love, but she needed his trust first. She turned cautiously and watched as he ran a finger along the spines. He pulled out a book and opened the cover, rejecting it and returning it to its shelf. The third book he tried he held for some time and then turned to see Kesta watching him. His cheeks flushed a little, grubby with dust.

She took him to the audience room, and they stood out of the way and observed Calayna, Jollen, and Rece dealing with the day's petitioners. They walked the gardens, sitting on Osun's favourite bench and watching young Ursaith taking her first riding lesson on the leaf-strewn lawn. They snuck back in through the kitchens and Kesta stole Alikan a sweet pastry and they ran through the corridor, the boy almost laughing as they ducked into a room to eat it.

Kesta studied him as he licked the caramelised, sticky fruit juice from his fingers. She reached out a hand to tuck a strand of his hair behind his ear but stopped herself.

'We should get you back to Trouble,' she said.

He didn't say anything as he walked with her to the dungeons, keeping pace at her side rather than following behind. The young guard opened the cell door for them and Kesta felt Alikan's delight and relief when he saw Trouble asleep. The boy hesitated in the doorway, turning a little to look back at Kesta.

'My father is in Navere; with my two brothers. They're here to take back the city. I failed my test. They'll kill me too.'

Kesta crouched to bring her head to the same height as the boy's. She reached out and placed her fingers beneath his chin to look him in the eyes. 'No, they won't. They won't get past me.'

***

Kesta ran a hand across the pristine tablecloth and nodded with a smile at the servants. She took in a deep breath to quell the nervous churning of her stomach. She regretted inviting the priests, not because she feared them, but because she had to postpone dealing with Voxen until they'd left. Several scouts had gone out to confirm Alikan's story and survey his place of hiding; a small house on the northern side of the city that belonged to an ex skin trader.

She reached up and touched her hair, checking it hadn't come loose, then hurried to join the others in the audience room. They'd decided not to call together all the Ravens who were present in the palace, wanting their dinner to appear welcoming rather than a display of power. Kesta had of course asked Calayna and Rece to be there, along with Ovey, Beth, Jollen, Sirelle, and Ovey's young half-brother, Neffy.

'Any news?' Kesta asked Rece at once.

He bent his head to confide excitedly, 'Yes. Our scouts confirm what the boy told you. Voxen and his two sons are holed up at Hallen's house on Stone Street. Only the older boy has left the building, he visited the temple. The other two have been glimpsed through the windows.'

Kesta straightened up and stared at Rece. 'There is a connection with the temple?'

'So it would seem, although he may have just been leaving a prayer with the gods.'

'Which would suggest they intend to act very soon.'

'Indeed. I have alerted the guards.'

Kesta smiled. He might be Chemman, but Rece was the very best of men.

One of the double doors of the audience room opened and a guard stepped in. 'The High Priest of Navere Temple, and Administrator Kerzin.'

Kesta gave a curt wave of her hand and the guard opened the door wider to admit the two men. She opened up her *knowing* at once, feeling the rebuff of the High Priest's amulet and the twisting, tumultuous anxiety of Kerzin.

Rece stepped forward at once. 'Please be welcome to Navere Palace.' He gestured to Zardin who came forward with a tray of glasses of dark, red wine.

'We are welcomed,' Bantu replied formally, exploring the room with his eyes.

Kerzin quickly accepted a glass of wine and sipped from it at once.

Bantu nodded his head to the large green banner hanging at the back of the room. 'Your choice of the raven emblem is interesting. Ravens are often used as messengers, are they not?'

'They are,' Kesta replied at once. 'They are intelligent birds who remember well who hurt them, and who helped them.'

Bantu raised his eyebrows with a smile. 'That is interesting. In Chem, the crow family are seen as somewhat evil.'

'In the Fulmers, Chemmen are seen as somewhat evil.'

Bantu barked a laugh. 'You are very quick, Kesta Silene.'

'And you have done your research, High Priest of Navere.'

Rece cleared his throat. 'Would you like to come through for dinner?'

They walked through to the large, formal dining room. Kesta had ensured she was seated beside Kerzin and opposite Bantu.

'Is it odd for you to be conversing at dinner with women?' Kesta asked as soon as they were all settled. Rece's face reddened and he took a large swallow of wine.

Bantu frowned, but he held Kesta's gaze. 'It is a little odd, yes, but I can't say that it's unpleasant.'

'And how are the visitors to the temples?' Calayna asked, gesturing toward the food to indicate Bantu should help himself. Kesta picked up a basket of bread and offered it to Kerzin.

Bantu paused, a frown on his face as he considered. Kesta noted that the only jewellery he wore was a small leather thong about his neck with a bloodstone hanging from it. 'There is a great mixture of people coming into the temple as is always the case.'

Kesta sensed those around the table relax a little, all but Kerzin who remained tense, anxious, a touch angry even.

'Some are happy, excited by the changes in Navere,' Bantu continued. 'Others are afraid and resentful. Their opinions depend on whether they've lost, or prospered, naturally. I'm impressed at the way you have minimised disruption and poverty.'

Rece turned the conversation to safer subjects; the weather, the harvest, the fact they had not had any earthquakes in Chem for some time. Although he mostly kept still and was polite, Kesta could sense Kerzin's agitation growing through her *knowing*. She wished her father were here, he had a way about him that could put anyone at ease.

She cleared her throat and turned to the priest. 'How long have you been administrator to the temple?'

The man's eyes widened a little, however he recovered quickly. 'A little over six months, um…'

'Just call me Kesta. If that feels uncomfortable, many of the men in the palace prefer "sister".'

Kerzin frowned. 'In the priesthood, we only call each other brother, and name no one but a Coven Lord, Master. I'll, er… I'll try "Kesta".'

She didn't need her *knowing* to recognise his embarrassment, his cheeks flushed a bright red. With a jolt, she realised there was no anger, no animosity aimed at her. But if not her, then who?

They finished their meal with Bantu seemingly transfixed by Beth and Jollen's accounts of their visits to the Fulmers and Elden. The women gave away nothing of their training, describing only the land they'd seen and a little of the culture.

'Shall we retire to the library?' Rece suggested.

'I have heard much of the library of Navere Palace,' Bantu said eagerly. 'I believe Dryn Dunham was a great collector of books.'

Kesta wanted to say that Jorrun was too, but her tongue didn't move. She knew Jorrun would hate any comparison or link to his father. When they reached the library, Bantu stood in the middle of it and turned about, gazing at the shelves.

'My!' Bantu exclaimed. 'It really is quite a collection. I imagine there is a vast amount of knowledge to be found here.'

Kesta opened her mouth to tell him he could take a look, she'd started to warm to the High Priest, despite not being able to read him with her magic; but Kerzin stepped up behind her.

'Don't let him have any books!' he whispered.

A chill ran down Kesta's spine and she immediately thought of the small green book that had saved her life and led to the destruction of the demon, Hacren.

Rece beat her to it. 'You are welcome to take a look.'

Kesta gritted her teeth. 'My husband is very protective of this library.' She tried to put a smile in her voice. 'He wouldn't even let anyone but me in for several weeks after we liberated the palace.'

Bantu laughed, but it sounded hollow.

While Calayna and Rece escorted the High Priest around the lower floor of the library, Kesta poured some camomile and chicory tea into a mug and took it to Kerzin. She tilted her head and raised her eyebrows at him but didn't say a word.

'Not here,' Kerzin hissed, glancing toward Bantu. 'I'm due to visit the women's temple in three days. Find me then.'

She nodded, handing him the tea, and catching up with Bantu. Ovey and his half-brother were sitting in some of the comfortable chairs, their young faces flushed with wine and good food as they chatted quietly together.

'How does one get to all those books on the upper level?' Bantu was asking.

Kesta stepped in quickly. 'With a very tall ladder.' She grinned, but the priest's eyes narrowed. 'Seriously, though, there is a passage accessed from elsewhere. So, do you have any advice for us?'

From the way the man's mouth opened and closed she could tell she'd thrown him. 'Well… Well you're already sensitive to the impact of your changes. How about… it has been a long time since the city has seen any kind of festival. In just under a month it is considered Domarra's Day, to coincide with the completion of most harvesting. Perhaps you could arrange something and we of the temple could bless it, and the city?'

'That sounds like a good idea.' Calayna looked from Kesta to Rece. 'Although we would have to look at the expense, of course.'

'The temple would be willing to help with that, eh, Kerzin?' Bantu gestured the administrator over. 'We receive many donations at the temple, more than enough to keep us priests, we would be happy to donate toward a celebration of Domarra.'

Kesta folded her arms and shifted her weight onto one hip. As much as she hated the Chemman worship of what she considered imaginary gods, it was an essential part of their culture and one she had to respect if she liked it or not. Even so… She looked toward Kerzin, but the man wouldn't meet her eyes.

'I'll look, of course, most revered master.'

Bantu waved a hand and laughed. 'Kerzin likes to count the money, but he doesn't like to hand it out! We will help.'

It was quite late before Bantu politely made his farewells and the Coven members were left alone to discuss their impressions. All of them were shocked at Kesta's revelations. Only Calayna had been wary still of Bantu and refused to trust him, the others had all allowed themselves to be charmed.

Once in the privacy of her room, Kesta risked calling Jorrun, her heart expanding painfully within her chest at the sight of his reflection in her scrying bowl and the vibration of his voice in the pendant clasped in her hand.

'Kes, I don't like the sound of this festival. I might be being paranoid, but it worries me.'

Kesta drew in a deep breath. 'The festival itself will be a good thing. It will boost trade and allow us to provide alms for those struggling before winter sets in. However, I agree, any involvement of the priests and the gods we'll have to keep a close eye on.'

'Do so. Good luck with tomorrow. Please be careful.' He reached a hand toward the water without quite touching it.

'And you. Will you contact me in a couple of days?'

'No, please try to contact me tomorrow, I want to know how it goes.'

She nodded. 'I love you.'

He smiled and the worry fled from his eyes. 'I love you too.'

The water darkened and Kesta sat back on her heels. Her eyes narrowed as she thought of Kerzin and all the mixed-up emotions she'd sensed from him. Who was he and what was he up to?

***

Before their raid on Voxen's hideout, Kesta had Alikan moved from the dungeons up to one of the women's rooms on the top floor of the palace. Most of the locks had been removed from the outside of each door and been placed instead on the inside, although two had been left, the bars still present outside the windows. The young guard escorted him, taking up his post in the corridor. They didn't lock the door and left it open a crack, but Alikan didn't seek to come out.

They chose to make their raid during the day, to demonstrate that the Ravens were not afraid and had nothing to hide. While Rece took his guards with Beth and Jollen to the front of the house, Sirelle took Raven scouts and her magical trainees around the back. Kesta took Ovey on a treacherous route across the rooftops, waiting until Rece was close before jumping off the edge of the roof. She caught the eaves with her fingers as she fell, swinging in and blasting the glass out of the window before her feet hit the pane. She landed in a crouch among the broken glass on the floor, drawing her dagger. Ovey landed beside her a moment later, stumbling to his knees before scrambling to his feet.

The door to the bedroom burst open and Kesta sensed the man call up his power. He was young, not more than eighteen. Guilt burst briefly in Kesta's chest as she created a strong wind and hurled him back, the fireball he'd formed slamming against the wall behind him. Manipulating the air, Kesta held the young magic user fast, while Ovey darted in and hit him hard around the back of the head with a small cosh. He slipped to the ground.

They heard shouting and a woman screamed as the front door of the house was broken in. From the sound of the footsteps Kesta guessed several people were heading for the back door. With a glance at Ovey, Kesta quickly checked the upstairs rooms. There was a woman in one, and she ducked down behind the bed, eyes huge.

'Stay where you are,' Kesta ordered.

She called her magic ready and reached the top of the stairs. A man stood part way up it, holding up a shield of power to deflect Beth's attack. The fireball he sent blazing toward Rece was powerful and Kesta cursed under her breath. Both Jollen and Beth managed to deflect it as Rece instinctively ducked. Nausea swept through Kesta as she realised it was unlikely she could let this man live. Someone with that much active power would be almost impossible to detain long term. She shielded, calling flame ready to the fingers of her left hand.

'Voxen.'

He twisted around to regard her, his face creasing with hatred. 'You.'

'You know you won't get out of this.' She held his gaze. 'Surrender and tell us what we need to know and you and your sons will live.'

He didn't reply but blasted her with an inferno. Her shield held, but behind her Ovey cried out. She expanded her shield, pushing forward against the pressure, the muscles of her legs straining as she descended the stairs. The walls and ceiling were aflame, blackening and blistering, sending choking smoke back up the stairway. Rece bellowed for everyone to get out.

Ovey!

She had to hope the young man had the sense to have got himself away. She called up a huge wind, swirling it around her in a maelstrom and blasting it down the stairs. Most of the fire went out, but the wooden structure of the house creaked and groaned. Through the smoke she sighted Voxen and leapt without hesitation, stabbing her dagger down into the man's chest. She spun about and sprinted back up the stairs, one of her feet snapping through a damaged board and raking the skin off her shin. She pulled herself up.

'Ovey!'

'Here, I'm here!' His voice was breathless.

Kesta leapt up the last steps and found the young Chemman dragging Voxen's unconscious son toward one of the windows.

'I couldn't leave him.' Ovey panted, coughing into his sleeve.

'The woman?'

Ovey swallowed and gestured to the window. The woman was huddled beneath it, too scared to make the jump.

'Come on,' Kesta told her firmly. 'We can get down the stairs now but watch your footing.'

Rece's worried shout came from downstairs. 'Kesta?'

'We're okay, can you help us carry this man down?'

Kesta grabbed the woman by the wrist and pulled her to the top of the blackened stairway, the walls cracked in places. Rece set his feet carefully, bracing himself to take the hand of the female slave and help her down, before assisting the others.

'Voxen's other son?' Kesta asked breathlessly.

'Sirelle and the Ravens have him under control,' Rece told her.

'Let's get everyone back to the palace. I guess the dungeons will be busy for a while. Let's have the scouts check over the building, we may find something useful in here.'

'I'll see to it.' Rece gave a slight bow of his head.

Chapter Eleven

Dia; Fulmer Island

'Icante!' A young warrior came hurrying into the hold, shoulders heaving as he caught his breath. 'A boat has arrived from Elden. Your grandchildren are onboard.'

She stood, the wool and carding brushes tumbling from her lap. 'Are they on their way here?'

The warrior nodded.

Dia turned to Eidwyn, the girl who'd replaced Pirelle as her apprentice. 'Please have Kesta's old room made ready for her children.'

Dia hurried from the great hall, one of her bodyguards, Gilfy, falling in behind her as she strode past the small slate-roofed houses to the gate in the high wall. From the causeway she could see down to the beach and the small ship that had anchored close to the shore. She met the Elden party where the high cliff path came up from the dunes, the little dark-haired girl breaking away from the others to run to her.

'Grandma!'

Dia crouched, holding out her arms to hug Arridia. As she looked up, she saw Azrael fly up out of the lantern Rosa carried and her insides went cold. If the little spirit had travelled over the sea, something had to be very wrong.

'Icante.' Kurghan gave a polite bow, Nip letting Joss down off his shoulders to run after his sister. The two Eldemen warriors also bowed, Rosa giving the briefest of curtseys before hurrying forward.

'Icante, we've brought the children here for safety,' Rosa said, worry creasing the skin of her face. She was pale and had dark shadows under her eyes.

Dia kissed Joss, then straightened up. 'Let's get you into the hold.'

Rosa swallowed and nodded, then remembered her courtly training. She introduced the two warriors. 'You remember Kurghan and Nip from Northold?'

'I do.' Dia gave them a warm smile despite her fear. 'And Azrael, of course. Doraquael will be happy to see you.' Why did she have a sinking feeling this was something to do with the drakes?

'Can I go to him now?' Azrael asked.

'No,' Dia replied sternly, and the fire-spirit spun back a little way. 'Stay with us and Doraquael can hear your news when I do.'

Azrael made himself smaller. 'Yes, Icante.'

'None of you are hurt?' Dia asked Rosa as they headed back toward the hold, the two children skipping excitedly ahead.

'Oh, no. But I found I don't travel too well by sea.' Rosa's cheeks flushed a bit, a high contrast to the rest of her skin.

'I have some tea that might help,' Dia told her kindly. 'And Tantony, he's all right?'

'He is,' she replied earnestly. 'The last I saw him he was intending to seek Temerran in Taurmaline.'

Dia regarded Rosa, then turned her attention back to the steep path. Arridia had taken hold of Joss's hand as they approached the high causeway.

'Please excuse me,' Nip muttered as he passed the women to catch up with the children.

'He's a good lad,' Dia observed.

Rosa nodded, a little out of breath. 'His father will be lost without him in the stables.'

Both Heara and Arrus were waiting for them in the great hall. Dia quickly arranged food and drink for the two Eldemen warriors and for Worvig to make them welcome. A messenger was sent to fetch Vilnue to meet the rest of them in Dia's room.

As soon as Azrael entered the room, Doraquael came flying to meet him and the two spirits flew loops around each other just below the ceiling. While Eidwyn made them all tea, Dia took some ginger and other herbs from a chest, blending them carefully for Rosa.

'Talk to me,' Dia said, mindful that the children were with them.

Both Kurghan and Nip turned to Rosa and the former lady-in-waiting's cheeks coloured again. She didn't falter though as she recounted everything that had happened, pausing only to sip gratefully from the tea Dia made for her.

When she'd finished, Dia turned to the two fire-spirits. 'What do you two have to say for yourselves?'

'We are ssorry, Dia!' Doraquael wailed. 'We really knew none of this. The ancient ones don't talk of the old dayss. In fact, they won't talk to Azra and me at all.'

'Because you're earth-bound?'

'Yess.' Azrael drooped. 'The ancient ones forbid it but would not ssay why. Siveraell found out for us. He cares for humans more than most.'

'If it's forbidden, why did you both make the exchange to become a part of the earth realm?' Dia demanded.

'For Naderra,' Azrael whispered, his eyes burning a fierce blue. 'For Jorrun and Osun. I guess Naderra was my fire priestess.'

'And you mine.' Doraquael pulsed a little closer to Dia.

'All right.' Dia's shoulders sagged. 'We will have to assume these Geladanians will find their way here. Azrael, you stay by Arridia. Doraquael, you stay by Joss. No excuses, you don't leave the children for a second.'

'Yes, Dia,' they chorused.

She turned to her husband. 'Get the warriors on alert, I want all the longships launched and patrolling our coast unless the sea threatens their lives. Eidwyn, send word to the other holds, I need as many *walkers* as possible here on Fulmer Island.' She turned to Vilnue. 'Have you heard nothing from Bractius?'

Vilnue shook his head with a puzzled frown. 'No. It seems odd he'd send warning to Northold and not here.'

'And Temerran would have sent you word,' Arrus pointed out.

Dia sat down on the end of her bed. 'We will have to assume the Geladanians would have intercepted messages.'

'I'll post scouts on the cliff below the hold.' Heara straightened up. 'I don't want anyone creeping in through windows here.'

Dia nodded distractedly. 'I'll have to get word to Kesta and Jorrun, they need to know their children are in danger.'

'The bad men aren't here yet,' Arridia whispered from where she sat on the floor with her brother.

'Oh.' Rosa covered her mouth with her fingers. 'There's something I needed to tell you, Icante, but...' She glanced at the children and the others in the room.

'It's okay; and please, Rosa, you know to call me Dia.'

Rosa drew in a deep breath. 'It's too early, but I wondered... is there any chance Arridia might be coming into her powers?'

Dia froze, turning slowly to study her granddaughter. 'I would say no, but you obviously have reason to think so.' She slipped off the bed to kneel beside Arridia. 'Look at me a moment, my honey.'

Arridia turned to blink up at her.

Dia's breath caught in her throat. One of the little girl's eyes had deepened in colour, it was almost violet.

'Dia?' Arrus asked in concern.

It was a moment before Dia forced the words out. 'She's a *walker*!'

'No.' Eidwyn almost dropped her cup. 'She can't be.'

'What's wrong, grandma?' Arridia asked.

Nip stepped hastily forward and stroked her hair. 'Everything's fine, Riddi. Shall we go and feed those goats we saw out in the hold?'

'Oh, yes please,' Joss spoke up at once.

Arridia looked up at all the adults with narrowed eyes, but she got to her feet and took Nip's hand.

'Thank you,' Dia mouthed to the young man. As he left the room with the children, Dia cleared her throat and pointed a finger at the fire-spirits. Azrael gave a squeal and both drakes went flying out the door.

'She's too young,' Eidwyn sounded anguished.

Dia was silent, wrapping her arms around herself. The fact Jorrun was her father might go some way to explain it, but Arridia was at least two years too young even for someone of powerful Chemman decent. And it wasn't just her age. It was hard for a *walker* to conceive a child, rare for that child to have power. A third-generation *walker* was… it was unheard of. They'd considered Arridia and Joss might inherit some of their father's power, but never their mother's.

'Could it be the danger that triggered her magic to come early?' Vilnue asked.

Rosa stirred. 'I think she had it before then. She knew something was bad about the assassin the moment he knocked.'

Dia sighed. 'I'll talk to her and ask Everlyn to carefully direct her training.'

'Won't you train her yourself?' Eidwyn asked in surprise.

Arrus gave a loud sigh. 'I imagine my wife intends to rush off and save Elden again.'

'Is Elden actually in danger though?' Vilnue asked. 'If they are here for *walkers*, perhaps Elden is of no consequence.'

Dia chewed at her thumbnail. 'If Bractius tries to help or shield the islands in any way, then he has no one there who can defend him or his people, if they have the magical strength Azrael warned of. There's also Temerran. He'll be careful, but he'll also feel obliged to protect the Fulmers.'

'And if we have to fight, it's best if we don't wait until they come here, where the *walkers* and children are.' Heara's mouth quirked up in a grim smile.

'Exactly.' Dia straightened up and placed a hand on her hip. 'Heara, how many Ravens with power are you and Everlyn training that have no obvious Fulmer heritage?'

'There's three.'

Dia nodded. 'They will come with me. We will go first to Northold to get news from Tantony. Vilnue, you will go to Temerran and the king.'

'Yes, Icante.' Vilnue gave a bow, though she wasn't his commander.

'I'm coming,' Heara challenged.

Dia shook her head and Heara tried to protest. 'No, Heara, I want you here with the children, at least until Kesta and Jorrun get here. I'll take Gilfy, you trained him well.' She met her husband's eyes and he said nothing, knowing they'd discuss things in private later. She turned to Kurghan. 'We'll get you and your men back to Elden. The Fulmers owes you a great debt.'

Kurghan gave a shrug. 'From what I recall, we owe you more. Anyway, Jorrun's my Thane. Do you want to use the fisherman who brought us here?'

'It would make sense if we want to go unnoticed.'

'I'll sort it.' The carpenter nodded firmly.

Dia glanced at Arrus. 'Okay. I'll sort you all some rooms for tonight. Rosa, are you staying?'

She saw the conflict in the woman's eyes, but Rosa nodded. 'I'm staying with the children.'

'I want Heara to sleep in their room, but I'll put you nearby with Everlyn. Thank you, everyone, we'll speak again tomorrow before I leave.'

The others filed out, Heara leaving last with a reproachful look over her shoulder at Dia and a bang of the door.

'She thinks you think her too old.' Arrus chuckled.

Dia scowled at him. 'She knows very well I just want my best to protect the children.'

Arrus's expression became serious. 'And what of me?'

She studied his face. 'I want you here with the kids, but… but I'd like to have you with me to keep my head straight, stop me trying to do anything too brave.'

Arrus frowned and stepped forward to touch her cheek with his warm palm. 'It's not like you to be unsure.'

She placed her hand over his. 'Arridia has thrown me a little. More importantly, this seems like a fight we can't win.'

He opened his mouth to protest.

'Arrus, think about it. The Geladanians have sent a small delegation. What do you think will happen when we defeat them?'

'Ah.' He slumped a little.

'Exactly.' Dia exhaled loudly. 'We buy time, no more. Our best hope is not to beat them, but to persuade them their prophecy is nonsense.'

Arrus winced. 'They worship what they believe is a god, they are unlikely to doubt her word.'

An awful thought entered her mind, that if they believed they'd succeeded in their mission, these Geladanians might spare the lives of the rest of them. She shook her head and gritted her teeth. 'We'll find a way.'

He grinned and lent forward to kiss her. 'You always do.'

She shoved him away with a laugh. 'Go update your brother on what's going on. I need to spend time with our granddaughter.'

***

She found Nip and the children out at the goat pen; the young stable hand was lifting Joss so he could feed grass to the animals. Arridia turned at her approach. She looked much too serious for a girl of her age. Both the fire-spirits hovered above them, Doraquael a little higher than Azrael as they scanned the surrounding hold.

'Nip, would you look after Joss a moment?'

He frowned, glancing at Arridia. 'Of course.'

Dia reached out a hand toward her granddaughter. 'Walk with me a while, Arridia.'

Azrael didn't need any prompting, he came after them, making slow circles above.

'Have I done something wrong, Grandma?' Arridia looked up at her.

'No, of course not.' Dia squeezed her hand. 'I'm just a little worried about something.'

'The bad men?'

'Yes.' They made their way out of the hold and onto the causeway, Gilfy and another warrior following at a discreet distance. 'How did you know the man who came to the Raven Tower was a bad man?'

Arridia shrugged. 'I felt it.'

'How did it feel?'

Arridia screwed her face up a little. 'He was concentrating really hard, but it made me feel bad inside.'

'And do you sense things in other people?' They turned right, taking the high coastal path westward.

She nodded. 'You feel scared, Grandma, I've never felt you be scared before.'

'I am a bit scared, my honey. How long have you been able to feel other people's emotions?'

'Always. I thought everyone could. Is that bad?'

'No, no, it isn't bad, just unusual. *Walkers* don't get their powers until they're much older than you.'

'Oh, I can't do magic or anything, Grandma.'

Dia almost laughed at her indignant tone. 'My honey, feeling the emotions of others is a magic of fire-walkers, in fact it's the only one...' She halted, pivoting to look up at Azrael.

'What, Grandma?' Arridia tugged at her hand.

'It's a magic unique to fire-walkers, as is walking the flame.'

'Am I a fire-walker like you and Mumma, then?'

Dia nodded distractedly. 'Azrael, do you know if any of the magic users in Geladan can use what we call *knowing*?'

Azrael shot down to float just in front of her. 'I'm sorry, Dia, I don't. Siveraell might be able to find out, but he is in Elden.'

'Tell me, Azra, what is unique about a fire-spirit who is earth-bound as opposed to one who is not?'

'An earth-bound sspirit cannot live in the fire-realm anymore,' Azrael wailed dramatically. 'But they can live without having to renew themselves in the fire-realm, living insstead on the things of the earth. Coal, oil, biscuits.'

'Biscuits?' Dia narrowed her eyes at him. Arridia giggled. 'So, the benefit is you can stay here all the time, protect a human every moment.'

'Yess, Dia.'

'It's quite a sacrifice though, with no real benefit to you.' She felt a renewed love and respect for the crazy little drake.

Azrael made a low, buzzing sound, but said nothing.

Dia drew in a deep breath. 'I have to leave tomorrow, Arridia, to help Tantony at Northold, but in the meantime, I need to teach you how to use your *knowing* properly. Everlyn will carry on your lessons.' She sat down on the grass near the edge of the cliff and Arridia sat beside her. Gilfy headed further down the path to check ahead. 'Okay. *Knowing* is a gift given to us by the spirits of nature, and one we must respect. We have to be careful not to let other people's feelings hurt us, or overwhelm us, and we must also honour the privacy of others. It is rude, invasive, to take in another's private feelings without good cause.'

Arridia blushed a little, but she nodded.

'Have you learned how to turn your *knowing* on and off, block emotions?'

Arridia chewed at her lower lip, a motion that immediately reminded Dia of Kesta. 'I can a bit.'

Dia was almost scared to ask her next question. 'And do you push your emotions on to others?'

She shook her head at once. 'I can tell when Mumma calms Joss, but I can't do it myself yet.'

'Well, thank the spirits for that much,' Dia muttered. 'Okay, let's try turning your *knowing* on and off.'

184

They sat together for nearly three hours, Gilfy and his partner patrolling the path behind them as Azrael kept watch above. Heara quietly joined them, climbing a little way down the cliff and keeping her eyes on the sea below. By the time they stopped to take a break, Arridia's eyelids were drooping and her stomach was making gurgling noises, but she could do an adequate job of blocking her *knowing*.

'Come on.' Dia stood up. 'Let's get you back.'

'I'm tired,' Arridia grumbled. 'Can Nip carry me back?'

'Nip isn't here and you're a bit big for me to carry.'

'I'll do it,' Heara said as she climbed up the cliff. She held out her arms and Arridia ran to her with a grin, Heara crouching so Arridia could clamber onto her back.

'You and Joss seem very fond of Nip,' Dia said.

'The horses say he is like hay, or a soft blanket,' Arridia said. 'He's kind and warm, not like most silly boys. He's still on the outside, but his thoughts go deep and deep, like a well.'

Dia and Heara glanced at each other, eyebrows raised.

'What about me?' Heara asked.

'You're like lots of sharp sparks, like a hot, red log on a fire.'

Heara laughed out loud. 'Thanks. I think.'

'You're welcome, Aunty Heara.'

***

Anxiety danced in Dia's chest and made her pulse race as the Elden sailors rowed her away from the beach. Her grandchildren were between Rosa and Nip, the fire-spirits above them, Heara off to one side. Worvig stood with his arms folded. He hadn't held back on his opinion of her going straight to their enemy. Was she doing the right thing? It was hard to be sure, and while part of her wanted to stand up in the boat and order them to turn back, her muscles didn't move and her mouth remained closed.

The boat bumped up against the side of the fishing vessel, and the captain stood first to catch the rope ladder that was thrown over. Dia didn't particularly like the man, but he was no danger to them. Still, it would be a long journey on a crowded ship.

The small cabin was offered to Dia and the two other women in their party. Shevi, who'd been rescued from Caergard, was very strong in elemental magic and had a mixture of Elden and Chemish blood in her ancestry. Mayve was weaker, her ancestry a combination of Borrow, Fulmer, and Chem, although her skin was pale enough to hide her island heritage. The third Raven in training that Dia had brought with her was a young man who'd been a boy when they'd taken Mayliz to the far north of Navere. He'd been hostile for months before he'd come to trust Jagna and Estre, who later moved on to Arkoom. Belir had black hair in short, tight curls and pale green eyes; not as strong as Shevi, he'd come into his powers late in his teens.

'You all right, Kurghan?' Arrus placed his arm companionably around the carpenter's shoulders.

'Yeah, just thinking Nerim will miss his boy in the stables this winter. He won't admit it, but Nerim's losing the sight in his remaining eye.'

'Is there no one else in the Hold he could take on?' Dia asked.

'I've got a couple of grandchildren I might nudge in his direction.' Kurghan scratched at his beard.

Dia turned her eyes away from the shrinking shore, raising her hand briefly to acknowledge her own grandchildren who were still waving madly. She winced when she imagined Kesta's reaction to the letter she'd sent.

The crossing was rough. Arrus, Gilfy, and Kurghan lent the Elden fishermen a hand while the rest of them kept out of the way as best they could. Dia was more than a little relieved when they reached the harbour of Taurmouth at the end of the next day.

'Will we head straight to Northold?' Kurghan asked. 'I left a boat moored here that we can all squeeze into.'

'Let's have a moment on dry land,' Dia replied, and several of their party sagged in relief. 'We'll take a meal and see if we can gather any news.'

'I'll nip to the Green Inn and see if Tantony has left any messages, but I suggest you eat at the Ship's Lantern.' Kurghan hurried off at once.

'It's this way, my lady.' One of the Elden warriors indicated the main road that ran alongside the harbour.

Dia paid for their meal with three island pearls taken from a soft pouch on her belt. She was sure they were worth far more than the food and drink, but the Fulmers didn't trade in money.

One of the Elden warriors slipped off to seek gossip around the docks, and Arrus wandered off to mingle in the tavern's common room. Kurghan found them, shaking his head when Dia looked up to regard him.

'No messages from Northold or the castle.' Kurghan picked over their still plentiful leftovers. 'Either they feared to send birds or didn't expect us to come back to Elden.'

'Or possibly there is no news,' Gilfy suggested with a shrug. The young man had tied his long black hair back in a tail, though a strand fell across his dark eyes.

The Elden warrior slipped back into the room with a nod at his colleague. 'Gossip in the docks is that the young prince and princesses are visiting their maternal grandmother here in Taurmouth. The Queen didn't come with them.'

'It seems to be the season for grandmother visiting.' Dia swirled the wine in her glass. She looked up sharply at Kurghan. 'Aren't Eleanor and Scarlett a little young to go off without their mother?'

The carpenter shifted in his seat. 'They're not much more than two.'

'Bractius is scared,' Dia whispered, more to herself than the others. 'But he's trying not to show it. Finish up, I'd like to get going within an hour.'

'I'll fetch Arrus Silene,' Gilfy offered.

As they made their way through the dark streets to Kurghan's boat, Arrus put his arm around Dia, bending his head to speak close to her ear. He smelt of ale, but she knew he was a long way from drunk.

'Trader in the tavern has just come down river from Taurmaline. He says the king has guests from a foreign land that he's treating like royalty. Bractius has been giving them tours of the city and lake. The trader said he got a glimpse. The strangers were dressed in rich colours and he thought they looked like Fulmer Islanders, asked me if I knew anything of them.'

'Did this trader seem to think anything was amiss?'

Arrus shook his head. 'He said that Temerran was still at court though.'

It was a bit of a squeeze getting them all into Kurgan's boat with the small amount of baggage they'd brought with them.

'Set the sail as soon as we're clear of the town,' Dia instructed Kurghan.

'There's not enough wind to push us upriver,' one of the warriors commented.

Kurghan grinned. 'I suspect there will be shortly.'

As the men rowed hard against the current, Dia watched the town slip by on either side with painful slowness. As tempting as it was to call her magic sooner, she didn't know who might be watching the harbour and river. She recalled Arridia's ability to sense 'badness' and narrowed her eyes. Reaching with subtlety, she called up her *knowing*, stretching her senses toward the shore. There was plenty of furtiveness and secrecy, and she brushed against lust, but no concentrated desire to kill.

As they left behind the lights of Taurmouth, she called power from within her to her hands, agitating and shaping the air to form a strong wind that filled the sail. Kurghan quickly set it, taking up position at the rudder.

'I can take a turn for you,' Shevi offered.

Dia smiled her thanks to the trainee Raven.

Even with the assistance of magic, it took two days for them to reach the lake, stopping every few hours to stretch their cramped legs and relieve themselves. As they drew close to the lifting bridge that spanned the river, a man shouted down to them, demanding to know who they were.

'That's new,' one warrior murmured.

'Kurghan of Northold, you know me, man.'

'Aye, I do Kurghan. Who's with you?'

Kurghan swore under his breath. 'Family from Taurmouth!'

Dia's wind swept them closer and she made out the shapes of several warriors, all with their bows trained on them. One of them stiffened when he caught her eyes and recognised her.

'Let them through,' he told his men at once.

Dia heard the sound of the winches being turned and the long frame of the bridge split in two and slowly rose to let their mast through. They moved out onto the wide darkness of the lake, Kurghan steering them toward its eastern bank. Dia sat up straighter, leaning out a little over the side of the boat as she saw the shore drawing closer and heard the light rustle of the trees. She could only just make out the silhouette of the Raven Tower. No lights were lit in its leaded windows. She sensed, before she saw, several warriors patrolling the lake shore, their emotions changing as the boat was sighted.

As they reached the small wharf, a group of twenty men came from the hold, headed by Tantony. Kurghan stood up, waving a hand over his head.

'Merkis, it's me!'

'Kurghan!'

There was a muttered exchange of words, and most of the men backed away from the wharf. The boat bumped up against the wooden pilings and one warrior threw a rope which Tantony caught and tied.

'Did my wife and the children make it safely?' Tantony asked.

'They did,' Kurghan reassured him.

Tantony surveyed the others in the boat with a frown and he froze on recognising Arrus. His eyes met Dia's.

'No! Why are you here? Did you not get Temerran's warnings?'

Dia raised her hands to calm Tantony, then stood, stepping over Mayve and taking Tantony's hand as he helped her onto the wooden planks of the small wharf. 'I received no communication other than the words Rosa brought.'

'Both the king and Temerran sent you messages, warning you of those people and the danger to you. They said for you not to come!'

Dia shook her head slowly. 'No birds, no letters… nothing came to the Fulmers.'

Tantony swore, then flushed slightly. 'The messenger birds must have been intercepted somehow. The ravens made it here, but pigeons would have been used for the Fulmers. But that means…' He swallowed, his eyes widening as he stared at Dia. 'That means they know we know why they're here and what they want.'

Chapter Twelve

Kesta; Free city of Navere

It had only been two days, but keeping the two Chemman sorcerers captive was already taking its toll on the magic users of the Navere Coven. If they weren't able to persuade them to their cause soon, they'd either have to kill them, or let them go. The first option made Kesta's stomach churn and her palms sweat. The second would be a display of weakness as far as the people of both sides of Chem were concerned. They'd kept Alikan away from his two half-brothers. From what Kesta had learned from the boy, these young men hadn't treated Alikan any better than their father had.

Kesta shook herself, pulling herself back into the present and taking more notice of the surrounding street. The first rush of the market had subsided somewhat, but the main street was busy, with a few venders calling out the last of their fresh wares. There were still two empty shops and Kesta sighed at the sight of them; they had once been skin shops, their owners having left Navere province rather than take up another trade. An idea struck Kesta and she smiled. She'd speak to Calayna about it later, but right now she had other things to attend to.

She halted at the women's temple. It was a large building with three stories and a black marble front. Tall, iron candelabras stood outside with fat, white candles; the flames fighting against the chill wind. Unlike the traditional, male only temples, there were no priests standing in the street throwing words of guilt and fear toward passers-by. This temple was quiet, almost peaceful, even so, Kesta shuddered as she passed through the wide-open door.

There was only one priest seated within, a thin, annoyed-looking man with close-shaven hair. He sat at a desk behind which was a large, locked cabinet where he secured the offerings from the women who came here. The ground floor had been divided into alcoves by thick wooden walls and small statues of Seveda, Warenna, and Domarra occupied this floor. There was no sign of Kerzin, so Kesta took the stairs up to the next floor where she knew the priests had an office. The door was closed, so she knocked. There was no reply, but a chair scraped, and a moment later the door opened. Kerzin peered out at her. It was a moment before he moved aside and let her in, closing the door behind them.

There was no one else in the room and the curtains were closed over the small window. The only furniture was a desk, two chairs, a narrow bed, and a row of almost empty bookcases. She had to stop her hand from moving closer to her dagger hilt.

'You wanted to speak to me?'

Her words seemed to startle Kerzin and he cleared his throat. 'I did.' He sat in the chair behind the desk, avoiding her eyes, then leapt up as though something had stung him, causing Kesta to flinch. 'Oh, forgive my manners, please sit.' He indicated the other chair, then sat down slowly again as Kesta did. Kerzin stared down at his desk, the muscles of his jaw moving. Kesta opened up her *knowing* and was assaulted by a confusing tumult of emotion; fear, anger, embarrassment.

'Maybe start by telling me who you are?' Kesta suggested gently.

Kerzin continued to stare down at the desk. He didn't look up as he started speaking. 'I am Kerzin Irren. I believe you met my brother, Gerant, who served Feren Dunham. I myself never served the Dunhams, but as all those with power do, I had to serve my father. I developed my power early, not long before I was eight. I'm sure you've heard this story too many times, but in Chem they ensure a powerful son obeys his master.'

'There're better ways to win respect and loyalty,' Kesta muttered. 'Brutality is more likely to breed hatred and revenge.'

Kerzin gave a snort and almost smiled. 'Indeed. I was fifteen when I was given my first woman to strengthen the coven. She wasn't much older than me. I still see the terror and hate in her eyes. I couldn't do it. We sat and talked. We talked every night for months until my father learned I hadn't touched her and took her for himself. She killed herself the next day, slicing through her wrists with a blunt knife.'

Kesta's hand moved to her mouth and he looked up at the movement.

'I challenged my father believing he would kill me, but I won. I killed him. I should have taken the Coven, but I was a coward, I ran.'

'You were a child,' Kesta said.

Kerzin sighed and looked away again. 'I cut my hair, exchanged my fine clothes for practical ones, and signed up with some mercenary guards in Parsiphay province. I... it wasn't work I enjoyed and as it involved dealing with traders who came into contact with Covens or those who knew them, I was constantly risking being recognised.

'I've always been a devout worshipper of Warenna, and one day while visiting the temple it struck me that I should be a priest. I told a few more lies and got accepted by the temple. For a while I was happy. I took on the most menial of chores, living a quiet life, mostly existing in silence. But then...' He winced. Kesta was tempted to send the man calm through her *knowing*, but he drew in a deep breath and took control of his emotions. 'Women were sometimes gifted to the temples. Some were sold on to make money, some were used by the priests and some...'

He stood up, going to the curtained window and rubbing at his face with one hand. Kesta waited, knowing she wouldn't like what she was about to hear.

Kerzin cleared his throat. 'Some were sacrificed as a blood offering to what turned out to be a demon.'

'Hacren.'

Kerzin nodded. 'I tried to stay out of it, but I... I just couldn't. I didn't realise it was a demon back then, I really thought they'd bring Hacren through, which to me seemed to be an appallingly bad idea. Who could I go to for help, though? Not the Covens, and not the Heathens from across the sea who had taken Navere. I did what I was able to, I gave the women pain-free release from the world. Do you think me a monster?' He turned to face her.

'I think you are a man who has lived in a world of monsters.'

His eyes widened briefly and he looked away again. 'When the plot to raise Hacren failed, I applied for a transfer here. I wanted to find out more about the people who had defeated a demon, who freed women, and who dared to try to change the land. The temple was reluctant to let me go because of all the menial chores I did for them. Navere was happy to accept me as they'd lost many priests after Navere's capture and the demon's defeat.

'Once here I studied and observed the city's new masters. There was plenty I admired, much I approved; but then there was you and your irreverence toward the gods, my god, Warenna. I don't... I couldn't like a people who disrespected my god. And...' He clenched his teeth and curled his fingers into fists. 'I was so conflicted between what my heart and head said, and what was preached from the old testaments of the gods. Women were meant to serve, and yet...'

'Your heart told you it was wrong.'

Kerzin walked back to the desk, leaning against the chair. 'It did. And it left me in torment. I spent hours, days, months praying to Warenna for strength. Then Bantu came to Navere and was appointed High Priest. His words were inspiring, thoughtful, soothing, revolutionary. Some priests hated him and left, I followed him like a starving dog. He saw my potential, my educated and organised mind, and made me his administrator. Over time...' He sat in the chair and managed to maintain eye contact with Kesta for almost a minute. 'Over time, I realised he was a liar and a fraud of the worst kind.'

Kesta leaned forward. 'What do you mean?'

'I mean he is a devious, evil man. He was involved in the attempt to raise Hacren. He is a practitioner of blood magic, and I suspect he is behind the Disciples of the Gods.'

Kesta sat back in her chair. For a moment she forgot to breathe. 'You are sure of this?'

Kerzin nodded. 'I have seen things that prove it is so.'

'Why have you trusted me with this?'

'Having lived some time in Navere, having met you, despite your disrespect of the gods, I believe, I hope, you are the person I need you to be.'

A huge weight seemed to press down on Kesta. 'I don't know about that, but I will protect those I care for and fight against what I perceive as evil.'

'And the gods?'

Kesta rubbed at the back of her neck with both hands and leaned back in her chair before regarding Kerzin. 'In the Fulmers we believe in each other. We have faith in ourselves. We understand right from wrong. We live in harmony with the life around us, with the land beneath the sky. As for your gods, if they abide by that, they will find peace with me. If they upset the balance of the land, if they threaten anyone I love…' She leaned forward. 'I will do to them what we did to the false Hacren.'

'You are so sure of your beliefs.' There was a hint of admiration in Kerzin's voice. 'You are uncompromising.'

'Actually.' She gave a slight shake of her head. 'Much as I hate it, I've learned to accept when I'm wrong.'

Kerzin frowned down at his hands clasped together on the desk. 'Where do we go from here?'

Kesta chewed at her bottom lip. 'Kerzin, my friend, what is it you want, what is it you need? You took a big risk to meet me; what was it you hoped for?'

'Peace.' Kerzin's whole body shuddered. 'Forgiveness.'

'From the woman your father killed?'

He froze, breathing hard. 'Is it true you can see inside a man's soul?'

'Only you can do that,' she replied softly. 'Only you can truly judge yourself. But I can get a sense of your emotions. The question remains, how can I help you?'

'We need to stop Bantu.'

Kesta regarded him, chewing at her lower lip. 'I can't just send Ravens into the temple to attack a priest, it would destroy years of effort to get the temples to work with us and turn devout worshipers against us. We need evidence and proof. Can you get me any?'

Kerzin opened his mouth and winced. 'The only proof I have is my own testimony. I have no co-conspirators. Bantu is cunning and careful and has made himself popular and trusted here.'

'Does he have power, like you? Do any of the other priests?'

Kerzin shrugged and shook his head. 'I don't know. People of power are not meant to join the priesthood, but I don't imagine I'm the only one who has.'

Kesta gave a distracted nod. 'Bantu wore an amulet that prevented me reading his emotions. I suspect he has power, though it may be that he just knows about mine and is preventing me discovering his truths.'

'What are you going to do?' Hope shone in the priest's eyes.

'Nothing hasty,' Kesta replied. 'We need to plan carefully how we'll discredit him. I'll speak to Calayna and Rece. Can you find out who else is involved, who his contacts are?'

Kerzin nodded. 'I have some ideas; I'll make a list.'

'Thank you. How can I contact you?'

'I come here on this day every week, or send a man you trust to Warenna's shrine in the temple.'

'All right.' Kesta stood and reached out a hand. Kerzin instinctively recoiled, but he slowly recovered and took her hand briefly, a look of guilt on his face. 'Be careful,' she warned him.

He said nothing as she left the room, but she felt the press of his still mixed emotions against her back.

***

Calayna and Rece were busy in the audience room, so she paid Alikan a quick visit before relieving the three Ravens who stood guard over their magic-wielding prisoners in the dungeon. It was about an hour before Rece and Calayna came to find her, and they moved down the corridor to where they could speak quietly.

Rece gave a loud sigh. 'I agree we can't go storming into the temple to take out Bantu. Perhaps we can invite him here again?'

'That's a good idea, but we'd still need plenty of evidence before we arrest a High Priest.' Kesta narrowed her eyes. 'I'll see if any of our prisoners have any connection to him. It's likely.'

'If we can ascertain the names and locations of his supporters, we should move against them and capture as many as we can while Bantu is at the palace.'

'That's a good plan,' Kesta agreed. She drew in a deep breath. 'What are we going to do about Alikan's brothers? We can't hold them indefinitely and we can't let them go.'

Calayna gave a shrug. 'We have to kill them.'

Kesta's hand went to her stomach. 'I don't like it, but sadly you're right. Give me three more days. If I make no progress, we'll slip them something in their food, give them as quick and painless a death as possible.'

'Agreed,' Calayna replied at once.

Rece shifted his weight on his feet, but he silently nodded.

'Did the Ravens find anything of use at the house?'

'They did.' Rece raised his eyebrows. 'Nothing to connect the family with anyone else, but they had a small shrine to Hacren and several books on blood magic.'

Kesta's heart gave a jolt. 'They're necromancers?'

Rece glanced at Calayna. 'We have to assume so.'

'Please tell me they were checked for sharp objects and amulets before being left in cells?'

Rece drew himself up. 'Of course, they were.'

'I'll try with the younger one first.' Kesta steeled herself and walked to the cell door. When she glanced back, she saw Rece and Calayna were still watching her. She drew up her power ready to defend herself before pulling the bolt across. The young man sat in the scattered straw, a few dried sprigs of lavender peeping out from the yellow stalks. The Chemman necromancer lifted his head a little, one arm balanced loosely on a knee, his hand drooping.

'Damel, my name is Kesta, I think you know who I am.'

His nose wrinkled in a sneer and he looked away without a word. Kesta realised her error at once. She was a woman, someone as indoctrinated as him would never speak to her. It would have been better if Jorrun had been here. The only male they had in the Coven who was strong enough to deal with another magic user was Ovey, and he was younger than this necromancer. An idea came to her, and she smiled.

'I'll give you some time to consider whether you'll tell us what you know. If not, we'll let a priest in to hear your last prayers before you die.'

'I can kill you all, bitch!'

Kesta threw him back against the wall with a flick of her wrist. 'Yeah, I don't think so.'

She took a step forward and his eyes widened. He struggled against the pressure of the wind she controlled, his face reddening as he tried to gasp for air. Kesta let him drop.

'Have a think about it.'

She closed and bolted the door, moving down the corridor to his brother's cell. As soon as she drew the bolt, she felt a rise in his emotions and the surge of his power. She shielded quickly as the door flew back. Fire came billowing out to engulf her. She pushed into the flames, then sidestepped and threw out a blast of energy. The young man grunted as he hit the wall, his magic spluttering momentarily before he gained control. As he hit the ground, he sent out another stream of flame. Kesta closed her eyes as she sent fire back, a fierce, concentrated inferno that incinerated him in seconds.

She stood for a moment, catching her breath, her eyes watering in the smoke, leaving tracks down the soot on her cheeks.

'Kesta!' Calayna and Rece's worried shouts came from the corridor. Rece appeared in the doorway, sword drawn.

'I'm sorry.' Kesta shook her head. 'Had it been a guard or one of the other Raven's they'd be dead now, and the necromancer free. I had to kill him.'

Calayna regarded her for a moment, then stepped forward to wrap her in a hug.

'What of the other one?' Rece asked.

'He isn't as strong, and I think he'll be scared to act without his brother, but he won't talk to me. I want to see if he'll confess anything to Kerzin.'

'Won't that risk exposing Kerzin?' Calayna frowned.

Kesta's shoulders sagged. 'It might. We could say the boy is a worshipper of Warenna.'

'But he worships Hacren, won't Bantu object?' Rece said.

'If he hears of our request, we'll try to be discreet.' With a last glance at the burned body, Kesta stepped out into the corridor. 'If Bantu tries to come here instead, or objects on the basis that the boy worships Hacren, then we'll know the two are known to each other. I'll stand guard here myself until morning. Would you do me a favour and send me a book and some food? Also, my scrying bowl in case Jorrun contacts me.'

'Of course,' Calayna agreed at once.

***

It was almost evening three days later before Kerzin arrived at the palace. He was breathing hard, his colour high. He glared at Kesta, nostrils flaring.

'I trusted you.'

Kesta's own cheeks warmed as guilt flooded into her heart. She glanced away. 'This could give us the proof we need of Bantu's involvement with the Disciples of the Gods. It might also mean a young man doesn't have to die.'

Kerzin drew in a deep breath and sighed it out. 'Take me to him.'

202

Ovey and Beth had taken over guarding the dungeons to allow Kesta a rest, and they moved out of the way for Kesta and the priest. Calayna and Rece hurriedly arrived as Kesta paused outside the young man's cell. She held Kerzin's gaze for a moment before drawing back the bolt and stepping aside as she opened the door.

She heard a scuffle inside the room and a loud gasp.

'But… but your holiness, h–how could you? How could you work for these people?'

'I don't,' Kerzin replied softly. He left the door ajar and Kesta remained out of sight. 'I work only for the gods. I was told that there was a soul here in peril.'

'They will kill me, your holiness, for I won't betray Hacren.'

'You have been misled,' Kerzin told him. 'These people you work for, it is not your god they seek to summon, but a demon. One such was called before—'

'Oh, no, master. We know that an evil being slipped through before, but the priests got the invocation wrong. It has to be done at the right time.'

'How can you be certain Bantu has it right? He may be mistaken as well.'

Kesta held her breath.

'He is wise and Hacren speaks to him, but you would know that.' There was doubt in the young necromancer's voice. He was starting to sense something was wrong.

Kesta yanked the door open, hoping Kerzin would understand. 'That's enough, priest, time for you to go.'

The young man paled. Kerzin's mouth opened and closed, then he stilled, his eyes widening just a little as he met Kesta's gaze.

'The boy has a right to make his peace with the gods,' Kerzin said angrily. 'How dare you interrupt, woman? Leave us.'

Kesta glared at him, trying not to smile. She stepped back out of the room and closed the door almost completely.

'Listen,' Kerzin began urgently. 'I'll do what I can for you, try to buy you time until we raise Hacren on, um …' He blinked and clicked his fingers, giving his head a little shake.

'On Hacren's Day,' the boy supplied with an impatient frown, leaning closer to the priest in his hope.

'Yes,' Kerzin rolled his eyes at his own supposed moment of forgetfulness. 'Give them false information if you must, but try to cooperate and don't give them any cause to kill you. I'll try to visit when I can. We'll get you out.'

There was no reply, but Kesta assumed the boy nodded.

'Very good. I must go now. Blessings, my son.'

'Blessings, holiness.'

Kerzin stepped out into the hall and Kesta slid the bolt across. They waited until they were upstairs and away from the dungeon before they spoke.

'I fear we will never gain his trust after what I have done, but I will see what I can do over time,' Kerzin said sadly.

Kesta noted his use of 'we,' but said nothing.

'You did well, thank you.' Calayna gave a thin-lipped smile.

Kesta cringed. 'Excuse my ignorance, when is this Hacren's Day?'

'The day of the dead.' It was Rece who answered. 'I think in the Fulmers it is Midwinter. The longest night, the shortest day; Hacren's Day.'

'So, we have nearly three months, and the name of the man in charge.' Kesta's muscles relaxed a little. 'If we gather information and act quickly, there should be no chance of those idiots trying to bring another cursed demon through.'

'Excuse me, master Kesta.' A young page came hurrying up; she held a tiny roll of parchment in her palm. 'Two birds have flown in, both carrying the same message from the Fulmers.'

Kesta's heart stopped, then beat again faster than before. Two birds meant something urgent, something her mother wanted to be sure she knew. Her hand was unsteady as she peeled away the tight roll to read the tiny writing. Her legs went from under her, her palms hitting the floor hard as she just managed to stop herself smashing her head on the carpet.

'Kesta!' Calayna cried in alarm, darting forward to help her up.

'What is it?' Rece demanded.

Kesta could barely get the words out. Anger swept through her initial shock and her vision turned red. 'Someone attacked my children.'

'What?' Calayna's hand flew to her mouth.

Kesta scrambled to her feet. Her fists and jaw clenched as she breathed hard through her nose. 'Someone attacked my children. They are safe now in the Fulmers with my mother, but there are others who might try it. I have to get to the Fulmers.'

She took five rapid strides before she halted, pivoting to face Calayna, Rece, and Kerzin. 'Oh, but Bantu—'

'We'll handle it,' Calayna said firmly. 'Go.'

Chapter Thirteen

Cassien; Free City of Caergard

Cassien sat patiently, hand on his sword, gazing at the Raven banner adorning the wall. It had become almost a tradition when Ravens took a city; the women they freed sewed the emblem of their liberators.

Kussim, Pirelle, and Dalton dealt with the long line of petitioners in the audience room, and Cassien's admiration for the three of them grew as the day wore on. All of them were calm, patient, but unbendingly firm when it came to upholding the laws of the Free Provinces. As one man stormed out, and a smiling woman walked away with one of the palace servants to start a new life with her own wage, a guard stepped in; his face flushed, eyes wide.

'Masters, you have visitors. Master Jorrun Raven, Raven Tyrin, and, um, master Rothfel.'

Kussim stood at once, breathing faster. The double doors were pushed open and Jorrun strode in, his usually controlled face glowing with a smile at the sight of his niece. Cassien got to his feet politely as Kussim almost ran to hug her much taller uncle, her head barely coming up to his chest. Jorrun kissed the top of Kussim's head, keeping an arm around her as he shook Dalton's hand and kissed Pirelle's cheek. He only let go of Kussim as he approached Cassien, clasping his wrist and then leaning in to hug him briefly. Cassien swallowed, a sharp pain searing his heart.

'Have you met Tyrin?' Jorrun introduced the young, red-haired man who accompanied him. 'And of course, you all know Rothfel.'

The unassuming man sauntered forward to shake hands, and Cassien couldn't help but smile at his grin.

'Cass, you're doing well?'

'I am, thank you,' he replied politely.

'You've come to free my mother.' Kussim blinked up at her uncle, her blue eyes glistening in the light of the high windows.

'I have.' Jorrun breathed. 'But tell me first, how are things here on the frontier?'

'Both good and bad.' Kussim filled him in and Cassien hovered out of the way, feeling a little awkward. One of the side doors burst open and Catya stood there. She took two steps into the room, then hesitated, her eyes fixed on the man who had been her guardian for many years. Ruak sat on her shoulder and regarded them all with a clumsy regality.

Jorrun stood slowly, but it was Rothfel who spoke first. 'My best student.'

Ruak chose that moment to launch himself up in the air with a shriek. 'Cat!' he croaked several times before settling on a windowsill.

Catya laughed and Cassien's muscles relaxed.

Catya hurried into the room to hug Rothfel. Cassien frowned and looked away as Jorrun then held her for a long time. Jorrun stepped back, still holding Catya's arms as he gazed down at her. 'Are you well, Catya?'

'I am.' She smiled up at him.

'Do we have many more petitioners?' Kussim asked her steward.

'There are five more, my lady.'

'We can deal with them,' Pirelle offered quickly.

'Thank you.' Kussim's smile lit her face. She took Jorrun's arm and indicated which way he should leave the audience room. Tyrin and Rothfel followed with Catya.

'Cass?' Jorrun halted to look back at him.

Cassien turned to regard Pirelle and Dalton. He should really stay with them.

'Go on, Cassien,' Pirelle reassured him with a smile. 'We'll send for Senai to join us.'

Weight seemed to drop away from Cassien and his heart eased as he hurried to follow the others.

Kussim showed their visitors into Caergard's library, her eyes sparkling with mirth as her uncle went straight to the shelves, taking in a deep breath of the library's smell. 'Have you found anything useful?' He turned to ask.

'Plenty,' Kussim replied eagerly. 'I've set aside some texts you'll want to see in my room.'

Catya hopped up to sit on a table, Ruak fluttering from her shoulder to perch on the back of a chair. 'What's your plan for Uldren?'

Jorrun regarded her, worry lines creasing the skin around his eyes. Cassien wondered if it was worry about infiltrating Uldren, or concern that Catya's bloodthirsty nature had not subsided at all.

Jorrun sighed. 'We can't hold Uldren. We just don't have the people, and with winter coming it would be a bad time to throw the civilian population into any kind of war. We've decided on a different approach.' He glanced at Rothfel. 'Sabotage their strength. We'll hit

Uldren's Coven, take out as many as we can, but our priority will be to get Dinari and as many women out and safely back here as we can.'

'What about the people?' The words burst out of Cassien.

Jorrun took a few steps towards him. 'I'm sorry, Cass, but if we overreach, we could lose everything. We can risk a few Ravens, but not all the Free Provinces.'

'We could hold Uldren—'

Jorrun shook his head. 'We would likely end up under siege in the palace. Uldren Province is a frontier we don't presently have the resources and strength to hold. It would take a large army; large armies need food and equipment. More importantly, they need loyalty to the cause. We don't have that loyalty yet, not from the majority of men in the west.'

Cassien's spine sagged.

'I understand how you feel,' Jorrun said. 'We can only do what we can, Cass. As Osun taught us, patience and planning are what will free Chem.'

Cassien looked up and nodded.

'So, when do we go?' Catya asked eagerly.

'I'm intending to go as soon as possible.' Jorrun pulled out a chair and sat down. 'Tell me everything you can about Uldren.'

Both Catya and Cassien made their reports, with Kussim adding other intelligence the Ravens had gathered of their neighbours during their occupation of Caergard. When they'd finished, Jorrun and Rothfel exchanged a look. The thief nodded.

'I'll lead the rescue myself,' Jorrun said. 'Rothfel will take two scouts in before us and cause a few destructive diversions. I'll take all the male magic users we have, which isn't many, and hit the palace.'

Catya straightened up. 'What about me?'

Jorrun opened his mouth, but hesitated.

'You said yourself they are more suspicious of any group with women in it,' Rothfel pointed out. 'You might draw unwanted attention to any party you travel with. As it is, Jorrun's face is recognisable to anyone who served a Dunham.'

Catya scowled. 'I'm the best scout you have, you know it.'

Jorrun raised his hands. 'No one is disputing it, but you'd be risking your colleagues.'

Cassien shifted uncomfortably. Jorrun was right, but he knew how he'd feel himself if they had denied him the chance to help. He cleared his throat. 'What if I got Catya in separately?'

Jorrun flinched as though Cassien's words had hurt him.

'I might be able to put the two of you to use,' Rothfel mused. 'But you'd have to be prepared to die before giving us away.'

'Of course, we would,' Catya retorted at once.

Cassien glanced at Jorrun. The tall man looked sad.

There was a knock at the library door and a female page stuck her head in. 'Excuse me, Ravens, you have more visitors.'

'Who?' Kussim demanded.

'Master Jagna of Arkoom, and two of his Coven.'

Jorrun's face lit up and he stood.

Kussim smiled. 'Show them in here.'

Moments later, Jagna entered the library, heading straight for Jorrun and hugging him without hesitation. 'It's good to see you, brother.'

'And you.' Jorrun's smile brightened his blue eyes. He looked his old friend up and down. Jagna had allowed his once close shorn hair to grow longer, allowing its honey colour to show. 'How is Estre?'

'She's very well.' Jagna grinned. 'We're expecting our second child.'

Jorrun's own smile widened and he reached out to clasp Jagna's hand.

'Why do men always congratulate each other on getting a woman pregnant?' Catya muttered under her breath. 'It doesn't exactly take much effort on their part.'

Cassien rolled his eyes at her, stepping forward to greet Jagna and clasp his wrist. 'Brother.'

'Great to see you, Cass.' Jagna looked him up and down with a smile.

'What brings you here?' Jorrun tilted his head.

Jagna gave a slight shrug. 'Heard your sister has been found and wanted to give you a hand getting her out.'

'Thank you.'

Kussim stepped up beside her uncle, and Jorrun automatically put an arm around her.

Jagna turned and indicated the two young men he'd brought with him. 'This is Vorro and Meric. Vorro served a year in the Fulmers, Meric is due there this spring.'

Both young men gave a polite bow to Jorrun and Kussim. They were in their late teens, Vorro maybe a year or two older and much darker in complexion than Meric. Cassien guessed Vorro had Fulmer blood in his ancestry, Meric appeared more like an Eldeman, or even a Borrowman.

Jorrun gave them a polite greeting, then turned to Jagna with a frown. 'How did you know I would only take men into Uldren?'

'I guessed it would be the case.' Kussim looked up at him and Jorrun gave her a squeeze.

Catya scowled and hopped down from the table, raising an arm for Ruak to fly onto. 'Are we leaving first thing?'

'Yes.' Jorrun turned to regard her. 'We'll travel together until we get close to the river. I want to cross north of the fords, use rafts to get across.'

'Rafts will take a while to build, and also to hide when we get to the other side,' Rothfel pointed out.

'We tie ropes to them so they can be pulled back to the other side and re-used when needed. Kussim, would you send a party ahead of us tonight to start work on the rafts?'

'Of course.'

Rothfel grinned and nodded.

'Come on.' Kussim stepped away from her uncle. 'Let's find you all rooms to refresh yourselves and we'll eat together this evening. We have lots to catch up on besides politics and war.'

***

Their evening was a pleasant and happy one, and Cassien made an effort to get to know Tyrin, Meric, and Vorro. Tyrin was quiet-natured but friendly, Vorro was serious but quick and intelligent. Meric in contrast had a bright and bubbly nature which made him particularly easy to get along with. Rothfel entertained them with stories of his recent escapades, while Jorrun updated them with news of Elden, the Fulmers, and the Borrows.

'Have you seen Temerran?' Catya asked him.

'Not for a while,' Jorrun replied. 'We missed him by a few days, I think, when we left Elden.'

They continued their meal until long after the darkness pressed against the windows. Cassien started when Jorrun quickly got to his feet.

'You'll excuse me, please, Kesta is trying to contact me.' His hand went to something hidden beneath his shirt.

Cassien watched worriedly as Jorrun left the room, but bright conversation soon returned to the dining room.

When Jorrun returned a few minutes later, his face was pale and he held onto the doorframe, the joints of his fingers white.

'Uncle?' Kussim sprang to her feet.

'Someone has attacked my children.'

'Who?' Jagna demanded.

'Are they safe?' Kussim asked at the same time.

Jorrun stepped into the room, his fingers twitching into fists. 'It was a people I've never heard of; from a land I do not know. Geladan. They seem to believe my children are a threat to their god.'

'God?' Cassien sat up straight. 'You mean another thing like Hacren?'

Jorrun shook his head, sitting in the nearest vacant chair. 'Kesta says the fire-spirits believe this god—goddess—is real.'

'We'll go with you.' Jagna stood.

Jorrun shook his head slowly. 'Arridia and Joss are safely in the Fulmers and Kesta is on her way there now. She promised me she would keep them safe and made me swear I'd get my sister and take care of things in Navere. As much as it's killing me, she's right. Dinari deserves freedom, and I can't lose the Free Provinces after everything we've been through.' He looked up and met Catya's eyes. 'Cat, I need you to go to Navere and help them sort out the Disciples. Will you do that for me?'

She nodded.

Jorrun drew in a deep breath. 'Thank you.'

Jagna poured a glass of wine and took it to Jorrun.

'Shall we go to the library?' Pirelle suggested.

'That's a good idea,' Kussim agreed.

Jorrun was slow to follow and Cassien hovered in the doorway.

'I'm all right, Cass.' Jorrun stood, forcing a smile. 'This isn't the first time in my life I've felt helpless to save those I love, but it didn't stop me trying then, and it won't now.'

Cassien nodded. He folded his arms, then unfolded them again, wincing as he tried to think of something useful to say. He had an odd, empty feeling deep in his chest. 'After we get your sister, can I come with you back to Fulmer hold? I really want to help.'

Jorrun hesitated. 'I like knowing you're here to watch out for my niece. But if Jagna can stay in Caergard a while, then yes, I'd love for you to accompany me.'

Cassien pushed the library door open for Jorrun to proceed him. Catya was sitting in the corner, laughing with Meric. Kussim looked up from speaking with Dalton and smiled, her eyes finding Cassien's before Jorrun's. Cassien attempted to join the conversation, but Jorrun wandered the shelves, studying the books again. Cassien couldn't even imagine what he was feeling. Forcing his feet to move, he approached the Thane of Northold.

'Found anything interesting?'

Jorrun glanced at him. 'The library contains copies of many of the historical and geographical books that are held in both Arkoom and Navere. It has more stories and fanciful tales than either of those libraries. Azrael would love them.' He ran a finger down a spine. 'These are maps of old boundaries and roads. Are you trying to distract me?'

'I… um…'

Jorrun turned and smiled at him. 'I appreciate it.' He sighed loudly. 'But I'm going to my room, I need a bit of time alone.' He patted Cassien on the arm and slipped out of the library.

Cassien didn't stay much longer himself, politely saying goodnight to Kussim before heading to his room. He got into bed, gazing out through the window at the infinite stars until sleep slowly took him.

***

Cassien woke with a groan, his eyelids heavy and his head foggy. He splashed cold water on his face and dressed quickly, then double-checked the two small bags he kept packed and ready for missions. He stepped out into the hall a moment before Catya did. It wasn't her own room she emerged from, but Meric's. Pain and heat tore out from his heart, his anger rising in defence.

'He's not much more than a child.'

Catya snorted, tossing back her hair. 'We were younger, as I recall.'

Cassien's cheeks flushed. He had an overwhelming urge to break something, but he clenched his teeth and forced his breathing to slow and deepen, turning away from her and heading to the audience room to see if the others were readying to leave yet. Kussim was there alone, other than a page and four guards.

'Cass.' Her face lit up.

'I'm not late?'

'My uncle has been up for a while walking the gardens. Rothfel has been procuring his peculiar choice of supplies. You look tired.'

He opened his mouth in surprise. 'Yes, I… I guess I am a bit. To be honest, I can't remember when I last slept well. There's always so much to think about.'

'There is.' Kussim swivelled in her chair to watch him as he stood before the raven banner. 'I could never have imagined having this much responsibility as a woman in Chem.'

'You do a brilliant job—'

The doors flew open and Catya strolled in, Ruak on her shoulder. 'I'm ready to go, thought I'd better take my leave.'

'Did you want us to take care of your raven for you?' Kussim asked.

'No.' Catya turned her head a little and stroked Ruak's chest feathers. 'He'll be fine in Navere.'

She twisted to regard Cassien and his hackles rose. She knew very well her behaviour hurt him, he just wasn't sure if it was deliberate or if she honestly didn't care. He cleared his throat.

'Look after yourself.'

Her face grew suddenly serious. 'Yeah, you too.'

She strode forward and Cassien stood his ground as she grabbed a handful of his shirt and kissed him. Ruak croaked and flapped his wings to keep his balance. Catya stepped back and left without another word. Cassien turned, Kussim was looking away toward the corner of the room.

The door opened again and Tyrin came in, talking excitedly with Vorro and Meric. Rothfel followed more slowly, hands held behind his back. He spotted Cassien and nodded.

Kussim stood, straightening her spine. 'Are you ready to go?'

'We are,' Rothfel confirmed.

'I'd better grab my things.' Cassien hurried back to his room to pick up his bag, then headed straight to the courtyard where the horses were waiting for them. Both Jorrun and Jagna were already mounted. Cassien secured his bags to his saddle and swung up onto his horse as Rothfel herded the younger Ravens out of the palace. Cassien twisted his neck to look, but Kussim hadn't come out to say farewell.

'Quickly now,' Rothfel urged. He went to the train of five supply horses and gave them a final check over.

'Are we ready?' Jorrun asked impatiently.

'We're good,' Rothfel confirmed.

Caergard City was itself only a few miles from Warenna's River, and even with their north-eastward route they reached its banks before midday. Their two scouts checked the area was clear and came back to report their rafts were ready.

'Are we going to risk it in the daylight?' Cassien asked Jorrun in concern.

'There's no reason not to if there are no easterners around.'

The crossing point they'd chosen was a rocky bend in the river's course where a fold in the hills hid them from the north. Willows concealed the eastern bank and on the west was a small, boggy forest.

The scouts who'd gone ahead the previous night had constructed two rafts large enough to each take two horses. Jorrun insisted on going first, and Cassien quickly offered to go with him. They guided the raft to the far bank using long poles, Jorrun calling his power ready in case of attack. It took over an hour to get all their party across, but they did so un-accosted, although Cassien wasn't convinced they'd been unobserved.

'This is where I leave you,' Rothfel turned his horse to address Jorrun.

Jorrun nodded. 'Good luck.'

Rothfel nodded back, and he and the two scouts galloped away eastward, leaving Cassien, Jagna, and Jorrun with the young magic-wielding Ravens.

'How will we know when Rothfel has everything in place?' Jagna asked.

A smile ghosted Jorrun's lips. 'Oh, we'll know.'

Cassien took the lead, aiming for a trade road that ran between two of Uldren Province's larger towns, but leaving it to head back south-eastwards to avoid coming within sight of any guard posts. They passed a few people on the road, a solo trader with a heavy pack on his back who tried to convince them to examine his wares, a farmer and his three slaves, herding a small flock of sheep, and a band of mercenaries who thundered past them on urgent business of their own. They were stopped only once before making camp for the night, by a patrol of guardsmen watching over the estate of a Coven Lord they'd passed within a few miles of. Jagna took the lead in answering their questions and they had to stand aside and watch as two of the guards searched through the baggage on their pack horses, one of them helping himself to some valuable spices.

'I'm so sorry.' Cassien's cheeks flushed as they watched the guards ride away. 'I've never seen the patrols come out this far before.'

'A party as large as ours can't expect to avoid notice completely.' Jagna placed a hand briefly on his shoulder.

Even so, Cassien offered to take the watch as they set up camp and ate. Jorrun moved away a little, taking out his scrying bowl to talk quietly with his wife. The others chattered as they ate, and Cassien clenched his teeth at the sound of Meric's pleasant and innocent laugh. He shook his head at his jealousy; he was a better man than that, or hoped he was.

'Is everything all right?' Cassien asked Jorrun as he returned to the others.

'Kesta is just passing through the Borrows,' he replied. 'She is angry, and afraid, as am I.'

Cassien felt a moment of helplessness. Anything he offered would be a speculative promise at best. They had no idea what the next few days would bring. 'You have my help, for what it's worth.'

Jorrun smiled at him. 'Your support is worth everything, Cass.'

Cassien's heart lightened at once and he straightened his spine as he turned back to patrolling a wide perimeter around their camp. Jagna took over from him at midnight, but when Cassien awoke, it was Jorrun who was missing. He leapt up from his blanket, surveying the empty land surrounding them.

'Everything's fine,' Jagna reassured him as he stirred the oats, milk, and dried fruit he'd put together for their breakfast.

Jorrun returned as they were finishing up and Cassien's muscles relaxed. 'Anything?' he asked at once.

'There's a small village down in the dip of the valley where people are already stirring; nothing else,' Jorrun replied.

They packed up and Cassien once again took the lead, keeping to the wilderness until they got within seven miles of Uldren City. Most of the land here was cultivated, farms, villages, and a small town stood between them and the high walls.

'We can't hide anymore,' Cassien apologised. 'From now on we'll have to talk or fight our way to the city.'

From the dark frown on Jorrun's face, Cassien suspected he wouldn't be averse to the latter. All the young Raven sorcerers put on copper collars to pose as servants; Jorrun wearing a more ornate silver one. Jagna was to be the merchant, with Cassien as his guard and relative.

They were stopped three times on the road by patrols and by the time they drew close to the city gates even Cassien's patience was wearing thin.

'There aren't many times I'm tempted to draw on my family's name,' Jorrun muttered as he glared up at the walls. 'But now is one of those times.'

'We're almost there,' Jagna told his friend quietly.

The guards finally let them through, although Cassien noticed they were followed by one all the way to the inn they chose at random. They'd already decided to stay well away from Gunthe to ensure he wasn't linked to them after their raid. While Meric and Vorro saw to the horses and lugged all their belongings and supposed stock up to their room, the rest of them gathered in Jorrun's room.

'All right.' Jorrun's eyebrows were drawn downward, shadowing his eyes. 'As planned, we split into two groups and move closer to the palace after nightfall. We wait for Rothfel's signal, then meet at the wall opposite the silversmith. If anything goes wrong, try to return here and whoever makes it will take the stock, trade it, then get themselves back to Caergard. If you free a woman, but get separated, the same plan applies; disguise her as best you can and make your way back.'

They ate a hurried meal in the room, simple food but hot and filling; and possibly the last meal some of them would have. Cassien was to go with Jagna, Tyrin, and Vorro and their group left first, heading for an expensive wine and skin shop near the palace quarter. It took some effort for Cassien to keep a smile on his face and his hands from his sword and knives as the shop's owner served them a deep-red vintage and described some of his other wares.

The building vibrated, and a boom sounded nearby. Most of the patrons leapt to their feet and Cassien slowly copied. There were several screams and cries of 'earthquake', before many of the shop's occupants fled out into the street. With a glance at Jagna, Cassien followed, pushing through the confused and concerned men to make his way toward the silversmith. He glanced over his shoulder to ensure the younger Ravens were keeping up. Smoke billowed upward and across the city, the news spreading in whispers, then wails.

'The temple has exploded!'

Rothfel.

Cassien had to fight hard against the grin that wanted to form on his lips. He spotted Jorrun easily, his height giving him away. Their eyes met and Jorrun started moving through the crowd, not to the palace gate, but to where the main road spilt from the palace and a quieter, narrower way, followed the high wall. As they caught up to him, Jorrun called up his power and reached down into the earth as Kesta had taught him years before. He ripped rock upward and the wall cracked and collapsed. Dust billowed and there was a loud rumble as rocks tumbled. The remaining bystanders fled with more cries of 'earthquake'.

Cassien raised his arm to cover his mouth, blinking against the swirling debris, and scrambled over the ruined wall. Fire shot out from his left and right as Jorrun and Jagna took out the guards who came toward them. The younger Ravens joined in and only two men got as far as Cassien's sword. Jorrun destroyed the first door they reached, the stone frame cracking. It was a race against time now, to reach the women before the palace realised it was under attack and murdered them all.

The intelligence they had regarding the palace was old, but proved true, Cassien led them up three flights of stairs and they found themselves on the level of the coven's residences. Jagna, Meric, and Vorro spun about to guard the top of the stairs as the rest of them ran on. At this time of day, they expected the coven to be eating, not resting in their beds.

Even so, one door flew open and Jorrun roasted him as soon as he saw it was a man. They gained the next flight of stairs, Cassien's blood turning to ice as he heard a woman scream. Jorrun flew past him, taking the stairs two at a time. Cassien pushed his muscles harder, a burning pain searing them as he forced himself to keep up. Shouts told him that coven members had engaged those below.

As they reached the landing Cassien found guards, two of them were kicking in a door, a third had twisted a woman's arm behind her back and drawn his sword. Cassien drew a dagger and sent it spinning into the man's neck, Jorrun used his magic to sweep the other two off their feet and hurl them down the hall.

Jorrun drew air into his lungs. 'I am Jorrun Raven! Come out and follow us quickly if you want a chance of freedom in the west.'

Cassien darted forward and assisted the fallen woman to her feet. Her cheeks were wet, but she scrambled toward the top of the stairs. Two doors opened and eyes peered out.

'Quickly!' Jorrun called. 'We cannot linger long. Is Dinari with you?'

A third door opened and a woman stepped out. She was tall, elegant, her hair and skin dark, but her irises pale blue. Every inch of her skin was tattooed in swirling runes. Her eyes fell on Jorrun and she froze, but for her eyelids that fluttered as tears spilled over.

'I knew you would come for me.'

Jorrun couldn't seem to move, but Dinari did, almost flowing over the carpet to raise a hand to his bearded cheek.

Shouts and a dark plume of smoke pulled Cassien sharply back into the present.

'Jorrun!'

The tall man pivoted and ran to the top of the stairs. Cassien nodded and gestured frantically for the women watching from the shadows to follow him. As Cassien reached the staircase, he was in time to see Jorrun shield his fellow Ravens. Jagna was red-faced, sweat beading his skin. The younger sorcerers looked wide-eyed and terrified. Cassien raced to Jorrun's side, drawing another dagger. Three Chemman sorcerers and several guards blocked their escape.

'Down!' Jorrun bellowed.

The Ravens all hurled themselves to the ground as Jorrun blasted the defending Chemmen down the hall. Cassien turned to the women huddled behind him. Three of them had young children. 'Stay close to me. I won't be able to wait for you, so whatever you do, keep up.'

He didn't wait for a reply, but hurried after Jorrun. One of the Uldren Coven members stirred as they passed and tried to stand. Cassien gritted his teeth and made a small sound in the back of his throat as he pushed his sword up and under the man's ribs.

They fled down the stairs, Tyrin sending a ball of flames toward a group of guards who burst from a side door. They gained the outside, Jorrun falling back to shield them from behind as Cassien and Jagna took the lead. One woman stumbled as they raced across the grass and Meric stooped to snatch up her child, throwing it partially over his shoulder.

A wall of men blocked both the gate and the gap in the wall, their swords drawn. The three archers among them let loose. Jagna threw two off course, but the third hit Vorro in the shoulder.

A deafening boom set Cassien's ears ringing as the palace gates exploded, stone flying outward as the gate posts crumbled. Jorrun scattered the guards at the gap with a towering tornado. Cassien spun about, snapping the shaft of the arrow protruding from Vorro before engaging the four guards who remained standing. Jagna once again took the lead, heading not for the main street but further along the narrower way. Jorrun drew his sword, but Cassien waved him away.

'Go on,' he yelled.

With a look of pain, Jorrun ran after the others.

Cassien didn't have time to watch him go. He caught one guard's blade and twisted aside as another swung down towards his left shoulder. He leapt, his sword going out wide to catch the first man's blade again, his boot connected with the second man's chin, throwing his head back. Cassien landed, ducking and pivoting left to throw his dagger into a third guard's throat. The sword of the first whistled over his head and Cassien straightened, thrusting his blade into the man's sternum. He was forced to let go of his sword and leap back as the fourth guard hacked at him. He rolled, coming up onto his feet with his remaining daggers in his hands. He sprang, landing on one foot and spinning. One dagger embedded itself in the man's eye whose jaw he'd cracked, the other in the chest of the remaining guard.

Cassien winced, his aim had been slightly off.

He crouched to quickly retrieve his weapons and clambered over the rubble into the road. There was no sign of the others.

Instead of following them, he took the shorter route out onto the main street. Several men were still stumbling around in a daze, faces covered in dust. Cassien hurried to the inn. The streets were full of people panicking, many heading towards the gates. While some wailed about earthquakes and the Gods deserting them, others had understood they were under attack.

Cassien let the air out of his lungs when he caught sight of Jorrun. They were at the inn, one of the Raven scouts was finishing readying the horses. They had eight women and three children with them.

'Get the children up onto the horses,' Jagna instructed. 'Vorro, can you ride?'

The young man nodded, though he swayed where he stood, his coat stained dark with his blood.

'Do you have a spare cloak and hood?' Dinari demanded. 'And some trousers?'

Jorrun stared at his sister, then his eyes lit up and a smile spread across his mouth. He turned and rummaged in his bags, taking out some trousers and a hooded tunic. Dinari undid her skirt, letting it drop to the floor before scrambling into the trousers and pulling the tunic on over her head. The hood barely hid her tattooed face. She climbed clumsily onto the horse behind the injured Vorro.

'Can you ride?' Jorrun asked her.

She grinned at him and shook her head. 'I guess we'll see.'

Jorrun didn't return the smile. 'Hold tight to Vorro. You might need to take the reins if he loses consciousness.'

She shrugged. 'That was the plan.'

'Okay.' Jorrun turned to address the other women. 'Stay close and try to remain between the horses. If you can, keep hold of one of the stirrups. The gates will be very crowded and it will be hard to get through. This young man here is Cassien, he'll follow behind us. If anyone gets separated, keep a watch for him coming through the gates. Let's go.'

Jorrun got up into his saddle and twisted to hold Cassien's gaze for a moment before heading out into the street and using his mount to clear a way through. Cassien waited until they were almost out of sight before he followed.

Here and there, groups of guards were urging people to return home or at least get off the streets. Despite their efforts, there was still a crush of wagons and people fleeing on foot, afraid of a quake that might topple buildings or of the rumours of invasion.

Cassien briefly caught sight of Jorrun at the gates. He half expected to see the fire of his magic, but he disappeared from view with no sounds of confrontation. Cassien soon discovered why. Several guards lay dead around the gate. Cassien drew in a sharp breath when he saw one of their Raven scouts among the fallen. He forced his way through the panicking people, eyes frantically searching the backs of the veiled women's heads for any that might be from the palace.

He was through. He moved aside off the road, heading for a slight rise, aware he was making himself stand out and was very visible from the city walls. A woman caught his eyes, not from the palace, but a slave who'd been separated from her master. She carried a child on her hip. Cassien darted back toward the crowd and grabbed her arm.

'Raven,' was all he said.

Many of the city's occupants came to a halt, milling around and staring back at the walls. It was mainly travelling merchants, farmers, and visitors to the city who continued to flee down the road. Cassien spotted Jagna and the others; they were quite some way ahead.

'Got something that doesn't belong to you?'

Cassien let go of the woman to grab for his sword hilt as he pivoted, only to be confronted by the grinning face of Rothfel.

Cassien rolled his eyes, his heart still hammering.

'It's all right.' Cassien turned to reassure the woman. She had dark-brown eyes, and blonde hair peeped out from below her headscarf. 'He's with me.'

They hurried, but the others stayed ahead of them.

'How did you destroy the temple and the gates?' Cassien asked the thief when they were out of hearing of anyone else. 'I didn't think you or any of your scouts had magic.'

'It's a different type of magic.' Rothfel glanced at the woman, but she didn't seem perturbed by their conversation. 'It's called Alchemy. I have a friend who has a friend.' He winked.

'I, um… did you know you lost one of your men at the gates?'

'I did.' Rothfel grew serious, his eyes distant. 'He understood the risk and was willing to take it.' His eyes fell on the child. 'What's your name?'

The child looked at its mother, who nodded.

'Topei.'

'Well, Topei.' Rothfel bent to meet her eyes. 'Have courage, you're nearly free.'

Cassien glanced at the women; her eyes were bright, the skin around them creased with worry, although it was hard to be sure of her expression beneath her veil. 'Can I take Topei a moment,' Cassien asked. 'We need to run a bit, if you can?'

The woman responded by lifting the girl and holding her toward Cassien. As soon as he had her secure against his own hip, he set off at a jog. It was Meric who turned and spotted them, alerting Jorrun who led them off the road.

'Cass, Rothfel,' he greeted them, his eyes passing over the woman and child. Their priority may have been rescuing the palace women with power, but Jorrun would never begrudge Cassien saving another slave. Rothfel lifted Topei up onto one of the baggage horses.

'You're not followed,' Cassien reassured him. 'But I think we should stay on the road for now and slip off it after dark.'

'Masters,' Dinari called out. 'You need to tend to your man before we go any further if you want him to live.'

Cassien stared at her in awe. In the west he'd gotten used to women speaking freely, but here in the east it was punishable by death. Dinari had spoken out more than once now. This woman had courage and intelligence. Vorro slumped over in his saddle, and it was clear it was only the tattooed woman's strength that was keeping him in place.

'You're right,' Jorrun said. 'Let's get off the road.'

They moved toward a small stand of trees, helping the four children down and allowing the horses to graze. Jorrun himself eased Vorro down onto the ground and Cassien grabbed his healer's kit of his horse which Tyrin had been leading. Before anyone could stop her, Dinari had worked her fingers into Vorro's torn shirt and ripped the fabric open. Jorrun drew a small knife from his belt and used his magic to heat the blade while Cassien took out a small flask containing a mixture of painkiller and strong alcohol.

Jorrun glanced up. 'Jagna, can you help Cass hold Vorro down?'

Dinari moved aside to let the men work, a frown on her un-veiled face. Cassien gave Vorro the end of his belt to bite down on as Jorrun cut into his flesh so he could pull out the arrow. Having endured so far, Vorro couldn't help but scream as Cassien poured alcohol onto the open wound, before pressing down a thick wad of cloth and binding it in place.

'Will you not heal it?' Dinari asked.

Jorrun frowned at her, not understanding.

'With your magic.' She held a hand out to gesture towards Vorro.

'You can't heal with magic,' Jagna said in confusion.

It was Dinari's turn to appear confused. Her eyes travelled over Jorrun's face. 'Our father learned how, but it was one of the secrets he guarded in his library. Mother saw the book in his room, and I later sought it out in the library with help from Osun, but... but you were very young.'

Jorrun's mouth was open, his eyes watered and the skin around them reddened. 'You knew me as soon as you saw me.'

'Of course.' She smiled, reaching out a hand to touch his bearded cheek. 'You were only four or five when you promised me you would save me, but even then, I knew you would.'

'But I took so long.' A tear fell from his eye and trickled over her fingers.

Cassien sniffed and looked away, swallowing against the painful lump forming in his throat.

Dinari shook her head. 'But you found me.'

Jagna cleared his throat, wiping quickly at his nose. 'You say magic can heal; do you know how we can heal Vorro? He's lost so much blood.'

Dinari turned to the Chemman and Cassien's heart sank as she shook her head. 'It was many years ago. All I remember is that it's blood magic.'

'Blood magic.' Jagna shrank back. 'How can something evil heal?'

'Because it isn't evil.' Dinari looked around at them all. 'I mean, it can certainly be used as such, it is an element used in necromancy, certainly; but blood magic is simply that, magic of the blood. Understanding the blood and using its power is the key to healing, that much I can remember.'

'But the fire-spirits see it as something evil, as did our mother,' Jorrun protested.

'Yes.' She held out her arms, turning her hands to reveal the tattoos that covered even her palms. 'It's hardly surprising a woman with the potential for power would fear blood magic. It is the same for the fire-spirits, blood magic can bind and trap them, so they would want to prevent its use.'

Jorrun sat back on his heels, rubbing his face with his hands. 'I avoided looking through my father's books on blood magic as I didn't want to know any more about it than I do.' He gave a frustrated growl. 'The little I learned was from old Elden texts.'

'Jorrun.' She touched his arm. 'The books father had revealed how to remove blood bindings, including for dream traps, and for tattoos.'

His hand fell away from his face and he grabbed for her fingers. 'Are you saying we can remove these, that you could get back your powers?'

She nodded.

Cassien stood up, exchanging a glance with Jagna. His first thought was of Calayna, denied her magic for so many years.

Vorro groaned, bringing them back to the present.

'He can't ride like that.' Jagna shook his head.

Cassien closed his eyes and sighed. 'I'll stay with him.'

'And I,' Rothfel volunteered.

Jorrun rubbed at his beard and regarded Cassien for a while before reluctantly agreeing. He held out a hand. 'Get to Caergard when you can. I must go on to Navere and won't be able to wait for you.'

Cassien grasped Jorrun's wrist. 'I'll be with you as soon as I can.'

Chapter Fourteen

Temerran; Kingdom of Elden

It was one of the most uncomfortable weeks of Temerran's life. They were running out of ideas to keep the Geladanians entertained and, so far, they were showing no desire to move on or discuss their purpose.

'We can't go on like this.' Temerran ran his fingers through his red curls. 'And where in the spirits' name has that Lorev got to?'

They'd met as always in the early hours of the morning in Bractius's private study.

It was Teliff who answered. 'No one has seen any sign of the man. I think we can all guess where he's headed.'

'And what happens when Lorev fails and the next one of their party wanders off?' Temerran realised he was pacing and forced himself to stop. He'd spotted Linea only twice since following her to the lake, and always in public. His need to see her again in private was driving him to distraction, but according to the men and servants he had watching her, she hadn't left the castle. Perhaps that was it. Perhaps if he reduced the watch on her, she would slip away to see him. For a moment he was tempted by the idea, before reason reminded him he was being a fool.

'I don't like it that we've heard nothing from the Icante,' Bractius said. 'Messenger birds are coming into the castle, but we have no way of knowing those we dispatch are reaching their destinations.'

'Perhaps we should send a human to the Fulmers, rather than just a bird,' Dorthai suggested. Bractius had finally brought the Fulmer man into their council five days ago, although they'd avoided introducing him to the Geladanian officials. 'We don't even know for sure that Arridia and Joss made it safely there.'

Temerran met Bractius's eyes. The king had paled to an almost green shade. 'Jorrun would never forgive me. And Kesta will burn all of Elden down.'

Temerran grimaced, he probably wasn't far wrong. He turned to Dorthai. 'Would you like me to send a few of my best men from the *Undine*?'

'I'd be grateful.' Dorthai nodded.

'I'll send some of my men too,' Bractius offered at once. 'It certainly wouldn't hurt.'

Dorthai glanced at Temerran before bowing his thanks to the king.

'Now, then.' Bractius scratched at his beard. 'I've been avoiding starting any kind of trade negotiations with them as, to be truthful, I'm not sure I want to encourage them back. The problem is, they're unlikely to end their visit and move on until we at least go through the motions of doing so.'

'Or we could just be honest.' Teliff gave a shrug. 'Declare ourselves friends of the Fulmers and say we can't trade with anyone who means them harm.'

Ayline's eyes widened. 'What if they use that as an excuse to attack us?'

'I have to agree with my wife.' Bractius sighed loudly. 'We may owe the Fulmers a great debt, but I can't throw my people to the wolves.'

Temerran realised he was grinding his teeth. Jorrun was meant to be the king's best friend, but it was amazing how often Bractius forgot that fact. Although… perhaps that's what it was to be a strong king.

'All right.' Bractius straightened up. 'I'll start talking trade, but I'll eek it out as long as I can, carry on buying us time.'

'Sadly, I think they are doing the same.' Temerran gave a slight shake of his head. 'Whilst Lorev goes about his mission.'

'Damn the man.' Bractius cursed. 'Well, let's get about our day. Temerran, will you be coming hunting with me, Ren, and Efrin, or will you be looking at Elden crafts and artworks with Ayline and the ladies?'

Of all the Geladanian's Temerran found Efrin's company to be the least grating and straining on his nerves, however hunting on land wasn't a particular strength of his. 'I'll accompany her majesty.'

Ayline didn't exactly appear pleased about it, he was hardly surprised.

***

Temerran went to find his men, Nolv and Sion, to arrange for someone to lead a small group to the Fulmers. He asked his second mate to row out to the Raven Tower to tell Tantony in person what they were doing. He squeezed in time for a hot bath, before presenting himself for a late breakfast where their guests were gathering for the day's entertainments. He missed Linea at first, dressed not in her distinctive red cloak, but in a plain blue dress. She was laughing with the queen and they appeared comfortable, like friends. He tried to recall if he'd seen them together before but was sure he hadn't.

He couldn't help himself, he walked over.

'Your majesty.' He gave a low and elegant bow, his eyes sparkling with a charming smile. 'I am very much looking forward to accompanying you today.'

Ayline's eyes narrowed a little. 'Have you met Linea?'

Temerran turned and inclined his head toward the Geladanian servant. 'I have had that pleasure. Will you be coming with us today?'

Linea shook her head, small dimples forming on her cheeks as she smiled. 'It would not be my place.'

'Oh, I'm sure no one would mind.' Temerran turned to the queen and was in time to catch her sharing a glance with Linea. Had she decided to confide in and trust the queen rather than him? His heart plummeted.

'Please excuse me.' Linea gave a bow to the queen, rather than a curtsey, and Ayline nodded her consent. Temerran watched her walk gracefully from the hall. As she reached the door, Linea twisted to glance at him, a smile curving her lips.

When Temerran turned back to the queen, he caught a look of amusement on her face. It made his hackles rise.

'Ah, my dear Kichi,' Ayline gushed suddenly, opening her arms wide in greeting.

Temerran sighed, he doubted there was such a room full of deception anywhere else under the sky.

'Your majesty.' Kichi hurried forward and took the queen's hand to kiss it. They turned their backs on Temerran, but he had no time to feel slighted. Teliff was entering the hall with Yalla at his side, he'd never been so relieved to see the Merkis.

Temerran bowed politely to Yalla. As always, she carried her staff and Temerran found it hard not to keep letting his gaze wander to its emerald eyes. 'Merkis, are you joining us?'

'I am.' Teliff smiled ruefully. 'I'm a bit old to go tearing about the countryside on a horse like a mad thing.'

'Oh, I don't know.' Temerran grinned. There wasn't as much as a flicker of a smile on Yalla's face.

Ayline clapped her hands together. 'Are we all ready?'

Anyone who wasn't quickly made themselves so. Ayline had chosen two of her more sensible ladies-in-waiting to accompany her, and they had an escort of six palace guards. The tour started in the castle itself, Ayline showing them into some less public rooms that contained old paintings and tapestries. They stopped in the queen's own private parlour so she could show off some of the best pieces in her jewellery collection. While Kichi gasped and commented over each item, Yalla frowned and remained aloof. It wasn't until they entered the small ladies' chapel that the High Priestess suddenly showed interest. She used her staff to point toward a large mural on the stone wall. The image of a woman smiled down at them, her eyes somehow both knowing and kind. The sun crowned her golden hair and the moon rested on a pendant at her breast. A hind lay in her lap, and a cat stood with its head beneath her hand. In her other hand, she held a landscape that represented the land beneath the sky.

'Is that your Goddess?'

'Yes, it is.' Ayline gazed up at it, hands folded before her.

'Have you ever seen any demonstration of her power?'

Ayline opened her mouth, and Temerran felt a moment of sympathy for her.

'We see such all the time, in the miracle of birth, of healing,' Ayline said firmly.

Yalla grunted, and Temerran's hand twitched with an urge to slap the arrogant and rude woman.

'And your god, have you ever seen him?' Yalla asked.

'To some people faith isn't about seeing,' Temerran said. 'It's about knowing. The gods of Elden give their people strength enough.'

Yalla narrowed her eyes. 'It was my understanding you don't believe in gods.'

'That doesn't mean I can't respect the beliefs of others, and spirits know I've seen my fill of false gods.'

Yalla straightened up with a hiss, her teeth showing.

Teliff quickly stepped in. 'Temerran here played a big part in the destruction of the false Chemman god, the demon posing as Hacren.'

'Oh, yes, you sang the binding,' Kichi joined in, with a glare at the much taller priestess.

Temerran forced his muscles to relax and slowed his breathing. He cursed himself silently; he'd let her rattle him. But then… he'd rattled her too.

Despite Teliff and Kichi's efforts to lighten the mood, the rest of the tour was somewhat tense and Temerran was happy to escape after their late lunch. He took a walk about the ramparts to take in the fresh air and clear his mind. As he headed back down into the castle, he saw the familiar red fabric of Linea's cloak. Her hood fell away as she turned to smile at him, her body pressed up against the stone where she'd been looking out over the lake. Temerran composed himself and approached her slowly.

'Good afternoon, Linea.'

'Temerran.'

'I take it this isn't a chance meeting.'

She shook her head. 'I came to tell you to be careful.'

He tilted his head to one side to study her face.

'You upset Yalla today. She isn't a woman to cross.'

'She isn't an easy woman to like.'

Linea gave a small bark of a laugh. 'No, I suppose not.' She breathed in, then took a step toward Temerran and placed a hand on his chest. 'You're aware why we are here. Jderha wants the fire-walkers dead. Whether you and Elden want to get dragged into it, or step away, well… well that's up to you and Bractius I guess.'

Temerran took a step back. 'Dia Icante is my friend.'

Linea looked away, the skin around her eyes creasing as though in pain. 'Then my people and yours are about to become enemies.'

'We don't have to be,' Temerran implored her. 'Is there not some way we can convince the others to just head back to Geladan?'

She was shaking her head before he finished. 'The word of Jderha is absolute, our devotion without question. Yalla can't let the fire-walkers attack Jderha.'

'But they wouldn't.' Temerran grabbed her arms, his eyes locked earnestly on hers. 'Jderha is nothing to them. They didn't even know she existed. Their history is long lost to them. The only reason the fire-walkers would hurt her is if she threatens them first, or sends assassins to kill innocent children.'

'Then it has already begun. It is prophesied—'

'Prophesy!' Temerran let go of her, throwing his hands up with a growl. 'Prophesy is nonsense, it only comes true if you make it. Stop making it, help us persuade your people to go home!'

He was breathing hard.

She strode forward, grabbing some of his hair in a fist and kissing him fiercely. It was some time before Temerran stepped back to gasp in air.

Movement in the courtyard down below caught his eye. A familiar figure made his heart surge in hope, then shrivel in fear. What was he doing here?

He turned back to Linea. 'I have to go.' He kissed her again, quickly this time. 'Please, help us.'

With a last look in her turquoise eyes, he headed for the door and ran down the tower steps. He cut the man off before he reached the king's private audience room.

'Vilnue, why are you here?'

The ambassador to the Fulmers turned. There was no smile in his greeting. 'Temerran. I think you know why.'

'Dia knows then? Are the children safe? Rosa?'

'They are all safe, or were when we left them.'

'We?' Temerran's relief was short lived. 'Please tell me you got our warning? None of the fire-walkers came here with you, did they?'

Vilnue swallowed.

'No.' Temerran shook his head.

Vilnue gave a wince. 'You know the Icante.'

240

Temerran clenched his jaw. 'Let's see the king. I have news for him too, and it isn't good.'

The two guards outside the king's study informed them Bractius was still out hunting, but they allowed Temerran and Vilnue to wait inside after finding a page to send for Teliff.

'Where's Dia?' Temerran asked as soon as they were alone. 'The Raven Tower?'

Vilnue shuffled his feet. 'Um, she's on the *Undine*.'

'She's in Taurmaline?' His eyes widened incredulously. 'What does she plan to do?'

Vilnue waved a hand at him to sit down and moved to the king's desk to pour them both a drink. 'You know Dia, she's made no plans yet, not until she has all the facts. She won't come charging in here attacking people, that's for sure.'

Temerran stared down at the drink in his hand. If anyone could solve this diplomatically, it was the Icante. Even so, nausea rose from his stomach to his throat. He put the glass to his lips but couldn't bring himself to drink.

'This is a mess. And it's my fault.'

'Yours?' Vilnue frowned at him.

'Yes.' Temerran stood and paced the room. 'I went sailing across the sea looking for adventure, exploring new lands. I'm the one who brought news of *walkers* to Geladan.'

'You couldn't have known—'

'Prophesy.' Temerran growled. He took a large swallow of the burning spirit.

The door opened and Teliff hurried in. 'What's going on?'

Vilnue gestured toward the desk with his glass. 'Get a drink.'

It was nearly an hour before Bractius came striding in, still in his riding clothes, his face flushed. Temerran filled him in, including his conversation with Linea on the battlement.

It was an uncomfortable few minutes until Bractius spoke. 'Gentlemen, we are out of time. I will summon Ambassador Ren to the audience room later this evening and we will have an honest conversation.'

'I think Dia should be there too,' Temerran said.

Bractius avoided his eyes. 'Perhaps it would be best for her to remain out of the way for the moment.'

'I think Temerran is right,' Vilnue said. 'Dia might convince Ren that the *walkers* have no interest in their supposed god.'

'Dia's presence could inflame the situation.' Bractius shook his head. 'If I can't persuade Ren, then we'll broker a meeting, perhaps at Northold.'

Temerran's eyes narrowed. What was Bractius up to? Surely the Elden king wouldn't sell out the Fulmers. Temerran understood Bractius had to protect his own people, but he wouldn't have a crown, or a country, had it not been for Dia.

Teliff shifted uncomfortably.

Vilnue stood up. 'I'll advise the Icante of what's happening.'

'I'll come with you,' Temerran said at once.

'Be back here for when I confront Ren.' Bractius regarded them both. 'Especially you, Temerran. If he has the powers you accredit him with, I don't want him using them to mess with my thinking.'

Temerran nodded, biting back the comment that if he wanted protection from magic, it was the Icante he needed.

He and Vilnue made their way through the castle, trying to appear calm and relaxed as they passed Efrin and the Geladanian warriors in the great hall, still riled from their hunting trip. They picked up their pace as they left the castle grounds and wound their way down to the harbour. Temerran's men looked sheepish as he strode aboard the *Undine*.

'She's um, in your cabin, captain,' one of the Borrowmen informed him.

Temerran gave him a glare that sent him scuttling to find something busy to do. The bard drew in a breath before opening the door to his spacious room. As soon as he saw Dia standing there, the knot in his heart eased. She was dressed in trousers and a green shirt, a long jacket buttoned at her waist.

'Tem.'

He hurried forward to hug her, while Vilnue stood leaning against the doorway. There was another woman in the room, one Temerran didn't recognise.

'I was so glad to hear the children got to the Fulmers safely,' he said. 'But you shouldn't have come here, we tried to warn you.'

They exchanged news quickly, Dia introducing Shevi, the young Raven from Chem. Dia studied Temerran's face. 'You don't seem to have much hope that this will not end in a fight.'

'These people are fanatical about their goddess.' He peered up at the castle through the leaded glass of the cabin window. 'I don't think reason comes into it.'

'I need to be there, at this meeting.'

Temerran glanced at Vilnue.

Dia sighed and unfolded her arms. 'You know I'm right. Bractius wants to avoid a magical battle in his castle, that's understandable, but what if these people take an extreme stance and attack?' She turned to Temerran. 'You seem to think it likely.'

'We'll get you into the castle, but the audience will be up to Bractius,' Temerran said.

'That will have to do.' Dia gave a shake of her head. 'Shevi, fetch the other Ravens, we'll go at once.'

'These people are powerful.' Temerran fell in beside Dia as she strode across the deck.

'I've met powerful people before.' She caught his worried glance and touched his arm. 'Have more faith in me, Tem.'

'It isn't you I'm worried about, but I can't help but worry *for* you.'

Dia was quiet for a moment. 'We can only ever do our best.'

***

Vilnue hurried ahead to fetch Teliff, who came to meet them, muttering and cursing under his breath. 'I could get strung up for this.'

'Sorry.' Vilnue winced.

'Right, come this way.' Teliff gestured to the door that led to the kitchen stores, and he took them through several servants' corridors to a small waiting room with plain wooden benches and no windows. Temerran recognised it as the private back way into the audience room. A single candle burned in a sconce on the wall.

'Stay here, please.' Teliff looked from Dia to the Ravens. 'Unless it sounds as though the king is in trouble.'

244

Dia didn't respond, she was staring up at the candle flame.

'Dia?' Temerran's concern grew.

Dia narrowed her eyes, speaking not to Temerran, but to the flame. 'I know you.'

The flame grew and split. Both Teliff and Vilnue took several steps away from it. The fire-spirit drifted closer to Dia, who barely blinked.

'Hello, Icante, I am Siveraell.'

'Siveraell!' Dia's face lit with a smile. 'Well met, my dear friend.'

'Sss, careful, Icante.' The fire-spirit made himself smaller. 'No one musst know I am here and helping you, least of all the worshippers of Jderha.'

'You bring warning?'

'I do.' He flared brighter. 'The ambassador, Ren, will seem alone when he meets the king, but there will be fire-spirits within the torches, sset there by the priestess. She has four captured spirits which are bound to do her bidding. I am not aware of their plan, I am ssorry. The drakes won't come to Elden while She is here, they will not risk capture. I... I will only take a little risk myself.'

'We are very grateful,' Dia told him. 'And you know if they ever captured you, I would come for you.'

'I do, Dia.'

'Get yourself to safety; and thank you.'

Siveraell bobbed, then shot away into the candle flame.

Teliff shifted his feet and cleared his throat. 'I'll warn the king and advise him you're standing by to assist.'

'Do you think he'll still meet Ren alone, knowing he might attack?' Vilnue asked his fellow Merkis in surprise.

Teliff drew himself up. 'The king isn't a coward.'

Vilnue raised his hands. 'That's not what I meant.'

'They may just be taking measures to protect themselves, not knowing what our intentions are,' Dia suggested.

Temerran met her eyes. She didn't believe that any more than he did.

'We'd better get in place,' Teliff prompted them.

Temerran glanced down at his clothes. He should have changed into something more formal—too late now. He turned back to Dia and she reached out to squeeze his hand. He nodded, his stomach twisting.

Two warriors stood by the main doors to the audience room, two more waited discreetly at the back of the room. Temerran's eyes were drawn to the harsh black seat which had been relegated to a corner. Bractius would miss Jorrun more than ever this evening. He couldn't help but wonder which Bractius regretted more, damaging the friendship he had with his Thane, or losing his control over him.

The ornate door at the side of the room opened and the king walked in, Teliff on his heels. Bractius was perfectly groomed and wearing a rich, purple shirt and a long black robe hemmed with white fur. He wore his crown, something Temerran rarely saw him do. The king's eyes went to the innocuous door behind which Dia waited, then snapped back to Temerran. He pointed to the rows of empty benches along the edge of the room.

'Be seated.'

Both Temerran and Vilnue moved to obey, sitting a little way apart in silent agreement.

There were three sharp knocks at the door and the king sat on his throne, Teliff hurrying to stand at the base of the three steps leading down to it. Bractius nodded to the guards and one stepped forward to open the heavy doors.

Ren walked in, wearing a suit of dark-green velvet. He made a quick check of the room, and Temerran noted that the man's eyes flickered towards the torches on the walls. As the guard closed the doors, Temerran glimpsed Efrin waiting outside. He hoped the rest of the Geladanian delegation weren't waiting there too. He shuddered.

'Your majesty.' Ren gave a low bow, a smile frozen to his face. 'I was intrigued to be invited here alone. I see that this is a formal meeting of some importance.'

Bractius shifted a little in his throne, leaning toward its right arm in a casual pose. 'Ren of Geladan, we welcomed you with friendship and trust. It is time for us to put the truth of your visit out before us. We are aware that you came here looking for what we call "fire-walkers".'

Ren blinked once, his smile not slipping for a moment. 'That is so.'

'It is our understanding you have come here intending to kill them.'

Ren hesitated for only the fraction of a heartbeat. Temerran stiffened as he sensed Ren call up his power.

'Your majesty.' Ren took a single step forward. All four guards immediately changed their posture and Ren halted; hands raised. 'We have no quarrel with Elden. You are a fine and good people; I had hoped that we might come to a beneficial trade arrangement.'

Bractius didn't miss his meaning and Temerran had to stop himself curling his fingers into fists.

'The people of the Fulmer Islands are my friends.' Bractius leaned forward. 'Their Icante and her daughter have saved this country from the attacks of powerful enemies. I will not betray them, nor aid anyone who would hurt them.'

Ren's face crumpled, but Temerran felt the man increase the power to his voice, turning his words to honey despite their content. 'We seek only to protect our most beloved Goddess. You know of the prophesy. A fire-priestess protected by an earth-bound spirit will slay her.'

Bractius's face was hard, and Temerran could see the tendons standing out on his neck. The king was fighting hard against the spell of the words. Temerran glanced around the room at the others. Both Teliff and Vilnue were watching Ren avidly, eyes wide and mouths slack. The four warriors in the room had all relaxed their stance, their guard dropped.

It took some effort for Bractius to get his words out, and Temerran found himself admiring the Eldeman.

'Go back to Geladan and leave the Fulmers alone, and your goddess will have nothing to fear.'

'The fire-walkers are traitors to the goddess, their way of life against the laws of nature—'

'Actually, their way of life is the way of nature.' Temerran stood up and Bractius sagged back against his throne.

'We seek only to reverse a wrong, to defend—'

Temerran sang, his voice clear and strong. Ren staggered, his own words trailing off. Temerran smiled as he sang, letting the power flow through him without reservation. It was a simple tale, as old as humanity, and he almost laughed at Ren's puzzlement. Slowly one, then two, then all four fire-spirits emerged from the flames, each of them wide-eyed and transfixed by Temerran's words. As his song ended, he regarded Ren, who stood glaring at him, breathing hard.

Temerran quirked his mouth up in a smile and shrugged. 'Spirits love a good story.'

'The Borrows will pay for this.' Ren growled.

'I think it's time for you to leave,' Bractius said from his throne, his voice once again steady. 'You are no longer welcome in Elden.'

Ren laughed and it made Temerran's skin crawl. 'We have no use for Elden, not at the moment. As for leaving, Yalla and Kichi are on their way to finish our mission; if Lorev hasn't already done so.'

Ren clicked his fingers and the fire-spirits darted toward the throne, their faces contorting as though in agony. The doors flew open and Efrin burst in, sword drawn. Bractius leapt off the throne to draw his own steel.

'Dia!' Temerran yelled.

Ren pointed towards the king. 'Kill him, then the bard.'

The fire-spirts wailed and cried, but they moved toward Bractius, only to be thrown back down the audience room by a strong blast of wind. Dia stepped into the room, forming a shield around the throne, the Ravens fanning out behind her. The two guards at the far doors were already down and dead, and Vilnue ran to engage Efrin. Teliff shadowed his king. As much as he ached to take out Ren, Temerran left him to the Icante, drawing his own sword to assist Vilnue.

The fire-spirits were hurling themselves at Dia's shield, but she held it steady, refusing to retaliate.

'Do something!' Bractius demanded.

'They are being forced against their will.' Dia glared at him. Her eyes narrowed as she turned her attention to Ren. 'I have freed spirits before; all I have to do is smash the trap that holds them.'

Ren showed his teeth in a chuckle. 'I don't hold the trap, that is many miles away by now, but Yalla has given them to me to obey.'

Dia gave the slightest of smiles. 'That's good information.' She gestured to the Ravens to hold her shield and advanced on the ambassador. He backed away, eyes widening, glancing over his shoulder to Efrin who was still busy with Vilnue and Temerran.

Calling up a small tornado, Dia sent it after Ren. The man tried to run but was swept up and hurled against the wall again and again. Dia darted forward, drawing a dagger and landing on Ren's chest.

'Tell the spirits to stop attacking the king.'

He shook his head, struggling to breathe with her weight on his lungs.

'Tell them,' she growled, pressing the tip of her dagger against his eyeball…

Vilnue let out a cry as Efrin's sword cut in and out of his side. Vilnue twisted and the move slowed the exceptional swordsman enough for Temerran to slash at Efrin's leg. Vilnue spun, bringing his sword down into Efrin's skull as Temerran stabbed through his back and into his kidney.

'Are you all right?' Temerran grabbed Vilnue as he staggered.

'The king!' Vilnue gasped, pressing a hand to his bloody wound.

Temerran straightened up. The fire-spirits were still battering at the shield of the Ravens; Dia knelt on Ren, blood poured from several wounds on his face. Temerran ran over to her, throwing himself to her side.

'What do you need?' he asked.

'For him to command the spirits to stop their attack.'

Temerran looked down at the Geladanian. 'You have some power, but you are no bard of the Borrows.' He called up his power and stared into the man's blue eyes. 'Ren, you will tell your fire-spirits to cease their attack.'

Ren froze, the muscles of his jaw moving before the words burst out of him. 'Stop attacking the king!'

Dia studied him for a moment, then turned to Temerran. 'Hold his jaw.'

The blood drained from Temerran, but he did as she asked. Ren screamed as Dia took hold of his tongue and sliced through it.

She threw the bloody organ to the floor. 'You will never use the power of your voice for harm again. Think yourself lucky that's all I have done to you.'

Dia stood, and the Ravens allowed their shield to drop. 'He's all yours,' Dia told the king.

Bractius didn't move a muscle, his eyes on her bloody hands.

'We need to get after the others,' Temerran said. 'With your leave, your majesty, we'll set sail on the *Undine* at once.'

'I'll ensure the castle is secure.' Teliff gave a quick bow and rushed from the room.

'What of these?' Bractius indicated the four fire-elementals who clustered together in a corner.

'The only way we can help them is to find and kill the High Priestess.' Dia shook her head sadly. 'They are not of this realm, while they're captive, they can't go home and eventually they will fade and die.'

All four fire-spirits began wailing. Bractius put his hands over his ears. 'They can't stay here.'

Inspiration struck Temerran. 'Do you know where the one who holds you captive is?'

One drake drifted a little closer. 'No. But sshe can summon uss.'

'You're coming with us then,' Temerran said. 'As soon as she calls you, you will tell us where.'

The diminutive spirit pulsed its agreement.

They all turned as Adrin and a group of warriors came charging into the audience room. 'Your majesty, we heard you were under attack!'

'Bit late,' Temerran murmured with a glance at Dia.

Bractius glared at Adrin, but didn't have a chance to speak as a red-faced Teliff strode in. 'They've taken my bloody ship!'

'What?' Bractius demanded, standing up.

Teliff shook his head. 'Your ship. I meant your ship.'

Bractius's cheeks flushed and his eyes blazed. 'You better not mean my warship.'

Teliff swallowed. 'And we found this.' He turned and made a beckoning motion with his hand. A warrior came forward, dragging a woman wearing a bright red cloak. Temerran caught his breath.

'Linea.'

At the sound of his voice she looked up, pulling away from the guard to run to Temerran. He wrapped her in his arms, holding her close.

'Who is this?' Dia demanded.

'She is Linea,' Ayline said from where she stood in the doorway. 'I agreed to hide her here so she could escape the others. She is just a servant.'

'She has been helping us.' Temerran looked appealingly from Bractius to Dia.

Dia studied the back of the woman's head, met Temerran's eyes, then turned back to the king. 'We need to go at once. I'll leave Ravens Mayve and Belir at the Raven Tower in case you need them. Vilnue?'

The Merkis swayed where he stood. 'I'll live.' He grunted. 'But I'll not be much use for a while.'

'If it's okay with you, your majesty, I'll drop Vilnue off at the Tower to recover and exchange him for Tantony when I pick up my husband.'

Bractius gave a dramatic shrug. 'As long as I'm clear of those people.'

'A thorough search is being made now, majesty,' Teliff said.

'Keep warriors by yourself and the queen at all times, though,' Dia warned. 'Don't forget their assassins.'

'I doubt their ship is still at Southport,' the king said. 'But if it is, I'll have every man arrested and the ship taken apart for timber.'

'We need to go,' Dia said. With a slight inclination of her head towards Bractius, she placed a hand carefully against Vilnue's back and helped him from the room.

Temerran gave a low bow. 'Fare well, your majesty.'

'Good luck to you, bard.'

Temerran took hold of Linea's hand and they hurried toward the *Undine*.

Chapter Fifteen

Rosa; Fulmer Island

Rosa watched as Joss drew a shape in the ashes on the hearthstone.

'Is it a wolf?' Nip guessed.

'No, silly.' Joss shook his head at the much older boy.

'Is it me?' Doraquael asked from where he hovered just above the flames in the fireplace.

Joss squealed with laughter.

'No.'

It had been days since Dia's departure and there had been no sign of the Geladanians; even so, Rosa couldn't quite relax. The hold was busy with the harvest and storing wood and bricks of cow dung for their winter fires. Heara had all those too frail to help with the work up on the outer walls, watching for ships and strangers. The warriors on watch were doubled at night, but Rosa had struggled to sleep. The slightest noise had her wide awake and straining her ears for any trouble.

She hoped Dia had made it to Northold, and Tantony wasn't too worried about her.

'Is it a frog?' Worvig leapt forward, grabbing up Joss and lifting him into the air. 'Is it a dancing frog?' He twirled the boy around and Joss laughed so hard he hiccupped.

'Are they on their way in?' Milaiya looked up from where she stirred food in a large cauldron.

Worvig set Joss down. 'They are.'

Rosa shook herself from her worrying and hurried to help Milaiya and the three other women who'd stayed behind set out the freshly baked loaves and the jugs of ale and water.

Then she heard it, faint at first, then growing stronger as the returning workers drew closer to the hold. Male and female voices twinned together in song and, as it had done every time since she'd first heard it, it stirred something in Rosa's heart. She'd experienced nothing like it before. It was almost mystical, certainly spiritual.

'I should be out there helping,' Nip grumbled.

'You have your own job, lad,' Worvig replied in a deep but quiet voice that brooked no argument. He placed a hand briefly on the top of Joss's head.

The doors burst open and the hold folk came dancing in, Heara at their head and Everlyn just behind holding Arridia's hand. Azrael flew above their heads, humming loudly.

They gave Worvig and Milaiya crowns made of wheat stalks, which they exchanged for horns of ale. With no further ceremony, the islanders spread out around the hall to eat and drink, the song hanging in the air long after it had ceased.

Rosa noticed that neither Worvig, Heara, nor Everlyn touched the ale. Their days of peace hadn't lessened their caution either.

'How did your lessons go today?' Rosa asked Arridia. It wasn't unusual for the girl to be quiet and thoughtful, but she hadn't said a word since she'd got back to the hold.

'Everlyn says I'm doing well, but... I find it hard to stop my *knowing*. I always had it, Rosa. Turning it off is like trying to turn off my hearing.'

'That does sound hard.' Rosa popped a blackberry in her mouth, wincing at the unexpected tartness. 'But… if you think about it, Arridia, sometimes you do almost switch off your hearing. You understand how listening to someone else's private conversation is rude, so you try not to hear? Well, I guess your *knowing* is the same.'

Arridia frowned, then glanced up at Rosa. 'That makes sense.'

One warrior started up a song and others quickly joined in. Rosa caught the exchange of looks between Worvig and Heara. Worvig got up and made his way out of the hold. When Joss began nodding off in his chair, Nip took him off to his room, Doraquael and Eidwyn close on his heels. Rosa turned to watch Arridia; the girl was wide awake and surveying the hall, small lines creasing the soft skin above her nose. Arridia's curiosity often got her in trouble, but Kesta encouraged it—much to Jorrun's concern sometimes.

Rosa cleared her throat. 'What do you think of the Fulmers at harvest time?'

Arridia looked up and smiled, her violet eye taking on a deeper purple hue in the firelight. 'I think it's wonderful. Can we have a harvest festival like this at home?'

Rosa imagined Tantony's face at such a request and almost choked on her nettle tea. 'I think lots of the folk there would love it, but some might not like taking on what they consider being foreign and godless ways.'

Arridia's frown deepened and she pursed her lips together. 'Actually, this reminds me a bit of the Elden goddess.'

'You're very intuitive,' Everlyn said. 'Such nature rituals would have been observed long ago in Elden, before they were associated with witchcraft, rather than with their gods.'

Rosa looked up sharply, her cheeks burning a little, but she clamped her mouth tightly closed. She herself was a firm believer in the god and goddess, though she tended to be private about it. She recalled some chapel paintings she'd seen of the goddess, and she was indeed often depicted with scenes of the harvest.

Worvig came back into the great hall, the cold night air sweeping in with him. He met Heara's eyes and gave her a nod. Rosa glimpsed stars before Worvig closed the doors.

'Have you eaten enough?' Rosa asked Arridia. Her own eyes were stinging, and she stifled a yawn.

Arridia looked down at her plate and gave a nod. 'Yes, thank you.'

Rosa stood and helped Arridia down from her chair. Everlyn and Heara immediately got to their feet as well.

'Oh.' Rosa put her fingers to her mouth. 'I didn't mean to interrupt your evening also.'

'It's fine,' Heara said, hands folded together behind her back. She had two short swords at her hip and a line of throwing knives on a belt strung across her chest. 'I'll feast later when I'm not on duty.'

Rosa realised she was staring at the Fulmer scout and looked away with a blush. Since she'd come here with the children, Heara had been permanently on duty, as had Worvig and Everlyn.

And herself, come to think of it.

They settled Arridia quietly in Kesta's old room, both the fire-spirits perched atop candles that stood on the mantlepiece. Heara held her thin blanket and mattress ready to lie before the door as soon as it was closed and bolted.

'Goodnight,' Rosa whispered as she stepped out into the hall and followed Everlyn to the room she shared with her.

***

'Rosa?'

Rosa startled awake. The room brightened suddenly as Azrael came flying in through the open door, and she blinked against the glare.

It was Everlyn who answered, already swinging her legs out of her bed.

'What is it?'

Arridia stood in the doorway. 'I know you told me not to eavesdrop on people's feelings, but I can feel some badness.'

Everlyn leapt to her feet. 'Does Heara know?'

'She does now,' the scout's voice came from the hallway. She didn't sound amused. 'Everyone, get dressed.'

She herself was ready and fully armed.

As Rosa scrambled into some trousers and grabbed a tunic, the heart-stopping sound of glass shattering came from the children's room. They rushed across the hall, Azrael flying ahead. Two dark-clad men stood in the middle of the room amid the shards of the window. Both fire-spirts flew at the intruders, growing larger, only to distort as they were sucked into boxes around the men's necks with despairing wails.

Rosa let out a startled scream.

Heara sprang forward, wrenching Joss from his bed by the arm and throwing him to Everlyn. One of the assassins got in a deep slash across her arm before she drew her weapon. As Heara's blade came free, she flicked out with her left hand, but the second assassin batted her knife away with his own blade.

Everlyn gave Joss to Rosa and placing herself between the men and the children she called up her power; it was impossible for her to strike without also hitting Heara. Angry cries came from the great hall behind them, and Rosa's heart thundered harder. Surely assassins hadn't gotten into the hall through all the warriors in the hold?

Heara drew another short sword, her movements swift despite her wound. She caught the swords of both men with her blades and kicked out with both feet. The man to her left staggered and she twisted as she fell, plunging her dagger into the side of the man to her right. She landed behind him, letting go of her dagger to grab for a throwing knife.

The other assassin was quicker, slashing across her back with his sword.

Heara screamed. 'Get the children away!'

Feet came pounding up the steps from the guest rooms and Nip appeared, his sword already drawn. He glanced toward Rosa and the children before charging into the room.

Rosa grabbed hold of Arridia's upper arm and tried to pull her away.

'Nip!' the little girl cried out, struggling to break free.

Rosa bent and picked her up, trying not to turn at the sound of clashing steel. 'Which way?'

Everlyn's eyebrows shot up and she shifted Joss against her hip, improving her grip on the quietly crying boy. Without a word she headed down the stairs to the great hall, calling up her power again to form a shield before pushing the doors open a little. She gasped at what she saw. Rosa moved forward to peer over her shoulder.

Several unknown warriors had engaged those of the hold, and Rosa saw with horror that islanders had already fallen. Worvig stood between three men and Milaiya, who was pressed up against the wall.

Worse still was the magical battle that was raging in the centre of the room. A tall man with long grey hair was battering at the wavering shields of Eidwyn and two other *walkers*.

Everlyn handed Joss to Rosa and yelled above the battle sounds. 'Eidwyn! Hind!'

As Everlyn ran forward into the room, Eidwyn backed toward the door. Everlyn sent a fierce blast of air, not at the sorcerer, but at the doors at the far end of the hall. The heavy bar across them snapped and they burst outward against their hinges. Rosa stared in wide-eyed shock, thinking for a moment the woman had betrayed them. Then she realised the warriors pouring in were Islanders who'd been locked out.

As Everlyn engaged the sorcerer, Eidwyn slipped back through the door to join Rosa. Milaiya spotted them and, taking a chance, ran out past the two warriors who still fought a bloodied Worvig.

'With me, quickly!' Eidwyn panted.

'What will we do?' Rosa asked, allowing Milaiya to take Joss so she could take Arridia's hand.

'Hind.' Eidwyn repeated Everlyn's command. 'We run. We hide.'

She took them rapidly down the stairs to the guest rooms and the storerooms. The sound of feet on the floorboards above them was loud.

'What about Nip?' Arridia fought against Rosa, but she tightened her grip. She didn't reply. What could she say? Heara was injured and Nip... well, Nip was barely more than a boy himself.

Both Milaiya and Eidwyn set to work moving some sacks at the far end of the room. Joss clung to Rosa's leg. The boy still hadn't uttered a word, and Rosa stroked his dark hair.

'There are fewer bad men,' Arridia said suddenly.

Eidwyn paused, turning to look at the stairs.

Arridia sucked in air, biting in her lower lip. 'He's coming; and I can't feel Everlyn or Uncle Worvig anymore.'

Milaiya let out a cry. Eidwyn glanced at Rosa, then found the edge of a hidden door with her fingertips. Behind it was a dark, narrow passage, shored up with wood. It smelt earthy and damp.

'Go on.' Milaiya's gaze locked with that of Eidwyn.

The young *walker* nodded, kissing Milaiya on the cheek and hugging her briefly. 'Thank you.'

Eidwyn called some flames to her fingers and strode into the passageway. Rosa herded the children in front of her, then hesitated when Milaiya didn't follow.

The Chemmish woman raised her chin a little. 'Someone has to close and hide the door behind you. I owe Kesta my happiness.'

Before Rosa could protest, Milaiya closed the door firmly.

Eidwyn had already moved ahead, descending a steep set of stairs, and Rosa urged the children to hurry.

'Where's Azra?' Joss sniffled.

Rosa couldn't bring herself to answer, but Arridia did it for her.

'He'll find us when he can, Jossy.'

Rosa shifted her grip on the boy and forced her feet to move faster to catch up with Eidwyn. The stairway was only wide enough for one person, so she kept Arridia in front of her. As the darkness closed in behind, cold fingers walked up and down her back and she strained her ears for the sound of the secret door opening.

Her feet and her knees were already aching, and her shoulder was burning from carrying Joss, but she gritted her teeth and forced herself on. The stairs ended and the tunnel stretched before them, the small light of Eidwyn's magic chasing back the blackness.

'Where are we going?' Joss asked.

'Eidwyn is taking us somewhere safe,' Rosa told him, longing to ask the same question herself. 'But we must stay quiet.'

Eidwyn glanced over her shoulder but said nothing. They reached what appeared to be a dead end, and Rosa's muscles trembled as she breathed out; but young Eidwyn took a sharp turn to the right.

They'd been walking for about ten minutes when Rosa felt a slight vibration beneath her feet and soon after a soft continuous roar. Eidwyn halted and extinguished her small flame. Rosa stopped at once, taking a moment to put Joss down on his feet and stretch her back.

She heard wood grating and the creak of a hinge. The roaring sound grew louder and Rosa realised what it was. A waterfall.

'I can't use my magic or risk light,' Eidwyn said, making Rosa jump. 'When we leave here turn left and keep close against the wall.'

Without waiting for a reply, Eidwyn slipped out of the tunnel.

'Keep hold of my hand,' Rosa warned Joss. 'Will you be all right, Arridia? I need to keep a hand free to feel where I'm going.'

'I'm fine, Rosa,' the little girl replied.

Rosa put her back against the jagged rock of the cliff, feeling with her feet as well as her hand. Cold spray from the waterfall quickly coated her skin and clothing in a fine dew, and she resisted the urge to take her hand from the wall to wipe her face. She almost fell over Arridia in the darkness when the girl stopped.

'We have to climb,' Eidwyn whispered. 'Up to the coastal path then a quick run into the woods. I'll help Arridia.'

Rosa nodded, forgetting the *walker* couldn't see her in the darkness.

The cliff wasn't as firm as Rosa had expected, areas of softer earth mixed with the dark rocks. She didn't dare look down at the pounding surf far below. She kept Joss close in front of her, following the route Eidwyn took as best she could. The *walker* reached the top of the cliff, silently bidding Arridia wait while she crawled on her belly to check the path. She moved into a crouch and leaned over to help up first Arridia, then Joss. The young boy swayed on his feet, and Rosa prayed they wouldn't have to run much further tonight.

'Okay, we need to move quickly. Straight across the road and into the trees…' Eidwyn's eyes grew huge and her face was lit up with the blaze of a distant fire. Rosa spun to see a plume of flames rising from the Hold.

'Goddess!' Rosa exclaimed.

Arridia made a quiet whimper. 'He's coming.'

'The trees, now.' Eidwyn grabbed Arridia's arm and Rosa snatched Joss up off his feet, running as fast as she was able until she stumbled over the roots and twigs scratched at her face.

'Stay close,' Eidwyn hissed. She hesitated, regarding Rosa and Joss. 'Let me take him for a while.'

Rosa didn't argue, feeling a little guilty at her relief as she handed the heavy boy over. She took Arridia's hand and they followed Eidwyn's fast pace. Rosa tried not to think of the Hold, of how much of the harvest was destroyed, of how many people had fallen.

'We need some horses,' Arridia said suddenly.

Rosa shushed her.

'I can't feel Nip.'

Eidwyn pivoted. 'Are you using your magic?'

Arridia stared up at her wide-eyed and nodded slowly.

'Oh, Arridia!' Eidwyn put her hands over her face. 'The sorcerer can sense magic. He'll find you if you use it.'

Even in the darkness, Rosa saw the girl's skin grow pale. For the first time, her eyes filled with water and a tear fell from her lashes.

'It's all right.' Rosa squeezed her in a quick hug.

Eidwyn looked as though she wanted to cry as well, Rosa had no doubt the *walker* knew their flight was hopeless. If Everlyn was gone, there was no one else on the island strong enough to stop the sorcerer.

Eidwyn turned on her heels and headed deeper into the trees. Arridia and Rosa hurried after her, each of them with one hand out in front of them to feel for low branches. A loud snap to their left made them all freeze; Rosa's pulse was loud in her ears. Another snap of a twig followed an odd bleat.

'They came!' Arridia whispered.

'What? Who?' Rosa strained her eyes for any movement between the trees.

'The ponies couldn't come because they were shut in, but the goats said they'd help.'

Several patchwork shapes appeared in the darkness. A dark goat with a wide forehead trotted straight up to Arridia and gave her a soft butt.

'Gramma goat,' Joss said.

Eidwyn was staring at Arridia. She shook herself. 'Quickly then. Arridia, see if she'll carry you.'

Arridia stroked the goat's nose, then climbed up onto its back. One of the others approached Eidwyn, and she swung Joss from her hip and onto the goat's shoulders. The animals set off at once, the rest of the small herd fanning out through the trees. Rosa and Eidwyn hurried to follow, picking up their pace to a jog. Despite her terror, Rosa allowed herself some hope again. If they could get to one of the other Holds, maybe even a ship, they had a chance to evade the Geladanian assassins.

The goats took them down to a stream and Eidwyn jumped in, taking the horn of the one Joss rode to steer it into the narrow channel. She headed upstream, away from the Hold. Rosa gasped at the cold as the water came up over the tops of her boots, filling them to soak her stockings. They followed the water for some time before Eidwyn climbed out on the southward bank. The sky lit up behind them and above the trees as fireballs shot across the sky, not toward them, but back toward the hold. The trees swayed and shook as a blast of wind went rampaging through the forest.

'It must be Evelyn,' Rosa exclaimed.

Eidwyn shook her head, holding out a hand to help Rosa out of the water. 'It's fire-spirits.'

A fierce gust bent the trees and there was a booming crack and whine as one tree gave way and crashed over. Rosa was hurled off her feet and several of the goats scarpered, blaring their alarm. A small ball of fire came skimming close, then circled back.

'I found you, I found you!' Azrael cried in delight.

'Azra!' Joss held his hands out toward the little drake, almost falling off his goat.

'Does Heara live?' Eidwyn asked as Rosa scrambled up onto her knees.

Azrael made a quiet buzzing sound and dropped lower. 'Sshe's bad, in a terrible way. But she ssmashed the traps to set us free! The sorcerer has more traps, we can't get close to him, but we'll try to delay him from a distance, waste his power.'

'You can't let him get to the children,' Eidwyn said. 'You might have to risk being trapped to try to stop him—'

'Eidwyn doesn't understand,' Azrael wailed. 'If Azra and Doraquael are trapped, they can make us hunt you, make us kill the children.'

Rosa swallowed, twisting to look at Arridia. The little girl's face was serious, her chin raised a little as she sat astride the goat, her skin glowed a rosy colour, reflecting Azrael's light.

'It's all right, Azra,' Arridia said. 'We'll know it isn't really you.'

Azrael wailed again. 'I musst go help Doraquael. Go quick as you can to Eagle Hold. Take a sship to Shem, they have the strength to protect you there.'

He shot closer to Joss, then hovered briefly in front of Arridia, before hurtling back toward Fulmer Hold.

Rosa got to her feet. Her boots squelched. 'How far is it to Eagle Hold?'

Eidwyn held her gaze. 'Almost two days.'

Rosa's mouth fell open and she quickly snapped it shut. 'Come on, then.'

She caught up with the leader of the four remaining goats, resting a hand on its back to help keep from tripping or sliding over. Behind them the hiss, rumble, and bright flares of the magical battle continued for almost half an hour. Then everything became dark and still.

Rosa rubbed at the centre of her chest with one hand, hoping the pain there wasn't her heart. Her knees were screaming at her and her throat raw from breathing hard through her mouth. She couldn't go on much further.

'Eidwyn,' she panted. 'Take the children on. I'll catch up when I can.'

Eidwyn protested, but when she saw Rosa's expression she stopped. Eidwyn nodded slowly, once, then turned, continuing south with a determined, if exhausted stride. The goats followed, but Arridia twisted about.

'Aunt Rosa, come on!'

'Go on, Riddi, I just need a breather. I'll be with you in a moment.'

'Promise?'

Rosa nodded; her fingers crossed behind her back.

She sank to the cold ground and let a sob escape. She hoped she would see the children again, but it didn't seem likely.

'Oh, come on, you silly woman,' she growled at herself. 'You're tougher than that.'

She took off her boots, wrung out her stockings, and put them back on straighter. She let down her hair, twisted it back up into a tighter knot, and pinned it back up. She stretched her spine and pulled back her shoulders, taking in several slow, deep breaths.

Rosa got to her feet.

Movement caught her eye and she pivoted to see a man stepping out of the shadows. He was tall, thin, with olive skin and long grey hair tied neatly back. Recent burns had ravaged the left side of his face.

'Well,' he said. 'You're not what I was expecting.'

Rosa drew her small dagger.

The sorcerer laughed.

Chapter Sixteen

Kesta; The Borrow Sea

Kesta realised she was pacing the deck and forced herself to stop, gripping the rail to stare out across the miles of grey, rippling sea. The three warriors who'd come with her to allow her a break from sailing Jorrun's ship, had quickly learned to stay out of her way. She'd balanced her power to speed them along without straining the hull and the mast or burning her reserves. She had no doubt her mother was better protection for her children than she herself was, but it wouldn't hurt to conserve her strength.

She'd spoken with Jorrun again briefly in the early hours. The guilt and worry on his face, in his voice, still tore her heart. He was as desperate to be with their children as she was. Tonight, he would strike at Uldren to save his sister and deal a heavy blow against those who refused to abolish slavery. Her palms itched with the need to call magic, the desire to be fighting at his side. Why did their lives never go the way they planned?

'Silene?' One of the warriors cleared his throat. He held out a clay mug; steam rose from it.

She smiled, the tension in her muscles easing a little. 'Thank you, Yorik.'

He gave a nod of his head, moving with ease across the tilting deck back to the cabin.

Kesta raised the mug to her face and drew in a deep breath. The warm vapour and scent of apple and ginger seemed to clear her head.

One warrior began to sing, and she put her mug up on the roof of the cabin before climbing up after it. She sat with her legs crossed, and joined in the warrior's song, as though it would somehow draw them closer to home.

Slowly, the sun set beyond the sea and the sky deepened in colour, grey, to blue, to black. Few stars came out to peer at them. The moon was a silver glow that teased behind thick clouds.

A plume of fire lit the southward horizon. Kesta got slowly to her feet. The silhouette of the walls of Fulmer Hold was burned into her retinas and she saw it long after the fire subsided. She was breathing hard, her fists clenched. Her power thrummed through her veins. With no regard for the strength of the ship's wooden frame, she created a tempest to drive them toward the beach. The three warriors did their best to hold the rudder and control the sail. Jorrun's ship rose on a high wave and was thrown onto the beach above the tide line. Kesta vaulted over the rail and landed in the sand. Her fingers twitched. Fury pressed out against the boundary of her skin.

Someone had attacked her home.

Someone was going to die.

She didn't wait for the warriors but sprinted for the dunes, scanning the beach as she did so. There was no enemy ship, no footprints of raiders. As she gained the path up to the causeway, she sighted a scout and two warriors hurrying toward her.

'Kesta Silene!'

'What's happened here?' She demanded.

'We were attacked by a sorcerer. He just appeared right in the middle of the hall with his men.'

'My children?'

The man turned pale. 'I don't know. We were sent—'

With an angry growl, Kesta shoved past them, pushing her muscles hard to gain the high causeway. The guards at the gate straightened up on seeing her, swiftly stepping out of her way. People were milling about outside their homes within the outer wall of the hold. Many of them still wore their finest clothes and wheat-stalk crowns from their harvest celebration. Someone called out Kesta's name, but she ignored it, slowing down as she saw the buckled and broken doors to the great hall. Inside, it was smoky. Men were still fighting the remnants of the fire. She stepped within and gasped. A huge hole had ripped through the building from the storeroom below to the vaulted ceiling. Bodies lay still about the wreckage of the room; men, women, and… Kesta swayed on her feet.

'Silene!' someone said in shock.

'Where's my mother?' Kesta turned to come face to face with Milaiya. The Chem woman's face was blackened with soot and a nasty bruise swelled her cheek and eye.

'The Icante isn't here, she went to Elden.'

'What?' Kesta's voice was quiet, but hard as flint.

'The children got away.' Milaiya reached a hand toward her, then quickly pulled it back. 'Eidwyn took them through the escape tunnel with Rosa.'

'Not Everlyn?'

Milaiya shook her head, tears breaking free in a flood down her cheek. 'She stayed to try to defeat the sorcerer.'

'And did she?'

Milaiya shook her head again and swallowed. She pointed toward the side of the room, and Kesta saw healers and warriors

272

working on a large group of injured. As the smoke cleared a little, she saw Everlyn lying unmoving, her left side scorched and blistered. Worvig was also there, a bloody stump where his right arm had been.

'Uncle!' Kesta flew across the room to throw herself to his side.

One of the already exhausted healers twisted to look at Kesta over her shoulder. 'He might live, but don't hold your breath,' she said, not unkindly.

'Who's taken charge?' Kesta forced the words out past her painful throat.

'That would be me.' Heara struggled up off the floor a little.

'Oi, don't you move,' the healer scolded, as she moved on to the next person.

Kesta's eyes ran over Heara's torn and bloody clothing. The scout's arm was bandaged, and a heavy wad of cloth was tied tightly across her back.

'All the Geladanians are dead save the sorcerer himself,' Heara reported breathlessly. 'There was no one here left who could stop him, though we tried. He's gone after the children. I sent out scouts and warriors, but other than monitoring his progress and sacrificing their lives to slow him down, there's not much they can do.'

Kesta stared at her, unable to speak.

Heara swallowed, closing her eyes against the pain. 'I managed to free the fire-spirits. Two of the assassins had them in traps. They were good, but not good enough.' Heara gave a low chuckle, her grin turning into a wince. 'They are doing what they can.'

'Do you know which way?'

'Eagle Hold would be my guess.'

Kesta didn't wait, but fled the great hall, snatching up a fallen sword as she went. As she drew close to the causeway, she saw a familiar figure on horseback trying to push his way through the bewildered crowd.

'Nip!'

The boy turned in his saddle, halting the pony.

'Lady Kesta?'

She ran, swinging up onto the pony behind him. 'When you get to the road, turn right, then fast as you can until I tell you to stop.'

'Yes, my lady.'

He spurred the pony forward, urging it into a gallop despite the darkness as soon as they reached the open road. As she held onto the Elden boy, something soaked into her sleeve. Blood.

'Where are you injured?' Kesta demanded.

He gave a quick shake of his head and said through gritted teeth, 'It's nothing.'

'If you collapse on me, I'll have to leave you.'

'Understood, My Lady.'

She quested out a little with her *knowing* despite her words, Nip had a nasty gash to his ribs, but right now the pain was just driving his anger and determination. There was nothing this boy could do against a sorcerer, but nothing under the sky was going to stop him trying.

'Here!' Kesta called out.

Nip reined the pony in and Kesta jumped down, calling a little fire to her hands to examine the ground. She nodded to herself. They'd fled not to the obvious closest Hold, but southward through the woods toward Eagle Hold.

'Wait here,' Kesta told Nip.

The boy gave a snort and slipped down from the pony, trailing her at a distance. She shook her head but didn't stop him.

The sky lit up as several streaks of fire blazed above the trees to the south.

'Azrael,' Kesta murmured to herself.

But it also meant the sorcerer had tracked the children.

She halted, something odd catching her eyes. She crouched and ran her fingers over the ground.

'Have you found something?' Nip whispered.

'Goats,' Kesta replied with a puzzled frown.

'They must have fled the hold.'

Kesta straightened up, scanning the trees. She sensed, before she saw, another flare of power and sprang forward in that direction, keeping to a steady jog.

Her initial fury had faded, a cold determined anger settled in her belly, sharpening her senses. She could smell the rotting leaves, the beginnings of a frost, and the sweat and blood on Nip. They came to a stream and Kesta jumped it to check what she assumed; sure enough, there were no tracks on the other side.

She chose upstream and followed the bank until she found the trail again; Rosa's boots, Eidwyn's softer shoes, and the hoofprints of several goats. She came to a point where the tracks split, some goats had broken into a run and fled. Her breath caught in her throat when she spotted a new set of prints. A man's large feet with a long stride.

Nip was falling behind.

Small, fiery lights darted between the trees. There was only one creature she knew that moved in such an erratic way. A frightened fire-spirit.

She took a risk. At worst, she'd draw the sorcerer toward herself and away from her children. She called her power, sending a flare up, but no higher than the trees.

Two lights sped towards her at once. Small, pale, almost shapeless. Even their eyes seemed to hold little fire, pale red now rather than blue.

Pity and concern squeezed Kesta's heart.

'We tried Kesta!' Azrael wailed. 'He's too strong.'

Kesta swallowed back the lump in her throat. 'Get back to the Hold. Ask for some oil to replenish yourselves.'

Both the drakes started up their mournful crying.

Kesta clapped her hands together loudly. 'Enough. Go and replenish yourselves at once, then come back and help me.'

Both fire-spirits flew up, then wove quickly northward.

Nip caught up to her, leaning against a tree and breathing hard.

'I guess it's no good me ordering you to go back.' She raised an eyebrow at the stable boy.

Nip said nothing, just pushed himself away from the tree and started trudging toward what he guessed was south.

Kesta shivered, not at the chill air, but with a sense of foreboding. She'd fought alongside Azrael many times, and she'd never seen the little spirit so drained. Then there was Everlyn. The *walker* was almost as powerful as Kesta was and experienced in fighting with magic, yet this man had left her for dead.

She caught up with Nip and overtook him. The tracks of the sorcerer now mixed in with those of the goats and her friends. She drew in a sharp breath at the sound of a voice not far away.

'Well. You're not what I was expecting.' A man's voice followed by a laugh.

Kesta ran, calling up her power. He was tall. Shadows sharpened his aquiline face as he called a ball of blue flame to his hand and spun to face Kesta. Rosa gasped, taking a few staggered steps backward.

Kesta raised her shield as Lorev hurled his fireball, but instead of deflecting his attack, she stole it, pushing her own power into his missile and sending it back against him. Again, he attacked, and again she made it her own. His grin turned into a snarl, and he hesitated as he considered how to get around her unusual tactic. Kesta didn't. She pushed her power down into the ground and ripped upward. Rosa almost fell, but Nip reached her just in time, both of them running out of the way of the two trees that toppled. Rock thrust like a solid geyser from the earth, spraying dirt and debris. Lorev shielded, creating a vortex of angry air to catch up the rocky splinters, and sent it at Kesta. She stood firm, holding her shield with her left hand while with her right she added fire to the tornado and wrested it from Lorev's control. Something burst in her nose and blood trickled over her lip, her muscles were shaking.

With a cry she ripped the tornado apart, the wild wind and debris spinning off in all directions to shake the trees. She hurled Lorev backwards, her heart huge and painful in her chest as it strained to endure. Fire caught in the branches and from those flames small creatures emerged, rapidly growing in size and ferocity. Three fire-spirits battered at Lorev's barrier; the sorcerer staggered as he fought to keep his waning shield. He reached for a box that hung about his neck.

Nip darted in and snatched it. The sorcerer hurled the boy and he tumbled across the forest floor to land in a broken heap, his body curled around the spirit trap.

Kesta's vision blurred as tears of rage spilled from them.

'Azrael, move!'

She reached out her power, thrusting it through Lorev's shield and reaching for his bones as she'd reached for the granite bones of the island. With shrieks, the three fire-spirits spun away. Kesta pulled out, Lorev's body was ripped apart, blood, muscle, and shards of bone sprayed out across the forest.

Kesta swayed on her feet, breathing hard. Rosa scrambled over the broken ground on her hands and knees, feeling in the darkness for the stable boy.

He gave a small moan and a sob came from Rosa. 'He's alive.'

'Kesta, Kesta, Kessta!' Azrael was making crazy loops around her head.

She sucked in a breath. 'Azra, go find Eidwyn and the children; bring them back here.'

Azrael bobbed, he and the unnamed spirit shot away, while Doraquael remained to illuminate the forest.

Kesta forced her feet to move, and she dropped to the floor at Rosa's side.

'Whatever were you doing trying to fight a sorcerer with a dagger?'

'It was that or a boot,' Rosa muttered in reply.

Kesta reached out to check Nips pulse. It was faint, but there. 'He's lost a lot of blood.' She turned and met Rosa's eyes, then flung her arms around the older woman to hug her fiercely. 'Thank you,' she sniffed, wiping at her nose and eyes with the back of her hand. 'Thank you for saving my children.'

Kesta felt Rosa shrug. 'Of course.'

Kesta sat back on her heels to regard Doraquael. 'Why did my mother leave the islands when she knew there were dangerous people hunting for Riddi and Joss?'

'The people were in Elden,' Doraquael replied, drifting closer. 'The Geladanians. The Icante went to confront them with the aid of Temerran and Bractiuss. She thought we could protect the children until you got here.' The fire-spirit sunk almost to the ground, his shape collapsing into an inverted teardrop.

Kesta nodded, although there was still a remnant of anger at her mother that tucked itself stubbornly in the centre of her chest.

'Who was the fire-spirit who came to help?'

'Tyrenell.' Doraquael perked up at once. 'Dia rescued him from a trap long ago, resscued him from Relta. Tyrenell owed your family a debt, I collected it.' The fire-spirit reddened in colour.

'Thank you.' Kesta sighed, twisting to see the wound across Nip's lower ribs that Rosa was examining.

'It's still bleeding.' Rosa looked up at her in concern.

'We need to bind it.' Kesta looked at the boy's torn and bloody shirt, then down at her own clothes.

'Oh.' Rosa straightened up. 'Excuse me a moment.' She pulled her tunic up over her head. Underneath it she still wore her long nightshirt, tucked into her trousers. 'I didn't have time to get changed properly.'

Kesta smiled. 'It will do for now.'

They had just finished tearing up Rosa's nightshirt and binding up Nip's ribs when light grew between the trees to the south. Kesta leapt to her feet. Eidwyn approached slowly, her shoulders slumped, her young face drawn with exhaustion, the two fire-spirits hanging back behind her. Around her trotted four goats and the two small figures riding them made Kesta's heart stop. She sprinted forward, grabbing Joss up off his goat and twisting to hug Arridia as well.

'Are you hurt? Are either of you hurt?' She breathed in the scent of them.

'No, Mumma,' Arridia spoke into her neck. 'I knew you'd get the bad man.'

'They've both been so brave.'

Kesta looked up at her mother's apprentice. She tried to speak her thanks, but she emotion caught the words in her throat. Eidwyn nodded, pursing her lips in a smile.

Kesta squeezed her children again, kissing Joss's forehead as she put him back on his goat.

She cleared her throat. 'The Hold is secure. I know it's a long way, but we need to get back.' She looked up at the fire-spirits. 'Tyrenell, thank you for your help today. Azra, can you fly to the Hold, get warriors to bring ponies and a litter for Nip.'

'Nip's here?' Arridia sat up straight.

Kesta tensed, someone was calling power. She threw a shield up around them, her hand going to her dagger as she spun about to try to see who was attacking them.

'Kesta!' Eidwyn stepped towards her, shaking her head and holding out her hands. 'Kesta it's okay, it's… it's Arridia.'

Kesta stared at the woman in confusion, pivoting to look at Arridia. Her daughter blinked up at her, cheeks a little flushed. It was the expression she wore when she was worried she was in trouble. Then Kesta noticed her eyes.

'Riddi?'

She knelt and held her daughter's face in her hands, gazing into her beautiful, violet coloured eye.

'How?' Kesta stammered.

Eidwyn swallowed loudly. 'We think she may have always had some power, that it was so normal and natural to her that it seemed a part of her. The attack triggered her to realise her powers as a *walker*.'

Kesta sat back on her heels. 'How did we not know?'

'It's all right, Mumma,' Arridia said, tears starting in her eyes. 'Everlyn and Rosa have been teaching me. I'll learn how to not feel into other feelings, I promise.'

Kesta rose onto her knees and hugged her tightly. 'You haven't done anything wrong, my honey, mummy has.'

'You haven't,' Eidwyn said softly. 'Why would you suspect a child is a *walker* when we've been taught such a thing isn't possible?'

'But Jorrun is her father. He was Arridia's age when he developed his power.'

'I didn't ssee it, neither did Jorrun,' Azrael interrupted.

The fire-spirit's words didn't ease her guilt, she felt sick. She glanced over her shoulder to the light of Doraquael, patiently waiting with Rosa and Nip.

'We should join the others and start heading back to the hold.'

Azrael took his cue and shot off.

'I'm not sure if Nip can walk,' Rosa said as they approached.

The boy stirred, trying to push himself up. 'I can,' he said hoarsely.

'If we wait, there's a pony coming,' Arridia spoke up.

Kesta listened, hearing nothing, then realised with a jolt. 'Do you sense the pony, Riddi?'

She nodded. 'Sorry, Mummy. When you said Nip was hurt, I wanted to find him. The pony was a long way away, by the cliff. It was on its own and scared, so I told it to come here.'

'Spirits,' Kesta swore, pivoting to stare at Eidwyn. 'She can reach that far?'

Eidwyn winced, shaking her head with a shrug.

Kesta calmed herself and smiled at Arridia. 'That was very kind, and the pony can carry Nip.'

***

They met the pony by the stream and Nip climbed up into the saddle without protest, drooping forward over the animal's shoulders. If she could be sure the way was safe, Kesta would have sent him on ahead with Eidwyn and one of the fire-spirits; protecting him at their slow pace was keeping him from the healing he desperately needed. Either choice was a gamble with the boy's life. Azrael came flying back to join them, circling the children several times as though to reassure himself they were there.

'Azra, how is the hold?' Kesta asked.

'Sad.' Azrael dropped to fly at Kesta's shoulder. 'Sshocked. But they are already rebuilding.'

'And… and my uncle?'

'He is hanging on, Kessta.'

Kesta took in several slow, shaky breaths, breathing out through her mouth. She stepped closer to the pony, placing a hand on its shoulder and sending warmth, love, and calm to Nip. Out of the corner of her eye she saw Arridia relax, but she herself could not. Arridia was an enigma. Third-generation *walker* and daughter of a powerful Chemman sorcerer. Was that what made the Geladanians fear her? But how could they know? Was it possible their goddess was real? Kesta clenched her fists. Real or not, the creature would have to go through her.

Torchlight bounced up and down ahead of them, and a little of Kesta's tension slipped away. Moments later twenty mounted warriors came surging through the trees, pulling up on seeing them.

'Silene,' one greeted respectfully. 'We are most heartened to have you here. The spirit said the sorcerer is dead?'

'The sorcerer is scattered across the forest floor,' Eidwyn replied before Kesta.

Nip sagged, almost falling, and Kesta reached out to hold him up. 'I need half of you to ride as swiftly as you can back to the Hold with this young warrior. Ensure he is seen to promptly.' She looked up at the fire-spirits. 'Tyrenell, if you would be so kind as to guard them, I would be most grateful, and consider your debt not only paid, but my friendship absolute.'

Tyrenell flew a loop, then moved ahead to light the way.

'Can I go with Nip, Mumma?' Arridia asked.

'No, my darling,' she told her gently. 'But we will follow fast behind. We'll ride the ponies with these brave warriors. Would you tell the goats for me that they should hurry back to the Hold? Tomorrow morning we'll feed them lots of treats for their loyalty and bravery.'

Arridia straightened up. 'I will, Mumma.'

They quickly organised themselves into two groups. Arridia rode with Kesta, Rosa with Joss, and Eidwyn behind one of the warriors. As they neared Fulmer Hold, deep exhaustion swept through Kesta, but she held her head up and greeted the many people who were still up and working on helping injured friends, or repairing their defences.

When they reached the great hall, the warriors led the ponies away. The grey tendrils of dawn were creeping up from the horizon.

Kesta turned to Rosa and Eidwyn. 'Would you settle the children? Then get yourselves some sleep.'

'Yes, Silene.' Eidwyn gave a bow which she struggled to straighten up from. The young woman was dead on her feet.

Rosa placed a hand on Kesta's arm. 'Come join us soon?'

Kesta nodded, but already her mind was racing ahead. She checked with the warriors to ensure everything was secure and advised them her recent battle with the sorcerer had yielded timber with which they could start repairing the Hold in the morning. She joined the healers, lending a hand where she was able, stopping to check on Nip whose wound was being stitched. She found Milaiya at Worvig's side and knelt beside her friend.

'How is he?'

Milaiya held her hands to her face. 'He is very weak, but stubbornly holding on. They cauterised the bleeding, but tomorrow will try to cut away the bad flesh and sew a flap of skin over the stump.' Her voice broke into a sob and Kesta put her arms around her, kissing her cheek.

'My uncle is the strongest man I know, he'll be fine.'

Worvig groaned, sweat beading his forehead. 'The children…'

'They are safe, uncle.' Kesta leaned forward and brushed back his damp hair. 'Sleep in peace.' She opened up her *knowing* and sent him calm, relaxation, and freedom from pain.

She found Heara next, stubbornly fighting to stay awake. 'The hold is secure,' Kesta reported.

'The sorcerer?'

Kesta showed her teeth in a grin. 'I tore him apart.'

Heara laughed, then blanched in pain. 'I failed—'

'Heara.' Kesta grabbed her hand and squeezed it tight. 'You have no magic, but you still beat them. You're the most amazing woman I know.'

The scout shook her head, but Kesta could feel her pride and peace returning.

'Get some sleep.' Kesta leaned forward to kiss her forehead. 'I'll need you tomorrow.'

Heara nodded, wriggling into a more comfortable position under her blanket as Kesta sent her sleep through her *knowing*.

She left the ravaged great hall and climbed the stairs. Her children had been put to bed in her mother's room. Eidwyn was curled up on the floor beneath a blanket, already sound asleep. Azrael drifted slowly along the length of the long window, his eyes on the sea below, while Doraquael watched the door. Rosa sat at the foot of the bed, wiping her eyes quickly as Kesta entered.

'Hey, come here.' Kesta hurried forward to hug her dearest friend. She was desperately in need of a hug herself and wished with all her heart that Jorrun were there. She'd been raised to rule, but that didn't mean she didn't need support. She longed to call him, but he had been due to attack Uldren and she had no idea how it was going, distracting him might prove dangerous. She would have to wait to speak to her husband.

Kesta glanced at the children; both appeared to be sleeping. 'Tell me everything,' she whispered, letting Rosa go but keeping hold of one of her hands. Rosa did so, starting with the messages from Teliff and Temerran.

'I owe you my world.' Kesta held her friend's gaze, while Rosa blushed a bright red.

'It's only what you taught me.'

'Nonsense.' Kesta squeezed her hand. 'You have always been clever and much stronger than you give yourself credit for. Come on, get yourself to sleep.'

Rosa nodded, stretching out along the foot of the large bed, and Kesta pulled a blanket up over her. She ensured four warriors remained on guard outside in the hallway, then made her way back down to the great hall to help the healers.

Chapter Seventeen

Catya; Free Provinces of Chem

Tucked safely within the boundaries of a tangled wood upon her horse, Catya gazed down on the valley, the cold wind blowing back her hair. Ruak flew low over the meadow, chasing his shadow as the sun sank behind the opposite hills. He lifted higher on reaching the trees, stretching out his legs to land on Catya's raised arm. Her eyes narrowed, her gaze following the line of mounted men who hugged a strip of trees on the bank of the narrow river. They had no supplies with them she could see and wore none of the emblems of a Free Province patrol. They were heavily armed, possibly bandits. The sun glinted on something silver.

Wolves?

Catya straightened in her saddle. If these men were indeed scouts from Eastern Chem, they were a very long way across the border—and they were heading for a village.

'I don't like that, Ruak.' She gave the raven a gentle push to shift him onto her shoulder. 'I don't like that one bit.'

She urged her horse forward, keeping a distance behind the men as she moved lower into the valley to follow their tracks. Her concern soon proved true as screams pierced the quiet evening. Ruak recognised the sounds of battle and knowing the bounty it might yield, lifted off Catya's shoulder and flew off towards the chilling sounds. Catya urged her horse into a gallop, but stopped short of the village, vaulting down, and unclipping her bow and quiver. She crept closer, staying low. The fight already seemed to be over. Several men lay dead on the ill-kept road. Two of the raiders came out of one of the small houses, one swigging from a skin and the other carrying a single, silver candlestick and some other loot. Catya shot the one with the wineskin through the throat. Less than three seconds later her next arrow burst through the looter's eye and into his brain; he didn't even have the time to cry out before he and his treasures hit the ground. Catya crept forward, her fingers finding the familiar silver brooch, still warm from the dead man's body heat.

She drew in a long, slow breath, shutting her emotion down, feeling nothing in response to the sounds coming from inside one of the buildings. She darted to a window, rising just enough to peer within. Two men, both occupied. She crept to the corner of the building, keeping her back to it as she slipped around to the front. Two terrified women ran from one house to another, carrying food and clay jugs. As soon as they disappeared, she moved to the door of her building, placing her bow on the ground and drawing a dagger. Catya eased the door open with painful slowness, stepping on her toes to reach the first man. She grabbed a handful of his hair to yank back his head and slit his throat.

The woman he'd been trying to force himself on screamed as his blood gushed out over her face and hands.

The second man scrambled to his feet, trousers around his knees. Catya flicked her dagger and it thudded into his chest. She leapt at him, pulling the dagger free and cutting his jugular.

'Stay in here and hide,' Catya hissed at the two women, not looking at their faces.

She peered out the door. Three men had come out, alerted by the scream, but hearing nothing else they laughed it off. Catya's blood boiled, heat burning her cheeks and throat. She took three arrows out of her quiver with her left hand and pushing open the door snatched up her bow. One man caught her movement. He was the first to die. She got the second, but the third was quicker. Catya dropped her bow and cartwheeled out of his way as his sword swept out. She drew two daggers, pivoting to face him, knees slightly bent. His lip curled a little as he adjusted his grip on his sword.

Catya made a feint and he fell for it, swinging his sword up to bring it down two handed toward her head. She flicked her right wrist and her dagger spun toward him; he batted it aside with a clumsy block. But not the second dagger she threw with her left hand. It caught him just below his sternum, and he staggered back with a grunt of surprise. Catya pushed up off her feet, springing onto her left hand and swinging both legs to kick him hard in the face. As her feet touched the ground, she backflipped, landing beside her bow. She snatched it up, nocked an arrow, and shot him through the back.

'Not another step, bitch.'

Catya pivoted, the last two men had stepped out into the open; one of them held a young boy in front of him, a knife to his throat.

'Drop your bow,' the man demanded.

Slowly, Catya did so, her eyes fixed on the raider's. As the bow lowered to her waist, she grabbed an arrow from her quiver and shot it at him. She wasn't quick enough. As her arrow penetrated the man's shoulder, he pulled the knife across the boy's throat. Blood soaked his tunic in a fast-growing wave. Catya froze, then rage pushed out from her chest, heating her body.

She charged, the bow falling as her fingers found her daggers. The injured man dropped his knife, reaching awkwardly with his wrong hand for the sword at his hip. Catya threw a dagger and it hit him just below his Adam's apple. The last raider swung his sword at her head, and she dived, rolling under his blade and up onto her knees to slice back-handed at the backs of his. He roared out a scream, crashing forward. Catya spun up onto her feet and slammed her dagger down into his back, again and again, fury trying to drown out her feeling of shame. Heara had warned her time and time again that her arrogance and over-confidence would get innocent people killed. She staggered back, panting, shaking her head. She should have been quicker; she should have been smarter.

She couldn't bring herself to look at the boy, averting her eyes as she quickly searched the men. Almost all of them wore a wolf insignia; and something else. Several of them possessed the six-pointed star of Warenna, the combining of the four triangles of earth, air, water, and fire, in the centre a gem that represented spirit.

She frowned, her eyes glazing over as she recalled the scouts who'd attacked herself and Cass at Warenna's river. One had worn a pendant, and another a ring with the symbolism of the Chemmish God of Magic. She couldn't recall any paraphernalia of the other gods.

The hairs prickled on the back of her neck and she glanced around. Some surviving villagers had crept to their doors to peer out. Catya couldn't bring herself to meet their eyes. She collected her weapons, tore a pendant from one of the raider's necks, then hurried to her horse and Ruak.

***

A smile came unbidden to her lips as she rode up over the high ridge and looked out across the vast valley. The river was a seemingly infinite silver snake, flowing down from the mountains that surrounded distant Arkoom, past Margith, then onward to Navere by the sea. It was a heart-wrenchingly beautiful sight, and she breathed it in, the cold dawn air burning the back of her throat. Condensation swirled up from her horse's nostrils as it too scented the air. Catya clicked her tongue and urged it forward down the narrow, steep track.

It took another two days to reach the harbour city, Ruak muttering and ruffling his feathers at the constant noise of the gulls. She acknowledged the salutes of the guards at the gate, observing the progress of the young runner who dashed ahead to announce her arrival to the palace of Navere.

It was two girls who came forward to take her horse from her when she reached the stables, and Catya headed for the guardsman's entrance to the palace rather than the front door. She grinned when she found Rece there waiting for her; the Chemman knew her too well.

'Cat.' He reached out his hand and she clasped his wrist.

'What's happening?'

A smile curled one side of the captain's mouth. 'Your report first, if you please.'

She looked up at him, her grin widening as they hurried through the corridors side by side, toward Osun's study. 'Of course.'

She gave him news of Caergard first, then all she knew of the proposed attack on Uldren. Beth and Calayna were both waiting in the study, and Catya drew her collection of wolf brooches and religious symbols from her pouch to show all three of them.

'We should show Kerzin,' Beth suggested. 'See if he knows anything.'

'Kerzin?' Catya regarded the woman with a frown.

Rece quickly filled her in.

'I knew a little of the situation.' Catya hopped up to sit on the edge of the desk, her eyebrows drawn together above her nose. 'Jorrun sent me to help.'

'What are you thinking?' Rece asked.

'I'm not sure I can get anywhere with Bantu myself. Kerzin is the obvious key there and Kesta has already won him over. Sadly, a man would be needed to infiltrate these Disciples. Also, I don't think they would let any woman near their plans. The young lad you're holding…'

'Alikan,' Calayna supplied.

'Yes. How much can we trust him now? Do you think we have his loyalty yet, or is it too soon?'

'What are you thinking?' Rece asked again.

'We let him and his brother escape, get Alikan to feed us information about who's involved and what they're planning.'

'No.' Calayna shook her head vigorously. 'He's just a boy.'

'And one who might be easily persuaded back to his own cause,' Rece added. 'His half-brother though, that might be an idea. Let him think he's escaped, see where he runs to and to whom.'

'What field Ravens do you have?' Catya regarded them all.

Rece shifted in his chair. 'We only have young trainees left, which is probably why Jorrun sent you back. We have Ovey, Neffy, Harta, and Charis.'

'Ovey and Neffy were on the raid on Alikan's family,' Beth said. 'So, they have some field experience.'

'They're just teenagers though,' Calayna warned.

'I'll need them,' Catya replied at once, raising an eyebrow; Ovey was about her age. 'Where are you keeping Alikan? I'd like to speak to him first before we put this plan together.'

'He's on the women's floor,' Rece told her.

Catya saw Calayna wince at the use of the palace's old name for the top floor.

She went to her room and quickly washed and changed before going up to meet the boy. She opened the small window to let Ruak out, but the raven stubbornly remained on her shoulder.

There were two guards outside the boy's room, Catya frowned, annoyance prickling her spine. The boy had power, if he turned out to be a spy, or was playing them to win his freedom, they'd regret not having a magic user watching over him. Even one Chemman sorcerer could destroy the palace, child or no.

She halted as an idea occurred to her, an idea that she knew the others would hate. Child Raven assassins could do a lot of damage in eastern Chem. She'd have done it. Perhaps there were other children who were like her.

She realised she was glaring at the guards and softened her expression. One of them recognised her and nodded to his younger colleague, and they moved aside. She knocked at the door, then stepped in. Ruak immediately spread his wings and set up a raucous cawing. Two pairs of wide eyes stared up at them, the blue eyes of a kitten, and the amber ones of a brown-haired boy. He scrambled to his feet, snatching up his kitten and turning protectively to put himself between Ruak and Trouble.

'Ruak!' Catya scolded.

The bird made a show of settling his feathers, but continued to mutter to itself, making a croaking sound in the back of its throat.

Catya smiled, aware she wasn't the best at being friendly. 'I'm Catya, I'm a Raven Scout. This is Ruak.'

The boy swallowed. 'I'm Alikan. This is Trouble.'

Catya did grin then. 'What a great name. Can we come in?'

The boy glanced at his kitten. 'Okay.'

The room was small, furnished only with a bed, a desk, and chair, and a cabinet barely taller than the boy. Bars obscured the window on the outside. Catya took hold of the back of the chair, pulling it towards the door to keep some distance between the bird and the cat.

Alikan put Trouble down on the floor. The kitten darted behind his legs, tail lashing.

'I've come here to help, with Kesta and Jorrun being away. I was their ward for several years; they took care of me.' Without going into anything too personal, she told the boy a little about herself, emphasising how much of a family the Ravens had become to her, surprised at how much it hurt to say it. 'I've been told you've been helping us, can I ask why?'

Alikan regarded her for a long time before he answered. 'Trouble told me to.'

Catya drew in a deep breath. The boy tensed, obviously expecting derision or disbelief. 'But you must have had reasons of your own, otherwise you would have said no to the cat.'

Alikan gazed down at the kitten. It was nodding off, still sitting up, but head drooping and watery eyes almost shut. 'Before I was caught, I was afraid every day. Since Trouble found me, since... since Kesta talked to me, I've felt safe.'

Catya swallowed, she knew that feeling all too well. She'd lived her life in terror until the day Jorrun had struck her uncle's head off his shoulders without a word. He'd hugged her, then taken her hand and led her into the Hold's keep and told her, 'No one will ever hurt you again while you're under my protection.'

She'd stepped out of that protection of her own free will, and although she tried to deny it, she missed that wonderful sense of security.

'I don't have magical powers,' Catya told him. 'But I can teach you lots of things—'

'Does Ruak talk to you?' Alikan interrupted.

'Oh, um. A bit.' She glanced at the bird on her shoulder, its eyes still fixed on the cat. 'He can say my name.'

'Really?' Alikan brightened.

Catya cleared her throat. 'Alikan, there are some bad people who want to hurt us, make us go away so things go back to how they were years ago in Chem. To how your family want things. Is that how you want them?'

The boy screwed his face up, his eyes following the pattern on the carpet. 'No, I don't think I want that. It's much nicer here.'

Catya shifted forward in her chair, unsettling Ruak. 'Then we need your help. I need you to tell me everything you can remember of the places you've lived, of the people your father and brothers met, and of any missions they sent you and them on against the Ravens. Would you do that?'

'What, everything?'

Catya nodded.

'Then can we… can we go outside?'

His face was so vulnerable, so open, Catya's heart gave a squeeze. 'Come on then. Best leave Trouble though.'

She held the door open and Alikan darted through, with a glance back at his sleeping kitten.

'Would you like us to accompany you, Master Raven?' one of the guards asked.

'Oh, but what about Trouble?' Alikan gazed up at the young man, then turned appealingly to Catya.

'One of you come with me and follow at a distance. The other can guard the cat.' Catya gave a bemused shake of her head.

'I'll take care of Trouble, young master.' The younger guard bowed toward the Chemman boy.

Alikan smiled at him. 'Thank you.'

They spent nearly three hours walking the gardens, Ruak flying off to do his own thing. Alikan chattered away, telling of his life in no particular order, growing slowly in confidence. Catya watched for any signs of duplicity, but either he was genuine, or the best actor Catya had met. Would Alikan have been able to fool Kesta and her *knowing*? Probably not, but she couldn't take any risks. Everything the boy told her would have to be backed up by evidence from the scouts before they acted on it.

Catya halted, watching as leaves drifted slowly down around them. 'Alikan, do you think we might persuade your half-brother to join us one day?'

Alikan kicked at the fallen leaves with the toe of his boot. 'I don't think so. I don't like him very much.'

'If he were to escape,' Catya said slowly. 'Would he try to rescue you, take you with him?'

'No.' Alikan looked up and scowled at her as though she were an idiot.

She almost laughed. She took in a breath and relaxed her face. 'And how likely would it be that you would break him out?'

'I wouldn't do that.' His face reddened, his amber eyes hardening.

'But,' Catya said quietly. 'Would he believe you would? If we pretended?'

Alikan's eyes widened. 'I… I don't know.'

'Come on.' Catya turned back toward the palace. 'It's getting late. Shall we find you some dinner?'

He nodded, hurrying to keep up with her longer stride.

'Where do you normally eat?'

'My room.'

Catya sighed. 'Where would you like to eat?'

Alikan shrugged. 'Maybe with Ovey, and Duco.'

'Duco?'

'My guard.'

'The young, handsome one?'

Alikan frowned at her. 'He's not as old as the other ones.'

Katya smiled to herself. 'I'll see what we can do.'

***

Rece wasn't convinced by her plan to get Alikan to help his brother escape, and Calayna flat out refused. She suggested instead that they make use of the priest's visit. They dispatched several scouts to look into the places and people the boy had mentioned. They also allowed Alikan to eat with them all that evening in their ornate dining room. The priest, Kerzin, was due to visit their prisoner the next day, and Catya made sure she was introduced to him.

She waited to one side of the audience room as the temple's administrator was announced. He didn't even glance towards her as he strode toward Rece and Calayna, greeting the captain first. Despite his supposed empathy, years of conditioning still made him dismiss women automatically. Catya grunted to herself, pushing away from the wall and walking silently up behind him.

'I'm Catya.'

Kerzin flinched, pivoting on his heels to stare at her wide-eyed.

'I'm a Raven Scout, from Elden.' She held out her hand and he leaned back as though she'd offered him a snake. It was hard not to grin.

Calayna didn't seem amused, her lips pressed together in a thin line. 'Kerzin, I apologise, we haven't had time to tell you yet. Kesta was called away to an urgent matter in the Fulmers, Catya was sent here to take over the matter of Bantu and his disciples.'

'This child?' Kerzin exclaimed.

'This child could slit your throat before you had time to blink,' Catya muttered.

Rece clapped his hands together and stepped between them. 'Catya is a very experienced scout and is very good at what she does, you need not worry about that. We have a plan regarding Bantu and need your help for it.'

Kerzin stopped scowling at Catya to regard Rece. 'Tell me.'

Rece did so, and the priest took two steps backwards, raising his hands. 'Oh, no. You want me to lie? To deceive and use the boy? It's bad enough that I'm giving him false hope.'

'You'd be no worse than the people he'll run back to,' Calayna said. 'And you're not giving him false hope, you gave him a chance to step away from the Disciples, a chance for us to grant him life. He hasn't taken it, has he?'

Kerzin reluctantly shook his head. 'He hates women of power with a passion.' He sighed. 'When did you want to try this plan of yours?'

Rece winced. 'During your visit today. Follow the directions we give you to get out, Catya will be waiting to trail you. As soon as you get him outside, tell him you have to go back to the dungeon and pretend he'd overpowered you also so you can avoid our suspicion.'

The muscles of Kerzin's jaw moved as he thought it over.

'All right, let's get this done.'

With a nod at Rece, Catya hurried to her room to grab all her weapons and shut Ruak out of the way. The raven wouldn't be impressed, but she couldn't let the bird give her away. It was a risky plan and involved several people, so there was a lot to go wrong. Ovey was to play dead in the hallway above the dungeons, his magic ready should anything go wrong. Three guards carefully picked by Rece would also pretend to have been taken out by Kerzin.

It was the priest himself that concerned Catya the most. Kesta trusted him, and that counted for a lot, but he wasn't a scout, and he certainly wasn't a Raven. A lot rested on whether the man could lie convincingly, and from what she'd seen, he abhorred deception almost as much as Cassien did. And yet... hadn't the man survived, surrounded by people he professed to hate and had subtly worked against?

Perhaps she should give the miserable-looking man a little more credit.

She hurried through the corridors to her appointed place, a door where tradesmen made their deliveries to the kitchens. She stepped away from the building, then ran at it, leaping to grab the thick branch of a sleeping wisteria that had been allowed to grow up around the door. She clambered up, perched and waited, her muscles beginning to strain before two figures burst out of the door.

'I can't go any further,' Kerzin panted. 'If they know I helped the heathens might attack the temple! I'll go back, pretend you overpowered me.'

The young sorcerer stood staring at Kerzin, eyes wide, shoulders rising and falling.

'You have somewhere you can go?' Kerzin prompted.

The boy nodded and swallowed. He looked frantically around the garden, his eyes lingering on the guarded gate before he spotted the two gardeners with their wooden ladder conveniently left propped against a tree. The gardeners themselves were really guards and had wandered away, as instructed by Rece, leaving the means of his escape unattended. Damel made a dash across the lawn, clumsily dragging the ladder and tipping it up against the wall. Catya jumped down from her perch and strolled after him.

When he gained the top, Damel pulled the ladder up and placed it over the other side. Catya raised her eyebrows, she'd have jumped it herself. She broke into a sprint, dashing through the gates and stopping out in the street. The ladder lay across the granite flagstones, Damel just disappearing down a side street. She should have brought Ruak after all.

Springing into a run again, she caught up just in time to see him take another turn. The boy was already out of breath and slowing; she wasn't surprised, according to the guards he'd done little but sit about and mope in his cell. She eased back a little, keeping a distance of a few yards. Damel didn't look back once, Catya shook her head at his arrogance, then remembered her own with a sharp stab to her heart. She gritted her teeth, and concentrated, surveying everyone around and behind her as often as she discreetly could; there was every chance the Disciples themselves had a watch on the palace.

Damel halted suddenly, looking quickly around himself, his eyes glancing over Catya. She continued her steady pace toward him, eyes slightly downcast. He'd never met her, never seen her as far as she knew. She let the air out of her lungs as he darted up some steps and hammered on a door. It was a building she knew; it belonged to a trader who'd been awarded a lucrative place in the foreign market that had been set up near the docks, replacing the evil slave trade with goods from Elden and the Fulmers.

The door opened and a short, tubby man stepped out, his thinning hair combed across his head. Catya couldn't quite catch their first words, but the man's face and neck reddened and he didn't seem too pleased to see Damel. The trader grabbed at Damel's arm and dragged him in with a rapid check of the street.

'You better not have compromised me, boy—'

The door slammed shut.

Catya sauntered past, taking a turning back towards the palace.

It was time to plan their move against the Disciples.

Chapter Eighteen

Dia; Kingdom of Elden

Tantony ushered them into Northold's great hall and Vilnue slumped into a chair, while Dia exchanged a quick hug with her husband.

'Brandy, quick!' Tantony waved to one of the hovering women. 'Tell me.'

It was Temerran who answered, rather than Dia, recounting everything that had happened at the castle.

Dia perched on one of the tables. 'If we leave Vilnue here with two Ravens to take care of Northold, will you come with us on the *Undine*, chase down the king's ship?'

'Of course.' Tantony straightened up. 'I take it they'll be heading for the Fulmers.'

Dia sighed. 'No doubt. They have two ships, their own has slipped away from Southport. We have to assume their high priestess is the greater threat.' She turned to glare at Linea through narrowed eyes. 'Were there any other magic users left at Southport we need to be aware of?'

Temerran moved closer to the Geladanian servant.

Linea shook her head. 'There were several assassins though. I can't be sure if any were still on the ship, or if they all left to hunt Elden for... for news of your family.'

Dia continued to hold her gaze, Temerran shifted his weight onto his other foot. The woman was guarded, frightened, but her words felt true. When Linea glanced at Temerran, Dia experienced the sharp wanting of Linea's attraction to the bard, and the tentative budding of love. Heat rose to Dia's own skin and she turned to Tantony.

'We need to go at once.'

Tantony nodded. 'I'll grab a few things and catch you up.'

Dia hopped off the table and reached out to squeeze Vilnue's hand. 'Thank you, Merkis. I'll send word as soon as I can.'

Vilnue winced. 'Sorry to let you down, Icante.'

She scowled and shook her head. 'You haven't at all.'

He forced a smile, looking from her to Arrus and Temerran. 'Good luck to you all.'

With a glance at Linea, Dia pivoted on her heels and strode out of the hall. The others followed, and Temerran's warriors scrambled to ready the rowboat to depart. Tantony hurried down the path to the lake, face red, his gait hitched as he struggled on his damaged knee. As soon as he was in the boat, they untied and pushed away, rowing swiftly to the waiting *Undine*. Temerran was shouting instructions before he pulled himself up onto the deck, and Linea's eyes barely left him. Concern swept through Dia, and she was amused at herself at the little twinge of jealousy. She loved Arrus with all her heart, but there was a place there for her close friend also.

Temerran turned to nod at her and she called up her power, creating a wind and filling the sails. The already lithe and swift *Undine* seemed to revel in the addition of magic, cutting across the lake like a hawk through the air as the sun rose on the horizon. Linea turned to Dia, her eyes wide and her lips slightly parted.

Temerran stepped up to Linea's side. The grin on his face and the light in his eyes was infectious.

'We should catch them in no time,' he said.

Dia drew in a deep breath, less optimistic than the bard. 'They too have magic, remember.'

He clicked his tongue. 'The king's ship is a lump of lead compared to the *Undine*.'

'She is a beautiful vessel.' Linea looked up at him and Temerran almost glowed in her approval.

Dia cleared her throat. 'Tem, we need to catch up. Alone.'

His smile faded, his eyebrows drawing together. With a glance at Linea he stepped away from her and toward Dia. 'I'll be back soon,' he told the servant.

Dia exchanged a look with Arrus and he gave the slightest of nods, before approaching Linea with a bright smile and some friendly words.

It was Temerran who broke the silence first as he and Dia entered his cabin.

'Linea, what do you make of her?'

Dia tried not to smile and sat slowly in Temerran's chair. 'There is a certain guardedness to her emotions, but then she is alone in an enemy country.'

'Can we trust her?'

'That remains to be seen,' Dia replied seriously. 'But her affection for you seems genuine enough.'

'Really?' His smile returned and Dia couldn't help the laugh that escaped from her mouth. Temerran straightened his spine and he gazed out through the window momentarily, before stepping forward to crouch at Dia's side. He took hold of one of her hands in both of his. 'Dia, I've been going mad. I think… I think I'm in love with Linea, but that would be crazy, I barely know her.'

Dia pulled at one of his red curls with her free hand. 'When I first met Arrus, I thought he was an oaf. I was actually much more drawn to calm, intelligent Worvig.'

'Really?' Temerran sat back on the floor to listen.

She nodded with a chuckle. 'Really. But I found that Arrus's playful nature, his loyalty, his outgoing friendliness somehow complimented my own personality perfectly. We brought out the best in each other, but for me it was a love that grew over months. If you ask Arrus, though…'

'What?' The corner of his mouth quirked up and he regarded her eagerly.

Dia gave a shake of her head. 'Arrus insists he fell in love with me at once, that the moment he saw me he knew he wanted me to be not just his lover, but his wife.'

She saw Temerran's muscles relax as he contemplated her story. His frown slowly returned. 'I know little of her, and from what I've learned, I don't much like the people she comes from.'

'The Fulmers were your enemy until you got to know us.'

Temerran winced. 'Actually, it was us who was always your enemy, until my people were desperate and needed yours. It was easier to raid a people we knew nothing of and could believe inferior heathens.'

Dia made a noise in her throat, he'd made an interesting observation. 'The Geladanians consider us and those of Elden in the same way. It's a shame diplomacy failed so badly.'

'From what Linea has told me, their devotion to their god is fanatical and absolute. Even if they thought us the best people under the sky, they'd still carry out her orders.'

'That's what scares me the most. Even if we beat off this assassination attempt, we will only win a reprieve. Unless they either think they can't beat us, or...'

'Or they think they've won,' Temerran finished slowly. 'Dia, do you have a plan?'

She leaned back in the chair. 'I have the beginnings of one, but I'm not sure of the details.'

'Tell me.'

Temerran listened, the concern not leaving his face.

'There are obvious flaws to the plan already,' she concluded quietly.

Temerran rubbed at his face with one hand. 'There are.'

She stood, squeezing his shoulder. 'I'd best get back out and create more wind, if possible, I'd like to take on the king's ship before we reach the open sea. I'll send Linea in.'

Temerran smiled, his face flushing a little. 'Thank you.'

Dia headed out onto the deck, immediately calling back her power. They'd already left the lake and were speeding down the wide river northwards.

'The watchmen on the lifting bridge said the king's ship had a two-hour head start on us.' Arrus joined her as Linea slipped into Temerran's cabin. 'And they were moving unnaturally fast.'

Dia clenched her jaw as she sent wind into the sails again. 'They will want to outrun any messenger Bractius sends to warn the Fulmers.'

He rubbed her back. 'You can catch them.'

'I'll certainly try.'

Arrus remained at her side as the shore sped by on either side. The day wore on with no sign of the king's ship, and the light faded from the sky. Tantony brought them over some food and drink.

'We should have brought Kurghan,' Tantony said. 'He knows the river better than I.'

Dia let her magic dissipate, her shoulders sagging. 'I need to save power to fight.'

'What if they reach the Fulmers before us?' Arrus held his mug before his lips, hesitating to drink.

'Heara and Everlyn will have to protect Fulmer Hold until we reach it. Arrus, would you fetch Temerran? He needs to guide the *Undine* while I get some rest.'

Arrus exchanged a glance with Tantony.

'Oh, for spirits' sake!' Dia growled. 'This is important.'

With a wince, Arrus swigged back his ale and hurried toward Temerran's cabin to knock firmly at the door.

Tantony cleared his throat. 'Rosa will keep your grandchildren safe, Icante.'

Dia smiled at him. 'I don't doubt it. I need to sleep. Wake me if you sight the king's ship.'

***

Dia's stomach churned. They reached Taurmouth without glimpsing the king's ship and worse still, the warriors who kept watch over the harbour insisted it hadn't passed through.

'Well, you must have been asleep!' Tantony all but bellowed, Dia had never seen the gruff, but kind-hearted man so riled.

The three warriors looking down on them from the high harbour wall all drew themselves up indignantly. 'I can tell you now, Merkis, we are very vigilante here. The king's ship never passed.'

Dia turned her gaze to Temerran. The Borrowman was leaning against the ship's rail, a deep frown over his green eyes. He sensed her watching and looked up. 'I swear, Dia, we did not miss that ship on the river.'

She nodded, narrowing her own mismatched eyes as she regarded Linea. 'What is your explanation for this?'

Temerran immediately straightened up, Linea lifted her chin a little as she held Dia's gaze.

'Icante, there are sorcerers in Geladan who can cast a small glamour to make themselves go unnoticed. I do not think they could hide a whole ship though.'

There was truth in the woman's words, but… Dia gave a slight shake of her head.

'Kichi.' Temerran strode across the deck towards Dia. His eyes were unfocused, concentrating on some other sense. 'She is much stronger than Ren was, she could have put the city to sleep or persuaded them they never saw the ship.'

'A bard can do that?' Fear locked her spine.

Temerran nodded, turning to Linea.

Was that the slightest hardening of her eyes, or had Dia imagined it?

Linea smiled at the bard, reaching out to place a hand on his chest. 'For you that might be possible, but a whole city would be a big ask for even a strong bard.'

Dia clenched her jaw and sighed. 'Whatever the case, we go on to the Fulmers.' She waved a hand towards Tantony and the Merkis reluctantly stood back from the rail, the skin of his face still flushed. She stepped away from Temerran and Linea to approach the four fire-spirits who huddled above a brazier close to the mainmast. Their colour had dulled during the last day. She didn't know how long they'd been kept captive away from their realm, but her heart bled at the knowledge these little creatures didn't have long left.

'Hello, Dia.' One of them made a small, tired loop.

Dia sat on the deck, cross-legged. 'Tell me all you can of Jderha. Is she really a God?'

The little drakes all clustered closer and Dia had an overwhelming desire to hug them all, fire or no.

'She really is,' one spirit said. 'Ass far as we understand it. Jderha is an ancient being of extraordinary power.'

'And yet she fears a child and an earth-bound spirit?'

'Sshe does.' Another spirit came forward. 'She has known the means of her death for many years and fears it obsessively. Earth-bound spirits were murdered in Geladan, along with their priestess.'

'Tell me more of that.' Dia shuffled to make herself more comfortable and closed her eyes. 'If I understand, I might find an answer.'

She felt the warmth of the other two drakes as they moved in.

'In Geladan, sometimes when a beloved fire-priestess grew close to death, she would give her soul to allow a willing spirit to come through to the earth realm. That spirit would then find a new fire-priestess to sserve. They worked together to grow in wisdom, but they alsso grew to love each other very much, and to fear and question the will of Jderha. When the prophesy was told, the High Priestesses and the sorcerers were told to slay the earth-bound spirits. The fire-priestesses fought to save them and were also cut down. One of the most ancient spirits made a pact with a fire-priestess, and she gave her soul for him to come through. He led those who survived and they fled in a ship, north, across the sea, many, many years ago. The spirits lied and fought against Jderha's will—'

The three other fire-spirits wailed and shrieked, Dia felt them dart around her frantically.

'—and we ssaid that the ship was destroyed. It was not. It came to the Fulmer islands.'

Dia opened her eyes and blinked at the deck. 'And Temerran unwittingly gave us away.'

'He did.' One of the spirits hovered before her face.

'Can we really kill this god?'

The fire-spirit hissed. 'Prophesy says so.'

'And what of the High Priestess and bard we pursue?'

'Icante, I could not ssay. But we believe in you.'

The other three squealed their agreement.

Dia's heart was a tight, painful knot in her chest, but she drew in a deep breath and stood up. She met the eyes of her husband, who was waiting close by. She called up her power and filled the sails.

'Temerran, call your sea spirits, I want to know where that ship is.'

Temerran gave a low bow. 'Yes, Icante.'

'Dia,' one of the fire-spirits whispered. 'If we sstay, when we catch up with the High Priestess, sshe will make us fight you.'

Dia rubbed at her face and nodded behind her hands. To free the spirits, to protect her grandchildren, the High Priestess had to die. 'Do you want to stay behind?'

'We want to help, if we can,' one spirit replied.

Dia nodded.

Temerran had climbed over the railing at the prow and balanced behind the figurehead, Linea watching him with wide eyes as he sang. The *Undine* rose suddenly, tilting to the right as a large wave formed below them. The deck tipped and Arrus darted forward, grabbing Dia around the waist with one arm and taking hold of a line with the other. The ship dropped, leaving Dia's stomach behind as sea sprayed up over the sides, washing across the deck. Linea lost her footing and Dia tried to pull away from Arrus to help her, but his grip was too tight. She drew in a breath to cry out, but Temerran's first mate, Nolv, slid across the wooden planks to snatch at Linea's hand and kept her from going over the side.

'Tantony!' Dia looked around frantically, almost collapsing in relief when she saw the Elden Merkis was somehow still standing despite his damaged knee.

The sea calmed, becoming as flat as a mirror for about a mile in each direction.

Temerran ceased singing and Arrus let Dia go, following as she ran across the deck to the prow.

Three figures were rising from the water, all feminine in shape, their features as varying as one human's from another; hair streaming in an endless fall of white, foamy seawater.

'Why do you trouble us, bard?' one of the sea-spirits whispered sibilantly. 'Already you and the fire-witch owe us a debt.'

'Mighty queen of the sea.' Temerran gave a low bow. Movement caught Dia's peripheral vision and she saw Linea was creeping forward beside Nolv. 'There are some who have come from the south who enslave spirits. We wish to stop them before they do you harm.'

'He speaks truth.' One sea-spirit turned to her sisters. 'What do you want of us?'

'Your help.' Temerran leaned over the figurehead. 'We must destroy their ship.'

The three spirits turned to each other, forming a circle facing inward. Dia heard no sounds, but from their changing expressions they clearly conversed. After a moment, they broke apart to drift closer to the *Undine*.

'We will not go near them,' one spirit said. 'We will not risk enslavement.'

Dia's anger rose and she had to restrain herself from calling up her power, recalling the painful lesson one of the sea-spirits had taught her for threatening it many years ago when she'd helped save the Borrows. She saw Temerran stiffen, but before the bard could speak, one of the spirits did.

'We can tell you the Elden king's ship followed the coast and has headed southwest, not toward the Fire Islands you call the Fulmers.'

'Do you think they are returning home?' Arrus asked.

Temerran glanced at Linea before replying. 'The Geladanians are fanatical, they won't return home with their mission incomplete.'

'They are likely meeting their other ship, captain,' Nolv suggested.

Temerran nodded. 'And despite the *Undine* being the better ship, they've accrued quite a head start.'

Dia's skin tightened with a flush of heat to her cheeks. She didn't like failing, and she didn't enjoy the feeling of guilt it bought. She cleared her throat. 'I'll call to the whales, ask them to track the two ships for us.'

'Call them, fire-witch,' one spirit hissed. 'And we will take the *Undine* closer. Hold tight.'

'Get below!' Temerran called out in warning.

The bard barely had time to climb back over the rail before the sea rose again into wild waves. Dia took Arrus's hand and they hurried into Temerran's cabin. Tantony and Linea followed, but Nolv stayed out on the deck with his captain. The *Undine* gave a single groan, then was lifted onto a towering wave that threw them west along the coast. Dia dreaded to think what its aftermath would do to the shoreline. Linea went to the window, placing her hands against the leaded glass, her breath misting the small panes.

'Can you call the whales without touching the sea?' Arrus asked Dia in concern.

She shook her head. 'I'll have to wait until the spirits put us down. Where's Shevi?'

'She was helping down in the galley,' Arrus replied. 'I, um… I think she's taken a shine to one of Temerran's Borrowmen.'

Dia rolled her eyes, her gaze falling on the silent Linea. 'Do you have friends on the ships we pursue, Linea?'

314

The Geladanian servant stiffened ever so slightly before turning to smile at Dia. One hand gripped the window ledge and Dia realised the young woman was afraid.

Dia softened her tone. 'The sea-spirits are wild and sometimes malevolent, but they won't harm the Bard of the Borrows.'

'In Geladan, the spirits are not so... wild,' Linea replied. 'They obey and have no ill will of their own.'

'I imagine they have plenty of ill will,' Tantony muttered. 'They are just not allowed to show it.'

'Sit, please.' Dia indicated one of the chairs and Linea scurried over to take it. Dia took the other chair and Tantony sat heavily on Temerran's sea chest, stretching out his knee. Arrus helped himself to the bard's brandy. 'Do you know anything of Yalla's plans?'

Dia's abrupt question seemed to take Linea off guard.

'Oh... oh, no, she was not a woman to confide in others.'

Dia carefully drew up her *knowing*. Linea was nervous. She was also clearly thinking of Temerran. Dia placed her hand over her mouth, withdrawing her *knowing* to compose herself. 'But you were her servant?'

'No, I served the whole delegation. I'm sorry, if I knew more, I would tell you.'

Arrus handed her a glass of brandy, then sat on the table behind Dia. The ship tilted suddenly, briefly, both Linea and Tantony crying out in alarm.

The cabin door opened and swung back with a bang as the ship's momentum tore it from Temerran's hand. 'Everyone okay?' He headed straight to Linea, placing a hand against her cheek. 'We've just turned south.'

'Turned my stomach, too.' Tantony swigged back his brandy.

'The spirits think the High Priestess is using captive air elementals to move so swiftly. They will take us to where the two ships were last sighted,' Temerran told Dia. 'Then it will be down to your whales to track them.'

'And what then?' Arrus's eyebrows almost bristled.

'A sea battle.' Temerran shrugged and then grinned. 'What a Borrow ship was made for.'

***

Dia held fast to the rope, leaning out over the water as the *Undine* lifted and plunged. Temerran gripped the other end of the rope, his legs braced against the ship's railing. Cold salt spray stung her face and she blinked rapidly, trusting her friend as she stretched out further to touch the skin of the whale. It was cold and surprisingly rough, like the shell of an egg. She reached out her *knowing* and the whale reached back, showing her images of two ships as seen from below, the light dancing across the surface of the moving sea like constant ribbons of lightning. The ships came together, tiny shapes clambered across, then the ships parted, one going south, the other west.

'Thank you, my friend.'

Dia withdrew her hand and the whale sank below the surface.

She cursed under her breath.

'Dia?' Temerran's eyebrows drew together in concern as he helped her back over the rail.

'They've split up,' she told him through gritted teeth. 'We can only pursue one ship.'

316

'Fulmer Hold?'

She nodded slowly, nausea swelling uncomfortably in her stomach. 'Although… the Hold is reasonably protected, and if I know my daughter she will be there by now, possibly Jorrun too.' She closed her eyes and clenched her fists. 'We chase the ship heading south.'

Temerran wet his lower lip as he regarded her, but he nodded slowly. He pivoted on his heels to shout his commands while Dia moved carefully across the rolling deck. Arrus held out his hand to her as she joined him and Shevi.

'Shevi, if I guide you, could you fill the sails? I need to hold back my power to fight.'

The novice Raven gave a single, firm nod, calling up her power and manipulating the air.

'What is it?' Arrus touched her arm.

'I've had to make a choice; I can only pray it was the right one.'

'If it isn't, we'll deal with it, anyway.' He quirked his bearded mouth up in a smile and stepped forward to hug him.

'Sail!' One of the Borrowmen yelled down from the crow's nest.

'Keep going,' Dia urged Shevi.

Temerran's voice cut above the wind. 'Archers to the deck!'

Tantony hurried over and Dia pointed toward Shevi. The Elden Merkis changed direction at once, halting at Shevi's back with his hand on his sword hilt.

'I have a feeling I'm going to really miss Heara,' Dia muttered.

The Borrowmen scrambled to the railings, many carrying spears as well as bows. Temerran took the helm himself, Nolv striding the deck to shout commands.

Dia had to slow her breathing as they drew closer, the ship looming larger. Not the ship of the Elden king, but a sturdy-looking vessel of a dark, almost black, wood. Dia reached out her *knowing*, impressed at the calm of the *Undine's* crew. The four fire-spirits in contrast were in turmoil, and she tried to quiet them.

'What do we face?' Gilfy and her other bodyguard joined her and Arrus, both carried bows.

'They have but one air elemental,' Dia replied without turning. 'It seems they may have bet on us pursuing the king's ship or heading to Fulmer Hold.'

Her stomach shifted, tightening into a knot.

Or perhaps they were the decoy.

The distance closed, Shevi straining to keep up her power. Dia drew up her own, forming a huge ball of flames between her hands. She blasted it toward the Geladanian ship, but it hit an invisible wall, spreading and dissipating. She threw another and again it struck the magical barrier. Dia smiled slowly. The Geladanian ship was slowing and the *Undine* swiftly gained. It appeared the air-elemental was alone in being able to defend the ship and was unable to do both that and drive the sails.

Then a voice rose, as pure and hypnotic as moonlight, carrying across the sea against the wind. The muscles of the warriors grew slack, some of them dropping their bows. The frantic fire-spirits stilled, their colour dulling to orange. The sails flapped loosely as Shevi's arms dropped to her sides.

Dia withdrew her *knowing*, clamping it down tight. She looked around frantically. Even Arrus was staring straight ahead with glazed eyes. She caught sight of Temerran at the wheel, his green eyes wide and alert, his forehead creased in fear. Their eyes met.

'Dia, take the wheel!'

Temerran let it go, leaping down onto the lower deck as Dia sprinted for the stairs. The ship tilted and lurched and she lost her footing, rolling across the deck to land hard against the cabin wall.

Where's Linea?

She had no time to wonder. Her arm and thigh throbbing she pulled herself up and attempted to gain the stairs again. She used her hands to pull herself up and staggered to the wheel. She grabbed for the spokes and the muscles of her arms tore as she tried to wrestle control.

Temerran's voice rose, strong, deep, as powerful as the sea.

The warriors stirred, Nolv glancing about, eyes widening at the sight of Dia fighting the wheel. Gilfy reached the Icante first, cheeks flushed with embarrassment.

Something struck the mast and it gave a crack, then a groan, before slowly falling back. The lookout dived from the crow's nest into the water.

'Ware!' One of the Borrowmen screamed.

They scatted as the mast smacked down onto the side of the ship, shattering the railing. The *Undine* tilted alarmingly. Tantony grabbed Shevi's ankle as she slid across the deck, trying to halt their slide using his fingers and boots.

'Cut it away!' Nolv bellowed. Even as he did so, Borrowmen snatched up axes, climbing the upright stump of the mainmast to chop at the thin sliver of wood that still held, and the ropes that would drag them down.

As Temerran sang to counter the spell of Kichi, Dia called back her own power. The four fire-elementals had flown higher above the ship, circling something like crows harassing a hawk.

There.

Barely visible, she caught the ripple of the air-elemental. She had no idea how to destroy it, but the fact it was playing a dodging game with the drakes suggested fire might work.

Or perhaps water.

She called flames to her hands, waiting until the elemental was clear of the remaining masts, keeping her balance as the mainmast slipped away over the side. There was a hum and a buzz as several arrows were loosed. They were almost upon the Geladanian ship.

She sent a blast toward the air-elemental, her heart clenching at the knowledge the creature was most likely attacking against its will. A blast of cold met hers and she felt the impact, her feet sliding on the sea-drenched wood. Hands pressed against her back and young Gilfy grunted with effort as he braced her. The fire-spirits tried to join in, but they were weak, one of them dropping and pulling up just in time before it hit the deck.

'Fire!'

With Temerran and Nolv occupied, Arrus had taken over directing the warriors. Thuds and screams told that they were now within shooting distance of their enemy.

Whistles filled the air as the Geladanians struck back, but their arrows were thrown aside as Shevi called up wind. The young woman collapsed to her knees, Tantony pulling her out of the way, as she drained the last of her power.

Dia forced more power into her blast, aware that the singing had changed. Both Kichi and Temerran's words came faster, the pitch and tone altering.

'Ware the water!' A Borrowman warrior pointed down.

'Fire when you're ready!' Arrus drew his sword. They would be alongside in moments.

A murmur went up among the warriors. 'Sea-spirits.'

Dia's power wavered, and for a moment the air-elemental pushed closer. Who were the sea-spirits here for, Temerran, or the Geladanians?

With a cry she drew more power and sent the air-elemental hurtling back to rip a burning hole through one of their enemy's sails. Both ships exchanged arrows, some Borrowmen hurling their spears. Dia quickly threw up a shield, but several Borrowmen fell and around them the sea seethed and boiled.

There was no time for a conscience.

Dia drew in air and blasted a hole in the Geladanian ship, just below the waterline. She drew more power and threw several fireballs at their sails before the air-elemental swept in to put them out with bursts of frozen air.

The *Undine's* hull gave a wooden scream and Temerran cried out as though in pain.

Dia ran to the railing while the fire-spirits circled the air-elemental. She looked down into the furious black eyes of a sea-spirit, its body a swirling, dark green. Its liquid fingers were reaching into the minute gaps between the *Undine's* overlapping planks. Dia's own anger rose, along with her fear. As Temerran's singing started up again, ripples ran across the spirit's liquid skin like a shiver. It tried to withdraw from the ship, a gurgling scream ripped from its throat, and Dia knew the bards were fighting to control it.

She shook her head, nostrils flaring, and she backed away across the deck. Several Geladanian warriors had leapt or swung over onto the *Undine*, and Arrus had already engaged one. Gilfy flanked Dia, knife and sword ready, as she reached again for power, stilling and cooling the air, then rapidly heating it. Clouds built, the air grew heavy, a thunderhead formed above the battling ships. Dia poured all of herself into it, building the pressure, then she drew it down.

Fork after fork of lightning struck at the Geladanian ship, one of them striking the air-elemental as it shielded Kichi. Another hit the sea-spirit, lighting it up from inside as it sprang back from the *Undine*.

'Cut the ropes! Cut us free!' Nolv commanded as warriors fought around the first mate, who still clung to the wheel.

The Borrowmen obeyed, cutting through the ropes and removing the grappling hooks that tied them to the burning Geladanian ship that was sinking from the stern.

Kichi's voice increased in volume.

Temerran closed his eyes, struggling for the calm he needed to control his voice.

Dia raised her hands above her head.

Lightning lashed down, striking Kichi. She convulsed, seeming to fold inward and collapsing to the deck. She didn't move. Smoke rose from her corpse.

'Get us clear,' Temerran yelled.

The last few Geladanians were still fighting fiercely, but the *Undine's* crew worked around them to get away from the stricken

322

enemy vessel. Dia ducked aside from a swung sword, leaving Gilfy to take on the desperate man while she leaned back over the rail.

The sea-spirit was there, glaring balefully up at Dia. Three others slowly rose to join her.

'Are you all right?' Dia called down.

The spirit who'd been forced to attack the Undine sank below the waves without a word. One of the others spoke.

'You saved our bard, fire-witch.'

'He endangered himself and his crew to help me,' she replied. 'He is my friend.'

'Fire and water cannot be friends.'

'Why not?'

The spirit's hair flowed in an endless stream while she regarded the Icante. 'I have no answer for that.' Without another word, she melted away, her sisters with her.

Dia coughed as smoke drifted across from their enemy's vessel, only the fore-deck now above water; then the waves closed in and it was gone.

'Dia?' Arrus grabbed her arm, turning her to look closely at her face.

'I'm fine.' She forced a smile. 'The *Undine*?'

'Tem has lost a few good men.' He shook his head. 'And the ship is damaged. I'm not sure which hurts the bard more.'

Dia straightened up. 'I imagine there's healing to do.'

Movement caught Dia's peripheral vision and she turned to see Linea open the cabin door. As soon as she saw it was safe, the turquoise-eyed servant ran across the deck to throw herself at Temerran.

Dia chastised herself for her scorn, the woman wasn't from the Fulmers; she wasn't a fighter or a magic user; out of the way in the cabin had been the best place for her.

Temerran caught Dia's eyes and hurried over, his arm still around Linea. 'What now?'

'We need to get to Fulmer Hold as quickly as possible.'

Temerran surveyed his ship and winced. 'We can sail, but not at the speed they were moving.'

Dia reached for her power. She had some left, but it stung to draw it through. 'Make ready, we'll have to do the best we can.'

'What if we don't get there in time?' Gilfy asked.

Dia turned to look out across the sea. 'If Fulmer Hold has fallen, we'll just have to take it back.'

Chapter Nineteen

Jorrun; Eastern Chem

'Kesta?' Jorrun peered into the bowl, leaning low over the water. His heart lifted as his wife's image formed, then a spiked fist squeezed it when he saw the dark bruising on her skin. She wiped a stray tear from her lashes.

'Kesta? What's happened? The children—'

'Safe.' She raised a hand. 'Fulmer was attacked by a Geladanian sorcerer. I defeated him; but the Hold was badly damaged. Uncle… Uncle Worvig may not make it.'

Jorrun closed his eyes. 'I'm so sorry, Kesta, I should have been there.'

She shook her head. 'Your sister?'

His mouth automatically lifted with a smile. 'I have her, along with eight women and four children.'

'I wish I could kiss you.' Kesta grinned.

'Likewise.' His smile slowly faded. 'I've a few things to clear up here, but I'll be with you as soon as I can.'

'I look forward to it. Jorrun… Arridia is a *walker*.'

'A…' He frowned and shook his head, sure he must have misunderstood. 'I was around her age, maybe a year older, when I manifested—'

'No, Jorrun, she is a *walker*.'

'But I thought …'

'*Walkers* only gain their powers close to puberty.' Her mismatched green eyes were wide. 'That has always been the case. And there has never been a third-generation *walker*. I think it… I think it's your blood, Jorrun.'

He shook his head. 'Not just mine, you are the daughter of Dia, and powerful in your own right.' He wondered for a moment if there might be any truth to the Geladanian god's prophecy, but dismissed it at once. 'Stay safe, I'll be with you when I can.'

She nodded, reaching two fingers toward the water; then her image was gone.

It was a while before Jorrun was able to bring himself to move. He allowed the assault of emotions to flow through him, before taking control and straightening his spine. He tipped the water from his scrying bowl and made his way back to the camp, Jagna giving him a thin-lipped smile. He quietly told his friend what had happened in the Fulmers and the Chemman cursed.

'Would you like me to go with you to the Fulmers?' Jagna placed a hand on his shoulder.

Jorrun shook his head. 'No, my friend, I need you to help Kussim hold the border, if you're willing?'

'Of course.'

Jagna moved away to check the perimeter of their camp and settle the horses.

Jorrun's gaze fell on his sister and remained there. It was a while before he realised he was staring and he forced himself to turn away. If he was honest, he didn't remember Dinari, but the lifting of her chin, the curve of her neck, her confident efficiency, were all their mother's. The moment they'd stopped, Dinari had the women organised into preparing supper and setting up temporary shelter from their supplies. Tyrin, Meric, and Rothfel's remaining scout divided up the watch between them and Jorrun observed the young men with pride.

He was prouder still of his sister.

Sensing she was being watched, the tattooed woman glanced up. With a final quiet word to Topei's mother, she got up and approached Jorrun.

'You look so much like her,' Jorrun whispered, a painful lump in his throat. 'Are you aware how our mother died?'

Dinari held his gaze a moment, then shook her head. 'Tell me.'

Jorrun did so, unable to meet her mismatched eyes. Guilt clawed at the inside of his stomach when he told of how Naderra had given her life to save himself and Osun.

Dinari was silent for a while, then she settled to sit more comfortably. 'You and Osun were in a position to change Chem in one direction or another, I was not.'

'But I took so long—'

She placed two fingers on his lips. 'I am well, brother, I have survived.'

'But the life you had…'

'Take a look, little brother, at the women here, with us. They are silent because they don't yet know or trust you, but see how they work together in that silence, how the children are comforted, how they support each other. Observe how even Seren, Topei's mother fits in to the elegant dance, knowing what is needed, helping as she can. The women of Chem learned to build their own world, in secret, with strength and pride.

'There is pain, there is fear; there are always those. But we also find life; sometimes we even find joy.'

Jorrun clenched his teeth, anger and guilt pushed against his ribs. 'Even so—'

'Even so.' Dinari slapped her hand hard against his chest so it made a hollow sound. 'The fire-spirits knew, our mother knew, that you and Osun needed to change the world. Perhaps I have a part, perhaps women do—'

'Oh, but they do!' Jorrun grabbed her hand in both of his. 'Let me tell you about my Kesta, about my wife. And her mother.' He grinned. 'I can't wait for you to meet them.'

They talked long through the night, while the clouds drifted over the faces of the stars. Their small fire burned down to low, warm, red embers as Jorrun spoke of his children, and of his scatter-brained but heart-wrenchingly loyal friend, Azrael.

He sat bolt upright, as though someone had shot lightning through his spine. 'Oh, but you don't know!'

She scowled at him in feigned annoyance. 'What?'

'Kussim, your daughter, we freed her years ago. She now runs the Coven in Caergard.'

Dinari's eyes grew huge. 'Kussim?'

Jorrun nodded, glancing around to ensure he hadn't woken anyone. 'You'd be so proud of her.'

Dinari's expression stilled, and the fading firelight seemed to cast her face in deep shadow.

'Sister?' The word was both strange and honey on his tongue. 'What is it?'

'I have borne six children in my life, Jorrun. Four daughters and two sons.'

Fear froze his jaw, but he forced it to move. 'Do you have any word of the others?'

She rubbed at her face, breathing out loudly. 'My eldest boy died fighting for our father.'

'Fighting who?' Jorrun asked in alarm. He grabbed her arm when she didn't answer. 'Fighting who, Dinari?'

'He served his father in Mayliz.'

Jorrun swore and leapt to his feet. She caught at his hand to stop him walking away.

'He was lost to me years ago. Some sons can be saved, some cannot.'

'And the others?' he asked without looking around. Nausea pressed up against his sternum, and he held his breath. There was every chance he himself might have killed his nephew.

'The son I bore in Parsiphay is still there as far as I'm aware. He would be nine now. His name is Jereth.' Jorrun forced himself to turn and found her smiling up at him. 'One of his sisters I also left there when I was sold; she is named Eila. My other two daughters are, Ylena – who is thirteen and full sibling to Jereth and Eila. She was sold to Telloch when she was only seven. My youngest, Dierra, I have no news of. I had to leave her behind in Farport when I was sold to the trader who brought me to Uldren.'

'We'll trace their records.' Jorrun crouched, placing a hand against her cheek. 'We'll find them.'

She smiled and nodded, but there was no hope or belief in her eyes. Like most of the women in Chem, she'd learned to live without either.

He sighed. 'We should get some sleep.'

'Brother, stop tearing your soul to shreds,' Dinari said as he slowly stretched out on the blanket beside her. 'Tonight, because of you, I sleep in safety and hope for the first time in my life.'

***

A patrol awaited them on the western bank of Warenna's river, their captain reporting to Jorrun as soon as they gained the shore.

'Has there been trouble?' Jorrun asked in concern.

The man winced, glancing over the group that followed behind him. 'We have found a few more of those men bearing the wolf insignia. They seem to be worshippers of Warenna.'

'Not Hacren?' Jorrun sat up straighter in his saddle. 'A new faction then.'

The man gave a curt nod. 'Raven Kussim has been researching and studying the reports. She's found no link between Warenna and the wolf. She was concerned about your return and we were sent to escort you.'

'My thanks.' Jorrun swallowed back any pride. It was better to be cautious than overestimate your own ability. 'We had to leave Cassien and Rothfel behind with an injured comrade. If you can spare men to watch for them, I'd be grateful.'

'I'll patrol the riverbank myself with four others,' the captain offered at once.

'Should I stay with them?' Young Tyrin offered.

Jorrun hesitated, rubbing at his beard. 'No, come back with us. As much as I'd like to, I can't linger in Caergard and must get back to Navere, and to Fulmer. I'd prefer for you to return with me, Tyrin.'

Tyrin gave a nod, and Jorrun didn't blame the young man for relief in his eyes.

The sun was low as they reached the city gates of Caergard and they were ushered straight to the audience room. While Pirelle and Dalton stood formally on the raised dais, Kussim hurried forward to meet them. Her thin coat of chainmail was hard, but warm, as Jorrun hugged her.

'Kussim.' Her name caught in his throat as he stepped back. 'We have your mother.'

She stepped back, standing on her toes to peer past him. He couldn't turn around, afraid his careful control would slip. Kussim ran to her mother and the tattooed woman enveloped her in her arms, the swirling tattoos showing as her sleeves were pushed back.

Dalton cleared his throat. 'How did it go?'

Jorrun snatched gratefully at the distraction, speaking around the painful lump in his throat. 'We took out a large portion of Uldren's coven and, as you see, liberated several of their women of blood.'

'Where's Cassien?' Kussim's worried voice cut into their conversation.

'He stayed behind to help an injured friend,' Dinari replied.

Jorrun drew in a breath and turned to face his niece. 'Cassien is an excellent scout, he won't be far behind.' But her wide, watering eyes made Jorrun doubt his own words, and his choice to leave Vorro, Rothfel, and Cass.

'I'll advise the kitchen we have more family for dinner this evening,' Pirelle said. 'Let's get everyone settled in, then we can go from there.'

Jorrun gave the *walker* a slight bow.

Kussim turned to him, still clutching her mother's hand. 'Thank you, uncle.'

'It was the very least I could do,' he replied. An empty hole formed inside him and grew. He wished for all the land beneath the sky that his brother had been here to see this.

***

Jorrun went first to his sister's room, then Kussim's, finding both empty. One of the helpful guards suggested the library, and a smile crept across Jorrun's lips. He found both women inside, up on the higher balcony on the left side of the room. It was a moment before the women saw him, their faces were lined with concentration as they searched the spines of the hundreds of volumes, Kussim holding a small flame in her palm to better read the text.

'Come up.' Dinari invited with barely a glance.

Intrigued, Jorrun took the narrow iron stairs two at a time to join them. 'You're hunting,' he said.

'We are.' Dinari's eyes lit with a smile and he marvelled again at his sister's resilience, at how well she bore the scars of her life without bitterness.

Kussim was biting her lower lip, her eyebrows drawn together, low over her eyes. She gave an exasperated sigh. 'I don't think it's here.'

Jorrun straightened up in realisation. 'The book on blood magic healing?'

Dinari nodded. 'Indeed. I hoped there might be a copy here, but it seems not. Our father's library in Navere is the only place I've seen the text.'

'I'll send a message to Calayna—'

'No.' Dinari gripped his arm. 'A message might be intercepted and the book is incredibly valuable — not just to me. You are heading back to Navere yourself, are you not?'

'First thing tomorrow.'

'Then I will go with you.'

'But…' Jorrun looked from Kussim to his sister.

The two women glanced at each other; Dinari smiled. 'My daughter is safe, I've seen her, and held her, that is more than many mothers have in Chem. If the book is still in our father's library, then…' She held out her arms, turning them to show the dark-brown ink. 'I could have the power to fight with you.'

'And Calayna.' Kussim took a step toward him. 'Imagine if she had power, she is already formidable.'

'And my children,' Dinari's voice broke a little. 'They are all strong. If we took Uldren, Parsiphay, and Farport, we'd hold the coast and the majority of Chem.'

Jorrun held up his hands, his heart beating fast. 'No one wants to take all of Chem more than me, but if we take more than we can hold, we will lose it all. You know that.' He turned to his niece.

She lifted her chin to hold his gaze. 'I do. We're not talking about tomorrow, or a week, or even a month. It will take the tattooed women a while to learn to use their powers, and we'll have to plan carefully. And we shouldn't do it alone.'

Jorrun tilted his head to regard her, but it was Dinari who spoke next. 'It will take an alliance. Western Chem, The Fulmers, Elden, The Borrows, and the Fire-Drakes.'

Jorrun realised his mouth was open and he closed it quickly. 'We have considered such a thing, but the division of land after would be a nightmare.'

Kussim shook her head. 'No, not with the friendships forged. The Icante and Temerran. Yourself and Bractius. Kesta and that elder drake, Siveraell. Forget politics, forget the rest. If all of you, and maybe Rece and Calayna, sat down together, you could do it. You can make a fair agreement out of friendship.'

'For the protection of all of us, four lands united.' Dinari gazed up at him. 'Four lands who might stand up to Geladan.'

Jorrun drew in a sharp breath. A dreadful thought struck him, that it would take time to unite, time to conquer all of Chem —too much time. Kesta had fended off the Geladanians, but who knew how many more would come.

'We can't be hasty,' he replied.

Both women shook their heads, their wide eyes fixed on him.

Jorrun couldn't help it, he laughed. 'I'm cursed with being surrounded by strong, bloodthirsty women. I'll discuss it with Calayna and Rece when I get to Navere and see if we can find this book before we get too carried away.'

Dinari smiled, with another glance at her daughter. 'Good. And I'm coming with you.'

Chapter Twenty

Cassien; Eastern Chem

Vorro gave a small cry in his sleep, and Cassien shifted onto his knees to reach out and touch the younger man's forehead. His skin was dry, but cold. Cassien sank back on his heels in relief, lifting Vorro's jacket to check the skin around his wound just to be sure. There was some heat and swelling to the skin, but no infection that he could detect. Not yet, anyway.

'How is he?' Rothfel stepped out of the darkness, his voice as deep as the shadows between the trees.

'In pain, but he seems okay. How are we?'

Rothfel gave a grunt. 'Too close to Uldren for my liking, but they don't seem to have sent any patrols out in pursuit. I imagine they must know they were struck by Ravens.'

'Probably wondering why we didn't stay to occupy the palace.' Cassien yawned, flexing his shoulders and back.

'Let's get a litter built and be on our way.'

Cassien stood up at once, fetching a small axe from his saddle. He glanced at Rothfel's horse, at the strangely shaped packages it still carried.

'Rothfel, you teach certain, um, skills to us Ravens, but have you ever taken on an apprentice in your – what did you call it – alchemy?'

The much older man regarded him, the rising sun behind him somehow making his silhouette thinner. 'Not as yet, boy. Are you asking?'

Cassien gave a shrug. 'I think so.'

Rothfel's mouth curled up in a smile. 'Alchemy is powerful stuff, as powerful as magic, I wouldn't want to teach the wrong person.'

Cassien's heart sank, but he refused to let his posture sag.

'How old are you?'

Cassien winced. 'I believe I'm twenty-three.'

Rothfel gave a snort. 'A puppy still. And a puppy that prefers a master.'

'Hey.' Cassien bristled with indignation.

Rothfel held up his hands. 'I meant no offense. Some people like to learn from others, others have to learn on their own.'

Cassien's thoughts flew immediately to Catya.

'I'll teach you, Cass,' Rothfel decided. 'If I can't trust you, then there's no one under the sky that I can.'

They worked together on the litter in silence, sacrificing Cassien's blanket to create it. When it was done, they attached it to Rothfel's horse's saddle, leaving Cassien's mount free should he need to fight for them on horseback.

'So, who was it you learned from?' Cassien asked as they made their way steadily west.

'A man called Ignaya.' Rothfel instinctively surveyed the open meadow around them as they crossed toward a dip in the land that might hide them for a while. 'He lived in Snowhold Province, up in the mountains, on the edge of the treacherous trail from Snowhold to Gysed. Resources in Snowhold are scarce and there is little to do in the winters when the snow lies as deep as a man is tall, except learn and experiment.'

'I didn't know you'd been to Snowhold.'

Rothfel smiled slowly, his gaze fixed on the path ahead. 'Few know my whole story.'

'Does Jorrun?'

Rothfel nodded. 'And Rece, Calayna, and Kesta.'

Cassien dropped his horse's rein and fell back a little to check on Vorro; the young Chemman appeared to be sleeping. He quickened his pace again, taking hold of his horse's halter as he rejoined Rothfel.

'Asleep?' The supposed thief regarded him.

Cassien nodded. 'So, Ignaya…'

Rothfel grinned. 'You learned herblore here, and in the Fulmers?'

'And in Elden.'

'Alchemy is not dissimilar. Instead of mixing just plant ingredients to create cures and poisons, Ignaya would experiment with anything. Rock, mineral, metal, even magic. He created interesting alloys in his furnace, and various salts and tonics. He learned a lot by observing birds and animals, experimenting on himself more often than any other living thing.

'One winter I found myself snowed in with him and he came to trust me, offering to let me help him in his work. There was much of use I learned, including the explosive powder you saw the results of in Uldren. It was a recipe he kept completely to himself, fearful of its destructive power in the wrong hands. If I teach it to you, Cassien, I must have your word you will use it for defence, for protection of the innocent, not for conquest, not for power.'

'Of course, you have my word.'

The corner of the man's mouth twitched. 'I need not have even asked you, Cass, but I needed you to understand. There is something else. You must teach no one else, unless I am dead.'

Cassien looked up sharply; at the man's small, stubbled chin, at his unremarkable nose, at his hazel eyes.

'I mean it, Cassien. And whoever you train must be trustworthy without reproach. Never teach Catya.'

Cassien opened his mouth to protest, but stopped himself. Rothfel was right. Brilliant as she was, Catya was too volatile, too selfish.

'I agree,' he said.

'Good.' Rothfel examined the high banks to either side of them and Cassien instinctively checked behind. 'I'll start as we walk, I know you can take in information and still remain alert. We'll have to leave any practical experiments until we are somewhere safe, and private.'

Rothfel kept his voice low as they travelled, Cassien often repeating things back to ensure he had it right. Instead of heading west by the fastest route as Jorrun had done, they took a more north-westerly path, taking the time to rest the horses, check Vorro's wounds, and cover their trail. Cassien snuck away into a farm to steal some winter greens.

They made camp almost an hour after nightfall, risking a fire for Vorro's sake and to cook a hot meal. Cassien checked Vorro's pulse and skin, relieved there was still no sign of fever.

'I have an iron tonic to put in the stew for him,' Rothfel said quietly.

'Iron?' Cassien looked up sharply. Vorro stirred.

'Yes. Blood has a metallic smell, an iron taste does it not? Ignaya believes that blood is of iron, and that blood loss through wounds and… um… from a woman's flow, needs to be replenished with iron. It wouldn't hurt,' he finished with a shrug.

'In the Fulmers they teach that eating dark-green leaves, salty broths, and drinking dandelion and nettle tea help with blood loss.'

'We'll try both, then.' Rothfel took a small vial from one of his packs, while Cassien woke Vorro. The young Chemman sat up groggily, seeming confused at the darkness. Cassien handed him the broth, quickly spooning down a bowlful himself before relieving Rothfel at keeping watch. They'd chosen a small dell that hid the light of their fire from all but a narrow opening to the north. Cassien climbed the slope, using the spindly trees to help pull himself up. He glanced down at the camp to see Rothfel checking Vorro's bandage, before concentrating on the surrounding land.

He'd almost made a complete circuit of the dell when the hairs stood up on the back of his neck. He held his breath, straining to hear anything. One of the horses snorted down below. A pidgeon startled away to his left. Slowly, Cassien drew his sword, then stepped stealthily along the ridge. He widened his eyes to allow in as much light as possible, movement catching his attention at once. Cassien froze in place, watching as the men crept past, counting their number. Eight. Eight men and all armed and armoured in leather and mail. He caught the shape of a silver wolf insignia. His eyes narrowed and he gritted his teeth. One man gestured without speaking, Cassien's eyed followed the direction of his finger.

They'd spotted their camp.

Cassien switched his sword to his left hand and drew a knife, taking it by the blade and hurling it toward the men. It hit one in the side of the neck. His second knife embedded itself in an eye as the warrior turned. His third knife was thrown hastily as the men charged, slicing into a thigh. Cassien threw his sword to his right hand and drew his last knife. One man swung at him, two handed, overhead; Cassien ducked and spun as he caught the blade, plunging his knife into the man's belly. Cassien jumped back, then took several cautious steps, choosing his ground as three men came it him together, more cautiously this time. Two launched themselves forward, impeding the third. Cassien turned sideways on as he parried their blades, but the weight of their attack pushed him back.

Light flared suddenly, and Cassien risked closing his eyes as he ducked and rolled. Flames blazed between the trees, engulfing two of the warriors. Cassien scrambled to his feet, taking everything in with a rapid glance. Vorro stood a short way down the slope, another ball of fire ready in his hands, his dark skin almost grey as he swayed. One warrior who'd stayed back collapsed to his knees, a flow of red pouring from a gaping wound in his throat as a shadow slipped away.

The two remaining attackers exchanged a glance, then went for Cassien, choosing him as the easiest option. Cassien gave a slight shake of his head, then sprang at them. His sword licked out, engaging, parrying, then cutting in and out of the first man's chest. The deep wound in his leg hampered the second man, and he tried to use his greater bulk. Cassien sliced his hand, and as their swords met on the second stroke, the sword slipped from the man's bloody grip.

Rothfel stepped up behind the warrior and hit him hard on the back of the head with a piece of wood. The Chemman wolf crumpled.

Cassien made a quick check of the area, then helped Rothfel drag the warrior down to their camp. Vorro followed, his feet dragging, his breaths ragged. While Rothfel tied their captive to a tree, Cassien fetched Vorro some now cold tea.

'Are you all right?' Cassien asked.

Vorro nodded as he gulped his tea. 'Just a little dizzy.'

'Thank you for your timely help.' He turned to Rothfel, who was standing over their captive, hands on his hips. 'What's your plan?'

Rothfel grunted. 'I thought it was about time we got some answers.'

Cassien grimaced and Rothfel raised his eyebrows. Though he said nothing, torture wasn't something Cassien approved of in the slightest. Drawing in a deep breath, Cassien climbed back up the bank to make a search of the bodies. From the smell and the horsehair on their clothing, it was obvious they had mounts nearby. More horses would be useful, but there was also a chance the Chemman warriors had left their camp guarded. He found a wolf insignia on each of the men, almost burning his fingers on the metal of one brooch on a charred body. There was something different about it. The metal was gold, rather than silver.

Cassien retrieved his knives, cleaning them before returning them to their sheaths in his wide belt. When he returned to their camp, he found Rothfel had built up their fire and was brewing something over it in a small pot. Vorro was watching, his eyes wide. Their prisoner still slumped forward against the tree. Rothfel looked up, holding Cassien's gaze for a moment before pouring some of the brew he was making into a cup and walking over to their prisoner. He kicked the man's leg twice to wake him up.

'We'd like a little information,' Rothfel said, his voice steady and low, his face impassive.

The warrior glared at him, then spat.

Cassien stepped forward, but Rothfel held up a hand to halt him. Rothfel smiled ever so slightly.

'Cass, I'd like you to hold this man's nose so he opens his mouth.'

Both Cassien and the warrior looked at the cup held in Rothfel's hand.

'Oh.' Rothfel glanced at the cup as though only just remembering it was there. 'This contains a slow, but deadly poison. It's incredibly painful and will cause horrific hallucinations before destroying your will so you'll tell me anything and not even realise you're doing so. I have an antidote, so as soon as you're ready to talk, let me know.' Rothfel turned to look at Cassien. 'Cass.'

Cassien realised he hadn't moved and forced his feet to take him toward their prisoner, who instinctively pulled against his bonds. He crouched and reached out his hands. The goggling warrior tried to pull away. Cassien's heart quailed and he turned to Rothfel.

Rothfel held his gaze. 'Remember why it's you I am teaching, Cass.'

Cassien's own eyes widened as he realised. Clamping his jaw tightly closed, he seized the prisoner's jaw and grabbed his nose, pressing hard to seal his nostrils. The man fought, his face reddening, until his lungs could take no more. He gasped in air, and Cassien dug his fingers into the corner of the man's jaw to keep his teeth apart while Rothfel poured his potion into his mouth. Most of the liquid spilled away as the man choked and spluttered.

Rothfel stepped away and Cassien rocked back on his heels, regarding his new master.

'We wait.' Rothfel answered Cassien's unspoken question. 'Soon the hallucinations will start, then the pain.'

They strolled to their fire, where Vorro was struggling to make them some nettle tea with his one good arm.

'Come on, you'll tear your wound open.' Rothfel gently moved the young man aside. 'I'd best check it, anyway.'

Cassien finished the tea, while Rothfel tutted over Vorro's arrow wound and changed the bloodied bandages. A groan made Cassien turn toward their prisoner, but Rothfel silently shushed him. They finished their tea and persuaded Vorro to try to sleep before Rothfel stood and approached the Chemman warrior. The man's head was thrown back against the tree, his mouth slack, but his eyes wide and his pupils dilated. He let out another cry.

'Something wrong?' Rothfel asked innocently.

'The ants.' The warrior struggled against the ropes that held him, trying to move around the tree. 'They're so big!'

'I see,' Rothfel replied.

Cassien checked around them with a frown. There were no ants that he could see in the darkness.

Rothfel crouched and the warrior tried to recoil. 'No! Your eyes… your eyes are holes.'

Rothfel raised his eyebrows. 'And they'll swallow your soul if you don't tell us what we want to know.'

'Why is everything so bright?' the warrior muttered. He gave a groan and hunched a little.

'Has the pain started?' Rothfel asked. 'Better answer quickly then. The wolf insignia you wear, what does it mean?'

'We are the Wolf Guard.'

Cassien drew in a breath, letting his excitement get the better of him. 'Who do the Wolf Guard serve?'

'Warenna, Warenna, Warenna.' The prisoner kept repeating the word as though tasting it on his tongue. He closed his eyes and gave a strangled groan. 'The lights are so bright, why won't the lights go out?'

Cassien gave a growl of frustration. 'Who gives the Wolf Guard their orders?'

The warrior groaned again, eyes still tight shut.

'There isn't long left until it will be too late for the antidote,' Rothfel said.

The words burst out of the warrior. 'Bullcren of Teloch!'

'Teloch.' Rothfel glanced at Cassien. 'Intelligence suggests Bullcren's Coven was making a play for becoming the new central seat of Eastern Chem, but both Parsiphay and Uldren wouldn't agree to it.'

'What has Warenna got to do with Bullcren and Teloch?' Cassien demanded.

The warrior stared at him in horror, his eyes growing impossibly wider.

'Answer him,' Rothfel snapped.

The prisoner gave a small whine in the back of his throat. 'Bullcren worships Warenna and wishes to restore magical power to

344

Chem, pure, clean, magic. Not that of necromancy, not that of women.'

'Are the fools planning to summon their God like they did in Arkoom?'

'No, no.' The warrior tried to rock back and forth. 'They trust Warenna's will.'

Cassien spoke to Rothfel over his shoulder. 'But if Uldren and Parsiphay have declined to accept Bullcren as Overlord of their covens, why so many of these Wolves in Uldren province?'

'Information from deeper in East Chem is old news, and not necessarily reliable.' Rothfel gave a slight shake of his head. 'Perhaps the uprising in Parsiphay prompted Uldren to accept help, and Teloch rule.'

Cassien regarded the warrior whose head was thrashing from side to side. He reached forward and grabbed the man's jaw to still him. 'What was your mission here in Uldren province?'

'Spies.' A small amount of saliva dribbled from the man's lips. 'We are to seek out and kill Raven spies, disrupt their raids, stop them stealing our property. Give me the antidote.' He finished with a whimper.

'And those in Caergard province?' Rothfel persisted.

'To scare the populace, to stir up support for the east, and hate for the Ravens. The antidote, please.'

Rothfel gestured for Cassien to follow him and returned to the fire. He sighed loudly. 'It was what we suspected, I suppose, but it's good to know who's behind it.'

'And they're not trying anything stupid regarding the gods.'

'Unlike those in Navere, it would seem,' Rothfel murmured.

Cassien looked toward their prisoner. 'Shouldn't we give him the antidote?'

It shocked him when Rothfel laughed.

'Give him some nettle tea, if you like, Cass. I didn't poison him, not really, although a larger dose of mushrooms might have killed him. He'll have a bad belly in the morning, and an aversion to ants it would seem, but nothing worse than that.'

Cassien stared at him incredulously, then snorted out a laugh of his own. 'I'll give him the tea; it won't hurt for him to believe he had a lucky escape from death.'

Rothfel's face grew serious. 'We should probably slit his throat.' Cassien protested, and Rothfel interrupted him. 'We should, but we won't. I no more have the stomach for killing a helpless man than you do. Get some sleep, Cass, I'll watch for a while.'

***

The following day, Vorro insisted he was well enough to ride, so they dismantled the litter and Cassien helped the young man up onto his horse. Their prisoner had soiled himself in the early hours, and he yelled curses and threats after them as they left.

They kept to a cautious pace, wary of meeting more Wolves, or alerting any Eastern Chemmen to their presence. They reached Warenna's river at nightfall two days later, forcing the frightened horses to swim it in the dark. Cassien made a quick check of the western bank. He could see no signs that anyone had been here recently, so they found a sheltered spot to make camp, Vorro using his magic to dry their clothes rather than risk a fire.

It was almost midday as they reached the walls of Caergard City. As soon as they reached the palace, Cassien asked for news of Jorrun and learned he'd missed him by a matter of hours. Disappointment washed through him. Although he understood Jorrun wanted him here in Caergard to watch Kussim's back, he'd really wanted to go to Fulmers to fight these 'Geladanians'.

'Cass?'

Kussim broke into his thoughts and he realised his mind had wandered.

Rothfel raised an eyebrow at him and answered Kussim's question for him. 'I agree, I think we need to get more spies into Teloch and somehow strengthen our border along Warenna's river.'

Cassien shook himself. 'I suggest we build watch towers along the river. Let them do the same if they want. It will make it harder for people to make an escape in one direction or the other, but as winter sets in, fewer people will make a move, anyway.'

Kussim nodded with a glance at Dalton and Pirelle. 'And we can make no more strikes at the eastern cities for a while, anyway. We'll start drawing up plans, look at materials and manpower.'

Cassien dug into the saddlebag he carried and took out the silver and gold brooches. 'This might help a bit with costs.'

Kussim stepped forward to take them from him, her cheeks flushing slightly as her eyes met his. 'Will you stay here for the winter, Cass?'

He shook his head. 'I really want to catch up with Jorrun, help him defend his family. They, well, they're kind of my family too. And I need to know Catya is safe and not doing anything too reckless.'

Kussim nodded, not meeting his eyes and turning slightly away. 'Go to her, then. Jagna is staying until spring with Vorro and Meric, so we have extra protection here. Take care of yourself, Cassien.'

Rothfel gave a loud sigh. 'I'd best come with you too if I'm to finish your lessons.'

'I'd be grateful, and for the company.' Cassien turned to smile at him.

It was only as they were on the road toward Navere that evening, that Cassien realised with a jolt what Kussim had said.

Chapter Twenty-One

Kesta; Fulmer Isle

'Ready, Kessta?' Azrael turned a slow loop between her and the fireplace.

Behind her, Eidwyn sat on the bed with Arridia. It was hard for Kesta not to be distracted by her daughter's presence, but she wanted her to see what it was to be a *walker* – even if she wouldn't let her daughter *walk* for many years yet. Kesta shifted on the carpet, relaxing her spine, then opened one eye to peer at the fire-spirit.

'Are you and the other drakes going to get into trouble for this?' she asked.

The brightness of Azrael's flame intensified in a brief pulse, and she knew whatever he said next would not quite be the truth. 'We want to help, Kessta, the younger drakes are ready.'

'Hmm.' She regarded him a moment longer, before turning back to the fire. She slowed her breathing, falling easily into a meditative state. She triggered the part of her brain that allowed *walking*, her spirit slipped free to join the consciousness of one of the fire-spirits. Unable to travel through the fire-realm himself, Azrael had left it to one of the others to carry Kesta to where she needed to go.

Northold.

It took some time, passed between three fire-spirits as far as she could tell from the change in the feel of their alien emotions. Then an image grew before her eyes; the great hall of Northold lay before her, several warriors sat at the tables eating. Amongst them was the Elden ambassador, Vilnue, and a woman she recognised, wearing a Raven insignia. There was no sign of Tantony – or her mother.

'The king,' she prompted the fire-spirit.

She was plunged at once into a fiery vortex, the bright colours flashing rapidly as they shot through the air across the lake rather than delving down into the earth towards the fire-realm. The flames cleared to reveal the king's audience room. Bractius was there with Teliff. They appeared to be receiving a report from one of their warriors.

'Can you address the king?' Kesta asked the fire-spirit. 'Tell him I'm here and find out what's happened?'

I will try, Kessta.

The king grew larger in Kesta's vision as the fire-spirit drew closer. Bractius was the first to spot it, leaping off his throne and backing away.

'Peace!' the little fire-spirit hissed. 'I am a friend, I carry Kesta Silene with me.'

King Bractius froze, his hand still on his sword hilt. Teliff moved quickly to his side. 'Kesta?'

'She cannot sspeak,' the young drake explained. 'But I can ssay her words. Is all well in Elden? Is the Icante still with you?'

Bractius frowned up at the fire-spirit, his eyes searching its flaming body as though trying to discern Kesta within. 'Elden is safe, the Geladanians have left, the Icante pursued them. She…' Bractius glanced at Teliff. 'She should have reached the Fulmers by now.'

'If the Fulmers was the Geladanian's destination,' Teliff muttered.

'Was there a tall, thin man in their party, a ssorceror?' the drake asked for Kesta.

Bractius shook his head, letting go of his sword. 'No, that sounds like Lorev. He left some time ago. Of the main delegation, there were two women left; a bard and a High Priestess.'

'Kessta defeated this Lorev.' The fire-spirit turned in a loop, momentarily forgetting Kesta. The room swirled in front of her, making her dizzy.

We must go, Kesta, you have been walking *too long.*

Reluctantly, she agreed.

She was pulled at once into the vortex, moving so swiftly all colour blurred into one bright tunnel of orange. Again, she was aware as they passed her from one spirit to another, until she sensed the familiar and comforting aura of Azrael. He slowed, allowing her to come back to her body gently. Even so, she was immediately hit by an intense headache and overwhelming nausea.

'Kesta?' Eidwyn darted off the bed, grabbing a mug of tea which she pressed into Kesta's hands. 'You were gone nearly two hours.'

'Are you okay, Mumma?' Arridia slipped off the bed.

Kesta quickly held out a hand to ward her off. 'I'll be all right, Riddi, but please don't touch me a moment.'

Arridia placed her hands behind her back. Kesta found herself momentarily lost in her little daughter's stunning, violet eye.

'Did you learn anything?' Eidwyn prompted.

The young woman's words were like a punch to Kesta's stomach. She tried to stand. 'I did. My mother set off in pursuit of a ship full of Geladanians. Bractius believed they were headed here, but they should have arrived by now.'

Azrael, who'd been keeping watch out the window, gave a squeal of alarm.

'I'll tell Heara at once.' Eidwyn gave a slight bow and hurried from the room.

'Is it the bad men?' Arridia asked.

'Bad women, this time.' Kesta raised her eyebrows. 'Azra, tell Doraquael and Nip, ask them to come in here, and return yourself at once.'

'Yess, Silene.' The little drake squeezed through a gap in the window and was gone.

'Will we have to fight again?' Arridia asked, hands still behind her back.

Kesta held out her arms, ignoring the throbbing of her head. Arridia darted forward at once. 'It's likely, my honey.' Kesta stroked her daughter's dark hair.

Azrael wriggled into the room and was about to speak when a ball of flames burst from the fireplace. Kesta turned instinctively, placing her body between her daughter and their attacker as she shielded.

There was no surge of power, the bright flare faded.

Kesta looked up to see a large fire-spirit hovering before her, its attention not on them, but on Azrael, who was cowering and wailing.

'Siveraell!' Kesta sat up straight, still shielding Arridia.

The elder fire-spirit ignored her, his focus still on Azrael. 'What are you up to, Azrael? We have been ordered to stay out of the earth realm. Why are you risking the young drakes, getting them in trouble?'

'You know why.' Azrael made himself small.

Sivaraell's flames shivered in a sigh. He turned to Kesta. 'I will fight with you, Kessta, but the other drakes must stay in the fire-realm lest they be captured.'

Azrael gave a little shriek of delight.

'Siveraell.' Kesta got slowly to her feet, briefly placing her hand on Arridia's head. 'We are already indebted to you; I don't want you to risk capture and enslavement.'

'We thought we were free of Jderha,' Siveraell said. 'But she does not forget, and she does not forgive. More importantly, she will not rest until the threat against her existence is extinguished.'

Kesta glanced at Arridia, fear walking up her spine.

'Yesss,' Siveraell whispered. 'The southern god has made it them or her.'

The door opened, making Kesta jump, and Nip ushered Joss into the room. Doraquael floated in, coming to an abrupt halt when he spotted Siveraell. Joss went straight to his sister, sensing something serious was going on.

'Did you learn anything?' Nip asked at once.

'I did.' Kesta bit at her lower lip, a deep frown on her face. 'Would you please stay here and guard the children?'

'No.' Siveraell moved closer to her. 'These foolish sprites will guard the children; I will come with you.'

Kesta's heart sank a little. She wanted the elder Drake's strength and wisdom to watch over Joss and Arridia, but she nodded and held the door open for him to follow.

She went straight to the great hall. Work was already underway to repair the floor, and fabric and fir-tree branches had been stretched across the hole in the roof to keep out the rain. Heara sat on the raised dais, her stiff spine speaking of the pain she still endured. They had moved the most severely injured into the guest lodge, but a few were still resting and being tended in the hall's guest alcoves.

Heara looked around on hearing the door open. 'Kesta. I've sent messages to the other holds and have mustered the warriors to the longships. If the Geladanians are out there, we'll spot them. Shall I send word for the rest of the *walkers* to come to you?'

'No.' She hopped up to sit on the edge of the table. 'I don't want to leave the other holds defenceless, and having all the *walkers* in one place… well, it risks us all being wiped out.'

'If the High Priestess defeats you and the children, sshe won't stop there,' Siveraell warned. 'She will take the opportunity to kill all the Islanders.'

Heara and Kesta stared at each other. Kesta drew in a breath. 'Even so, if the ship lands elsewhere on the island, the people there will need time to flee. Heara, we should send word for everyone to have an escape plan in place, to make for Elden, the Borrows, or Chem, should any hold be breached.'

Heara opened her mouth, then closed her eyes and nodded. 'That would be prudent.'

Kesta regarded her mother's closest friend. The skin beneath her eyes was dark and her forehead glistened a little with sweat despite the chill in the room. 'Heara, has anyone checked your wounds today?'

'They're fine.'

'I'll look anyway,' Kesta persisted.

Heara scowled, but she let Kesta examine her. The stitches seemed to be holding and she was relieved to find no infection; Kesta couldn't help but wince at the extent of the black and purple bruises.

'Have you taken anything for the pain?'

'Yes,' Heara replied, avoiding her eyes.

'Well, take more.' Kesta stood.

Heara huffed. 'You're getting too much like your mother.'

Kesta grinned. 'Why, thank you very much.'

Heara grinned back, but only for a moment. 'What's your plan?'

'At the moment? Fortify the hold, then defend the hold.'

'Will you call Jorrun?'

Kesta folded her arms around herself. 'He is too far off to get here, unless the Geladanians hold off their attack for some reason.'

'Can we find them a reason?'

Kesta regarded the older woman and glanced at Siveraell. 'Anyone we sent to delay them, would likely not survive, except…'

Heara paled a little. 'Except maybe you.'

Kesta nodded. 'It's something to consider.'

'No.' Both Heara and Siveraell replied at once.

Kesta raised an eyebrow. 'Offer me a better plan, then.'

'I'm working on it already,' Heara said.

Kesta drew in a breath. 'I'm going to visit Worvig and check on the healers.' She forced a smile at Heara, before striding through the great hall to the colder outside.

She spotted Rosa at once, handing out cups of honey water to both the injured and the healers. Kesta kissed her friend's cheek, then crossed the long room to the dark corner in which Milaiya sat beside Worvig.

'How is he?'

Milaiya rubbed at her face, her copper hair fell about her shoulders in unwashed tangles. 'The healers are keeping him asleep.'

Kesta sat carefully on the edge of the bed. Worvig lay still, his skin more grey than olive. His hair had been brushed back from his forehead and fanned out around him on the pillow. The muscles of his chest had given way a little to fat, but his shoulders were still broad and strong. Kesta caught her breath at the wad of bandages that had replaced the arm which had once lifted her in and out of trees, the arm which had taught her to fight dirty, the arm which had shielded her and her mother.

A surge of pain took her unawares and her eyes spilled over. She quickly wiped at her face and glanced at Milaiya. 'Sorry.'

Milaiya said nothing, but reached out to squeeze and hold her hand. They sat together, observing Worvig's chest rise and fall, Sivaraell's light casting a warm glow.

Kesta cleared her throat and freed her hand. 'I have to go.'

Milaiya swallowed. 'The warriors are saying we're still in danger.'

Kesta held her gaze. 'We are. Keep the hold steady, bring people together to eat, invite the musicians to play. Instil calm and courage, if you can, Milaiya.'

The freed slave stood as Kesta did. 'What will you do?'

'Shield our people.'

Siveraell gave a hiss. 'You are not the Icante.'

'The Icante isn't here.' Kesta surveyed the room. Everlyn was still in the same place and Kesta headed toward her. 'The Silenes are in no fit state to fight. There is only me.'

'Kessta, the children must be our priority—'

356

Kesta spun on her heels, her fists clenched, heat rising up her skin. Siveraell shrank back at her glare.

She forced air into her lungs, then turned and stepped softly up to Everlyn's bed. The *walker* was awake, the side of her face, neck, and shoulder covered in wet cloths slavered in a cooling and pain killing ointment. The silver-haired healer who was attending Everlyn placed her last strips of cloth, and with a meaningful glance at Kesta, quietly left.

'How are you feeling?' Kesta's heart gave another painful clench at the knowledge of the price this quiet woman had paid to protect Fulmer Hold, to protect her children.

'I never thought myself vain, but the thought of how I must look...' Everlyn's eye watered and Kesta had to swallow against the lump in her throat. 'I'm alive, I'll heal.'

Kesta looked away, steeling herself.

'It's okay.' Everlyn forced a smile. 'Ask me.'

Kesta rubbed at her chin and made herself meet the woman's mismatched eyes. 'Do you have your power?'

Everlyn raised her bandaged arm and called flames to her fingertips.

Kesta nodded. 'I might have to leave the hold, go to meet our enemy wherever they land.'

Everlyn frowned, her eyes full of pity. 'I'm sorry it's fallen to you. I'll do my best to guard your children.'

Kesta's nostrils flared and she was momentarily unable to find her voice.

'Kesta, is there any news?'

Kesta looked around to find Rosa standing beside her. 'I wish I could send you home to Tantony.'

Rosa straightened up. 'Tantony can manage without me for a while, I'm needed here.'

Kesta and Everlyn's eyes met, both knowing there was a high chance Tantony would have to be without her for more than a while if the Geladanians won.

'What?' Rosa placed her free hand on her hip.

'I'm going scouting with Siveraell,' Kesta replied, avoiding her friend's eyes. 'Nip and Doraquael will watch over Joss. I want you and Azrael to continue to guard Arridia.'

'Of course.' Worry lines creased Rosa's skin.

The door burst open and a warrior stepped in, spotted Kesta, and almost ran over. 'Silene, a ship has been sighted.'

Kesta stood slowly. 'Go on.'

The warrior swallowed. 'An Elden ship, to the south, on the far horizon.'

'Heading toward land?'

The warrior shook his head. 'They're heading west.'

Kesta held her breath, then let it out slowly. 'Have three ponies saddled for me and supplies for several days' journey. At once.'

The warrior straightened up and darted away.

Kesta didn't wait, ignoring Rosa, who called after her as she headed back to the great hall. She updated Heara, then went to her mother's room to say goodbye to her children. She hesitated outside the room, her heart heavy and painful, before thrusting it open.

Azrael and Doraquael flew towards her, pulling up sharply when they saw who it was. Nip was sitting on the carpet, playing pick-up-stones with the children. Her *knowing* was under control, but even so, Arridia knew at once something was wrong.

'I have to go scouting for a while,' Kesta said.

Nip narrowed his eyed but remained silent.

'For how long, Mumma?' Joss asked.

'A day or two.' She forced a smile and touched his warm cheek. 'Give me a hug.'

She held both her children tightly, then looked up to pin the two fire-spirits with her eyes. 'Look after them. If need be, get them to Chem.'

'We will, Kessta!' Azrael and Doraquael spun loops around each other.

Kesta reached out to clasp Nip's wrist, then strode from the room. Rosa was talking with Heara in the hall, her voice unusually raised. With a twitch of a smile, Kesta slipped past without her friend seeing her, though Heara met her eyes for the briefest of moments.

The warrior had the ponies ready and offered to accompany Kesta, but she declined, mounting at once and setting off at a fast trot through the hold and out across the causeway. As soon as she came to the coastal path, she urged the pony into a gallop, wishing she had her swift horse, Griffon. It was dark when she arrived at Otter Hold on the western coast and their Chieftain Ufgard, and Brae their *walker*, hurried to meet her. Like the Icante, Brae had a strong affinity with birds.

'Any sign?' Kesta's shoulders heaved as she caught her breath.

'They are staying out of sight of the island,' Brae informed her. 'But they are there. I sent three gulls to watch for them. They barely made it back. The Priestess has two captive fire-spirits who will let nothing close, had the gulls not had a big head start and kept their distance...' The *walker* shuddered. 'When they re-joined the gull colony on the cliffs, the fire-spirit seemed to give up.'

'It would not have known one gull from another,' Siveraell said. 'And may have decided the gulls were no threat.'

Brae nodded. 'I tried the magpie whales and the dolphins; none would answer my call.'

'The sea spirits would know to stay far away from the Priestess.' Siveraell pulsed brighter. 'All spirits would by now. The one she has, the oness she forces to fight, would be those captured early in Elden.'

'What of our longships?' Kesta asked.

Brae and Ufgard glanced at each other, Brae's face growing pale, the Chieftain's reddening.

'One which trailed the Geladanians at a distance was...' Brea blanched. 'Well, it was ripped apart. None of the warriors made it back to shore.'

Kesta cursed.

'Will you stay?' Ufgard asked hopefully.

'I must watch for where they make land and meet them.' Kesta raised her chin. 'But if I could temporarily trade for fresh ponies, I'd be grateful. And perhaps a meal and a bed for a few hours.'

'They are yours.' Brae gave a bow of her head.

***

Kesta woke with a start, throwing aside her blanket as the knock sounded again and the door opened. She rubbed at her gritty eyes. Surely it had only been a few minutes? She blinked as Siveraell increased in size.

'Please excuse me, Kesta,' Brea whispered. 'We've had warning from the gulls of the Redcliff colony. A rowboat came ashore there, carrying five men. From the images, I think they were Geladanian. I... we, we think they may be more assassins.'

Kesta grabbed her boots and fumbled to put them on quickly. 'You've sent messengers out?'

'Of course.'

'There's a chance they might be scouts, we need to make sure they send no information back to their ship.' She cursed. 'They would have split up by now.'

'I have scouts here readying to go. Two of them were trained by Heara.'

'Go with them, use your *knowing*, the birds and animals too. Those five men have to die – quickly.'

Brea gave a bow. 'At once. Would you like warriors to go with you?'

Kesta opened her mouth to say yes, but decided against it. 'I have Siveraell. I'll go toward Redcliff, track anyone heading east, but I'll need to keep a watch on that ship.'

'I understand.'

There was a cough just outside the door. 'We're ready.'

Kesta drew on her coat and buckled her long dagger to her waist. 'Let's go.'

The cold air hit her as she stepped outside, cutting into her wooziness. The Hold had only provided her with two ponies, but she didn't stop to argue, no doubt their other animals would all be put to use tonight.

'Good luck,' Brea called out as Kesta urged her pony down the dark road. She reached out her *knowing*, giving the animal confidence and courage to run in the poor light before Siveraell swooped down to illuminate their way.

Kesta closed her eyes and stretched her *knowing* out further, trusting the pony to follow the fire-spirit, and the fire-spirit to lead them. Despite the late hour, there was plenty of life from the deep hum of the trees, to the bright flitting sparks of the bats. The human emotions of the Hold were already far behind them, and she briefly touched the dreaming family of a small farm. An overwhelming need for her husband momentarily threw her, and the pony gave a whicker.

Then she felt it on the edge of her *knowing*, the sharp, focused intent of a predator. A 'bad man.'

She slowed the pony and signalled to Siveraell, who fell back to stay out of sight. The assassin was coming toward her, no doubt heading for the distant light of Otter Hold. As he drew closer, Kesta dismounted, instructing the ponies to go on as she herself slipped from the path into the trees. A surge of excitement from the assassin told her he'd seen the ponies. Cautiously, she called up more power. The man tensed, warning her he had power too.

One side of Kesta's mouth twitched up in a slow smile. She longed for a fight, to release and satisfy some of her nervous energy, her swallowed anger, but she was the last person on the island who could afford a foolish mistake. She used her *knowing* and found him easily. He was crouched within some dying bracken on the roadside, his focus on the approaching ponies. Even huddled, she could see he was tall and sinew thin, dressed in a patchwork of deep, dark greens, blues and browns. Kesta raised an eyebrow at the excellence of the design.

Then she drew on a vast reserve of power and blasted him with fire.

He sensed it as soon as she called it, raising a shield and turning toward her. The ponies shrieked and bolted in the direction of the hold. The assassin's shield buckled, then shattered. Kesta gave a gasp, covering her nose with her arm at the awful smell of incinerating flesh. She waited a moment, then put out the fire with a cooling, icy wind.

Siveraell drifted to her shoulder. 'He had power.'

'Yes.' Kesta stared at the assassin's charred remains, biting her lower lip. 'The first ones that came here for the children did not.'

'Perhaps they thought their task would be easier than it was.'

'Perhaps.' Kesta sighed and stepped out onto the road. 'I need those ponies.'

'I can herd them here.'

Kesta gave a snort. 'Well, I'd hate to think I'm not as strong as my six-year-old daughter.'

She called up her *knowing* again, reaching back down the path for the red panic of the ponies. Kesta stretched out her emotions to force what had come to Arridia naturally, calming them and calling them back to her. It took almost half an hour, but the ponies tentatively returned, snorting at the scent of ash and burnt flesh.

'We've lost time,' Siveraell said anxiously.

'We have, spirit, but not needlessly. Head straight to Redcliff. Can you track?'

'I can.'

363

'Let me know which direction the other four took, then come and find me. I… I'm going to take a guess and head northeast to the coast. I don't want to lose that ship.'

'I think that would be a good guess,' Siveraell said sadly.

Kesta swung up into the saddle of one of the ponies. 'If you come across one of the men on your own, do you think you could take them out?'

'Not if they carry spirit traps.'

Kesta cursed. 'No risks then.'

'You too.' Faster than an arrow, the fire-spirit sped away.

Kesta stroked the pony's neck, then taking the rein of the other, she turned into the trees, calling light to her hand so they could see their way. Once again, she summoned her *knowing*, her vision growing a little hazy as she concentrated on her magical senses. As soon as they reached the open meadow, she urged the ponies into a gallop; the moon was low on the horizon but bright enough through the fleeting clouds to cast long shadows.

She almost didn't feel him so calm and controlled was he, but his excitement at sighting her fiery guide-light was like a tug at a spider's web.

Kesta cut off her flame and dived from the pony's back, pushing out the command for both animals to roll, and lay still. She pressed herself against the cold ground, her fingers tangling in the stalks of the wiry grass. He was stalking closer, wary, but excited. He knew he'd found a *walker*.

Kesta drew in a deep breath and touched the long pendant beneath her tunic. She pushed up onto her hands and knees and circled seaward towards the man's right. He didn't change course, whatever magic he possessed, he didn't seem able to sense her; but the moment she called more power, he would.

Her heart was loud in her ears as she waited, and she had to force herself to breathe. His apprehension was growing, a little bitter twist of doubt. It made her own resolve falter. One drawback of using your *knowing* was it was incredibly hard to avoid any empathy for the one whose emotions you absorbed.

He spotted the ponies and his hesitation was swept away by anticipation of destruction, of victory.

With a shake of her head, Kesta reached down into her beloved island and finding rock, ripped upward. The assassin let out a scream, echoed by the ponies, as the ground surged beneath him. He tried to shield as he was thrown up, then tumbled down a newly formed monolith. Bracing herself, Kesta stood and threw enough power into her flames to make his death quick.

The island grumbled into silence and the light of the fire quickly died. It took her only a moment to retrieve the ponies, and riding the other one this time, she continued her gallop toward the northern coast. Siveraell found her on the clifftop.

'Brea and her scouts have dealt with one of the assassins who'd headed south straight down the coast,' the fire-spirit reported. 'Two headed inland, and the last east along this path.'

'There's only one left inland, we'll have to leave Brea to deal with him.' Kesta turned to gaze down the dark trail eastward. 'We need to catch the fifth one before he reaches Fulmer Hold. I have no doubt they can stop him, but they may not see him before he reports to the Priestess.'

She stared out into the darkness, the surf below loud in her ears.

Where was the ship?

Chapter Twenty-Two

Temerran; The Fulmer Sea

'It's no good, she's still taking on water.' Nolv threw his arms up. 'We've used caulk and tar; but that sea-spirit hurt her. The Chemmish sorceress, Shevi, is trying to block the sea with her magic, but she's tiring.'

Temerran's intestines turned to ice. He couldn't lose the *Undine*; she was more than a ship, more than a home. He turned desperately to Dia. The Icante's expression was calm, but her fingers clenched and unclenched at her side.

She met Temerran's eyes and his heart fell further. 'If I use magic to speed us to a safe harbour, it will further strain the hull.'

'Keep bailing,' Temerran growled to his first mate. 'We'll head straight for land.'

A small, soft hand slipped into his and he looked down to see Linea's turquoise eyes gazing into his. Her warmth lessened his fear and he drew air into his lungs. 'Put supplies in the boats and have them ready just in case,' he instructed Sion.

'But, Captain—'

'We won't abandon her,' he snapped; then winced. 'But there is more at stake here than the *Undine*.'

The young warrior, Gilfy, cleared his throat. 'We can't be far from Barnacle Bay. With the right tide, and, um, a little assistance, we might be able to beach the *Undine* for repairs.'

'We'll be a long walk across land to Fulmer Hold though.' Dia looked momentarily anguished, but she closed her eyes briefly and straightened up. 'It's the best option.'

'Better than drowning,' Nolv muttered.

Temerran glared at him, and the man flushed scarlet beneath his beard. 'Prepare the boats as I said; we can row to Fulmer Hold faster than we can walk, especially if you can help, Icante.' He gave a small bow, confidence returning to his voice. 'Gilfy, can you direct my helmsman at the wheel?'

The islander nodded.

'Dia!' Arrus yelled across the deck from where he stood toward the prow. They all turned and Temerran's free hand flew to his mouth. Only two fire-spirits remained in the red embers of the brazier, they'd lost another one.

Dia looked away, and Temerran pulled his hand free from Linea to place it against her back. 'There was nothing you could do.'

Her ribs expanded and contracted beneath his palm before she replied. 'Perhaps not. If I'd chosen the other ship, they may have destroyed the *Undine*, not just damaged her.'

Temerran drew his hand back. It was a sobering thought. He couldn't imagine anyone besting Dia, but Kichi almost had, and by all accounts Yalla was much more powerful.

He shook himself and glared around at his men. 'Didn't I give you orders?'

Nolv and the others scurried away, Gilfy already at the wheel.

'We'll make it to shore,' Linea said timidly.

He smiled at her, running a strand of her soft hair through his fingers.

'Is there anything I can do to help?'

Temerran bent his head and kissed her quickly. 'If you would pack me a change of clothes and some essential supplies in my cabin to put in one of the boats, while I take care of the *Undine*, I'd be grateful.'

She smiled, the dimples on her cheeks growing more pronounced. 'Of course.' With a glance at Dia, she hurried across the deck.

Temerran raised an arm to the helmsman, who turned the wheel with a nod. The *Undine* took the move like a heavy cog, not a sleek clipper, and she took a wave badly, eliciting shouts of complaint from several of the crew. Temerran sprang up the steps two at a time to take the wheel himself. The grey-whiskered helmsman relinquished it with a wince and a 'Sorry, Captain.'

He waved him aside, widening his stance and letting himself feel the ship. He had to remind himself she wasn't a living thing, but even so he felt her pain and distress thrumming through her wood.

'You can make it, girl,' he crooned under his breath, his grip on the wheel gentle, but firm. Her starboard list was becoming more pronounced as Nolv began to lose his battle against the encroaching sea. Temerran had always intended to die on this deck, one way or another, it broke his heart to think of her going down without him. But suicide would be pointless and help no one.

He adjusted the angle at which they hit the waves; the island growing with painful slowness on the horizon.

'About two miles north.' Gilfy pointed.

Temerran nodded, his muscles starting to ache, but he couldn't give the wheel to anyone else. Dia had joined her husband and the two remaining fire-spirits.

Gilfy followed his gaze. 'Poor little mites.'

Temerran didn't disagree, but gritted his teeth and concentrated on his lurching, wooden lady. The timbers gave a groan and a shudder ran through the ship. Dia left the fire-spirits to join him, her progress across the deck constantly halted by the sharp dip and rise.

'Just there.' Gilfy pointed again.

The cove was a small, sheltered crescent amidst high black cliffs, Temerran swore when he saw the sharp rocks that protruded out into the sea to either side of it. Even with good weather and an undamaged ship, it would take some manoeuvring to get them safely in.

Gilfy held out a hand to steady Dia as she joined them.

'That's really the best option?' Temerran glanced at them, turning the wheel a notch.

'Seal Harbour is about two hours away,' Gilfy replied. 'Think you can make it?'

Temerran didn't reply, straining his muscles to turn the wheel another two notches to take them toward the cove. A wave hit them, spraying up over the rail and reaching them high on the aftercastle.

'How well do you know the tide here?' Temerran demanded.

'Don't worry about the tide,' Dia called up her power. 'Lower me over the stern so I can touch the sea.'

Temerran opened his mouth, shaking his head in disbelief. 'You can't control the sea, it will tear you apart along with the *Undine*.'

Dia held his gaze. 'The *Undine* won't make it in without assistance, and she won't beach without my help, she'll smash. I can do this.'

Temerran bowed his head, hugging the wheel. 'All right.'

Gilfy darted forward at once to snatch up a long coil of rope.

'Take in sail!' Temerran bellowed. He almost lost his grip on the wheel as he watched Dia climb up over the rail. 'Spirits, this is a bad idea,' he muttered.

He sensed Dia draw up her power; it was phenomenal and he caught his breath. It seemed to infuse the ship, a tingling sensation deep in his bones, in his heart. The *Undine* rose and was somehow held by a wave. The wide-eyed Borrowmen hurried to tie back the sails. The cove drew closer and closer, and Temerran realised the wheel was no longer responding. He let go and ran to the rail.

'Dia, a little to port!' Gilfy yelled.

Temerran gripped the wood and leaned over. Dia hugged the hull, one hand stretched out below the water, her greying dark hair coming loose from its coils to cling to her cheeks and neck. The rope was wound around her in a secure harness and Temerran breathed a little.

Then one of the windows to his cabin opened below and a head poked out. He recognised Linea's glossy hair at once. Something in her right hand caught the light. She turned her head, then twisted around to look up, meeting Temerran's eyes. She smiled and drew away slightly, like him turning his attention back to Dia.

'Little more to port!' Gilfy cried out. 'Ten yards. Nine yards…'

Temerran thrust himself away from the rail and stared at the oncoming shore.

'Gently!' Gilfy called down. 'Five yards. Four…'

The wave subsided, then broke across the beach, crashing against the base of the cliffs. Temerran braced himself, a cry of alarm swallowed back by his pride.

The *Undine* hit the sand, listed to her starboard side, slid a few inches, then was still.

Temerran breathed in and out.

A cheer rose up from his men, those who'd been below tentatively climbing onto the tilting deck; including a very ruffled Tantony. Temerran forced his legs up the slope of the deck and grabbed hold of the rope below where Gilfy gripped it. In an instant Arrus was with them, the two remaining fire-spirits trailing him. He leaned over.

'Dia!'

There was no reply.

With a glance at Gilfy, they braced themselves and hauled. The fire-spirits flew down, returning moments later.

'Ssshe isn't conscious, but sshe is alive!'

As they pulled her up to the rail, Arrus leaned over to grab her and lift her into his arms.

'Dia?'

She stirred, her eyes fluttering.

Arrus relaxed, shifting his weight to keep his balance. He gently wiped the blood away from Dia's nose. 'Temerran, mate, we need to get to Fulmer Hold.'

'Of course.' Temerran straightened up, raising his voice. 'I want three boats manned with those prepared to fight for our brothers in the Fulmers and ready to go at once.'

Nolv hurried to report to him, Linea clinging to his arm to keep her balance.

'Linea.' Temerran reached out and took her hand, gazing into her sea-storm eyes. 'Whatever possessed you to lean out of the cabin window? You might have been hurt.'

She ducked her head, her cheeks flushing. 'I was worried when I saw Dia lowered past the window, and I admit I was curious too. I know little of fire-walker magic but for the wild tales told in my land.'

Nolv cleared his throat. 'Do I come with you, Captain?'

'No, stay with the *Undine*, see to her repairs.'

'Seal Hold is southward along the coast,' Arrus said. 'They'll help.'

Dia gave a soft moan and pushed against her husband's chest with one hand. He gently set her on her feet where she swayed and leaned against him.

'Dia, thank you so much.' Temerran gave a low bow, keeping hold of Linea's hand.

Dia shook her head, her voice a little hoarse. 'Not at all, it is helping the Fulmers that endangered the *Undine*.'

Temerran's own voice caught in his throat. 'We owe the Fulmers so much, particularly your family.'

'The boats will be ready shortly, Captain,' Sion called up.

'I have our bags.' Linea smiled at Temerran.

'No.' Dia straightened up. 'I'm sorry, Linea, but you must stay with the *Undine*.'

'Why?' The word burst from Temerran and he stared at his friend in surprise.

'Because she is Geladanian,' Dia said softly, her eyes apologetic as she faced Linea. 'With things the way they are and the attacks on the children, feelings in Fulmer Hold will be running high. When everything is calmer, Linea, you will be welcome, but for now it's best if you stay here. The fire-spirits must also remain so Yalla cannot use them against us. Tem... I understand if you feel you have to stay too, but I would appreciate some men to row for us.'

Every muscle in Temerran's body locked, his heart and lungs aching. He didn't want to leave Linea. But he had to.

'I'm sorry—'

'No!' Linea stepped back, her wide eyes filling with tears. 'Don't leave me here alone.'

'I'm sorry,' Temerran tried again, he reached for her hand but she pulled it out of reach. 'I owe Dia so much. All the lands do. Nolv will take care of you—'

Linea turned and fled down the stairs to the door to his cabin, slipping once, but keeping her balance before she disappeared from sight.

Temerran's face burned, and it was a moment before he could steel himself to look at the others. 'Come on, let's get to your Hold.'

Chapter Twenty-Three

Rosa; Fulmer Hold

'No.' Nip laughed as Joss whipped him about the legs with his withy stick. He tried to grab it, missed, and snatched the small boy up into the air instead. Joss squealed in delight.

'You fight like a girl,' Nip said as he tickled Joss.

Rosa lowered her sewing and cleared her throat loudly.

Nip blushed scarlet. 'Which is great, if that girl is like Heara,' he rapidly added.

Rosa smiled at him. She had no idea where Nip got his patience from, Goddess knew she'd tired of being trapped in the rooms in the back of the hall with two bored children.

'I'm hungry, Aunty Rosa,' Arridia said, not complaining, but politely matter-of-fact.

'Can we go to the hall?' Joss asked hopefully.

Both fire-spirits immediately shot to the door and hovered before it, making a loud humming sound.

'I think that's a no.' Rosa gave the two drakes a stern look. 'I'll get us something.'

Azrael and Doraquael lifted aside as Rosa left the room, closing the door quietly behind her. She nodded to the four warriors who stood guard in the corridor. Worvig had been moved into his room, but according to Milaiya, the burly warrior had refused to speak a word to anyone since waking yesterday. Rosa thought of her own husband, of the injury that had changed his life. There was still an occasional hint of bitterness when his knee prevented Tantony doing something as easily as he wanted, but for the most part he'd adapted and made the most of the life he had now.

She pushed open the door to the great hall. Many of the Hold's residents had gathered there for company, comfort, and courage. Heara had taken up her usual seat, still stiff from her injuries. Eidwyn was at her side, picking at a plate of berries, her eyes distant. As Rosa met Heara's eyes, the warrior shook her head. No word from Kesta then, and no news of the ship.

Rosa skirted the hall toward the large fireplace where they kept stew bubbling away for most of the evening.

'Do you need a hand?' a young woman asked her.

'Oh, thank you.' Rosa gave her a grateful smile. 'If you could bring some bowls and bread, that would be lovely.'

She picked up a small cauldron and ladled stew into it.

The doors to the great hall opened and many of the hall's residents tensed. A young warrior hurried in, his face alight with excitement. 'Silene.' He hurried across the hall, all eyes on him. 'We have captured a man, spying out on the westward coastal path. He's Geladanian.'

Heara sprang to her feet. 'Where is he?'

'Just outside.' The young man pointed back towards the doors. 'Shall I bring him in?'

'No,' Heara replied sternly. Rosa followed her gaze, taking in the faces of the children sat with their parents around the long tables. 'I'll talk to him outside.'

All conversation had ceased, but a few murmurs rumbled as Eidwyn and Heara trailed the warrior out of the hall. Rosa put down the cauldron. 'Please take the food to the children.' She didn't wait for the woman's reply, but hurried to catch up with the others before the warriors guarding the hall closed the doors.

The stranger was kneeling on the ground, his hands bound behind him. Seven warriors stood around him, one with his sword drawn and pressed against his throat. He gave a derisive snort as Heara approached. Rosa hung back.

'Well?' Heara demanded, a hand on her hip as she glared down at the Geladanian.

'Aren't you going to threaten me with torture?' The man sounded younger than Rosa had expected. His face was shadowed, but she glimpsed light-coloured eyes.

Heara gave a snort. 'I wouldn't waste my time. You're here to spy on us and report back to your ship. Your people want to kill mine. I don't need to know anything else.'

'Then why am I still alive?' His voice was calm and Rosa wondered if he were incredibly brave, totally sure of his faith, or… or did he know something they didn't.

Rosa edged closer, barely daring to breathe.

'Because my idiot men didn't kill you.'

The man gave a bark of a laugh. Several of the warriors shifted their feet. 'Are you what you heathens call the Icante?'

Heara's mouth curled up in a smile. 'Maybe.'

'Do you know where the term Icante comes from?'

'Out of my arse for all I care.'

The man stilled. A blush tightened the skin of Rosa's throat and cheeks.

'Icante was the name of the betrayer,' the man growled. 'The Fire-Priestess who turned against her god and betrayed her.'

Heara leaned back a little. 'From what I heard, the Fire-Priestess saved many people and innocent spirits from a paranoid dictator.'

The man tried to get to his feet, but several warriors grabbed at him to push him down.

'She's coming,' the man snarled, still struggling against the warriors. 'Jderha's priestess is coming here for the children.'

Heara waved a hand dismissively. 'Let her. We'll deal with her the same way we have the rest of you. You won't have a hair on the children's heads.'

The man's eyes widened and he threw back his head, his hood slipping to reveal dark hair and a face of around twenty-five years. 'So, the children are here.'

Heara froze, but only for a split second. Her hand flew to her dagger and she drew it, leaping forward.

The assassin called power, hurling the surrounding warriors across the ground, his somehow unbound hands coming around in front of him with a burst of flame.

Rosa let out a small scream.

Eidwyn shielded, only able to protect herself and Heara. Rosa turned, covering her face with her hands. The fire went wide, deflected around the *walker's* barrier. Three warriors weren't so lucky, their clothes, then their skin, catching fire.

The man reached into his coat and pulled out a box; he opened it, then dropped it. Rosa thought she saw the slightest distortion in the air, like an invisible being leaving ripples through the night.

'What was that?' Eidwyn demanded.

'That was my invitation to Yalla.' The young man grinned, showing his teeth.

Eidwyn blasted him with power. He staggered, moving closer to Rosa but keeping his shield and his feet. The remaining warriors had backed away, hoping for a chance, not stupid enough to engage.

'Get me to him,' Heara snarled, all signs of injury fallen away.

Eidwyn strengthened her shield and pushed forward. Rosa shrank back against the stone walls of the hall, her heart in her mouth. Eidwyn increased her power, but the Geladanian resisted, pouring more flames into his attack. Eidwyn countered with an icy wind and they circled; Heara with a dagger clenched in each hand.

The young man halted suddenly, blood sprayed out from his neck, then slowly, his head rolled from his body.

Rosa's hands flew to her mouth and she collapsed to her knees.

Eidwyn stilled her magic, then let her shield drop.

'What does a sick man have to do to get some sleep around here?' Worvig stood leaning on his sword, clutched in his left hand. He was pale and breathing hard.

Heara ran forward, placed her hands to either side of his face and kissed him hard, before stepping back and giving his cheek a mock slap. 'You're meant to be resting.'

'You're meant to be guarding my hold.'

Heara grinned, and Worvig smiled back.

'Seriously, though.' Eidwyn stepped forward. 'This priestess is on her way.'

Heara and Worvig maintained eye contact, then Heara spun about to face the *walker*. 'Milaiya will take charge of the children and anyone who can't fight and lead them into the woods to head for Eagle Hold. The rest of us will prepare to meet this priestess.'

'What of Joss and Arridia?' Rosa asked, using the wall of the hall to pull herself to her feet.

Heara glanced at Worvig. 'They stay here. We will defend them as best we can, but they can't go with the others. Kesta and Jorrun would never sacrifice hundreds to save two, not even their own children.'

Rosa felt sick, and hot, and cold; but she nodded her head.

'Get it done!' Heara yelled, making several people jump.

Everyone scrambled to obey, Eidwyn moving to Worvig's side to see him back inside the hall. Milaiya ran to him, tears streaking her face, pride glowing in her eyes.

'Time for you to lead our people,' Worvig said gruffly into her hair as he embraced her with one arm.

'Heara!' A voice tried to cut through the noise of the hold. 'Heara, a ship is bearing down on the bay!'

Rosa met Heara's eyes briefly, before Rosa broke into a run and pushed through the doors that led to the family rooms of the Icante.

'Bar those doors,' she panted to the warriors. 'We're under attack.'

Chapter Twenty-Four

Kesta; Fulmer Isle

Kesta stretched her *knowing* out further, frustration thrumming through her. The sun had risen and set, yet she hadn't found the assassin. He'd covered his tracks well and had either made exceptional progress without a mount, or they'd passed him somewhere.

'You should sleep,' Siveraell suggested. 'Renew your power, and your body.'

The weary pony stumbled to a halt, sensing her hesitation.

Kesta slipped from the saddle, stretching her back. She surveyed the meadows to her right, then the forest up ahead. As she cast her gaze to the dark sea, movement caught her eye. She took two steps toward the cliffs, her heart beating faster. Red sails. An Elden ship.

'Siveraell!' She ran to the second pony and vaulted into its saddle, grabbing the other's rein and forcing them into a run. The ship was heading inland, she had no doubt about its destination. Siveraell flew ahead to light the way and Kesta reached out her *knowing* once again. Shock jolted her spine. She felt fear, sharp and bright, fleeing outward away from the hold and into the woods.

'Siv, I think Fulmer Hold may have fallen, they're evacuating.'

She was desperate to go faster, but destroying the pony would gain her little time, and none at all if it fell. She opened up her hand to release the rein of the animal she led, letting it fall behind.

Braziers lit the high causeway, but the hold itself was dark. She could sense life within, a mixture of conflicting emotions, above them all… determination.

And something else. She jumped from the pony and sprinted past the causeway, her eyes searching the beach below. Several boats were landing, carrying warriors, their swords drawn ready to fight, black masks painted across their eyes.

Borrowmen.

But not only Borrowmen. She cried out, her feet flying down the coastal path. It was her father she reached first, throwing her arms around him.

'You're here.'

'Kesta.' Dia quickly joined them, Temerran and Tantony at her shoulders. 'What's the situation at the hold?'

'A sorcerer attacked us a few days ago. We lost warriors and they damaged the great hall. I've been out hunting Geladanian scouts and in that time the hold has been partially evacuated.' She swallowed. 'The ship is hard on your heels.'

'They'll most likely try to land here.' Arrus waved a hand at the beach.

'They have elementals,' Dia warned, glancing at Siveraell. 'Who do we have in the hold?'

'Eidwyn and… we have Everlyn, but she was badly hurt. Also…' She placed her fingers briefly over her mouth and looked from her mother to her father. 'Worvig was injured. He lives, but… Father, he lost an arm.'

Temerran sucked in air through his teeth, Dia seemed to freeze, but Arrus cursed and darted forward.

'Wait,' Dia barked. 'Tem, would your men defend the beach? I'll cover them with magic and try to prevent the Geladanians landing.'

'My men are yours.' Temerran bowed.

'Kesta.' Dia placed a hand above her daughter's chest. 'The priestess and her enslaved spirits might go straight for the hold.'

Kesta nodded, pushing down her fear.

'What of your plan?' Temerran asked Dia.

'Plan?' Kesta demanded.

Dia closed her eyes briefly and looked down at the sand. 'I had hoped to convince the Geladanians somehow that the children were dead, that they'd won. It was the only way I could see to prevent them ever coming back.'

'We may yet get a chance,' Temerran said.

Dia smiled grimly. 'If we do, we'll take it.'

Kesta nodded, her eyes meeting Tantony's. 'You'll come with me to the Hold? Rosa will be overjoyed to see you.'

Tantony hesitated, and she guessed its cause. The proud man didn't want to seem to flee a fight where his sword was needed. 'Please see me safely to the Hold.'

Tantony relaxed a little and nodded.

Dia straightened up. 'Let's get into position.'

Kesta turned and hurried over the dunes to the path. When she reached it, she turned, meeting her mother's eyes. They held each other's gaze for a moment, before Kesta broke into a jog she thought Tantony could match.

'Rosa, is she all right?' Tantony was a little breathless as they reached the causeway.

'She is. I'm sorry, Tantony, I should have said so at once. Rosa was very well when I left the hold a few days ago, in fact, she's quite the hero around here.' She glanced back to see that Tantony was beaming.

Kesta slowed to a cautious walk as she stepped into the light of the causeway's braziers. She held her hand high and called flames to her fingers.

'Trouble?' Tantony asked worriedly.

Kesta shook her head. 'I'm letting the Hold know it's me and I'm back.'

Siveraell slowly melded into the flames of the brazier, only his fierce blue eyes giving away the fact he was there. All three of them leaned over the rope railing to look down at the beach, then out to sea. The king's ship had drifted in closer and a growl rose in Kesta's throat. She felt the surge of power from her mother; the Icante wasn't messing about.

The winds rose and clouds swirled above the beach, the night darkening, the air heavy. The Borrowmen warriors had lined up, bows ready, although hitting a target in the storm would take an exceptional shot. Shevi was ready, arm slightly raised, to form a shield to protect the men.

Temerran took a few steps closer to the churning surf, Arrus at his side with his sword drawn. The bard sang.

Dia's storm grew and Kesta's own power thrummed in response, Temerran's words seeming to swell her lungs and her heart. Lightning struck down at the ship, but it hit an invisible barrier and ricocheted away, striking the sea. Flames blossomed on the ship then shot towards them, suddenly altering trajectory. Kesta realised with a gasp they were fire-spirits.

'I've got this.' Siveraell shot out of the brazier and intercepted them, growing huge and enveloping one of the spirits. The second tried to flee, but under some compunction of command, it swerved back with a wail towards Dia. Siveraell swooped and consumed it, then dove at the sand, his speed not faltering. Kesta gasped, gripping the rope tight as Siveraell vanished beneath the ground.

Dia's lightning hit the shield protecting the ship again and again, the afterimages dancing before Kesta with every blink. The ship drifted closer.

The hairs on the back of Kesta's neck prickled and she pivoted. Dark shapes were moving rapidly toward the causeway along the coast path. Kesta ran to the other side and looked down at the cliffs below the hold.

'They're scaling the cliffs!' She whipped her head around to yell at Tantony. 'The ship is a decoy, warn the Hold!'

'But—'

'Do it!'

With a hurt glare, Tantony set off in his hobbling run. Kesta clenched her teeth and called fire to her hands. She needed to get her mother's attention. She needed to hold the causeway.

The Geladanians on the coast path realised they'd been seen and sped their charge.

Kesta met them with a wall of fire, twisting to aim a blast of air at those climbing the cliff at the same time. There were screams as men fell, or were consumed. Where was their priestess? Kesta was confident she could hold the causeway herself, but it would take power, power she needed to save to face Yalla.

There was a twang and hum as several arrows were shot, Kesta shielded instinctively, her fire subsiding. A rumble of falling rocks made her grin and she glanced at the hold. The island warriors had seen the incursion and were repelling it from the walls of the hold. Kesta turned her attention back to the men on the coast path, they were waiting now, unsure of her reach. She took three steps back until she met the touch of the barrier rope and she quickly surveyed the beach. Dia was still feeding the storm, the winds holding back the ship even as the tide tried to carry it in. With a crack, lightning broke through the barrier and struck the deck. Fire licked up the foremast and ate hungrily at the sails.

Then a white blast of frost rose upward, stifling the eager flames.

The priestess?

Kesta pivoted to check the causeway, several men had crept forward and she rewarded their bravery with death. Desperation crept coldly through her adrenaline. She needed to get to her children, but if she didn't hold the causeway, her mother would be cut off from the Hold with the Borrowmen.

She steeled herself and called on more power, advancing toward the end of the causeway. In desperation, the Geladanian warriors charged. Below her on the beach, Temerran's voice rang out. 'Archers!'

Movement caught Kesta's eyes, her father was racing up the path from the dunes, Siveraell streaming behind him like a banner. She heard Arrus swear when he saw what she was fighting.

'Is the priestess on the ship?' Kesta yelled as she blasted out more flame.

The storm continued to intensify, the thunder so loud it vibrated the narrow spit of rock on which she stood.

'We don't know.'

It was Kesta's turn to curse. 'Siv, what happened to the fire-spirits?' Her flames wavered a little as she lost concentration.

'They are being held in the fire-realm. What do you need, Kessta?'

'I need to know where to be.' She poured more power into her flames as emotion rose from her chest to choke her.

'I'll find out.'

'No!' Kesta threw up a shield and pivoted to call after the spirit. 'Siveraell, you can't let her catch you!'

'Kes.' Arrus drew her back to the causeway.

'I need to save my power.'

He nodded, moving into a fighter's stance and stepping to one side to allow them both room to fight. Kesta drew her two long daggers.

'Let's dance, Urchin.' Arrus broke into a grin.

There were only about twenty men left, those who were wise enough, or cowardly enough, to hold back away from her magic. Three of them edged forward, and when Kesta didn't call her flames, they attacked.

Arrus caught a sword and then swung his up and high, bringing it down between the man's shoulder and neck. He placed his foot against the man's thigh to get leverage to pull his broadsword free and thrust it past him into the second man's belly as he raised his own sword to sweep it down. Kesta danced aside from the third man and spun; feinting with her left blade before plunging in the right.

The other men surged forward, seeing no magic was being used.

Arrus grabbed up one of the fallen men's swords and like Kesta he blocked and lunged, moving faster than his size would have attested. The narrowness of the causeway made it hard for the Geladanians to pass them, but their numbers pressed them back and three times Kesta had to use a little of her magic to stop them. Above, lightning split the sky and the Borrowmen joined in with Temerran's song. The eerie, deep sound sent a shiver down Kesta's spine as she sliced her dagger across one man's chest and stabbed the other into an unguarded throat.

A bright, fiery light suddenly illuminated the causeway. Unable to turn her back on the Geladanians, Kesta reached out to shield herself and her father, staring into the eyes of one of the terrified men to see what was reflected there.

Siveraell; grown almost to the size of three bulls, his visage more terrifying than any face Azrael had ever pulled.

The muscles of Kesta's legs went suddenly weak. She'd caught him. The priestess had captured Siveraell and had turned him against them.

Siveraell flew at them and Kesta poured more power into her shield, ducking and bracing for attack.

Nothing.

The fire-spirit flew straight over her and decimated the remaining Geladanians.

'Kessta.' Siveraell shrank quickly to his normal size. 'The priestess is not on the ship; it is guarded by air elementals. The Icante says she will finish them, then join you in the Hold.'

Kesta hurried to look back down on the beach. Flames were eating their way through the forecastle of the king's ship. Another fork of lighting lashed down, seeming to run the length of the mainmast until it blackened, smoked, and caught. Three boats filled with warriors were heading for the beach, already pushing through the surf. Her mother threw balls of flame, more testing than attacking, each repelled by the shield of an elemental. The Borrowmen were waiting, bows exchanged for sword and shield, their deep voices still raised in the bard's war song.

With a groan, Kesta turned toward the Hold. There was no choice, she'd have to leave her mother.

She didn't look back as she sprinted across the causeway, her shadow before her and the sound of boots telling her Siveraell and her father followed. As they drew close to the gates, they yawned open, the men on the wall above greeting them with cheers.

'What's the situation?' Kesta demanded.

'There were men scaling the cliffs, Silene, but none have made it to the walls,' one warrior informed them. He shook his head. 'How they thought they could scale the walls when they got there is beyond me.'

Kesta looked from her father to Siveraell, and from their expressions they were thinking the same thing. Another diversion.

'Where's Heara?'

'She's commanding on the wall.' The warrior pointed.

'And my children?'

'The great hall, with Everlyn.'

'I'll report to Heara,' Siveraell offered, and sped away at once.

Kesta hurried through the houses, the signs of the previous attack on the hold still evident. It was eerily quiet but for the occasional shout or cry from the seaward walls. The empty black windows of the buildings seemed to stare into her soul.

Several warriors stood guard outside the great hall. On seeing Kesta they called inside and stepped out of the way, greeting her and Arrus with clasped wrists. Kesta impatiently moved through them and into the hall. More warriors waited within, some standing, most sitting at the long tables. There were only twenty, but Kesta recognised them as the Hold's best.

'Kessta!' Azrael came shooting toward her, making rapid little yips as he turned somersaults around her head.

At the high table Everlyn sat, bandages still swaddling much of her body. Beside her Rosa and Tantony stood, catching up with each other's adventures. At the large cooking hearth Doraquael patrolled, while Nip read to Joss and Arridia, who sat at his feet. In a chair opposite him, Worvig sat, his sword balanced across his lap.

'Brother.' Arrus darted forward, grabbing Worvig in a hug.

A painful lump formed in Kesta's throat.

Worvig struggled to push his brother aside. 'Don't fuss, Arrus,' he complained gruffly.

Arrus gave a sniff and straightened up. 'What news?'

'None in here.' It was Everlyn who answered.

'Mumma…' Arridia sat up, her eyes wide.

'How goes it out there?' Worvig asked.

'The causeway is clear,' Arrus told him. 'Dia is holding the beach—'

'Mumma.' Arridia's voice came out in a frightened squeak.

Kesta met her daughter's eyes.

She shielded, stretching it out to take in those at the fireplace. Everlyn and the fire-spirits responded with shields of their own as a huge blast of power came from nowhere. Several warriors screamed, the bones of those outside the shields shattering, their lungs collapsing. The building groaned, the temporary repairs to the roof blasted away. Plates, jugs, and uneaten food tumbled to a halt. Kesta blinked, looking around at the devastation, searching for her attacker.

Joss was crying, Nip shielding the boy with his body. Arrus and Worvig stood back to back over Arridia. The little girl was pointing over Kesta's shoulder. Kesta pivoted, but saw only empty space. Then intuition prickled.

She called her *knowing* and at once caught the emotions of a stranger, feelings of triumph, feelings of hatred. A surge of power.

Kesta threw everything she had, her veins seeming to tear as her magic ripped through her. She felt the impact of it hit an invisible barrier, hurling whatever it was against the Hold doors. The heavy wooden bar cracked and the doors were flung open, scattering the warriors on the other side who lost their footing and tumbled.

As they scrambled to their feet, another figure also stood, turning slowly, her serpent staff in her hand.

'You bitch,' Kesta snarled.

'Mumma did a swear!' Joss chirped in surprise.

'I think under the circumstances she's entitled,' Arrus said.

The High Priestess straightened her dress, glaring at Kesta with glittering dark eyes. She opened her mouth to speak.

Kesta blasted her again. This time the priestess's shield held, but she was forced back out across the courtyard and Kesta advanced after her, aware that Everlyn moved carefully to her left, and Arrus to her right. A shuffling step told her Tantony was behind her.

The priestess raised her staff and both Kesta and Everlyn shielded, not just themselves but the front of the building. Fire seared past them, and within it were the wails of several trapped spirits. Kesta's anger boiled over to white hot rage, she could barely see as the blood roared through her ears. She pushed through the flames, drawing her dagger and advancing on Yalla. The priestess sensed her approach, showing her teeth in a contemptuous sneer as their eyes met through the conflagration. Yalla spoke words too soft for Kesta to hear and she released a fire-spirit from the staff; it went straight for Kesta, its blue eyes a broken, silent, cry.

Siveraell intercepted it, coming from nowhere and taking it down into the rock beneath the hold.

The priestess cursed, her grin slipping. She ceased her flames and shifted with uncanny speed to a ferocious blast of icy air. Azrael and Doraquael shot forward to hover beside Kesta and Everlyn, adding to their shield. Kesta's heart gave a terrified jolt.

'No, stay back! Don't let her capture you.'

Yalla looked from Kesta to the spirits, and Kesta knew she'd made a grievous error and shown the priestess a weakness. Yalla raised her staff, the emerald eyes of the golden head glowed.

Lightning forked down, striking Yalla's shield, leaving a tang of ozone. As the priestess twisted to glance over her shoulder, Kesta and

Everlyn both sent flames of their own at the staff, Kesta increasing the intensity of her heat, stretching herself to her limits. Blood trickled distractingly from her nostrils.

Yalla's shield held.

Again, and again lightning struck it.

'Everlyn,' Kesta panted. 'The staff. The storm.'

Everlyn nodded.

'My boys.' Kesta glanced at Azrael. 'Hold our shield.'

Kesta drew a breath into her shaking body. She reached up for her mother's storm and fed her power into it. She sensed the familiar signature of the Icante, and that of the Raven with her – but there was more. Eidwyn had joined her magic and... Siveraell eased up out of the rock beneath them, but he wasn't alone. Tears broke free from Kesta's eyes as several dozen fire-spirits streamed after the elder drake and up into the thunderhead, building its pressure, swirling the hot and cold air.

Kesta reached for it and pulled down. A tremendous barrage of lightning struck the staff, splitting her eardrums with thunder. White and black after images blinded her, but she felt the heat and sting of the lightning Everlyn called to follow.

Yalla's shield held.

The High Priestess pointed the staff at Azrael, the little drake gave a shriek as he was snatched from the air and dragged toward the snake's head.

'No!' Kesta closed her eyes, forgetting her body as she reached for the power of the storm as she would a waiting spirit within the flame. She took the lightning, a slippery, kicking fury that threatened to tear her apart and once again drew it down.

The staff shattered.

Blood dripped from Kesta's eyes.

Everlyn fell.

The sky burst, rain lashing down in drops so large they stung like hail. The ground sizzled and smoked where the lightning had struck. Yalla turned to Kesta, face red, eyes wide, teeth bared. She called power to her clawed hands.

Yalla screamed.

From the broken staff several spirits fled, air, water, fire, and even earth; but some of them remained, joining with Azrael and Doraquael as they ripped the priestess apart.

Kesta collapsed to her knees, a faint smile on her lips as she saw the silhouette of her mother through the driving rain.

'Kes?' Her father grabbed her shoulders.

'Okay,' she said. 'The children?'

'Safe.'

She let out a small whimper, tears falling to mix with the blood on her face.

'Everlyn?' Dia ran forward, landing on her knees beside the fallen *walker*. 'Oh, Eve, my friend.' The Icante's face crumpled as a sob broke her. 'We've been through so much together.'

Pain closed Kesta's throat, and she moved on her hands and knees to her mother's side. She couldn't speak, she couldn't ask.

Arrus leaned over them to check for Everlyn's pulse. 'She's alive.'

Both Dia and Kesta looked up at him incredulously, neither daring to hope. Arrus bent and scooped the injured woman up carefully in his arms, to carry her back inside the hold.

394

Azrael darted around them, whooping and cheering in crazy loops. 'We won!'

Kesta held her mother's gaze. Neither of them smiled. They hadn't won, not yet.

Kesta cleared her throat. 'Your plan. I have the rest of it. We need some of the Geladanians alive, if possible. Then we need Jorrun.'

Chapter Twenty-Five

Catya; Free city of Navere

Catya gazed down at the parchment, her finger running down the list of places they would raid tonight. She paused on the trader's name, the one who was still sheltering Damel. She'd been assigned there herself with Ovey and Harta. There was one thing they were waiting for…

'My lady.' A guard knocked at the door to Osun's study. 'They have arrived.'

Catya grinned, hurrying down the corridors to the audience room. The whole palace seemed to be astir, many busy with preparations for tonight's dinner. While the raids themselves were a closely guarded secret, it was common knowledge that the High Priest of Navere and his administrator were to eat with them this evening after Rece and Calayna held a meeting with them to discuss plans for Domarra's festival and the future of Navere province. During the meeting, the Ravens would strike, taking out all those they knew were associated with the Disciples of the Gods.

Their concern was Bantu. They suspected he had power, but didn't know how much.

The familiar, deep voice, made her heart swell as the guards opened one of the private doors to the audience room for her. Taller than anyone else in the room, Jorrun was easy to spot, as was Tyrin's red hair. Jorrun appeared deeply troubled, despite his smile, the skin beneath his eyes dark and puffy. She surveyed the room again, taking in the elegant, tattooed woman who looked so like her brother.

Catya drew in a sharp breath, searching a third time with her eyes, a sharp stab of fear jolting her heart. She hurried to Jorrun's side.

'Catya.' He smiled down at her. 'It's good to see you.'

'Cass, is he…?'

Jorrun's smile faded a little. 'He was well when I left him, Cat. He stayed with Rothfel to escort an injured Raven safely back to Caergard.'

She let out the breath she'd been holding.

'Catya, this is my sister, Dinari.'

Catya reached out a hand toward the woman and Dinari took it at once, her fingers long and the skin of her hand soft, unlike Catya's calloused one.

'I've heard a lot about you,' Dinari said.

Catya glanced at Jorrun, who gave one of his rare laughs.

'All good things,' Jorrun reassured her.

Catya shuffled her feet, aware there was plenty of bad he might have said about her had he wished.

Dinari cleared her throat. 'The library.'

Jorrun sighed, calling out to the elected head of the Navere Coven. 'Calayna, a moment.' He explained quickly about the book Dinari had found in their library as a girl. Calayna grew pale, looking down at her tattooed hands, then up at Dinari's blue eyes.

'I'd never even thought to hope I might lose my tattoos… or ever have power.' Calayna's voice was shaky.

'Can we look now?' Dinari turned to Jorrun.

Calayna shook her head. 'We need to brief Jorrun.'

'I'll do that,' Catya offered at once.

Calayna smiled tentatively at Dinari. 'The library is this way.'

'I think I remember,' Dinari replied softly.

Jorrun watched the two women as they left the room, then turned to Catya. 'Have you had news from the Fulmers?'

'Not for several days. Has something happened?'

Jorrun nodded, taking her arm and moving to the side of the room. 'The Hold was attacked again. Kesta and the children are safe, but I am needed there. I... I should have been there.'

Catya froze, her eyes growing wide. Jorrun was crying. She'd never seen him cry before, never. It made her feel helpless, afraid. She swallowed, reaching out to take one of his hands, larger and stronger than her own. The hand that has sheltered her.

'You can't be everywhere, Jorrun, you can't save everyone.'

'My family should have come first.' His skin flushed redder, the grip on her hand tightening briefly.

'You were protecting them from Chem. Kesta was protecting them from Geladan.'

Jorrun hesitated, his chest rising and falling. 'I can't see it like that. Chem could have waited, even Dinari could have waited.'

Catya shook her head. 'Bantu and his Disciples are ready to strike, to take Navere. If Navere falls, we all fall.'

Rece stepped up quietly beside them. 'Everything is in place.'

Jorrun drew in a deep breath, and nodded, wiping at his eyes with the tips of three fingers. 'The boy, Alikan, how is he?'

Catya grinned. 'He is having his lessons with Ovey.'

'I'd like to check on him.'

'Okay.' Catya drew herself up. 'Alikan, then your briefing, then I guess the library.'

Jorrun raised his eyebrows at her and she laughed, blushing slightly.

'I'll catch up with you in the library.' Rece clapped Jorrun lightly on the back.

***

They watched from a distance as Ovey, and his brother Neffy, demonstrated calling fire and shaping it into a missile, taking turns to attack and shield. The young guard, Duco, stood a little apart, a sleeping kitten balanced on one arm. He gave Catya a tentative wave and a flood of warmth coursed through her. With a glance at Jorrun, she held up a hand briefly in return.

Alikan stood up from where he observed on the grass, the two much older boys crossing to him. Jorrun drew in an audible breath when flames appeared above Alikan's palm, both Ovey and Neffy cheering and ruffling the boy's hair.

'He's found his magic,' Jorrun said.

'A few days ago.' Catya smiled. 'Ovey thinks he'll be strong.'

'Kesta thought so,' Jorrun agreed softly. 'Tell me your plans.'

Catya took him to the study and she briefed him on all the information they'd gathered, basking in his approval.

'I should come with you,' Jorrun said.

Catya shook her head. 'Rece and Calayna will need you in case Bantu does have power.'

She saw the muscles of his jaw moving as he ground his teeth. 'All the Ravens with magic here are very young.'

'And all of them have been trained exceptionally,' Catya pointed out. 'Damel is the strongest magic user we face, Ovey and Tyrin are more than a match for him.'

Jorrun made a noise in his throat, unconvinced.

'You have to let your fledglings go sometime.'

Jorrun turned to regard her. 'Before they rebel and leave of their own accord?'

She quickly looked away. 'Shall we go to the library?'

He sighed silently. 'Yes.'

Catya felt the silence grow awkwardly between them as they made their way back through the palace. She'd never regretted her decision to leave the Fulmers before, but for the first time, doubt wormed in her heart. She'd never admitted to anyone the real reason she'd run away on the Borrow ship, not even herself.

The library door was ajar and the sound of excited laughter came from within. Jorrun's pace quickened and Catya had to hurry to keep up with his long stride.

'Jorrun!'

Both Dinari and Calayna spun around to face him as they entered. Rece was sitting forward on the edge of his seat, a wide smile on his face, his hazel eyes sparkling. Dinari held the book balanced in her hand out toward Jorrun.

'It's still here.'

Jorrun swayed ever so slightly, then strode to his sister's side, looking over her arm at the pages. His eyes moved as he read.

'It's possible,' Jorrun breathed.

Rece stood up. Dinari and Calayna stared at him, hardly breathing. Even Catya found herself caught frozen in the moment.

Jorrun took the book from Dinari and turned the page. 'You're right that it's a type of blood magic, but there's no killing or invoking gods for this, only understanding how to use magic with the living body. It will take time to study and understand fully, but I should be able to do it. Brother, would you allow me to study our father's notes, learn what I can of the things which can be used for good?'

Jorrun hesitated, and gave a slow nod. He almost dropped the book as Dinari grabbed him in a hug. Rece stepped forward to put an arm around his wife.

Catya smiled and gave a quiet snort through her nose. These two women might be as powerful as Kesta, perhaps as powerful as Dia. It might be enough to tip the balance considerably in their favour.

She quietly slipped away to polish and sharpen her weapons.

***

Catya watched from her perch on the rooftops as Bantu and Kerzin arrived at the palace. They'd chosen to walk rather than use a horse or litter and Catya presumed the High Priest wished to look humble. Her insides tightened a little, but she dismissed her apprehension. Jorrun could handle them.

She crept to the edge, took hold of the eaves, and dropped to the road below.

'Time to move?' Tyrin asked.

Catya nodded.

They had two dozen palace guards with them, all of them dressed as civilians of varying financial status. Ovey was already in place opposite the merchant's house, disguised as a ragged drunk slumped up against the wall. Two city guards who were part of the plan strode up to Ovey, making a loud scene to draw attention. Catya smiled as a face appeared briefly in the merchant's window. Catya moved down an alley, then climbed a tree with the ease of a squirrel. She immediately checked the way was clear, then slipped over the fence. With a glance upward to make sure Tyrin was keeping up, she ran down a second alley to an innocuous looking gate.

'Quickly,' Catya urged. 'They're almost ready.'

Tyrin didn't have her grace, but he matched her stamina and she didn't hear as much as a breath from the younger Raven. Shouts caught her ears, brought to her on the wind from across the city. One of their other coordinated attacks had already begun.

They were out of time.

Tyrin sent a blast of air at the gate, smashing it in. Catya sprinted across the dirty flagstones towards the back door; it flew open and three men burst out. None were Damel.

'Go help Ovey,' Catya urged. 'I'll take these. Watch your back.'

She drew two knives; two of the men spun to face her, the third made a run for the alley. Catya gave a shake of her head, then leapt, tucked into a ball and rolled between the two men, placing a dagger in the belly of each. She came to her feet, snatched both her daggers, and threw one at the man who'd almost made it through the destroyed gate. The knife bounced off the man's ribs and clattered on the flagstones. Catya cursed. The man turned and charged her, spittle flying from his mouth as he gave a desperate cry. Catya's second dagger embedded in his throat.

She sprinted to the house, pausing in the doorway. The sounds of battle were loud inside, the building shook and dust fell. She couldn't sense magic, but she felt the push of a strong, hot wind. She was in a kitchen, a woman and a girl huddled together on the floor beneath a table. Catya nodded toward the yard door and rushed across the tiles. Three men lay dead in the hallway, one of them a Navere guard. She charged up the stairs, her heart stopping when she saw Tyrin lying unmoving on the ground. Blood oozed from a wound on the back of his head, but his chest rose and fell. She cursed; she should never have let him go in without her backup. Yet again she'd been careless with someone else's life so she could take a kill.

Several pale-looking palace guards stood at bay further down the hallway, one of them indicated a room in which light flickered and flashed.

'Get Tyrin back to the palace,' she ordered. Catya placed her back against the wall and took a quick peep into the room. Ovey was holding his shield and trying to fight not one sorcerer, but two. The teenager's face was red, the tendons in his neck showing his strain. Catya didn't hesitate. She braced herself, then launched herself into the room. She leapt, one foot landing on a cupboard to propel her into a somersault. She drew her daggers, stabbing them down into either side of one sorcerer's neck as she flipped onto her feet. Damel twisted to blast her with fire, but she was already rolling across the floor and up onto her feet behind Ovey.

'You can do it,' she urged.

Ovey renewed his attack, throwing Damel against the wall. Catya followed the blast, running in to kick Damel in the groin, then in the face.

She turned to see Ovey wincing. 'Ove, grab two guards and catch up with the ones taking Tyrin back to the palace.'

The boy straightened up and nodded, breathing hard. He didn't see Catya pick up one of her daggers and slice it across Damel's throat.

She went to the window and looked out. There was still some fighting in the street down below. The guards had captured two men, two more were engaged with a single Raven. There was only one man under the sky who could use a sword like that. Catya grinned.

She took the stairs two at a time, ordering the milling guards to make a last search of the building. By the time she reached Cassien, his two opponents were down; one injured, one dead. He wasn't even slightly winded.

'Cass.' She subdued her grin and raised her chin. 'How did you find us?'

'I just followed the scent of death,' he replied, the light in his grey eyes belying his stern tone.

Catya did grin then. 'Come on, Cass, we're late for dinner.'

Chapter Twenty-Six

Jorrun; Free City of Navere

Jorrun had to stop himself wincing when Kerzin gave him another nervous, wide-eyed glance. For a man who'd survived so long hiding with his enemy, he wasn't being very subtle. Jorrun forced himself to pay attention to the grey-haired High Priest. The polite deception was killing him inside, all he wanted to was blast the man into the next world and be on his way to the Fulmers. His family might be safe, but he desperately needed to see them, to hold them; and to beg their forgiveness for not being there. No matter how many times everyone told him he had more responsibility to the lands under the sky than his own children, his heart refused to hear it.

'Hmm.' Bantu frowned as he studied the two sketches. 'Playing music of the Fulmers and Elden in the foreign market sounds intriguing, but it might be wise to remember it's the festival of Domarra. We wouldn't want to offend anyone.' He looked from Rece to Calayna.

Rece scratched at his greying hair and sighed. 'You have a point there. Perhaps we should leave the cultural demonstration to another day.'

'The rest looks great, though.' Bantu beamed at them, his eyes meeting Jorrun's briefly. 'We shall be holding our hourly prayers in the temple, but I'll be sure to pop out and see as much as I can of the festivities. It will be interesting to see how many pilgrims come in from the outer province compared to other years.'

Jorrun couldn't help wondering how many of those pilgrims would be followers of Hacren – or even Warenna's Wolves – rather than simple pilgrims.

'Shall we go through to dinner then?' Calayna suggested.

'I would be delighted.' Bantu's eyes scanned the library and Jorrun followed his gaze. He had no doubt the High Priest would love to get his hands on Dryn Dunham's book collection.

Jorrun fell in beside Bantu as Calayna and Rece led the way, Kerzin following behind with Beth. Only one person awaited them in the dining room and Jorrun had to hide his surprise.

'Rothfel.' Rece stepped forward to shake his hand. 'We were not expecting you.'

'I have not long arrived.' Rothfel gave them all a polite bow. 'Raven Catya invited me, I hope I'm not intruding?'

'Not at all.' Calayna took charge quickly and introduced him. 'This is Rothfel, a trader whose travels have resulted in fabulous tales that keep us entertained.'

'Is that so?' Bantu cocked his head. 'I look forward to hearing them, then.'

Jorrun studied Rothfel through narrowed eyes. The many-skilled man had subtly informed them he'd seen Catya, but as yet they had no news of her or how their raids in the city had gone.

'Some wine, dear friends,' Calayna offered, and the palace steward, Zardin offered them glasses, his face still.

'Thank you.' Bantu took a sip of the dark-red liquid. 'Hmm. I don't recognise the vintage.'

'From Elden,' Jorrun told him. 'A town called Woodwick.'

Bantu raised his eyebrows. 'It's good.'

The door opened and a small group stepped in, Dinari at their head. Bantu froze, his expression seeming to darken, before he recovered and forced a smile. Had it been the sight of another woman with tattoos, Jorrun wondered, or the Dunham features so clear on his sister's face?

Catya followed on her heels with young Ovey, Sirelle, and Jollen; Cassien bringing up the rear. He saw Rece glance at him out of the corner of his eye, though he himself didn't react. It was supposed to be Tyrin joining them for dinner, not teenaged Ovey. Cold fingers ran down Jorrun's spine. Sirelle had some bruising to her face, so Jorrun guessed her raid also hadn't gone entirely to plan.

He quickly recovered and introduced Dinari to both Bantu and Kerzin.

'I wasn't aware you had a sister here?' Bantu did well to hold Dinari's gaze and not let his eyes wander over her terrible blood tattoos.

'I have but recently rescued her from Uldren,' Jorrun replied.

Bantu's nostrils flared ever so slightly and Jorrun wanted desperately to grin in satisfaction.

'You raided Uldren?' Kerzin asked, his voice raised, his face flushing. He'd known about the raid, only after it had happened, but was doing a good job at feigning outrage for Bantu's sake.

'Oh, calm down, administrator.' Bantu met Jorrun's gaze and made a helpless gesture with his hand. 'Although I cannot condone violence and am still – as you know – coming to terms with the huge changes to my country.'

'It's blasphemy,' Kerzin muttered.

'Maybe we should eat,' Jorrun suggested.

Calayna overheard and nodded to Zardin who waited to usher in the servants. Jorrun pulled out a chair for Bantu and moved around the table to sit opposite him. Catya sat to Bantu's left, and Beth to his right. All the servants left the room, Zardin closing the doors behind them. It was a moment before Bantu registered that something was wrong; all eyes had turned toward him.

'Catya, can I have your report please,' Jorrun asked.

Bantu didn't move, his eyes not leaving Jorrun as Catya spoke.

'The raids were a success. We have taken out every hiding place of the Disciples in accordance to our intelligence. There are thirty-one prisoners in our dungeons, two of whom have already started spilling their guts about everything they know.'

'What's this?' Bantu tried to smile, but his movements were twitchy. He glanced at Kerzin. 'I hope you have good reason to be attacking our citizens in their homes?'

Jorrun leaned forward and the High Priest leaned back. 'We have very good reason. The so-called Disciples of the Gods have been murdering the people of Navere, people under the protection of the Ravens. And they have been plotting to try again to call their god through to this realm, as you know yourself, Bantu.'

'And I assured you, if I heard anything, I'd tell you.' Bantu raised his hands. 'I hope—'

Jorrun stood slowly and the smile slipped from Bantu's face. 'Bantu, we accuse you of causing the deaths of many innocent people, inciting riot, and most importantly, seeking to raise a god – or a demon – who would have enslaved and murdered thousands.'

'Nonsense.' Bantu pushed his chair back from the table. 'I'm not a fool. What evidence do you have? Who has accused me?'

'I have.' Kerzin's voice was quiet, but silenced Bantu at once.

Bantu stared at him, his eyes growing wider. 'No.' He began to stand, but stopped himself. He shook his head vigorously. 'No, you have got this all wrong. I have been working to stop the Disciples, to calm things in Navere. There.' He pointed at Kerzin. 'There is your traitor, your plotter! Kerzin has power, I know it, he is the one who wishes to raise a god! He has accused me to throw you from his own trail, to rid you of me, who would help the Ravens bring peace to Chem—'

'You're the deceiver, you have power too.' Kerzin's face reddened and he scrambled to his feet.

'Sit down,' Jorrun warned.

The administrator ignored him.

'Kerzin, what have you done?' Bantu stared at him wide-eyed. 'Are you really foolish enough to try to raise a god?'

'Shut up!' The tendons stood out on Kerzin's neck. 'Don't believe him.' The administrator tipped his chair over, almost falling over it as he backed away from the table. He met Jorrun's eyes and saw the doubt there. Kerzin growled, calling his power.

Every magic user in the room called their own power in response, Rece, Catya, and Cassien reaching for their weapons.

Kerzin shielded, calling flames to his hands.

Both Ovey and Sirelle aimed a blast at Kerzin, and his shield collapsed. Beth was a second behind them, choosing flame. It shot toward Kerzin in a narrow jet.

Kerzin's eyes remained fixed on Bantu, his flames directed at the High Priest.

Jorrun moved, darting in front of Kerzin to protect him with his own shield. Beth screamed, cutting off her power, breathing hard and almost collapsing when she saw her blast had no effect on Jorrun.

He pivoted in time to see Bantu lift a vial to his lips, a drop of blood falling on his chin.

'It's Bantu,' Jorrun said, his voice calm.

'What have you done?' Kerzin demanded, his raised finger pointing towards the drop of blood.

Bantu grinned. 'Just asked for a little help in destroying this little nest of abominations.' He gasped and doubled over, his face going red, then almost purple. Beth backed away from him and Cassien pushed Ovey behind him, toward the door.

Bantu grunted, his skin stretched and moved.

Dinari snatched a bread knife off the table and stepped close to Calayna and Rece.

Bantu flung his head back and let out a roar, his arms, legs, and spine all stretching out in an impossible way, his darkening red skin scaling over, even his hair rapidly lengthening. Then fire erupted from his mouth and hands.

'Get them out!' Jorrun bellowed to Rece. As Jorrun threw a blast of freezing air at the High Priest, Rece grabbed Dinari's arm and kicked open the doors to the garden to push her out, Calayna following at once.

Smoke began to fill the room as Bantu and Jorrun's magic met. Catya leapt up onto the table, landing in a crouch with her daggers ready. Beth, Jollen, and Sirelle came together, their shields merging in to one. Rothfel ghosted towards Cassien and Ovey. The priest continued to grow, and Jorrun heard Kerzin whimper, 'He'll bring down the palace.'

Realisation hit Jorrun hard in the chest; the man was right. He prayed Cass and the others would understand as he started to back toward the garden doors. Bantu's flames pursued them while Jollen worked hard to stop the table and walls igniting. As Jorrun backed up, Bantu followed. One of Kerzin's hands clutched at Jorrun's shirt as he continued to hide behind him; Jorrun gritted his teeth but shied away from making any judgement.

Bantu laughed, the sound hollow and rolling, like thunder in a valley. He increased his flames, blasting the doors and part of the wall out into the garden. As he advanced after Jorrun, Catya sprang from the table, landing on Bantu's reptilian back. She stabbed down with her daggers, but both blades screeched off his scales, barely leaving a score mark. She landed on her feet, diving aside as Bantu twisted to flail at her with his growing talons, flames still spilling from his palms. Cassien stepped in, his blade flicking out to pierce Bantu's wrist, slipping beneath a scale which snapped and took the tip of the blade with it.

Ovey and the three female Ravens pushed at the monstrous creature, their magic sending it staggering a few steps forward. Jorrun backed away, letting it come. The marble floor gave way to grass as he stepped over the threshold. Calayna had moved to the shelter of a yew tree, gripping Dinari's arm tightly to keep her back. Rece shouted commands to the guards who'd come running.

Bantu burst from the dining room, stone, glass, and timber raining down around him. Relief flooded through Jorrun and he drew himself up. As he shoved Kerzin out of the way with his right hand, he raised his left and drew the rest of his power. He aimed at Bantu's right leg, taking it out from under him. As the creature toppled, it called up its shield, deflecting the flames from the Ravens who clustered behind him in the broken doorway.

Cassien and Catya split up, circling, waiting for an opportunity.

Bantu dragged himself up, and reached for Jorrun with an opening claw, the black nails now as long as a man's forearm. Jorrun continued his stream of flames, but the blood-beast appeared immune. He glanced toward his sister; she was the only one of them with more knowledge of blood magic than he, albeit from years ago. Would this spell wear off in time? They couldn't count on it.

Bantu swiped at Jorrun and he rolled aside. The High Priest rounded on Kerzin, whose eyes grew huge. He didn't run, calling a weak shield to stand his ground. Jorrun swore, reaching down into the earth, risking the stability of the palace to rip a rock up from beneath the earth.

Bantu almost toppled, his arms flailing and missing Kerzin by a fraction. The creature leapt away from the moving ground, landing clumsily close to Dinari and Calayna. Rece led a charge with his guards and Jorrun tried desperately to throw Bantu off balance again with a strong blast of air, but the monstrosity scattered the men like wheat stalks. Calayna screamed out the captain's name, searing Jorrun's heart.

There had to be a way.

Firelight reflected off Bantu's scales. Bantu turned, searching for Kerzin, his eyes glistening as they caught the light of the Raven's attack.

His eyes.

Jorrun drew in air and bellowed, 'Ravens!'

Cassien was first to his side, stepping into the shelter of his shield, guiding young Ovey to join them. Jollen, Beth, and Sirelle came more cautiously, dodging the fiery breath of Bantu. Jorrun's heart gave a painful skip, pumping hard as Dinari dragged Calayna toward him, through the fallen men. He renewed his attack, drawing the High Priest's attention until the women were safe behind him.

Two missing. Two who worked best alone.

'Hold the shield.' Jorrun glanced around breathlessly. 'Cass, his eyes.'

Cassien nodded, sheathing his broken sword and drawing two daggers.

'Jollen.' Jorrun turned to the tall, brown-eyed Raven. 'Help me break his shield.'

She nodded, flicking her brown hair away from her sweaty face.

Bantu charged them, so large now the ground vibrated with every thud of his hooved feet. Jorrun and Jollen threw everything they had at him and he slammed up against the force of their blast of air, howling in frustration. A small figure came leaping out of the darkness, mud smeared across her face to hide her pale skin. Catya sprang onto her hands and into a somersault that took her between Bantu's legs. She drew her dagger and slashed upward.

Jorrun winced, his own muscles constricting. It was an inspired move, but the screech of the blade told them every part of this obscenity was scaled.

Nearly every part.

Catya sprinted to join them, shaking her head. 'I'm sorry,' she panted.

Bantu reached around to tear a tree out of the earth; he threw it at them. The Ravens instinctively ducked, Beth pushing more power into their shield. Jorrun swirled air into a tornado, sweeping the tree up and away, then back toward the priest.

'Dinari.' Jorrun turned to his sister. 'Have you read anything of this?'

'It's a blood curse,' she raised her voice. 'He sold his soul to his god for power.'

'How do we stop him?'

The paleness of her skin and her silence told him her answer.

Jorrun clenched his jaw, nausea rising from his stomach. He turned and met Cassien's eyes and the younger man nodded, shifting his weight in a fighter's stance.

'His scales are impenetrable.' Catya shook her head in frustration.

Jorrun ignored her, calling his power and forcing as much as he could through his protesting body. The other's joined him, Ovey stumbling a little. Bantu pushed against them, his hooves leaving deep scores in the scorched lawn.

Two figures moved in to either side of Jorrun. To his left, Rothfel, somehow wrapped in the night, handed four objects to Cassien. The young man's eyes widened, but he grabbed the objects and immediately began binding them to the handles of his daggers.

Alikan stepped up to Jorrun's right hip and raised his hands, adding his power to that of the Ravens. Jorrun shook his head, fear squeezing his heart.

'Alikan, no, get to safety.'

Alikan's nostrils flared and his eyelids fluttered over his amber eyes. The boy increased his power, ignoring Jorrun.

Their attack intensified again and Jorrun risked a glance behind to see Tyrin was with them, his head still bandaged. Around him were Harta, Charis, and Neffy.

Bantu's shield buckled, then broke. The creature let out a roar as it went flailing backward.

'Stop, just shield!' Jorrun called out.

As Bantu righted himself, Cassien threw his first dagger. It struck Bantu's scarlet cheek and spun off into the darkness.

Bantu bunched his muscles to charge.

Cassien threw his second dagger, but Bantu saw it, batting it aside as he sprang into a run.

'For the Gods' sake!' Cassien cursed. He turned. 'Cat!'

Cassien threw one of his daggers to Catya and she caught it by the blade. Cassien and Catya threw their daggers at the exact same moment, spinning on their heels as Bantu came at them. The daggers span through the air, their trajectory slightly erratic because of the load they carried.

Both daggers thudded into Bantu's eyes.

The creature screamed, its claws raising to pull the daggers free.

'Fire!' Cassien bellowed.

Jorrun drew the last of his power and threw flames at Bantu.

The creature's head exploded, the force of it throwing all of them off their feet and shattering what was left of the Raven's shield. Blood, bone, and gore rained down with the scorching heat.

Jorrun hit the ground hard.

His lungs refused for a moment to take in air, but he forced them, rolling onto his side. Red, white, and black after images danced before him and he could hear nothing beyond the ringing in his ears.

He scrambled to his feet, finding Alikan. Catya was also up, checking on Tyrin.

A wail of despair cut through the explosion-induced silence and Jorrun turned to see Calayna staggering toward the still body of Rece, Dinari chasing her unsteadily. Jorrun kissed to top of Alikan's head, then pushed him toward Catya. Dinari moved to allow Jorrun to kneel beside Rece. The man was still breathing, but a deep, bloody tear had laid his chest open. His eyes were locked on Calayna's, his hand clasped in both of hers.

'Jorrun,' Dinari said, her voice was calm, almost stern. 'This is a wound beyond normal healing, but not beyond magic.'

He stared at her, his eyes caught by the swirling tattoos on her face. He swallowed. 'I don't know how.'

'Then listen.' She smiled ever so slightly. 'According to our father's research, the body instantly tries to heal itself. Apparently, all you have to do is very gently add the flow of your magic to the flow of the patient's blood and… well, you kind of will the body to heal, you urge it on in repairing itself.'

Jorrun studied her face. 'That's all?'

She nodded, but looked away briefly. She was hiding something.

Jorrun turned to regard Rece, his friend, a kind gentle man whose courage was astounding. Rece didn't complain, didn't struggle or fight, he simply drew these last precious moments with his wife into his soul.

Jorrun choked, his vision blurring. He drew in a deep breath and called on the slow remnants of his power. Jorrun placed his hands carefully on Rece's chest, above and below the wound. He closed his eyes, trying to sense the flow of the man's blood. Not sure where to push his magic, he let it go, taking in a sharp breath when he felt his magic drawn from him as though Rece's body reached for it, and his blood did indeed understand what to do.

Dinari gave a breathy whisper. 'I knew it, I knew of all people it would be you.'

He didn't know how long he sat there, aware somewhere in the back of his mind of Cassien and Catya taking charge of the surviving guards and securing the palace. The flow of his magic was slow, somehow soothing, like a deep meditation, Rece's body not taking more than the weakened Jorrun was able to give.

'Jorrun.' Dinari placed a hand lightly on his shoulder. 'Jorrun, that's enough.'

He opened his eyes, blinking rapidly. The sun was just rising. Alikan was sitting a short distance away, his wide amber eyes fixed on Jorrun, his mouth slightly agape. Trouble lay curled up in the boy's lap and Catya stood protectively over him, Ruak on her shoulder.

The soft, muffled sound of crying made Jorrun look down. Calayna was bent over Rece, her face buried in his shoulder. The wound on Rece's chest had closed up, a vivid, angry, raised scar ran across his ribs. Jorrun winced, it wasn't neat, or pretty.

He met Rece's eyes and the captain nodded, mouthing the words, 'Thank you.'

Jorrun cleared his throat, looking away and rubbing his hands over his face and beard. He was exhausted.

'Come on, to bed.' Dinari helped him to his feet.

Jorrun didn't protest, but he looked around to check what was happening.

'All good, Thane,' Catya called out cheerfully.

Jorrun narrowed his eyes at her, then sighed and waved his hand in thanks. He let Dinari take his arm and help him towards the palace.

'Um.' Dinari glanced at him. 'You know our father was never able to heal anyone, though he tried. He thought it might be because he had the wrong blood, that his blood was too mixed—'

'But I am of mixed blood.'

Dinari shushed him. 'Dryn's research suggested healing and blood magic are an ancient magic of Chem, so he initially believed it was an inherited racial thing, like being a *walker*. Further study led him to believe it was more a matter of, um, purity…'

'Purity?' Jorrun looked at her sharply.

'Pureness of intent, pureness of spirit.'

Jorrun snorted.

Dinari squeezed his arm. 'That's what he wrote. Whatever the case, he couldn't do it, and neither could those he forced to try. He killed them, by the way, after they tried, to protect his secrets.'

'He would.'

'Yes, indeed. It's also apparently not possible to heal yourself, you can only heal another.'

Jorrun's eyebrows raised. That was interesting.

'Jorrun?' Dinari prompted as they reached one of the palace doors.

'Do me a favour.' He turned to meet her gaze. 'Have a ship made ready to sail, I don't care whose. As soon as I've had some sleep and can put one foot in front of the other on my own, I'm going home to my family.'

Chapter Twenty-Seven

Dia; Fulmer Hold

'No, your other left!' Arrus yelled, then muttered under his breath. 'Idiots.'

Dia turned away from the repair works, her eyes drawn to the house in which the Geladanian warriors were being held captive. Twenty warriors stood outside the building, the windows boarded up and a heavy beam barring the door. Twenty islanders to guard fifteen men; men who might guarantee the safety of her grandchildren, and the four nations of the north.

'Grandma?' Joss tugged at her hand.

'Yes, my honey?'

'Riddi says I can't be a *walker*. That isn't fair.'

Dia sighed and looked down at him, his blue eyes almost silver in the sunlight. 'I guess it isn't fair, my honey, but it is true, and we have to accept true things.'

'Why?'

'Because trying to change a true thing only brings you frustration and pain. Better to accept what is and make the most of it.'

Joss frowned at her and Dia laughed, feeling the tension fall away from her muscles, noticing the warmth of the sun for the first time. She reached down and took Joss's hand.

The door to the Hold flew open and Kesta came running out, ignoring her father's shout to sprint for the causeway. Dia turned to Arrus, who shrugged.

'Shall we see what your mum is doing?' Dia asked Joss.

He nodded; his face crumpled up in a worried frown.

They made their way through the Hold to the causeway. Temerran was leaning with his back to a brazier, gazing out to sea.

'A ship,' he said as Dia approached. 'A Chemmish ship.'

'Ah.' Dia joined him, keeping a tight hold on Joss's hand as he moved close to the rope railing. 'Any word from Nolv?'

'The cut timber has arrived from Seal Hold, so repairs are underway.'

'You should go to her.'

Temerran's face reddened a little. 'I sent Linea a letter—'

'A letter?' Dia turned to scowl at him. 'She wants you, not a letter.'

Temerran shifted his feet. 'It's a good letter. Anyway, I want to be here to see things through, before I head back to the *Undine*.'

Dia looked down at the beach, Kesta had come to a halt on the silver sand. She sighed. 'I suppose Linea could come here now things are a less fraught.'

Temerran gave a slight shake of his head. 'It's okay, you were right to keep her away for the moment. Every day I hear mutterings from your warriors about why we're keeping those Geladanian men alive.'

'When they're gone, you're welcome to stay here for the winter.'

'Thank you.' He smiled warmly, but the smile quickly faded. 'But I think I will take up Bractius's invitation to stay in Taurmaline.'

'Really?' Dia raised her eyebrows.

Temerran gave a bark of a laugh. 'I would much rather stay here, my dear friend, but the attacks on Fulmer have left you short of resources, you don't need my greedy men to feed. Bractius has a full larder that I won't feel guilty diminishing, and Ayline seemed to take a shine to Linea. I think – and I mean no offense – Linea will be more comfortable there. Just until things settle.'

Dia nodded.

The Chemmish ship had passed where the king's warship was anchored, carpenters removing some of its damaged wood. The mainmast had already been replaced, but as yet no canvas graced its spars.

Temerran followed her gaze. 'Bractius will be furious.'

The corner of Dia's mouth twitched upward. 'It's not our fault his men let the Geladanians steal his warship.'

'Isn't this the second of his ships you've destroyed?'

Dia narrowed her eyes at his grin.

The small Chemmish vessel was close to shore and launching its boat. She recognised Cassien at the railing, and the elegant, darker skinned woman was surely Jorrun's sister. Kesta moved closer to the surf and Dia smiled fondly; her daughter was often impatient. As the rowboat hit the breaking surf, Kesta waded out into the sea and a tall, black-clad figure leapt out of the boat to meet her, the sea swirling around them as they kissed.

Dia looked away, with a glance at Temerran.

Temerran chuckled. 'I believe the Thane will be busy for a while.'

'Indeed.' Dia squeezed Joss's hand. 'Come on, let's go annoy Uncle Worvig.'

'Is that Daddy?' Joss pointed down to the beach.

'It is. He'll be up soon, but he, um, has to sort some things out first.'

Temerran laughed aloud, and Dia gave him a withering glare.

'Sorry,' Temerran mouthed.

Dia rolled her eyes and led her reluctant grandson back to the great hall. She regarded the prisoner's accommodation again as they passed, gazing beyond it to the guest house where the injured were still being tended. Everlyn was doing well. It humbled Dia how much the younger woman had given for the islands. She'd overlooked her in the past as a possible Silene as Everlyn was shy and reclusive by nature. It was long past time to remedy that. With a sinking heart, Dia had to admit Everlyn would be the best choice for the next Icante, now Kesta had taken a different path.

They entered the great hall, having to skirt the building work. Azrael and Doraquael were darting around the large fireplace, making excited squeals. Worvig was standing with his back to the fireplace, fending off Arridia with a wooden sword, his face a little red and glistening with sweat. Arridia danced in and out with her own practice blade, her eyes sparkling, while Heara shouted instructions from where she reclined in a chair. Nip was whittling something, small slivers of wood falling into his lap.

Dia cleared her throat loudly. 'That doesn't look like resting.'

'Resting's for the lazy,' Worvig retorted, though he was out of breath.

'I'm winning, Grandma!' Arridia lowered her blade.

'Fool!' Worvig dropped his wooden sword and swooped in to grab Arridia up with his one arm. He spun her about and dumped her into the ashes of the fireplace.

'Worvig!' Milaiya cried in consternation.

'What have you learned?' Worvig leaned over the young girl.

Arridia stood up, brushed herself off, and regarded Worvig seriously. 'Never drop my guard.'

'Good.' Worvig grinned.

Arridia giggled. 'You're naughty, Uncle Worvig.'

'He certainly is.' Milaiya scowled at him, glancing worriedly at Dia.

'What have you learned, Uncle Worvig?' Arridia asked him.

Worvig drew in a deep breath and raised his bearded chin. 'Always do as women tell you.' He leaned in to whisper with a wink. 'But only when they're looking.'

Arridia laughed, both Milaiya and Heara protested loudly. Dia kissed Worvig on the cheek, narrowed her eyes at him, then took her grandchildren's hands. 'Come on, let's find Rosa and get you tidied up, your dad will be here soon.'

***

Jorrun turned away from them, gazing out through the window at the sea far below while Kesta watched him anxiously, barely breathing. Arrus opened his mouth to speak, but Dia raised a finger to shush him. The Thane of Northold was about the same age as Temerran, but to Dia, Jorrun appeared much older this evening, his face unguarded among those he trusted.

Jorrun swallowed and turned back to face them. 'What you ask is possible.'

Kesta let the air out of her lungs.

'But?' Dia prompted.

Jorrun took two long strides across the room to perch on the desk beside his wife. 'But. There are a lot of those, I'm afraid. Even if I successfully persuade them all through dreams that they won, that the children are dead, there is nothing to stop Jderha from sending others to check.'

'We can watch the seas,' Temerran said. 'After what Yalla and Kichi did, even the sea-spirits would be willing to help.'

Jorrun nodded, although he didn't look up. 'And if they believe they won, that they defeated the strongest of us, what is to stop them coming here to conquer the four lands?'

'It will take time for them to come back, Thane,' Tantony said. 'We can prepare.'

'You will hopefully have more strong sorcerers,' Dinari added, turning her hands over to study her tattooed palms.

'Prepare for a god?' Jorrun turned to her, then regarded them all. 'A real god, not a demon like Hacren, or an abomination like Bantu. A year won't be enough to prepare for Jderha, nor ten.'

Dia raised her hand. 'We must carefully consider the dream you will give these men. Let them think they killed the children, but let them also believe it only happened as many of us were away in Chem. Perhaps let them see Yalla being defeated with ease once one of us arrived here. Choose me as that person.'

Jorrun turned his ice-blue gaze on her, the warmth in his smile slowing her heartbeat. 'Never, Icante. If anyone should bear that target, it will be me.'

'No, me,' Kesta said at once.

Jorrun gave her a look and she quieted.

Siveraell drifted toward the centre of the room, Azrael and Doraquael giving excited squeals. One glance from the elder drake silenced them at once.

'It is a good plan, but you all know it will buy only a temporary reprieve.' The fire-drake's colour darkened to red. 'Jderha isss a seer. She sees what will be. The children live, the future she predicted hass not changed. At some point, she will know that.'

'Anything we try will be for nothing.' Kesta slid to her feet, her hand instinctively finding the hilt of her dagger.

Azrael and Doraquael started wailing. Worvig, Arrus, Tantony, and Heara all spoke at once. Dia searched out Everlyn, sitting quietly in a corner between Eidwyn and Cassien. The *walker* met her eyes and forced a smile.

'A moment!' Dia silenced them all. 'According to this prophesy, the children will defeat Jderha.'

'The future is a fluid thing,' Siveraell hissed. 'It can be undone.'

'What are you thinking?' Kesta looked at her mother with wide, hopeful eyes.

It was Jorrun who spoke. 'We must buy Joss and Riddi time. We must give them every advantage, every tool, all the support we can.' He stood again. 'As my sister entreated me several days ago, we unite the four lands beneath the sky, and not just them, but the spirits also.'

'That…' Temerran shook his head. 'That's some task.'

426

'But achievable.' Kesta took Jorrun's hand and gazed up at him.

'Okay.' Dia remained seated, but the room hushed at her voice. 'We plan the dream Jorrun will give the captives carefully, mindful of every detail, and we let them sail home in Bractius's ship. We spend the winter planning, talking, deliberating; then in the spring we come together. All of us, human and spirit.' She looked from Jorrun to Temerran. 'Bractius and Elden have to be on-board.'

'We'll see to it,' Temerran replied.

'And Chem must be whole and at peace,' Jorrun said quietly. 'We cannot afford division and to have enemies in our own homes.'

'Are you suggesting we conquer Eastern Chem?' Cassien spoke up. 'We still don't have the resources.'

'Oh, but we do.' Jorrun smiled slowly, looking up to meet Dia's eyes. 'We have the four lands.'

'Five.' Azrael made a mad dash about the room, coming to an abrupt halt at Sivaraell's fierce expression.

Dia opened her mouth, hesitated. She took hold of Arrus' hand. 'Yes, five. The Fulmers, the Borrows, The Free Provinces of Chem, Elden, and the Fire-Realm. We'll take Chem, then prepare for Geladan.'

The room fell into silence, broken only by the crackle of the fire, and Worvig breathing loudly through his nose.

'What will you tell the children?' Rosa's quiet voice broke into their thoughts.

Kesta looked up. 'The truth, always.'

Dia shook herself. 'Come on, we've had a hard few weeks, to put it mildly. And we'll have a tough winter to come. We'll meet in the spring to plan our conquest of Eastern Chem. In the meantime,

Tem, get yourself out in the hall and start singing, I don't know about the rest of you, but I intend to get drunk!'

Arrus and Heara gave a loud cheer.

Chapter Twenty-Eight

Cassien; Free City of Navere

Cassien strode through the market, his hood down, his four knives a reassuring weight on his wide belt. He nodded to a trio of guards who were patrolling the docks; they spotted his raven insignia at once and gave him a hasty salute. It was oddly good to be back in the busy seaport again. The Fulmers had been restful, healing, but the city enervated him, his senses somehow sharper. Seabirds wheeled overhead, their cries merging with the voices of Navere to make a unique song.

He reached the guard post overlooking the harbour, its captain diligently standing out on the porch observing the busy wharves.

'The crew of the *Undine*,' Cassien called out. 'Have they not disembarked?'

'They did.' The captain frowned. 'The bard said he would settle his men and then head for the palace.'

'Do you know which inn?'

'Chimera.'

Cassien gave a snort. It was the roughest of the inns in the docks, but probably very much to the taste of Borrowmen.

He raised a hand in thanks and hurried toward the inn, surveying the wharves himself out of instinct. The *Undine* stood out like a swan among chickens, and he had the uncanny sense that the sleek ship was watching him back. There were two Fulmer longships moored side by side, one of which he'd sailed in himself to get here just two days ago. Jorrun's small ship was the only one of Elden design he could see, they weren't expecting the king for at least another day.

He heard the inn long before he reached it; it seemed the Borrowmen were already making themselves at home. Cassien drew in a deep breath and closed his eyes briefly, before pushing open the door and stepping into the gloom.

The inn smelt of roasting meat, stale ale, and staler sweat. Despite the noise, the Borrowmen were mostly seated and doing nothing worse than uttering an occasional curse.

'Cassien?'

He turned and spotted Temerran leaning against a worm-eaten wooden pillar.

'Cass, it's good to see you.' The bard strode over and held out his hand.

Cassien shook it at once. 'How was Elden?'

Temerran winced. 'Elden was… Elden, but it was a comfortable place to stay and Linea loves the royal court.'

Cassien glanced around. 'Did she not come?'

Temerran grinned. 'She did. She is waiting on the *Undine* with Nolv until I get this lot settled.'

'Not a quick job.' Cassien smiled and nodded toward the ale in Temerran's hand.

The bard's grin widened. 'No, and thirsty work, too. Can I get you a drink?'

Cassien hesitated, but his instinctive politeness took over and he agreed.

'Have you met young Prince Lucien?' Temerran asked, his gaze so firmly fixed on Cassien he shifted his feet uncomfortably. 'His father has him training already as a warrior and the lad hates it. I told him about you. I know you're not overly fond of Elden, but if you ever find yourself there, I'd consider it a great kindness if you'd check up on the prince.'

Cassien gave a slight shrug. 'If I'm ever in Elden—'

The door opened, briefly letting in a little more light and fresher air. Catya sauntered in, her mouth curling up in an almost predatory smile when she saw the Borrowmen.

Cassien sighed. 'I think I'll need that drink.'

'Me too.'

He turned to see Temerran had become very still, only his eyes moving as he followed Catya's progress across the room. Cassien stiffened defensively.

Most of the Borrowmen appeared to recognise Catya, greeting her with a clasped wrist, enquiries after her latest kills, and offers of ale. Catya basked in their attention; then she turned and saw Temerran and her demeanour altered. Her face softened, her posture relaxed, her movements became more hesitant. For a moment, Cassien thought she looked almost vulnerable.

Then she smiled and sashayed over, completely ignoring Cassien.

'Tem, it's great to see you.'

'You look well, Catya,' Temerran replied.

'More like a woman?' Catya raised her eyebrows and placed a hand briefly on her hip. Temerran didn't have time to answer; Catya stepped forward swiftly and placing a hand against the bard's chest, she tried to kiss him.

Temerran averted his face, stepping back. 'Cat…'

Catya's skin reddened and her nostrils flared, her fingers folding into fists as she dropped back onto her heels. She quickly glanced around to see who had witnessed her humiliation. Cassien averted his eyes.

'You didn't miss me as much as I'd hoped then?' Catya tried to make a joke of it, but Cassien could hear the hurt in her voice.

'I did miss you, Catya,' Temerran replied without a smile.

Catya gave a snort, her expression hardening. She pivoted on her heels and went back to the Borrowmen, accepting a jug of ale and standing very close to one of the younger men. The young man, and several of the others, kept glancing over at Temerran, like dogs wary of a scolding.

Cassien looked up to see Temerran watching him. The bard beckoned over a serving maid and asked for both geranna and ale.

'I'd better go,' Cassien growled.

Temerran sighed. 'Would it help you to know none of my men will touch Catya?'

Cassien looked up sharply.

'Sit, please.' Temerran indicated the chair that had its back to the room.

Cassien slowly took it.

Temerran sat opposite him. 'I'm sure you have heard the tales of Borrowmen raids on the Fulmers and the shores of Chem. I won't try to pretend that those raids weren't often evil. My ship, the *Undine*, is different. I'll not take a crewman on-board who doesn't adhere to my code of morality, lacking in parts though it is. Catya was on my crew. The men were, and are, forbidden to touch her. They disrespect her, and they disrespect me and my ship.'

Cassien cleared his throat. 'And you, did you adhere to those same rules?' Something burned inside him and he shifted in his seat. He realised it was jealousy.

Temerran opened his mouth and hesitated. 'Cassien, did Catya ever tell you why she left the *Undine*, or why she joined my crew in the first place?'

The serving woman placed two cups, a bottle of geranna, and a jug of ale on their table.

Cassien shook his head.

Temerran rubbed at his face and glanced at Catya. She was flirting outrageously, but the men either appeared uncomfortable, or laughed and called for tales of blood and war. 'Cassien, she packed up and left the Fulmers because she thought herself in love with me.'

Cassien froze, his cup full of sweet, but potent, geranna liqueur not quite touching his lips.

Temerran met his gaze. 'I was unaware at first, but when it became clear, I did everything I could to deter her. In the end, I had to put her straight. I met Catya when she was a child, in a way, I still see her as one. I love her dearly, but like a niece. Anything else feels wrong to me.'

Cassien took a large swallow of his drink, which caught in his throat and set him coughing.

'It hurt her pride more than her heart, I think.' Temerran looked down into his own cup. 'But I thought you should know.'

It was a moment before Cassien could force the words out. 'Thank you.'

Temerran shook his head. 'I'm going to ask you something, Cassien. You don't have to answer.'

Cassien sat back, meeting the bard's green eyes. He nodded.

'Are you still in love with Catya?'

Cassien took another large swallow of geranna to hide his discomfort. Catya's too loud, too false laugh, made his muscles stiffen.

Temerran nodded and smiled, swirling his own drink around in his cup. 'For what my advice is worth, Catya is a special woman, but she will hurt you, and she won't let herself care. She doesn't know what she wants from life, and she won't shy away from using anyone for a moment's ambition. Mostly I think she's scared. She's so afraid of not being loved that she'll push everyone away. You can't change that, Cassien, only she can. You could wait for her, but she won't respect you for it, and I'd be sorry to see you waste your life.'

Cassien couldn't meet Temerran's eyes. The bard's words had cut too close to the centre of his soul.

'Want to get out of here?' Temerran prompted.

Cassien smiled, and some of the ache eased from his heart. 'Osun hated geranna, but he still drank it. I quite like it myself. I... I don't want to go back to the palace yet.'

'Hmm.' Temerran looked up at the ceiling. 'I still have a small amount of the dark spirit I brought back from my travels in the south. Fancy a tour of the *Undine*?'

'What about Linea?'

'Ah.' Temerran winced. 'I'm sure she'll forgive me.'

***

Cassien realised he was scowling and quickly relaxed his muscles. King Bractius had a way of filling up a room with his flamboyant gestures and his booming voice, as though he were trying to make himself larger than he was. Merkis Teliff shadowed the king, along with ambassador Dalton, and two Elden warriors resplendent in gleaming armour.

'My good friends.' Bractius beamed around at them all. 'Thank you for such a wonderful welcome. I am honoured to visit Chem at last.'

Much of the Elden king's welcome had been unplanned. The citizens of the city had gathered in the streets, more out of curiosity than respect.

'Your majesty.' Jorrun gave a slight bow. 'Let me introduce you to Navere's Coven. This is Calayna and Reece, who head the Coven.'

Bractius shook Rece's hand and kissed Calayna's. The Chem woman's mismatched brown eyes were strikingly prominent now her pale skin was free of the blood tattoos. It had been a long process, sometimes painful, but the inhibiting runes were gone and Calayna had found her power—a lot of power. Cassien glanced at Dinari. With her runes also gone and her long dark hair spilling down her back, he was reminded sharply of Kussim. A small ache started in his chest and he pushed it aside.

'This is Beth,' Jorrun continued. 'Jollen, and Sirelle, who helped us defeat Hacren. And these are our new and apprentice Ravens; Tyrin, Harta, Charis, Ovey, Neffy, and our Alikan.'

Bractius shook all their hands, stroking Trouble whom Alikan carried in his arms.

Rosa and Tantony had travelled with the king, patiently following his retinue, but exchanging smiles with the delegation from the Fulmers. Dia had brought most of her family and Silenes, leaving Eidwyn and Milaiya to run Fulmer Hold. Heara was rolling her eyes, her weight on one foot as she leaned back, hand on a dagger hilt. Vilnue stood beside her, sharing quiet words with Arrus. Everlyn's face appeared much better than when Cassien had last seen her, the scars smaller and whiter, no longer angry looking. He wondered if Jorrun had tried some of his new-found healing skills on the *walker*. Worvig followed the Elden king with his eyes, a frown on his face.

Cassien was one of only a handful of people who knew Kesta and Jorrun had brought their children with them to Navere for the first time. They were hidden away on the top floor of the palace with Nip, guarded by *walkers* and Ravens, and the two young fire-spirits. Cassien could understand them not wanting to let Arridia and Joss out of their sight. They'd heard nothing of the Geladanians since their captives had awoken on the king's ship, under the illusion they'd succeeded in their mission.

Cassien turned to regard Linea, who stood among the Borrowmen. She met his eyes and smiled, small dimples forming on her cheeks. He'd liked her at once, although part of that was down to relief that Temerran was completely in love with the woman and would never be interested in Catya.

'Thank goodness for that,' Rothfel muttered behind him, making Cassien jump. 'I'm starving.'

Cassien realised the king was being guided into the dining room. Bractius's face darkened for a moment, and Cassien couldn't help but smile. The tables were set out in Chemman fashion, a single long line all on the same level; no doubt the king had expected to sit above them all on a raised dais.

Cassien had arranged to sit toward the end of the table with Rothfel and the younger Ravens away from the politics. Tyrin was excited about his upcoming journey to the Fulmers to serve there for six months, both eager and scared at the same time at being trained by Heara and the Icante herself.

'I'm to go to the Fulmers too,' Alikan spoke up.

'Really?' Tyrin frowned.

'Oh, yes.' Alikan turned to the much older boy, his amber eyes wide. 'And to the Raven Tower. Kesta and Jorrun want me to stay with them until I'm older, but…' Alikan wriggled in his chair.

'Go on,' Rothfel prompted him.

'I shall miss Duco,' Alikan admitted.

'Your cat?' Cassien asked.

'No.' Alikan laughed. 'My guard.'

'We could arrange for him to go with you,' Rothfel suggested.

Alikan shook his head, his eyes on his plate of food, though he didn't move to eat any of it. 'Duco doesn't want to leave Chem.'

'I guess it is his home,' Rothfel said.

'I've spent time in all four lands as part of my training,' Cassien told the boy. 'As much as I love the Fulmers, I still think of Chem as my home.' As he said it, his thoughts went from Navere to Caergard and his cheeks grew warm. He quickly took a swallow of his wine. 'As Ravens we belong to all the lands, but you'll probably find one in which you feel you most belong. And Chem is on the edge, well, we are on the edge of changing history again.'

The younger Ravens all exchanged glances, but it was Tyrin who asked. 'You knew him, didn't you? Osun, I mean. You were there when Jorrun and Kesta first took Navere.'

Cassien sat up straighter, leaning away a little. 'I was,' he replied quietly.

He was bombarded by requests of 'tell us.'

'Please?' Alikan gazed at him with his bright amber eyes.

Cassien turned to Rothfel, but the man just grinned and laughed at him.

Cassien sighed. 'Okay. Well, I was born a slave…'

***

The meeting was more formality than anything, a chance to get the leaders of the four lands together in the same room; the actual planning had already been done across the quiet months of winter. As a land of divided clans, the Borrows was to be represented by Temerran, and the matriarchs and chieftains of two of the larger clans, including Grya, who'd once been sheltered by the Fulmers. Bractius, Dalton, and Teliff were there for Elden, although the king himself wouldn't be leading his men into battle. Calayna, Reece, Jagna, and Tembre would speak for Chem. It had been a while since Cassien had seen the Chemman sorcerer who'd come close to betraying them in Arkoom. Cassien still didn't completely trust Tembre, he doubted any of them did, really.

Dia, Arrus, Worvig, and Heara represented the Fulmers.

It had surprised Cassien when Jorrun had asked him to join them, after all he wasn't really a leader; but the fondness in Jorrun's eyes had both humbled Cassien and answered his question. Cassien had been with them in changing Chem longer than anyone but Osun.

They had placed a table in the centre of the room on which lay a huge map of Chem, different coloured inks marking the shifting borders. Bractius was looking over it with Teliff, the king's voice for once subdued, his posture reserved. The delegates gathered, talking softly, the enormity of this moment weighing heavily on them all. It was time to take Eastern Chem, or lose everything they'd been fighting for.

Jorrun pulled his chair back, and Cassien guessed the loud, scraping sound had been deliberate. The room hushed, and as Jorrun took his seat, the others followed suit. Cassien chose the chair to Kesta's left and she glanced at him with a brief smile. Rosa, Tantony, Everlyn, and the drakes were guarding the children, but worry lines were still etched deep in the young woman's face.

One last representative joined them. A bright, flickering, fiery shape emerged from a single candle that sat on the edge of the table. Siveraell hovered briefly above the map, turning the cloth an almost golden colour, before drifting to take his place between Kesta and Jorrun.

Jorrun looked down at the floor for a moment. He opened his mouth, but glanced at his wife before he spoke. Cassien wondered if he was the only one holding his breath.

'My friends. We in this room have already been through a lot together,' Jorrun began. 'We are here today to try to finish what we started, to make our four lands safe, to unite in peace, trade, and most importantly, in friendship. This is not about who's god is right or wrong, or whose beliefs are true, it's not about imposing, or restricting religion. What we do is a matter of simple right and wrong, of allowing all our peoples to live in freedom and safety.'

'Although to be fair,' Tembre interrupted. 'You are imposing a foreign way of life on Chem.'

Cassien had to stop himself from growling.

Several people protested, but Jorrun gave a small smile and waved a hand to silence them. 'That is, to an extent, the case; however, Tembre, it's more complex than that. Chem was already destroying itself before we became involved. Its system of rule set itself up for extinction and chaos. Even if the Dunhams had succeeded in complete rule, it was always only a matter of time before those who were oppressed rose up.'

'You are doing well enough, out of it, Tembre,' Calayna said warningly, her eyes narrowed.

Tembre raised both hands. 'Just saying what I see.'

'We digress.' Kesta uncrossed her legs and leaned forward. 'The absolute rule of sorcerers is over. Osun's laws are gently progressive mostly, except when it comes to the disgusting practice of slavery. I thought we were all on-board?'

'We are.' It was Jagna who replied with a glare at his reluctant ally.

'So, tomorrow we begin to move into position.' Jorrun raised his voice a little. 'We take Uldren, Parsiphay, and Teloch. We offer Dallaphon, Farport, and Gysed the chance to open their cities in surrender, or we take them too. Snowhold we will have to deal with when the passes through the mountains open. Rece.'

The captain gave a nod, then stood, stepping closer to the table. 'We will go through the plan one last time.'

As Rece's finger travelled over the map, and he outlined every detail of their strategy, Cassien regarded the faces of all of those in the room. Both Dia and Kesta were doing the same, and Cassien guessed the women would also be employing their *knowing*. He met Dia's eyes and the Icante gave him a warm smile which he instantly returned. Tembre fidgeted, but he was listening, his eyes fixed on Rece. Temerran was the first to ask questions, and several of the others followed. The silences gradually grew longer until no one else spoke.

'Is there anything else?' Jorrun looked around at them all.

Several people shook their heads.

Jorrun drew in a deep breath. 'Well, I don't know about you but I need some fresh air and a glass of wine.' He turned to Bractius. 'Would you like to join me?'

Cassien noted Jorrun's dropping of the king's title. He couldn't blame him for reaching for his friend, rather than the monarch. Cassien stood silently as the others left the room until there was only him. Forcing his feet, he walked across to the table and peered down at the map. He followed the line of the border with one finger, the land beyond it seemed vast still. His eyes moved left toward Caergard and there it was again, the empty ache in his chest. He realised his finger was hovering above the city and he drew it back quickly.

'Cass?'

He looked up sharply, his face warm. Catya stood with her hip against the doorway.

'Just coming,' Cassien muttered.

442

Chapter Twenty-Nine

Catya; Uldren Province, Eastern Chem

Catya screwed her nose up, her lip curling in a silent snarl. The Wolves were only twelve feet away, within easy reach of her daggers. Her palms itched, but she didn't move, watching as the men passed, then disappeared into the darkness. She looked to her right, catching the silver glint of Cassien's eyes. He gave her a single nod, then edged back down the slope to where the others hid. Catya closed her eyes briefly and drew in a deep breath before following.

'Have they gone?' Kussim asked, her gaze fixed on Cassien.

'They're gone,' Catya snapped. 'We need to move.'

Kussim's eyes narrowed, but she kept silent, gesturing to the others to get ready. Catya had to admit the young Raven looked exotic, even beautiful, in her dark-green trousers and shirt, and her loose-linked, hooded chainmail tunic. It did nothing but aggravate the frustrated rage that prowled and itched within Catya's chest.

They couldn't let anyone know they were in Uldren province. Theirs was to be an attack of stealth, which meant letting the Wolves move unopposed into western Chem.

They'd split themselves into three groups. Rothfel was leading his to come to Uldren City from the south. Jagna and Caergard's scouts from the north. Catya's group were taking the longest route to approach from the east. She glanced up at the moon; there were three days left until their coordinated attack on Eastern Chem. They'd delayed in Caergard, not wanting to risk having to hide within the eastern province any longer than they had to.

Cassien took the lead, moving slowly and looking for the signs left by the Fulmer scouts who were checking the way ahead. Catya allowed herself to fall behind, disguising their trail as much as possible, and ensuring no one followed.

By day they sheltered in deep woods, or in the few safe buildings the Rowen Order had procured for them. At their last camp, they waited just three miles from the city in a small croft that Gunthe had rented, supposedly for a son. They waited until after midnight before proceeding toward a lake within view of the closed city walls.

Kussim knelt beside the water and Catya tutted as Cassien quickly stepped in to stand over her, hand ready on his sword hilt.

Kussim drew in a deep breath, then called up her power. Slowly a mist formed, thickening over the dark water. Two of the other Ravens created wind; gentle enough not to break up the fog, but persistently herding the low, white shroud toward the city.

Catya shifted on her feet, her hands tightening on her dagger hilts. Ruak ruffled his feathers, brushing her cheek. She edged away from the others, her feet following the silver edge of the water. She could no longer see any light from the city.

'I think that's enough,' she called back, her voice dampened by the fog, but somehow carrying further than she'd intended.

Kussim glanced at her, but continued a little longer before reaching up to take Cassien's offered hand as he helped her to her feet.

The young woman regarded them all. 'You know the plan. Try to stick together, but if you find yourself separated, head for the palace.'

'Quiet as you can,' Cassien added.

Catya rolled her eyes and gave a shake of her head. The Fulmer scouts had already moved out around the lake, leaving only a swirl in the water droplets to show where they'd been. They moved within the mist, Catya's heartbeat seeming loud in her own ears. She somehow sensed the city wall before she saw it. The Ravens who followed gently eased the fog up and over the walls. They stood back, giving Kussim room. It seemed like an age that they waited, Catya clenching and relaxing her toes within her boots, over and over.

Then a boom sounded somewhere in the city, accompanied by cries and wails of alarm. Two more explosions followed, light flashing within the city and catching in the fog. Ruak flew up and away with a harsh caw.

Kussim drew her power, reaching it down into the earth. She heaved, and a large section of the wall collapsed inward.

Catya didn't wait for the debris to settle, she was up and over the rubble with a dagger in each hand, smearing the black ashes painted on her face with the back of her hand as the dust tickled her face. A dazed guard staggered out of the fog in front of her and she stabbed a dagger in and out of his chest. She paused for a heartbeat, gaining her bearings; they were a little further southward of their intended entry. Cassien appeared at her side, Kussim just behind him. Catya pointed and Cassien nodded, gesturing to the rest of their group.

Catya broke into the fast but energy conserving lope that Heara had taught her. A shadow came at her; not waiting to see who it was, she leapt, her feet landing on a soft stomach. The shadow gave a deep grunt, Catya pulled her blade across his throat and ran on. She felt the panic and fear rising in the city. Somewhere there was another rumbling boom, and in the distance, fire lit the palace in silhouette. Screams and shouts came like blunt arrows through the fog.

Some city folk barricaded themselves in their homes, others ran out into the streets, fleeing to the gates or towards the temples. The mist was dissipating, enough for Catya to see those who fled were all men. She flicked the handles of her daggers around her fingers so the blades lay back across her wrists.

It was time to dance.

While the others wove and dodged through the panicked people, Catya went straight for them, her blades punching into flesh, slicing through veins. She leapt, twisted; her speed and momentum felt as though she were flying. They didn't face more guards until they came to the palace, sections of the wall already lay in ruins from Rothfel's alchemy. Catya paused for only a moment to ensure she wasn't too far ahead of the others, before she charged the guards at the main gate. Arrows overtook her, the Fulmer scouts hitting their marks, then a blast of air threw several guards against the iron portcullis. Catya burst into a sprint, springing up to spin through the air. Arms outstretched, her daggers bit through two throats and as she landed in a crouch, she plunged her dagger into another man's kidney.

'Catya!' Cassien waved at her to follow, an angry frown on his face. The rest of her group were disappearing into the palace grounds over the broken stone.

446

With a growl, Catya stepped on one of the fallen guards and followed, unclenching her jaw and breaking once again into a run.

Jagna's group had beaten them to it. A magical battle was already well under way, fire streaming down from an upper floor window and curling around an air shield.

'Kussim,' Cassien yelled. 'We need to get you inside.'

Catya studied the building. Several of their warriors were engaged at the main entrance.

'Kussim!' She pointed to a window and didn't wait, her toes pushing off the soft grass of the lawn as she ran. The blast was cold and sharp against her right cheek. The window before her shattered inward and she leapt, her feet finding the ledge, then landing in a crouch on the wooden floor.

The room was empty.

'Clear,' she shouted over her shoulder.

She stepped to the door, hovering a palm over it to check it was cool, then pressing her ear to the wood. There were voices outside.

She glanced over her shoulder to check Kussim and the other magic users were close, then thrust the door open. Several servants huddled before her. She flicked out a dagger and caught one man in the eye.

'Out of the way, or die,' she growled.

The men and women fled, screaming. She grabbed up her dagger before the others emerged from the room behind her. There was a set of stairs not far ahead and she strode toward them, checking the way was clear. She took the steps two at a time, glancing down the first corridor in time to see two women duck inside a room with their arms around each other. Whoever had been holding off Jagna and his party had been on the next floor, so she started up the next flight.

'We should secure this floor first—'

Catya ignored Cassien and she heard him curse, but he followed.

Several guards stood outside a room. One of them spotted her and charged at once, raising his sword high and bringing it down toward her head. Catya ducked and rolled, plunging her dagger into the back of his knee. She got straight to her feet and ran at the others. Two knives flashed past her and she recognised Cassien's hilts; both found a mark. Another man fell to an arrow. The last was hurled down the corridor by a blast of magic.

Catya looked inside the room, keeping low. There were three sorcerers, two leaning out of the broken window, the third, smaller figure, holding back toward the room's corner. Catya threw a dagger and it thudded home, just below one man's ribs. He cried out, staggering, his shield faltered and a blast of flame from below incinerated him. Catya had to dive out of the way, the heat of the flames searing her skin.

Kussim stepped into the room with one of her Ravens and blasted the other man at the window. Pulling herself up against the wall, Catya fixed her eyes on the frightened face of the smaller figure in the corner.

Caught between two attacks, the elder sorcerer's shield crumbled and he was crushed between Jagna's flames and the blast of force from Kussim.

Catya leapt at the one in the corner. He tried to shield, then threw a panicked force spell at her. Catya's reaction was faster and she spun away, using the wall to launch herself at him.

448

'Catya!' Cassien bellowed.

She sliced at the figure's throat, his small hands flew up to try to hold in his blood, his eyes wide and round.

'Catya, no!'

Catya landed on one foot, pivoted, and plunged her other dagger into the small chest.

Kussim screamed.

Catya stood panting, a grin slowly grew on her face, she turned to survey the room and she caught the expression in the other's faces.

'Monster,' Kussim mouthed soundlessly. Her face was pale, her eyes wide.

'What in the Gods' names?' Cassien demanded. 'He was a child, Catya, a child.'

She scowled at him; he was being ridiculous. 'This is war. A child is as capable of killing as anyone else.'

'Look at him!' Cassien pointed. 'Look at him.'

Catya started to turn, but her muscles wouldn't seem to obey. A little doubt, a little fear, crept into her heart. She tutted and shrugged.

A tear slipped down Cassien's dust-stained cheek. 'You are evil, Catya. Evil. I don't know how I ever loved you.'

'Don't be ridiculous,' she spat. Nausea was creeping into her stomach.

Kussim continued to stare at her, Catya had an overwhelming urge to punch the pretty woman in the face.

'You're no Raven.' Cassien was shaking his head and took a step back. 'You don't belong with us. You're a monster.'

Catya scowled again, but she looked around. The body strewn on the floor seemed suddenly tiny, his face still contorted in shock and fear. It was a boy. He was only eight or nine.

Heat flowed through Catya's body, followed by an icy chill, but she gritted her teeth and forced a laugh to quell her need to vomit. 'You two are too soft, he'd have killed you.'

'We could have saved him,' Kussim almost yelled. 'Like Alikan, like Tyrin, and Meric. What's wrong with you?'

Kussim's words hit her like a blow to the stomach, and she had an overwhelming need to hit back. Her heart was hammering, the tears that prickled at her eyes increasing her fury. 'You can't save everyone!' Catya pushed past them out of the room, her feet finding their own way as her vision was lost in red and black, her chest tightening painfully. She left the palace, ignoring Rothfel's worried shout, her legs carrying her out into the darkness, out into the night.

Chapter Thirty

Temerran; Parsiphay, Eastern Chem

The *Undine* streamed ahead; the wind blowing Temerran's red curls across his face. To their portside two Borrow ships and a Fulmer longship fell behind; on their starboard side two Elden warships tried in vain to keep pace. Temerran had an urge to sing, but it wasn't a war song, or a song of enchantment that came to his lips, but an unseasonal harvest song.

Linea stepped closer to him and he put his arm around her. He still wished she'd stayed safely in Navere, but he had to respect her wish to be here. His voice faltered momentarily as eight ships detached themselves from Parsiphay's docks and head out onto the sea towards them.

'Go into the cabin,' he said gently.

'No.' Linea shook her head. 'I want to be with you.'

Temerran turned to gaze into her sea-coloured eyes. 'Linea, you will distract me. My focus will be on protecting you, not fighting the Chemmen.'

Linea looked down at the wooden planks, her forehead furrowed in a frown. 'All right.' She pulled away slowly, and he watched for a moment as she crossed the deck.

'Captain?' Nolv was standing stiffly at his side.

Temerran grinned. 'Archers and spearmen. If any of those ships survive, we attack and board. I need your sharp aim on the ballista.'

Temerran turned from his first mate and gripped the rails. One of the Chemman ships gave a shudder and listed hard to port. A second was pulled down into the sea and he winced at the brutality of it as the waves closed over as though it – and the lives aboard – had never been. The sea-spirits bobbed briefly to the surface, then disappeared.

A sudden, icy gale blew from behind and he turned to see Dia standing on the prow of the Fulmer longship like a living figurehead. Her hands were slightly raised, her eyes narrowed against the wind, power swirled through and around her as she called up her storm. One of the Chemman ships at least had a magic user on-board, Dia's lightning dancing across a shield instead of striking the masts. A third ship tilted sharply, its prow dragged downward as aquamarine, flowing shapes swarmed over it. Temerran winced at the groan of the ship's hull, and the loud, rending crack before it was sucked beneath the waves.

First one, then three, Chemman ships caught flame, Dia's storm reached the land and the bruised clouds released their rain. The distance between the fleets grew rapidly shorter, Temerran's heartrate faster. He gripped the railing tighter with his left hand, stroking the smooth wood with his right.

'Steady, my lady.' He held his breath, then bellowed, 'Make sail!'

As his men increased the canvas, the sails filled and the *Undine* surged forward, taking them between two of the Chemmish ships. The Borrowmen archers released, their fire-arrows thudding home. From the midship, Nolv let loose a huge iron bolt from their ballista, which tore through the starboard Chemman ship's mizzenmast. As the *Undine* cleared the ships, the Islanders and Borrowmen behind them began boarding to engage the Chemmen.

The Elden ship followed the *Undine* toward the harbour. Several sailors had jumped from the burning Chemmish vessels and swam desperately for the shore. Temerran clenched his teeth and looked away. There could be no room for mercy, not until they held Parsiphay.

Temerran glanced over his shoulder, Nolv was frantically winding back the ballista.

'Get ready to drop anchor!' Temerran raised his hand. They were coming close on the remaining two ships; he could see the wild eyes of those on-board. 'Now.'

They released the anchor, letting the chain run, the *Undine* making a sharp, swift turn to port. Nolv released his bolt and it tore through the upper decks on a Chemman ship. The *Undine's* crew needed no further command, they scrambled to pull the anchor back up, their beloved ship turned back hard to starboard to meet the Chemman ship broadside to broadside. They released arrows and grappling hooks, the men who remained in the rigging scrambling to take in sail.

Temerran drew his sword and leapt from deck to deck. The Chemmen sailors were desperate, defending not their land and masters, but their lives. Even so, it took only a matter of minutes to take the ship and lower its flag, as the Elden warship closed in on their final quarry.

'Captain?' Nolv looked at him, shoulders heaving.

Temerran drew in a long breath and briefly closed his eyes. 'Scuttle her. We can't spare the men to hold her.'

Nolv hesitated. 'The prisoners?'

'Tie them up and put them in a longboat, we'll tow them.'

Nolv posture relaxed a little. 'Aye, Captain.'

Temerran found a rope and swung back to the *Undine*. He strode across the deck and sighted Dia's ship. She still stood at the prow, chin raised, her black, silver-strewn hair blowing around her face. Temerran smiled to himself. The Icante was as magnificent as his *Undine*.

'Dia!'

She turned, her blue eye catching the light like a clear stream, her other eye darker than the ship's wood. She slowly raised her hands, palms together, a ball of fire forming between her fingers. Moving her hands apart, the fire grew, then she drew in a deep breath and blasted her fireball at the city walls. Temerran shielded his eyes and watched as the walls crumbled.

Arrows sprang at them from the harbour, but Dia pushed them aside, continuing to whip her wind into a tornado that ripped through the wharves. Several bright lights burst upward from the stone buildings, growing in size. Instead of attacking the Raven fleet, they turned back toward the Chemmen.

Siveraell.

'These people won't surrender,' Dia called across the water. 'I'll meet you at the palace!'

Temerran raised his sword, turning his attention to the docks. His men had disengaged them from the Chemman ship that was slowly sinking in their wake.

They cut a bloody path through the streets to the palace, the fighting swift and brutal. Magic users led each group; Dia flanked by

Heara and Arrus. The Icante didn't smile as she incinerated whole rows of men, each blast intense and as merciful as fire would allow. Drakes rose out of the burning ruins, seeking archers positioned on roofs and walls.

Temerran was an able fighter, but not exceptional, and twice Nolv stepped in to catch a blow that might have reached him. They passed the temple, its door firmly closed. Several fire-spirits gathered outside, flying off to melt into some nearby flames. It wasn't long before screams came from within the temple.

The fiercest resistance met them at the palace, wild-eyed and sweating warriors standing with their swords ready to meet them.

'Surrender and live,' Dia called out.

Several of the men glanced at each other, swords lowering just a little; but their leader let out a roar and charged.

Dia, her *walkers*, and the Ravens destroyed them in seconds.

They entered the palace grounds cautiously, Heara moving ahead. Temerran felt the subtle hum of the *walkers* reaching out their *knowing*.

Dia tensed and halted. Several people appeared between the crenulations on the palace roof. The magic users shielded, but Temerran lowered his sword and swore. Some of those on the roof were children, and they had knives at their throats. As far as they were aware, two of those children were Dinari's. Temerran wiped at his forehead with the back of his hand, his stomach tightening against the churning there.

One man shouted down to them. 'Leave the city, or we kill every woman and child in the palace.'

Temerran swallowed as angry murmurs rose from among their warriors.

'Can you sing something?' Dia asked without turning around.

'Anything I sing will affect us all,' he replied. Movement caught his eyes; Heara had somehow made it to the walls of the palace without anyone noticing. The scout made a quick survey, then used the small cracks in the stonework to climb her way up to an upper window.

Dia raised her chin slightly. 'Parsiphay is lost to you, killing women and children will not change that. What it will change is the way I deal with you.' She projected her voice with little effort. 'Let them go, and walk away from the city, or your death will be painful, and long.'

Temerran sang softly, subtly, words to ease the tension from the air.

'Let them go,' Dia continued. 'And we can negotiate a surrender which will allow you wealth and status, as well as your lives.'

'We won't be ruled by women.' The man spat. 'We are wolves, not cowardly lapdogs!'

Nolv sucked in a sharp breath. Temerran met Dia's eyes briefly. So that was where the 'Wolves' came from.

Dia's shoulders sagged and she shook her head slowly. 'Your Wolves are no more. It is not only Parsiphay that has fallen today, but Uldren and Teloch.'

'Teloch will never fall,' the man yelled. Even from his distance Temerran could see his face redden.

Dia raised a hand, and called quickly, 'Kill that child and it ends all negotiation.'

Temerran's singing faltered ever so slightly; had the Icante sensed the man was about to act through her *knowing*?

'Back away,' the man growled. 'Leave Parsiphay. You have until the count of ten, then we slit throats.'

'You'll be dead before you say eight,' Dia warned, calling her power.

'One...'

Temerran stopped singing, signalling to his men to ready arrows. He kept glancing at Dia. Surely she would never risk Dinari's children?

'Two...'

Everlyn and the other magic users also called up power, and Temerran felt the stirring of air as they readied to create wind.

'Three...'

Arrus shifted his weight from foot to foot, his eyes fixed on the men on the roof.

'Four...'

'Captain...' Nolv's voice was anxious. For a gruff man, Temerran's first mate was a softy when it came to children; it would kill the man inside to see these hurt and be helpless to stop it.

'Five... six...'

Temerran was breathing hard. His stomach churned. Did the Icante have a plan, or was she considering the hostages a cruel, but unstoppable loss?

'Sev—'

The child before the Chemman screamed, Temerran saw the flash of a knife, but it wasn't the Chemman's blade. Heara stabbed into his arm, at the same time as plunging a knife into the base of his skull. Temerran's breath caught in his lungs as the Fulmer scout pivoted and embedded her knife in another man's throat before any of the Parsiphay Chemmen could react. Temerran's heart was in his mouth. Even Heara couldn't stop every blade on that roof before it slit a child's throat.

She didn't have to.

The Chemmen lit up from within, flames licking from their eyes. Heara yelled at the children, grabbing at some to pull them away as the Chemmen burned from the inside out. A bright light shot upward as one body collapsed, then swooped down to hover before Dia.

'The palace iss secure,' Siveraell reported.

'Thank you.' Dia gave a small bow.

Temerran thought he would vomit as the bile of his repressed fear rose rapidly.

'Captain?' Nolv grabbed his arm.

Temerran cleared his throat. 'Go back and secure the docks, set a firm guard on the *Undine*.'

'Yes, Captain.'

Dia turned around to look at him, giving a small smile. 'Shall we go in?'

Temerran drew himself up. 'After you, my lady.'

Chapter Thirty-One

Kesta; Teloch Province, Eastern Chem

Kesta pushed air out slowly through her mouth. The intelligence they had on Teloch was sparse, but what they did know was it reputedly sheltered the most powerful of Chem's remaining sorcerers. An army had been impossible, not if they wanted to rely on surprise and cross eastern Chem without confrontation. Not that there hadn't been any. She looked around at their diminished group, her heart clenching into a tight knot. Jorrun turned and met her eyes, reaching out a hand to squeeze hers.

They both reached for their weapons as a shadow appeared before them in the darkness, relaxing when they realised it was Gilfy.

'All clear,' the scout and bodyguard informed them.

Jorrun stood without a word and Gilfy took the lead, guiding them across the open land toward the city. Kesta glanced up at the sky; they had about four hours until dawn. Unlike Parsiphay and Uldren, their attack was planned for the blackness of night. Their strike would come first, but not so soon they could warn the other cities.

Firelight marked the city walls and gates, and the corner of Kesta's mouth curled up in a smile. In the Fulmers, they'd learned long ago not to give themselves away with light. They halted to draw out their own shuttered lanterns, eight in all. Jorrun opened his a crack to peer in.

'Remember, you must be stealthy and quick,' he spoke to the little being inside. 'Don't let them raise the alarm.'

There was a hiss and the leaked glow of the lantern lost its intensity. Jorrun blew out the remaining candle flame and dropped the lantern.

Kesta turned to meet as many eyes as she could. Beth, Jollen, Tyrin, Meric, Dinari…

Kesta thought of Navere, of the five of them who'd first taken the palace, of their seemingly impossible dream to change the world. Her heart swelled and tightened painfully.

Fire flared at the gates and Jorrun got up slowly from his crouch. 'Keep your shields tight and watch the walls.'

As they sprinted for the gate, the fire-spirits flew up to take out the patrolling archers as noiselessly as they were able. The wooden gates themselves were already open, but an iron portcullis barred their way. Kesta had to place her arm across her nose to escape the stench of burned flesh.

With a rumbling rattle, the iron grid rose. Before Kesta could protest, Jorrun crawled beneath it on his hands and knees to assist the lone man who turned the winch. Kesta quickly followed with Gilfy, scanning the wide area just within the city.

'Thank you, Balten.' Jorrun shook the hand of the Rowen operative who'd been waiting to help them. 'Get yourself somewhere safe.'

The brown-haired man nodded, gave a small wave of greeting to Kesta, then darted away.

Once they were all through, they let the portcullis drop back down behind them.

'This way.' Gilfy indicated with his head, not waiting before he ran for one of the streets.

There was little light, just the occasional leaked lantern or candle through shutters and curtains. Kesta's *knowing* warned them of guard patrols, and they evaded them with relative ease.

A bell rang out, sharp, urgent, clamouring the alarm.

Kesta and Jorrun looked at each other. They'd lost the element of surprise.

Every second would count.

Kesta prayed the women and children would know they were coming and hide themselves.

Kesta led the charge over the last few yards to the palace, heading not for the gates, but for a section of unprotected wall. As Kussim would do in a few hours' time in Uldren, Kesta reached into the earth to heave up rock, throwing the wall down in a tumble of dust. Pride swelled within her when she sensed their combined shields merge into one solid barrier without command or prompting. As one, the Ravens clambered over the broken stone and stalked towards the palace.

Lights were coming on, spreading from window to window. A shout of alarm told them someone had spotted them. Jorrun and Tyrin turned aside to fend off the guards while Kesta blasted open the palace doors. By tradition the women kept for breeding were held on the upper floors, but as soon as Kesta started up the stairs, something felt wrong. She stopped, trying to block out the sound of fighting to concentrate on her *knowing*.

'Kesta?' Beth had halted a few steps above her.

Kesta closed her eyes, even as Meric and Jollen engaged a sorcerer who appeared on the landing above.

She sifted through the emotions, finding it among the fear and anger. Hope.

And around it was a slightly damp smell, cold, enclosed…

'The cellars.'

She opened her eyes, calling through her power and smashing the Chemman sorcerer against the wall. 'Down,' she commanded.

Jorrun and Tyrin caught up, and her husband fell in beside her as she hurried back down to the ground floor. The fire-spirits had been tasked with finding and defending the women and children, but they would have looked in the wrong place. A chill swept through Kesta. What if the Chemman had set traps for the little spirits?

'Kes?' Jorrun searched her face.

'They guessed we might come. They've moved the women below ground.'

The corridor suddenly filled with men, all wearing rough leather armour on which was embossed a stylised, snarling wolf. Their bearded leader drew his sword; he also drew up power. A golden chain around his neck caught the firelight, the star emblem of Warenna hanging above his open shirt. He surveyed them all, his dark eyes lingering last on Jorrun.

'You must be Dunham.'

Kesta felt her husband's growl. 'There no Dunhams anymore. We are Ravens.'

'You are attempting to rule all of Chem just like he did, you have the same lust for power.'

'I don't crave power, only peace for my family, and freedom for the slaves of Chem.'

The man straightened up into a fighter's stance. 'Your family will never know peace; you have made your family the enemy of every true-blooded man of Chem.'

A chill ran down Kesta's spine, even as the heat of her anger rose. Jorrun's stillness told her at once her kind-hearted husband had experienced a stab of doubt. To many, the Ravens were liberators, to others Kesta had no doubt they appeared to be a power-hungry enemy.

'If you accept the laws by which we live in the west,' Jorrun said, his voice and expression giving nothing away. 'You can keep Teloch to rule. Treat your women as equals, allow them to use their magic—'

'Blasphemy,' the bearded man spat. 'We all know you've been bewitched by your Fulmer whore.'

Kesta sighed.

Jorrun gave a slight shake of his head. 'Well, you've made your choice.'

Kesta and Jorrun acted in unison, both sending out a fierce blast of fire. As was usually the case, the Chemmen shielded individually, one of the weaker ones failing, his scream hurting Kesta's ears. She pivoted to Jollen and Tyrin. 'See if you can find a way down to the cellars, take Gilfy.'

Bullcren was strong, some of his men more than a match for the Ravens, and Kesta bolstered their shield instead of being able to attack. Jorrun picked off two of the weaker wolves, taking no pride in each victory. There was no finesse to Dinari's assault, but she battered at the Chemman, her strength easily matching that of her brother. A large crack appeared in the wall, snaking rapidly up and across the ceiling.

'Careful!' Kesta called out to Dinari. 'We'll bring the palace down around us.'

Dinari's face reddened a little, but she eased off her attack, pouring her power instead into shielding. Kesta stepped forward, surveying the wolves and picking a target. It took her a moment to steady her breathing, and as much as she wanted to close her eyes, she made sure she looked the young Chemman in the face as she threw him down the hall to break his bones against the far wall.

The Wolves' attack became desperate, Bullcren holding nothing back, Jorrun and Kesta countering his fire with freezing air.

'Surrender,' Jorrun offered one last time. 'You don't have to die.'

'No, but you and your evil do,' Bullcren growled.

Kesta felt Jorrun waiver as Bullcren's words wormed into his heart.

'Evil is what you do to your women.' Kesta surrounded herself in a strong shield and pushed forward into Bullcren's flames. 'Evil is what you do to your children.' She braced her feet against the floor, pushing harder, so close she saw the bloodshot veins in Bullcren's eyes.

Jorrun called out to her in concern.

Kesta called up her *knowing*, finding every strand of fear, pain, and despair she could within the palace, adding to it the memories of the cruelty she'd witnessed in Chem.

She spoke quietly, using her magic so Bullcren felt the physical impact of every word. 'Evil is what you do to each other, and to yourselves.'

464

She grabbed Bullcren's wrist, transferring the emotions of her *knowing* into the Chemman. He gave a strangled cry, his shield snapping as he crumpled to the ground. His eyes bulged; his face almost purple. Kesta didn't relent, pouring more emotion into him.

'Surrender.' She glanced around at the other Wolves. 'You don't have to die, just change.'

Bullcren convulsed, clutching at his heart; then he stiffened and grew still, the light slowly dulling in his eyes.

Two of the wolves stepped back, a third turned and fled, only one continued to attack and Jorrun destroyed him in a moment.

The crack in the ceiling splintered into two fast channels, dust raining down. Kesta threw up her shield at the same time as Jorrun, both of them trying to shore up the palace. Jorrun faced Kesta.

'Get everyone out.'

She shook her head, holding his gaze. 'No, I'm staying.'

'Kesta.' His eyes hardened; the Dark Man back. 'Get everyone out.'

A surge of anger that bordered on hate, shivered through her fear. He knew she couldn't leave him; he knew she'd have to.

'I'll stay,' Dinari offered.

'For a few minutes,' Jorrun agreed.

With a frustrated growl, Kesta turned on the two remaining Wolves. 'Lead us to the women and children, quickly.'

One man nodded and gestured down the hall. Kesta shoved him in front of her, ordering Beth to keep an eye on the other man. The Chemman wolf led them not to the cellars, but to an iron-clad door guarded by two men. Kesta's anger spread out from her chest. These were dungeons.

'The palace is taken,' the wolf informed his guards. 'And the building is about to come down. Get yourselves out of here.'

The two men hesitated, eyeing the Ravens dubiously, but relaxed their hold on their swords and walked away.

Meric darted forward and pulled back the bolts. As he swung the door open, fierce light flared toward them, the heat so intense it blistered the stone on the walls. Kesta shielded, reaching out to protect Meric and the others as they were engulfed in flames.

There was a terrified shriek and the fire died at once.

'Kessta! Kesta, we're sssorry!'

Three little fire-spirits flew up from the dungeons, darting about and pulling exaggerated mournful faces.

'Everyone all right?' Kesta surveyed the group before turning to glare at the remorseful spirits. 'You could have killed us all.'

'Ssorry, Kesta. We were protecting the children.'

'You have them?' Kesta looked past them into the darkness and saw frightened eyes peering back at her.

'We broke open the cells,' the fire-spirit swelled proudly.

The palace gave a groan and a shudder went through the stone. 'Get everyone up here, quickly.' Kesta rounded on the Wolf. 'Which is the quickest way out?'

The man pointed, receiving a glare from his companion.

'Come on, then.'

Kesta waited until the last woman was up the stairs and then pushed them to move faster through the palace corridors. Fleeing servants joined them as they jostled to get through a door out into the gardens.

'Get clear,' Kesta urged them, as she surveyed the lawns and flower beds, checking for danger. 'Keep your shields up, stay alert.'

She turned back to the palace as the building gave another loud groan and part of a wall crumbled. Kesta held her breath, her heart seeming to stop for a moment. She closed her eyes.

'Mother, take care of my children.'

She drew up her shield and sprinted for the building, just as Dinari emerged at a run from the main door, hurrying down the steps. Dust and debris billowed out behind her and Kesta skidded to a halt, mouth open. She instinctively ducked and covered her head with her arm as a huge section of the palace came down, stone spilling out across the lawn.

Too late.

Pain ripped through her chest.

A final few stones fell, clattering to stillness and silence.

Kesta straightened up.

A dark shape was moving toward her through the settling dust. Her pain faded, her muscles growing momentarily light before she hurried to meet him.

She slapped Jorrun's arm. 'Don't do that to me.'

He grinned down at her, then lent forward to kiss her.

'Mother?'

They turned at the emotion in the voice. A young girl had stepped away from the others, her blue eyes locked with Dinari's. The wind blew her long blonde hair across her face, the girl's nose and chin more familiar to Kesta than her own reflection.

'Ylena!' Dinari breathed, before running to embrace her daughter.

Chapter Thirty-Two

Dia; Free City of Parsiphay

The door burst open and Vilnue hurried in, waving a scroll in his fist.

'Word from Teloch; Gysed has offered its surrender.'

Dia sat back in her chair, some of the knots in her stomach and spine releasing. 'What terms?'

Teliff sighed and handed the scroll to Arrus. 'They asked for five years to implement changes.'

Arrus grunted. 'I can't see Kesta allowing that.'

'According to those dispatches, Kesta is already in Navere, and Jorrun has followed.' Vilnue said. 'Dinari is to head Teloch's coven with assistance from Jollen and Jagna.'

'At this rate, we'll be the last returning to Navere, and home,' Heara grumbled.

Dia sighed. Parsiphay had been far from an easy conquest, even three months after taking the city they were still arresting, and in extreme cases even executing, men who refused to accept the new laws. Dia hadn't dared leave the city before now, and they'd had to bring in extra warriors from Elden. The women and children they'd rescued from the palace had been sent on to Caergard; including Dinari's children, Eila and Jereth. The city was to be governed initially by Vilnue, Beth, Matriarch Grya, and Tembre; the latter another reason for Dia's reluctance to leave.

'Hopefully the surrender of another city will calm the populace.' Vilnue took a seat beside Heara. 'Perhaps we should have taken things slower here, like Teloch.'

Heara snorted. 'A soft hand would be quickly crushed here. Most of the male population are raiders and pirates.'

'Talking of pirates.' Vilnue raised his eyebrows. 'The *Undine* is loaded. Temerran is just waiting for confirmation whether you'll be aboard or not.'

Dia felt everyone's eyes on her. Arrus had but recently rejoined her, allowing Worvig to head back to the Fulmers for a while. Heara had been itching to get back to Navere and watch over the children since the day they'd conquered Parsiphay. Vilnue sat quietly, glancing down at the scroll in his lap as Dia's eyes found his. Of all of them, Dia's decision would affect the Elden ambassador most of all, taking away his lover, and leaving him with fewer allies at his side.

'Vilnue.' She leaned toward him. 'Do you think Beth and yourself can handle things sufficiently now? And by "things" I include Tembre.'

Vilnue drew himself up with a glance at Heara. 'If I'm honest, I would prefer to have you here, but… yes. We can manage.'

'Then I'll send word to the *Undine*.' She stood and left the room, finding a young servant to deliver her message before retreating to her quarters. Most of her belongings were already packed, and she quickly set about stowing the rest. The room brightened, and instinctively reaching out her *knowing*, she recognised the calm, alien presence, without the need to turn.

'Any news, Siveraell?'

469

'Only that there is none, which is good. No Fulmer or Elden patrol has seen any sign of ships from Geladan.'

Dia paused, glancing over her shoulder. 'Though it would be too soon, still, for the king's ship to have reached that land. And Navere?'

'The children are well. Kessta guards them now.'

Dia nodded, more to herself than the spirit. 'We have done all that we can. Except…'

'What, my friend?'

'We might consider sending a peace delegation one day, with Linea as an ambassador.'

Siveraell made a buzzing sound. 'I don't think so, Dia, as nice an idea as it is.'

She turned to regard the spirit and wondered for the first time how old it was. As far as she understood it, both Azrael and Doraquael were several hundred years old, but considered children compared to Siveraell.

'I'll heed your advice,' she said, giving the room one last check.

Arrus stuck his head in the door, and with a smile picked up the larger of her two bags, as well as his own. Dia gave a quick farewell to Beth, and a reluctant one, for the sake of politeness, to Tembre. She waved aside help from the servants, but accepted an escort of two guards.

Nolv was on the *Undine's* deck and hurried to welcome them aboard. Arrus and Nolv nodded at each other with a grunt that Dia supposed served as a handshake. The first mate knocked at his captain's cabin and muttered, 'You'd best have my cabin, Icante.'

She smiled. 'You're very kind, but the small guest room will do.'

The door flew open. 'Dia. I wasn't sure if you'd get away.'

She gave a loud sigh, Temerran's grin infectious. 'I had to leave them to it at some point and I won't be able to relax until I'm back in Navere with my grandchildren.'

'Grandchildren?' Linea stepped up behind Temerran.

Dia cursed herself, her jaw tightening. They'd been so careful to keep the children's whereabouts quiet.

'Are you wanting to sail at once?' Temerran asked, putting his arm around Linea.

'Just waiting on one more,' Dia replied.

They didn't have to wait long for Heara; she came running up the wharf, hair in disarray and clothes hanging out of her bag. She grinned at them all, not looking the slightest bit apologetic. 'Sorry, I had to give Vilnue a proper goodbye.'

Temerran laughed and turned to Nolv. 'Get us underway.'

They moved out of the way of the Borrowmen sailors, Worvig and Heara following Temerran into his cabin for an offered drink. Dia hesitated outside for a moment, watching as they slipped out of the harbour and moved swiftly away from the battle-scarred city. She hoped she would never have to return here.

***

'Grandma!' Arridia and Joss flew across the room, almost bowling Dia over.

'Hello, my honeys.' She squeezed them back, noticing Nip sitting quietly in a corner with a book in his hands. 'Did you not go home to Elden, Nip?'

The teenager coloured slightly. 'I thought I ought to stay here, especially since Rosa and Merkis Tantony have had to go back to Northold.'

'Is everything well at the Raven Tower?'

Nip gave a slight shrug. 'I think so.'

The flames of the two candles on the mantelpiece suddenly grew, then Azrael and Doraquael detached themselves to hover closer.

'It iss good to see you, Icante,' Doraquael said.

'I hope the two of you have been behaving?'

'Of course.' Azrael swelled up to twice his size.

'They haven't,' Joss announced.

Nip put the book up over his face to hide his chuckle.

'We have sso!' Azrael buzzed indignantly.

Dia raised her hands. 'Children. Enough. I have things to discuss with your parents, but I wanted to see you first. I'll come up later to say goodnight.'

'I do the stories,' Azrael blurted.

'Of course you do.' Dia glanced at Nip, who rolled his eyes. She could see very well why Kesta loved to have the sensible boy around. 'I shall see you later.'

She closed the door and made her way back to the dining room where an informal welcome dinner had been set. Zardin opened the door and gave a small bow as she entered; the others stood, but she waved at them to sit. She made a quick check of the room. There was no one there she didn't trust. Cassien sat beside Jorrun, with Rothfel at his other side. Reece and Calayna were opposite them. Dia took a seat between Arrus and Temerran; Heara was already tucking into the food set out on the table.

Linea stood and politely poured Dia some wine, before offering the carafe around the table.

'No news on Catya?' Dia looked around the table.

Temerran and Cassien exchanged a glance.

'Nothing.' Kesta's forehead creased and Jorrun reached out to take her hand. 'We hoped she might come here, but there's been no sign.'

'Catya can take care of herself,' Rothfel said, not unkindly. 'She'll come home when she's ready.'

Dia met her daughter's eyes. The worry there didn't lessen, and Dia didn't doubt Kesta and Jorrun would blame themselves.

'This wine is nice,' Heara said around a mouthful of bread.

'So, did you get to catch up with Bractius's grumbling letters about us using all his warriors?' Calayna asked Dia.

'I don't know what he's so upset about.' Rece took a sip of wine. 'We're the ones having to find the resources to feed them all.'

'Yes.' Dia's mouth quirked up into a smile. 'I caught up with Elden's news, and the Islands'.' There had been three letters waiting for her from Everlyn, full of small news, dear news, of the folk of the Fulmer Islands. She had a sudden twinge of homesickness. 'I must go back soon. Would you like me to take the children with me?'

Kesta straightened; she and Jorrun looked at each other for several heartbeats as though speaking with their minds.

'Thank you, Dia,' Jorrun said quietly. 'And Kesta will go with you at least for a while.'

'Would you like me to take you?' Temerran offered. 'We'll be heading through the Borrows and to Elden soon.'

'We'll take Jorrun's ship,' Kesta replied. 'But you might escort us part way?'

'I'd be honoured.' Temerran raised his wineglass.

'How is Kerzin settling in as High Priest?' Dia asked Jorrun and Kesta.

'I don't think it's a position he particularly enjoys,' Jorrun winced. 'He is a man more comfortable remaining in the background.'

'He has thrown himself into my new project, though.' Kesta almost glowed, although her smile was subtle. Dia raised a curious eyebrow, and Kesta explained. 'It's an idea I had some time ago to make use of some empty shops and help guard against poverty. Surplus donations from the temple, and what we and other traders can spare, are held at the shops. People can trade what they have, what they can afford, including their time and labour. Ravens, as well as Kerzin, ensure everything is kept fair and reasonable and no one is exploited.'

'Or dragged unknowingly into a type of slavery,' Cassien added.

Kesta gave a shrug. 'It seems to work. Some priests hated it at first, but Kerzin says they are starting to enjoy the gratitude and adulation from the people for their magnanimity and seeming kindness.'

The evening passed pleasantly; the conversation turning away from politics to discussing how the youngest and newest Ravens were doing. Dia wasn't surprised to hear Kesta and Jorrun were intending to eventually take Alikan back to Northold to oversee his early training themselves.

Rothfel excused himself, Temerran and Linea shortly after.

'I promised the children I'd see them before they go to bed.' Dia stood.

'We'll come with you,' Kesta suggested.

They said goodnight to Cassien, Rece, and Calayna, and headed up to the children's rooms. The communal room was empty.

'Nip must have gotten them ready for bed,' Kesta said.

A warning prickled in the back of Dia's mind. She had an uncanny sensation something was still in the empty room, or perhaps the ghost of intent. Instinctively she called up her *knowing*.

'Mother?' Kesta froze.

Dia raised her hand and shook her head. 'It's nothing, I'm just being paranoid I think.'

Jorrun strode to the bedroom the children used and thrust open the door. Both Arridia and Joss were sitting up on the same bed in their nightclothes. The two fire-spirits were flying circles around the room and humming a silly tune. Nip was pouring water into cups to place beside the children's beds. As the door opened abruptly, the boy dropped the jug, his hand going for his sword. The jug hit the floor, the water splashing up his trousers.

'I'm so sorry.' Jorrun hurried into the room, picking up the jug and looking in consternation at Nip's soaked trouser leg.

'Is everything all right?' Kesta asked, surveying the room.

'I wass about to ask you the same thing.' Azrael ceased his antics to regard Jorrun and Kesta.

'We're just jumping at shadows, I think.' Jorrun forced a smile as Kesta sat on the bed between the children. 'You'd better get changed, Nip. I'll fetch more water.'

Joss gave a whimper, his hand griping his nightshirt over his stomach.

'Jossy?' Kesta smoothed back his hair, her spine stiffening. 'He's hot.'

'It's the badness in the air,' Arridia whispered.

Dia and Kesta both reached out at once with their *knowing*. Dia experienced the sharpness of Joss's pain, the fear of the others in the room, and Arridia's contrasting certainty.

Sweat broke out on Arridia's forehead.

'Riddi?' Jorrun swiftly knelt before her. 'Tell us more about the badness.'

Arridia made a small sound in the back of her throat that hurt Dia's heart. The little girl was in pain.

'Has anyone been here?' Kesta demanded, looking from Nip to the fire-spirits.

'No.' Nip shook his head vigorously.

'No one hass been here,' Azrael confirmed. 'We wouldn't let them.'

'Nip, did you fetch the food yourself?' Jorrun asked.

The boy nodded; his skin pale. 'And I ate the same, I feel fine.'

Dia stepped into the room, trying to divine what was lifting the hairs on the back of her neck.

'Mummy.' Joss curled up into a ball, Arridia reached out to grab her brother's arm, her own face flushed.

'Joss.' Kesta gathered her son up into her lap, her eyes wide as she looked helplessly at Jorrun.

Dia froze, her vision blurring. She stretched out her senses. It was subtle, but it was there.

'It isn't poison,' she said. 'It's magic.'

Kesta and Jorrun immediately shielded.

'Nip, alert the guards,' Kesta commanded. 'Doraquael, search the palace, see if you can find other spirits to search the temple.'

'You think it might be someone left from Bantu's Disciples?' Jorrun sat on the bed, putting his arms around his shaking daughter.

Joss was breathing hard, his eyes tight closed. Dia added her own power to their shield, but it didn't seem to have any effect. Arridia gasped, trying hard to be brave and not cry out. Azrael flew about the room in a mad, helpless panic.

'Riddi, can you try to shield yourself?' Dia asked, stepping closer.

Kesta looked up at her mother, hope and fear in her eyes.

'I'll try, grandma,' Arridia said through chattering teeth.

Jorrun smoothed back her hair. 'You can do it, Riddi. See if you can make the shield inside yourself and push the magic out.'

'But the badness is in my blood.' Arridia turned in Jorrun's lap to gaze up at him. 'It's flowing where my magic flows.'

'Blood magic.' Kesta looked from her mother to Jorrun. 'Where are Dinari's books?'

'I might be able to heal it.' Jorrun shifted on the bed to lay Arridia down, then shut down his shield to concentrate on letting his magic flow into his daughter. Dia took another step closer, her hands clasped tightly together. She forced herself to breathe more deeply,

477

trying to slow her racing heart. She knew she'd be more use searching the palace for the culprit, but she couldn't tear herself away from her family.

'I can repair the damage.' Jorrun's voice was strained, his skin pale. 'But I can't stop it.'

Joss cried out and Jorrun quickly turned from his daughter to his son. Joss uncurled a little, but within moments Arridia was whimpering, tears running down her face. Jorrun put his face in his hands.

'I can't save them both.'

Azrael wailed.

Kesta hugged Jorrun hard and kissed his forehead above his fingers, her own hands shaking. 'Keep trying, buy us time. I'll have another go at this healing magic.'

He nodded, turning back to Arridia. Kesta met her mother's eyes briefly before calling up her magic and attempting to channel it into healing. Despite months of trying, only Jorrun and Dinari had been able to learn Chem's healing magic, and Dinari was many miles away.

Dia pivoted at the sound of running feet; Calayna and Rece arrived with Doraquael.

'What can we do?' Rece demanded, his face falling as Dia shook her head.

'We need to find the source of the attack,' she told them, chest muscles constricting 'It's the only way.'

'Do we know who?' Calayna asked.

Dia shook her head again. Jorrun swapped from Arridia to Joss, who was completely limp and unresponsive. Kesta was still trying, but to no avail, the skin of her neck and face reddening.

'Cassien is leading the search,' Rece said. 'I'll go help.'

Light flared in the hallway and Siveraell flew out of one of the lanterns, shooting toward Dia.

'Icante, it iss magic of Geladan, can you not feel it? The magic of Jderha.'

Dia's heart gave a painful flip.

'The god is here?' Calayna cried in alarm.

'No.' Siveraell hissed. 'If she were here, we would know it. It is one of her servants.'

Azrael moved toward the elder spirit. 'But we destroyed all her sservants.'

'Servants.' Dia's hands flew to her mouth, the floor seemed to move beneath her. 'Oh no.'

'What, Dia?' Doraquael demanded.

'Spirits, come with me!' Dia broke into a run, taking the stairs down to the guest rooms two at a time. When she reached Temerran's room, she thrust the door open. The bard stood up from his desk, dropping his quill and almost knocking over his ink.

'Dia?'

'Where's Linea?'

'Linea?' Temerran looked from Dia to her entourage of fire-spirits. 'She went to take some air in the garden. What's happened?'

Siveraell shot away at once.

'She has betrayed us.' Dia growled. 'I don't think she was ever on our side. Someone is killing the children with magic. A Geladanian.'

'No.' Temerran shook his head. 'She was just a servant.'

'Yes, a servant of the god! She fooled us all.'

Temerran's fair skin turned paler. 'No, she loves me. You told me yourself it was true.'

Heat rose to Dia's throat. 'It is true, but she also serves her god.'

The window shattered inward and Temerran ducked, shielding his head with his arm from the shards of glass. Siveraell flew in, huge, burning a fierce red. 'At the fountain, I cannot break her shield.'

With a squeal, both Azrael and Doraquael darted out the window, Siveraell followed. With a glare at Temerran, Dia raced for the stairs, her lungs and leg muscles protesting. As she reached a door to the garden, Temerran caught up with her.

'You must be wrong,' he panted.

Dia didn't answer, but unbolted the door, stepping out into the cold night air. The garden lit up with bursts of angry fire and several guards ran out of the palace, led by Cassien.

'Stay back,' Dia called to them as she strode toward the fountain.

'Dia.' Temerran called after her, then ran to keep up.

Siveraell swooped toward Dia. 'She is too strong, Icante.'

Azrael and Doraquael continued to batter at the invisible barrier. Within, Linea knelt before the fountain, the hood of her red cloak fallen back. In her hands she held a skull, upside down with the jaw missing. A flame flickered, feeding off the dark liquid within the blackened bone. Linea wore a serene smile on her red lips.

Dia turned to whisper to Siveraell, 'She had no power. How is she doing this? How is she so strong?'

'She is a witch, Dia,' the elder spirit replied. 'She has no power of her own but takes it from the land, from the spirits, and somehow, from her god.'

'Linea.'

She looked up at Temerran's anguished voice.

'Leave my grandchildren alone,' Dia growled, calling up her power.

Linea appeared almost sad as she regarded the Icante. 'You can't stop me, I'm protected by Jderha's love.'

'Why are you doing this?' Temerran reached his hands out towards her. 'They're just children.'

'But they will kill my Goddess.'

'No, they won't.' Temerran took another step forward. 'You know that. You know us now, I... I thought you loved me.'

She tilted her head to one side, her eyes sorrowful. 'I do, I really do. Jderha told me I would find my love on this mission, but that I would have to choose. I always knew I'd have to choose in the end.'

'Then choose me!' Temerran begged. Pain squeezed Dia's heart, shooting through her anger like lightning.

Linea shook her head. 'I cannot betray my god.'

'But you can betray me?'

Linea got to her feet, carefully keeping the skull upright. 'There is nothing to stop you choosing me. Come with me, Tem. The sea-spirits won't dare stop you sailing where you will with Jderha's protection. You could be free, free to explore the seas with me at your side.'

'Free.' Temerran gave a bitter laugh. 'How would I be free with the blood of children on my hands? How would I be free with the stain of betraying my best friend on my heart?'

'I'm sorry, Temerran, the children have to die.'

'Don't do this.' Temerran dropped to his knees and Dia realised he was trying to use the power of his voice. 'Please, Linea. Don't make me hate you.'

Dia called her own power back, hopeless or not, she had to try. She reached down into the earth as her daughter had taught her; but the rock resisted and Dia staggered, blood dripping from her nose. Spurred by her attempt, the three fire-spirits began battering at the shield again like moths against the glass of a lamp.

Dia drew in a slow, deep breath, stirring the winds to form a storm. Calayna cautiously stalked toward her, Tyrin, Alikan, and the other young Ravens behind her. All of them struck at the barrier, but it didn't waver. Linea stood unmoving within it; her eyes fixed on Temerran.

'Please,' the bard said, getting to his feet. 'Don't do this.' A tear ran down his face, dripping from his chin.

'Come with me,' Linea replied, holding out one hand toward him.

'I can't.' Temerran shook his head, but he took three staggered steps towards her. 'If you love me, stop this.'

The corner of Linea's mouth curled up in a wry smile. 'If you loved me, you would come with me.'

'You're not evil, I know it.' Temerran took another step toward Linea, then another, he was almost within touching distance.

Dia gasped, almost losing her concentration, but she managed to control her building storm. She held her breath.

'I want to come with you.' Temerran took a small step. 'But I don't think I could forgive something so evil.'

'Is it evil to protect someone you love with all your heart?' Linea gazed into his eyes.

'No,' Temerran replied softly. 'No, it isn't.'

He reached out to touch Linea's face, then stepped in to kiss her. As he did so, he drew his knife from his belt and thrust it up into her heart.

The shield collapsed, Dia and Siveraell both threw barriers of their own up around Temerran, saving him from the accidental attack of his allies.

The skull tumbled from Linea's hand and hit the wall of the fountain with a crack, before tumbling into the water. The flame went out.

Temerran sagged to the ground, Linea's body still clutched to his chest. He let out a heartrending cry, then bent over the Geladanian servant, his body shaking with sobs, his hands clutching at the red cloak.

'Check on the children,' Dia said to no one in particular. Doraquael offered to go, as Dia walked slowly over to Temerran.

'Come on,' Cassien urged the others. 'Let's check the rest of the gardens and palace just to be safe.'

Dia glanced at the young man, nodding her thanks.

Only Siveraell remained, keeping a discreet distance.

The stone of the well was cold as Dia sat on it. She reached out to wrap her arms around Temerran, saying nothing, but laying her head against the back of his neck. Slowly he quieted, becoming still, his fingers caught up in the red cloak.

'I've been such a fool.' His usually beautiful voice was harsh.

'No more than the rest of us.' Dia sat up, rubbing his back in small circles.

'But I nearly cost you your grandchildren.'

'No.' Dia shook her head and smiled at him. 'Linea did. She made that choice, not you. You saved my grandchildren, Tem. Did you realise you could walk through her barrier?'

'No.' He sat up a little, his fingers still clinging to the red cloak. 'Not until I did it.' He turned to gaze at Dia with bloodshot eyes. He was trembling. 'Why do you think I was able to? It couldn't have been my magic.'

'No.' Dia's heart bled. 'I think it was your love.'

They sat in silence for a while, Temerran looking down at Linea's lifeless face. Dia sensed a presence and looked up to see Arrus meandering toward them, two glasses of spirits balanced in his hands and filled to the brim.

Dia smiled to him and nodded, slowly getting up and running one of Temerran's red curls through her fingers. 'I need to check on Kesta and the children. Arrus will stay with you until you're ready.'

Temerran barely responded. Dia gave Arrus a quick kiss on the cheek as she hurried past him toward the palace. The Ravens had gathered in the library, but Dia ignored them for now, climbing the stairs as rapidly as her aching knees would allow.

'I'm getting old,' she grumbled.

Azrael and Doraquael flew loops about Dia's head until Siveraell flared at them and they subsided to the corner of the room. Arridia

484

and Joss lay together in the same bed, a blanket snugged around them. Dia held her breath until she saw the rise and fall of their chests. Jorrun sat beside them at the head of the bed, shoulders slumped, his face pale and drawn. Nip sat in his chair in the corner, his eyes red and puffy.

Kesta ran toward Dia and threw her arms around her, holding her so tightly she could barely breathe. 'Doraquael told us what happened. Is Temerran all right?' Kesta stepped back to regard her mother.

Dia shook her head. 'Not really, but he will never regret what he did, as much as it's hurting him.'

'We owe him everything,' Jorrun said, smoothing his son's hair.

'He won't see it like that.' Dia drew in a deep breath and sighed it out. She nodded toward the children. 'Are they okay?'

'I put them into a sleep.' Lines appeared above Jorrun's nose. 'I healed them as best I could without burning all their reserves.'

'I couldn't help.' Kesta gazed at her mother, frustration and pain all over her face. 'I thought I was good at learning new magic, but I just can't seem to grasp it.'

'It's no fault of yours,' Jorrun reassured her. 'It's magic of the blood, and the fact Dinari and I can wield it, suggests the ability is also in the blood.'

'I guess time will tell.' Dia straightened up. 'I'll leave you to rest.' She held a hand out toward Nip.

'Oh.' The boy stiffened, glancing from Jorrun to Kesta. 'I… I need to stay.'

'Come on, then.' Kesta lifted the corner of the blankets on the second bed. 'Stay, but get some sleep.'

Dia left the room, closing the door behind her. For all her fiery nature, Kesta had a habit of creating a family wherever she went. Dia leaned back against the door, breathing slowly, allowing calm to flow into her body.

Light flickered beyond her closed eyelids.

'And you, Siveraell, will you sleep?'

'No, Icante. I will go to the fire-realm and speak to the other spirits of what has just passed. Then we will wait, and we will watch.'

Dia opened her eyes and regarded the drake. 'Thank you.'

Chapter Thirty-Three

Kesta; Kingdom of Elden

Kesta nodded to the guards as she rode through the gates, her eyes drawn at once to the highest windows of the Raven Tower. Griffon gave a snort as he scented his stable, and Kesta stretched to pat his long neck.

Nip was there to meet her as soon as she slipped from her saddle, and she followed him as he led her horse inside. As always, he had water and hay waiting and they unharnessed Griffon together, brushing the gelding down in companionable silence. At the far end of the stable, Nerim ground herbs for one of his cures, leaning close over his work, the dim light not helping the fading vision in his one eye.

'I wish he'd let Jorrun try to heal him,' Kesta whispered.

Nip gave a small smile, flicking his curly, pale-brown hair out of his own eyes. 'He pretends to be too proud, but I think he is afraid. Give him time.'

'What are you two plotting?' Nerim ceased his work to squint at them.

'I was asking Nip how his training with Cassien was going.' Kesta grinned.

'In my day we chose one trade,' Nerim grumbled. 'How can you do anything well, if you try to be everything?'

Kesta and Nip exchanged a smile. They both knew how proud Nerim was of his son.

'Thanks, Nip.' Kesta handed her brush to the stable boy and warrior.

She crossed the courtyard; her shadow long on the grass. One of the Hold's women was feeding scraps to the geese. The great hall was busy. Several children sat at one of the long tables, slates before them as Rosa ran through their letters. Most of them had lost concentration, more interested in the enticing smells coming from the large fireplace; their eyes following the dishes that came out of the kitchens to be set upon the tables. At the far end of the room, Tantony was talking with two of their foresters, the men nodding and laughing.

Kesta narrowed her eyes and spun about. Jorrun stood less than two feet behind her, quickly putting his hands behind his back.

'Thane.' She looked him up and down, raising her chin a little.

'My lady.' Jorrun's mouth twitched as he tried not to grin. He offered his arm and she took it, following him up to the raised dais. It was all the excuse the children needed. Arridia, Joss, and Alikan all ran after them, ignoring Rosa's protests, Joss struggling to climb into his chair alone. Rosa dismissed the other Hold children and made her way up to join Kesta with a shake of her head.

Tantony placed a jug of wine on the table before them and took his seat beside Rosa.

'Why the celebration?' Tantony asked. 'Not that I'm complaining.'

'We've had good news.' Jorrun glanced at Kesta and turned to his Merkis.

'Oh Gods.' Tantony reached for the wine. 'You're not pregnant again, are you? Two children are enough trouble for this hold.'

'Hey!' Joss protested.

Arridia grinned at Tantony, and the gruff, but kind man smiled back.

'I'm not.' Kesta scowled at him.

'Our news does involve children though.' Jorrun held out his glass toward Tantony. 'Dinari's youngest daughter has been sent to her as a goodwill gesture from Farport. Dierra arrived safely in Teloch a week ago.'

'So she has all her children now?' Rosa clasped her hands together under her chin.

'All but the son she lost when we took Mayliz,' Jorrun murmured.

Kesta took his hand under the table.

'Oh, Jossy,' Arridia exclaimed. She and Alikan exchanged a look and rolled their eyes as Joss picked up the slice of mutton he'd dropped in his lap. Arridia reached over before Kesta could react, cleaning up her little brother and cutting his meat into smaller pieces.

Kesta's eyes met Jorrun's and they smiled.

A tall, brown-bearded man stepped into the hall and wove his way past the tables toward them.

'Kurghan.' Jorrun stood to clasp his wrist. 'Any news from Taurmaline?'

'Aye, Thane.' The carpenter's eyebrows rose. 'The king has put trading taxes up again, blames it on the need to keep foreign shores safe.'

'Cheeky—' Kesta glanced at the children. 'Cheeky monarch. It's Western Chem keeping his warriors supplied.'

'With Farport conceding,' Jorrun said quietly. 'I guess there is no more Western and Eastern Chem, just Chem.'

Kesta had an odd sensation of the room expanding, as though the whole universe had just opened up before her. She reached for her wineglass and took a quick sip.

'Other than Snowhold,' Cassien spoke up from further down the table. 'We will have to deal with the northern province sometime.'

'I saw young Prince Lucien out by the docks.' Kurghan frowned. 'Looked like he'd slipped out of the castle alone again.'

Kesta's heart grew heavy and she met Jorrun's eyes. 'We must invite him here again soon to spend time with Riddi and Joss. And Alikan.'

'I'll find a way to persuade Bractius,' Jorrun agreed. 'Perhaps when his sisters are older, he'll feel less alone in the royal court.'

'Oh, and Teliff gave me a letter from the king to pass to you.' Kurghan held it out towards his Thane. 'And there's rumour the Borrow Bard will visit, but not until late summer.'

In the most recent correspondence from her mother, Dia had told Kesta that Temerran was still with her on the Island, but that the bard was feeling guilty for keeping his men from the sea.

'You'll eat with us?' Jorrun invited Kurghan.

'I'll grab something, but I'd best not miss my supper.' Kurghan grinned.

Kesta peered over Jorrun's arm as he opened the king's letter. She let out an exasperated sigh and shook her head at the words. 'He should have consulted us.'

Jorrun passed the letter down to Cassien, then turned to Tantony and Rosa. 'Bractius has executed Ren. He says he believed he'd get no further information from the man and was concerned he'd somehow warn Geladan of our deception.'

Tantony raised his eyebrows. 'I guess that makes sense.'

Kesta wasn't so sure. Ren was all they'd had left to learn and gather information.

Cassien passed the letter back, his grey eyes darkened by a frown. 'A rash move.'

Jorrun shifted in his seat, but said nothing.

As much as she was enjoying the celebration, Kesta couldn't quite relax, and when Jorrun suggested they take the children up, she agreed at once. They settled Alikan in what had once been Catya's room, then took their own children up to the next floor.

'Only one story.' Jorrun gave Azrael and Doraquael a stern glare.

'And not one that lasts for hours,' Kesta added. She kissed Joss, then sat on the edge of her daughter's bed, momentarily caught by how beautiful Arridia's blue and violet eyes were.

'Are you worried, Mumma?' Arridia asked.

'I am a little, my honey.' Kesta ran a strand of her daughter's silky, black hair through her fingers. 'I'm not worried about anything that is, I'm just thinking of things that might happen, which is foolish.'

Jorrun placed a hand on her shoulder. 'Being prepared isn't foolish.'

'It will be all right,' Arridia said, with such certainty in her young voice that Kesta smiled.

'Goodnight.' Kesta kissed her and walked toward the door, turning at the last moment to raise a warning finger at the two fire-spirits. Azrael and Doraquael both shot back in innocent affront. 'One, short story.'

Jorrun pulled the door closed, leaving it open just a crack. As they climbed the stairs to the highest room of the Ivy Tower, they heard Doraquael softly humming as Azrael began his tale.

Kesta went straight to the window that overlooked the Raven Tower, touching the cold, leaded glass with her fingertips. Jorrun walked up quietly behind her and put his arms around her.

'It will never be all right, not whilst Jderha lives.' Kesta looked up to meet Jorrun's eyes in their reflections.

Jorrun hugged her tighter. 'Even a god knows that prophesy must be a fluid thing. If it were set in stone, then why attack the children and risk making herself known to them? Why do that if she thought things couldn't change? Perhaps... perhaps we have done enough already to alter fate, to make Jderha believe she has won and is safe.'

'And what if we haven't?'

Jorrun stepped back and turned her to face him. 'We learn, we study, we find every tool we can to fight a god. And we teach the children, we teach them to be strong and wise. And we watch the seas.'

Kesta nodded. 'We watch the seas.'

Acknowledgements

Thank you for giving your time to read Raven Storm, I really do hope you enjoyed it. Please come and say hello on Facebook or Twitter, and as always if you want to support me and my writing, the best way to do so is to leave a review and tell your friends.

My thanks go out to my fabulous writing team. My beta readers, Kat, Maria, and Kirsty. My editor, Emma, and my blog tour organiser, Rachel. I'd be lost without you all.

https://www.facebook.com/EmmaMilesShadow
https://twitter.com/EmmaMilesShadow

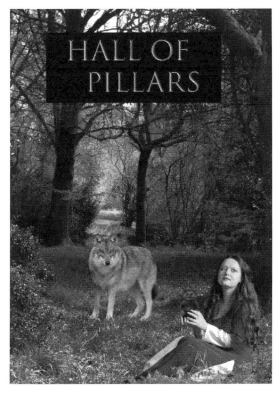

Life on the edge of the wilds where the fey roamed free was hard, but Mya did her best to protect and raise her nephew. The time of his coming of age was drawing close and as proud as she was of him, she was afraid to let him go, afraid that the truth of his mother's death would come back to haunt them. A chance meeting strikes up an unusual friendship that will sustain her through the hardest of times and of those, for Mya and her unexpected allies, there will be many; for a traitor arrives at the village, destroying everything she believes to be true and they must flee, or die

It will take more than friendship, courage or love, to save them this time.

Feather and Mya had fought hard for their peaceful life, defeating a Dark Fey queen so the people of their valley could be free; so they could put their feet up in their quiet cottage at the end of a day's work…

Of course, things won't stay that way long for Mya and her faithful brownie friend.

When visiting the Beltane fair in the wondrous tree city of Ashgrove, they hear rumours of horns, rumours of hoofbeats, rumours of slaughter. The Gentry are coming. Once again Mya and Feather must team up with the Wild Fey and the surly knight, Caelin, to defend the home they love; whilst her nephew, Jack, struggles to bring unity and order to the human city of Ayresport who refuse to accept the fey.

Only if they unite, will they survive.

Printed in Great Britain
by Amazon

75748166R00293